Selected Praise & Reviews
for
MATTHEW MATHER

"BRILLIANT...."
—*WIRED Magazine* on *Cyber* series

"Mather creates characters you've known your whole life."
—*BOING BOING* editor Jason Weisberger

"Relentless pacing...bombshell plot twists."
—*Publishers Weekly* on *Dreaming Tree*

"Another home run for one of the genre's top authors."
—Washington Post #1 bestselling author Steven Konkoly

"Prepare for the most thrilling ride of 2020 in *CyberSpace*."
—New York Times bestseller Nicholas Sansbury Smith

"Not only a great thriller, but a wakeup call."
—Brent Watkins, FBI Cyber Special Agent *(retired)*

Published by Pallas Publishing

isbn // 978-1-987942-13-2 // e-book
isbn // 978-1-987942-14-9 // paperback
isbn // 978-1-987942-19-4 // hardcover

first edition

CYBER SPACE

Also by Matthew Mather

Darknet
Part of the CyberStorm universe
Standalone novel

The Atopia Chronicles
Part of the CyberStorm universe
Three-book completed series

Nomad
Winner of "Science Fiction Book of the Year"
Four-book completed series

Polar Vortex
(now in development as a limited TV series)
Standalone novel

The Delta Devlin Novels
Two-book on-going series
Out of Time
Meet Your Maker

CYBER
SPACE

A CYBERSTORM BOOK

MATTHEW
MATHER

PALLAS
PUBLISHING

Acknowledgements

There are many people who helped in the development of this novel. In particular, I would like to thank:

Barry Matsumori
Vice-President, SpaceX *(former)*
CEO, BridgeSat

Brent Watkins
FBI Cyber Investigations
Special Agent (retired)

Richard Marshall
Global Director of Cybersecurity
US Department of Homeland Security

CYBER
SPACE

Prologue

Light flickered through smoke cascading down the rolling Kentucky hills that climbed to meet West Virginia. The sun rose blood-red over the Appalachians as a hot wind blew in from the southeast. The air sweltering and acrid. Burned my nostrils even through the soaked bandana across my face.

Not more than a mile away, flames licked the treetops.

The sky was literally falling. Spacecraft burning up in the atmosphere.

A slow-motion disaster was grinding mercilessly across America. Across the entire planet. All at the same time. Soon people would be going hungry. Natural disasters going unchecked, power failing, food supplies running out. The world's militaries on the trigger edge of disaster.

We had one long shot to maybe stop it all, to save everyone, and here I was driving a broken old tractor across a dusty corn field through the eye of a firestorm.

With the weight of it all on my beaten-down shoulders.

Chapter 1

The flickering silver beast exploded from the water in a muscular convulsion, twisting through the blue Louisiana sky before crashing back in the shallows near a stand of seagrass.

"Fish on!" I yelled.

Chuck buckled the gimbal belt, then clipped the kidney harness and straps to the reel lug under the fishing rod. Propping his left hand, the prosthetic one, under the rod, he used his right to operate the reel. He grunted as he strained to take the weight.

My eight-year-old son Luke danced around behind him.

"That's gotta be a two-hundred-pounder!" Chuck hauled back.

The reel whirred into a high pitch as the fish raced away. Grandma Babet threw the boat into reverse to follow it.

Keeping an eye on Luke, I sat in the front of the boat with Damon Indigo. Terek, his Ukrainian hacker friend, was proving to be the best tarpon wrangler. He wore VR goggles, which he used to navigate the hunting drones. The center aisle was occupied by six heavy-duty car batteries wired together to recharge the flying machines.

"Should we be worried?" I said.

Damon held one hand up to shield his eyes from the sun, his laptop on his knees. "Pretty sure Chuck can handle it."

"I mean these attacks. The news said India launched a missile at a Pakistani navigation satellite." I was halfway through scanning a news story.

"What would you be worried about?"

"This reporter says the impact is spraying debris everywhere up there."

"Are there new developments?"

"Hey," Chuck growled. "Put that away. Be in the moment, *not* in the Google."

"Right. Sorry." I put the phone down.

People staring at screens was his pet peeve, and he made us leave most of our devices in the car. The only exemptions were Luke's iPad and Damon's phone for the GPS—with strict instructions only to be used if absolutely needed.

Over the engine's growl, I detected the whine of the drones.

I pointed. "There."

Two dots against the blue. Terek guided them in.

"Come around, come around!" Chuck called.

The tarpon must have taken out two hundred feet of line, which bent around to the right, toward the front of the boat. Babet reversed the engine and we surged forward, but the fish was faster. It skirted a muddy island of grass ahead.

Chuck angled the rod around to follow it. "Clear the way!"

With the fiberglass shaft held high and bent almost ninety degrees, he made his way toward the front of the boat to keep the line from going under. The drones whirred twenty feet overhead. Terek still wore the VR goggles as he attempted to bring them down.

I held out one hand to keep Luke in the back while I leaned out of the way.

"Chuck, are you sure you know what you're do—"

Head still up, Terek swept one arm around to grab a descending drone. His elbow caught Chuck square in the temple. He staggered sideways and let go of the rod to brace himself as he

4

fell. The next instant, he shot forward. Jerked like a dog's toy as the huge fish pulled. He crashed into Damon, who flipped face-first onto the deck.

Chuck disappeared over the edge.

I instinctively reached to grab him, but Damon hit my legs and splayed me out as I lunged forward. Luke squealed. I shoved Damon aside and scrambled to my feet. Was my son overboard? Tangled in a rope? My eyes scanned.

Found him. Luke was in the back of the boat. Eyes wide. Arm waving.

"He's over there," Grandma Babet said. "Ev'body keep calm. Everything's okay."

I followed Luke's gesticulations. Everything was definitely *not* okay.

A surging brown shape broke the surface ten yards from the boat. Chuck gasped for air before going under again. One hand appeared and flailed through a churning swell that accelerated away from us. A thought flashed—I could jump in after him. But then I'd need saving as well.

And what about alligators?

Babet hit the throttle and the nose of the boat tipped up.

The rolling bump of water over Chuck crested. He appeared from the muck as he was dragged into the shallows. He struggled to his knees, his prosthetic hand dangling. A stringy mass of seaweed was slung across his shoulder. As he pulled the fishing rod from the mud with his right hand, it twitched.

"Let go!" I yelled.

He fumbled with the strap attached to the reel. A violent tug on the rod and he lost his balance. He flopped into the slime, then jerked ten feet forward and splashed straight back in.

I lost sight of him behind a stand of cattails.

Babet gunned the engine. We roared toward the small island, then swerved around the other side. Flat brown water crawled through a canyon of bald cypresses.

"Send the drones out," I heard Damon say behind me. "Give me the controls."

"Chuck!" I called.

Babet turned down the throttle and we drifted into the channel in silence.

"What happened?" Terek had the goggles off by now.

Damon was already sending one of the machines whirring high to search through a thicket of eucalyptus. "Did anyone see him?"

Luke cried little sobs. Wrapped his arms around my leg.

"Over here," called out a wheezing voice.

We all turned.

And there he was. Waist-deep in lily pads next to a gum tree on the next island. Covered in mud from head to foot, blood streamed down Chuck's face, but his teeth shone white as he smiled and waved.

Chuck called out, "Still got it on," and pulled back on the rod.

He slid forward, stumbling into the sludge again.

Chapter 2

The cathedral of the low country sky arced blue and cloudless over islands of scrub brush. A single gull squawked and hovered in a breeze that riffled the bayou water. Three of us sat in the back of the ten-seater jet boat—me, my son Luke, and our old friend Chuck Mumford.

Damon and Terek sat in the front, adjusting the drones for the next hunt. Damon's grandmother, Babet, was in the captain's chair in the middle, patching up a nasty cut on Chuck's forehead.

I said, "You're a crazy sonofabitch, you know that?"

Chuck grinned gleefully. "Show me the pictures again."

I held up Damon's phone. There was Chuck, chest-high in seaweed and holding a seven-foot tarpon up with both arms. The phone's screen was cracked. It must've happened when Damon was thrown to the deck.

"Bet you that was two hundred."

"You could have drowned."

"But I didn't."

"Or been attacked by an alligator."

"None here mean enough to bite me. Anyway, I'd give them this." He held up his prosthetic left hand, now strapped back on. "I'm Captain Hook."

"I can't believe that didn't break."

"Better than my real hand."

"You don't need to say that."

Chuck smiled. "When life gives you lemons."

"That was so cool!" Luke was all smiles again.

My son was terrified when Chuck had disappeared, but now it was the best thing he'd ever seen. Me too, maybe. I convulsed into a belly laugh, the last of the stress leaking out.

"Haven't seen you do that this whole trip," Chuck said.

"All it took was seeing you go ass over teakettle."

"Glad to be of service."

"I almost jumped in after you."

"Yeah, 'almost' being the operative word."

We released the fish after catching it, which disappointed Luke. To make up for it, we'd taken pictures of him with the big silver king. Messaged them to mom.

No response yet, but it was still the middle of the night in Hong Kong.

Luke asked, "Aunt Babet, can I feed the sharks?"

My boy scrunched his face up the way he did when he wanted to do something but wasn't sure if he should. With both forearms held tight to his chest and his shoulders hunched inward, he pointed one guilty-but-hopeful finger at the mess of barracuda guts on the cutting board at the back of the boat.

"Call me grandma, ev'body else do." Babet's gravelly Cajun accent drawled the words out. She glanced at me.

I smiled, and then nodded. *Why not?* I asked, "There aren't really sharks here, are there?"

"Does the pope poop in the woods?" Chuck joked.

"The pope does what?" Luke's nose crinkled. "Poop?"

"Uncle Chuck is being funny."

"Yeah, funny *looking.*" Luke giggled, his eyes going wide.

Chuck laughed and grabbed him to tickle his ribs. Luke shrieked and dodged away.

"Round the bayou," Babet said, lowering her voice so Luke wouldn't hear, "more likely a gator get you." She then turned to Luke and said loudly, "You go ahead, but you make sure to hang on tight with one hand. Always, you understand me?"

"Deal." Luke's chin wagged up and down, his gap-toothed grin widening.

On our flight from New York yesterday, his front right incisor had finally come out, the new tooth below it button-like. Almost all the kids in his class already had adult teeth, so he was happy to be joining that crew.

I was lucky to get a buck when I was a kid, but I'd slipped a twenty under his pillow at our hotel in the French Quarter. The tooth fairy was everywhere, I told him in the morning, and he was still young enough to half believe me.

Luke took three steps to the back, picked up some fish entrails, and peered over the side.

"Hey, what did Bab—" I paused. "What did *Grandma* Babet tell you?" I waved my empty beer can in my son's direction and squeezed illustratively, lightly crushing the aluminum shell.

"Right." Luke took hold of a side rail, planted both feet like a quarterback—just like I taught him—and sent the first gooey chunk into the drink.

He looked back at me.

I gave him the thumbs up.

Just like I taught him, I thought to myself and laughed. As if I were some kind of sports authority. I was always the kid that was picked last for teams in high school, and I didn't want that for Luke. We played catch, and I enrolled him in rugby. We got as much open air as we could.

Coming on this trip was part of that. I wanted him to do stuff outdoors, get out on the water, all the things I didn't get to do when I was young.

This expedition was important, I had explained to Lauren. It was a chance to see Chuck and Damon, and it would give Luke new experiences. My son was even more excited about it than I was. My wife gave us permission, but made me promise not to do anything stupid.

"Nice shot, Legook," Damon said.

I gave him a puzzled look. Why did he keep calling my son Legook? Had to be the tenth time he'd said it already.

Damon smiled back at me, seemingly not ready to divulge, and asked, "Hey, guys, are we going to try more fishing?" Our tech wizard was hunched over in the front of the boat, a towel draped over his head to create a tent where it was dim enough to work on his laptop.

Terek sat next to him. He said he was twenty-three, but he looked like a teenager with his giant mop of brown hair. Tall and lanky, he was probably six-two but less than two hundred pounds. His smooth skin was as pallid and lily-white as Grandma Babet's was dark and leathery.

He'd apologized about a dozen times after we'd hauled Chuck in, but the kid was still in shock. More affected than Chuck, that was for sure.

The young Eastern European was busy slathering on another layer of fifty-SPF sunblock. "Maybe we call it a day?" he said. His arms were a burnt shade of angry pink.

"I say we go again," Chuck countered.

My friend was now sprawled out on the back seat, beer in hand, body and clothes still caked in mud. In the four years since he and his family had moved to Nashville, he had become increasingly laid back. Permanent two-day stubble and shaggy hair. The bandage across his head completed the pirate look.

The persistent twinkle of mischief in Chuck's eyes hadn't changed a bit, but I couldn't help stealing glances at his left hand. The prosthetic. He said he didn't even notice the difference anymore, but I got a twinge of guilt every time I saw it.

Damon lifted the towel covering his head. Five-eight, he was more my height, but looked short next to Terek.

Where his grandmother had ebony skin, Damon's was more olive, his features almost Chinese. His father was Asian, he said, without adding more. I didn't pry. I knew his mother passed when he was young. Grandma Babet had raised him.

Damon said, "Hurricane Dolly is category five now. It's going to brush past Martinique."

"Should we be worried?" I asked.

"Not unless you have a villa there," Chuck said.

Damon said, "The track looks like it will come into the Gulf."

I scanned the lowland islands of the bayou and tried to imagine being here during a monster hurricane. Everything would be submerged, all the way to New Orleans. The thought of nothing but suffocating water all the way to the horizon was terrifying. I put it out of my mind. I never really learned to swim properly when I was a kid.

"Won't get near here for two weeks," Chuck said, "even if it does come this way. Average ground speed of a hurricane is ten miles an hour." It was the sort of arcane detail Chuck would know. "By then we'll be long gone. And hey, no more internet while we're out here. How many times do I have to ask?"

Damon shrugged an apology. "I'm adjusting the image recognition system to key off that last one you found. I'll set the drones to hover a little further out so they don't spook the fish."

Competing in the Grand Isle Tarpon Rodeo was on Chuck's bucket list. This boys' trip had been hatched after Damon suggested he could modify the drones he was working on at MIT. He altered their facial recognition systems to look for the telltale signs of huge tarpon laying up in shallow water.

Drone fishing wasn't a new idea, but the way we were doing it was.

We sent one out to hunt and followed in the boat. A second held the bait, attached to the line and rod. The idea was to drop the lure right onto the nose of the unsuspecting fish once the first drone found the target.

That was the concept. Problem was that the tarpons didn't like drones.

"Dad?" Luke had his arms close to his chest again.

"What?" I tilted my head.

"Can I play on the iPad?"

"Look where we are. Out on the bayou in Louisiana. Fishing with drones. You want to use the iPad *now?*"

He scrunched his arms in tighter and crinkled his nose.

I relented. This was a long-fought war of attrition. "Okay, but only half an hour. And no YouTube."

"Deal."

"Here we go," Damon announced from the front, holding the drone.

He released it. The six-legged, one-eyed monster lifted from the front deck and shot into the blue expanse on a blast of air that blew Chuck's hair back.

Chapter 3

"That's *it*?" Luke squinted into the binoculars.

A squat bunker of cement, topped by a white gantry and red-and-white striped crane, hunched a mile away across a flat of grass and sand. The horizon was flat. The SLS test engine didn't look like much from this distance, less like a rocket and more like an errant bit of an oil refinery.

In the sweltering heat, Luke and I, Damon and Terek had made the ten-minute hike from the Infinity Science Center back on Interstate 10 out to the test range with a knot of other tourists. Grandma Babet had wisely opted to stay behind in the air-conditioned lobby.

"That's the biggest rocket in the world," Chuck said to Luke.

"It is not," Luke protested.

"That's what the NASA man said on the tour."

"He was telling a fib," Luke said immediately. "The GenCorp Galaxy is the biggest. Look how *small* that is."

"He's not wrong," Damon said.

The GenCorp headquarters were only a few miles away. Damon had been there twice, he said, as part of a DOD—Department of Defense—contract he was working on with MIT. He joked with a smile that he could tell us what the project was, but then he would have to kill us. A secret, he whispered to Luke.

Chuck checked his watch. "That's going to light up in a few minutes. Then you'll see."

"Excuse me? Mr. Indigo?" A young girl and her friend addressed Damon.

They weren't more than fifteen or sixteen, both with braces on their teeth and wearing oversized tank tops over bathing suits and shorts.

"Uh, yeah, that's me," Damon replied.

"Can we have your autograph?" One of them held out a napkin from the science center cafeteria. The other handed over a pen.

"Sure, of course." He scribbled his name and a note.

They took back the napkin, thanked him, and ran back to their friends.

"That happen to you a lot?" I asked. His fame had grown, even though I knew he tried to avoid it.

"From time to time. I'm thinking of switching to my middle name to avoid some of it."

"What's your middle name?"

"Vincent."

My son watched the girls for a second, but then returned his attention to the test platform. "This is a rocket launch, right?" he asked.

"An engine test firing. No launch."

Luke handed the binoculars back to Chuck and scrunched his nose. Unimpressed. This was also the look he gave me when he wanted to go off by himself.

"Why don't you go play with some of those kids?" I pointed at a group of children about his age who were chasing each other around a wooden jungle gym near the waiting area.

He pouted. "I don't know them."

"Go and introduce yourself." I was a bit of an introvert. I wanted him to feel comfortable talking to people. It was important. So I pushed him.

"Okay." He waggled his head. "To infinity and beyond!" He made a rocket ship blasting off out of one hand and followed it toward the kids.

"I'll watch him," Terek said to me.

He and Damon wandered off behind Luke.

After mooring the boat at a wharf at the Port of New Orleans the night before, we had stopped right under the Mississippi Bridge at Dino's Grill for some shrimp and jambalaya. This morning, we'd met back at our hotel on Frenchmen Street for the drive up to the Stennis Space Center, the biggest rocket test facility in America.

Chuck had driven down from Nashville in his Jeep, but when we got into it that morning, the thing wouldn't start. He had it towed to the garage around the corner, and then we all took a taxi out to Grandma Babet's. All six of us had packed into her beaten-up '82 Monte Carlo, with Luke balanced on my knees in the back.

We'd driven out of New Orleans, eastward past Lake Pontchartrain, over the Pearl River delta, and into the State of Mississippi itself.

The Space Center was just on the other side, but in the hour drive both my legs had gone to sleep under the weight of my eight-year-old son. Not that long ago, he was a baby. Now he knew when NASA was telling lies.

Chuck and I stood in front of the chain-link fence and waited for the rocket test firing.

"We need to hitch a ride with Russia to even get into space," Chuck said.

I replied, "Isn't GenCorp sending up manned missions now?"

"Billionaires are almost worse than Russians."

"You have something against Russians? Because they're hacking our elections?"

Chuck rolled his eyes. "Has your Uncle Senator brainwashed you?"

"You don't think they are?"

"I'm sure we're messing with theirs, too. We even mess with our allies' elections—the last estimate I saw is that we've interfered in half of all the democratic elections around the world since World War II, and even more when it comes to undemocratic places. This is an old game, not a new one."

"And you're okay with that?"

"Within bounds, it's the norm. It's our job to keep them in check, and vice versa, but there's a big difference between that and basing a critical part of our national defense on Russia. They're still our biggest adversary. I agree with your wife's uncle on that."

"I'm not sure I do."

Six years earlier, I'd put my entire family in danger when I hadn't been able to see what was right in front of my eyes. I'd been blinded by my prejudices. Chuck had paid the price. His hand had been amputated as a result of the chaos and misunderstandings.

Chuck chewed on his lip. "I'm still not convinced what happened in New York back then was a big accident."

"Not everything is a conspiracy."

"These days it is. Seriously. Think about it."

It was my turn to roll my eyes.

"And it's getting worse," Chuck continued. "Real conspiracies. Like Snowden. And as Luke said, that right there"—Chuck pointed through the chain-link fence—"isn't the biggest rocket in the world. The world's most powerful rocket is owned by Tyrell Jakob, a billionaire who controls half the internet and most of the space over our heads."

"Careful what you say about my hero." I was joking. Sort of.

I had been promoted to partner at my venture capital firm in New York. I wasn't an ex-entrepreneur or a financial wizard, but I did have a talent for helping people get stuff done. We had branched out from social media investments into robotics and artificial intelligence, and Tyrell Jakob was the shining entrepreneur-in-armor on a hilltop we all admired.

Damon reappeared from watching Luke and latched his fingers into the chain-link fence. "I've met Tyrell a few times, at their HQ over here, and when he came to talk at MIT. A nice guy. I'm still in touch with people at GenCorp."

"That may be," Chuck said, "but putting that much power into the hands of one person? You think Russia is bad? Greedy rich people are worse. At least Russia has rules we can understand."

"I'm not sure that's true anymore," Damon said.

"It's about to start." Terek appeared with Luke on his shoulders.

My son waved at me, a hot dog in his hand.

"I hope you don't mind. He wanted one," Terek said.

"How much do I owe you?"

Terek waved me off. It was okay.

"So, you have a daughter as well?" Terek asked me.

"Olivia," I replied. "Antonia Olivia, but we use her middle name. My wife, Lauren, is in Hong Kong on a business trip. She's a lawyer. Big conference on international relations." I liked telling everyone who would listen. Guess I was proud. I had a feeling Lauren's career would be taking off soon. "Olivia is staying with our family in Washington."

"Senator Seymour, right?" Terek said. I must have looked puzzled about how he knew this, because he added, "Damon told me. The one that's on TV all the time? The one leading the Senate investigations into the Russians?"

"That's right. He's my wife's uncle. So, I guess Olivia's great-uncle or something. Lauren's mother, Susan, is in Washington for September."

This trip conflicted with Lauren's conference, but her mother had volunteered to take Olivia for two weeks. Susan was staying with her brother, the senator, at his Virginia estate.

"My wife and I just moved to Washington," Terek said.

"Government job?" About the only reason someone would move there.

Chuck asked, "Haven't you been down here with Damon all summer?"

"That's right. Babet helped me and my sister get jobs at the Port of New Orleans this past summer. I came down to spend time with her."

"You work at the port?" I had assumed Terek was doing his PhD at MIT, the same as Damon.

Damon held up his phone. "Have you guys seen the latest?" He flicked through the news on his phone. "That hurricane is the biggest they've ever recorded in the Atlantic basin. Huge tornadoes in the Midwest again. And fires everywhere. More in California—"

"There are always fires in California." Chuck could see where this conversation was going.

"Not before global warming. Not like this. Start of September, and we're already at the fifth named hurricane of the season. Record temperatures everywhere."

"The planet has been much warmer before. It's natural. It changes all the time."

"This isn't natural," Damon said, "not this time."

"You're saying humans aren't natural?"

"Fires in the Arctic? That's normal? There are fires all over Siberia right now. And look at this. A huge forest fire in Appalachia, across West Virginia. That's near your cabin."

"That is unusual," Chuck admitted. "But forest fires are nature's way of regaining balance."

"Until your cabin burns down."

"If that gets anywhere near my place, you can be sure I'll be drafting all y'all to help me cut fire breaks."

"Speaking of fires," Damon said. "India and Pakistan are heating up. Over a hundred were killed in clashes in Kashmir yesterday. And Mike, look at this."

I took his phone and read: "*India launches second anti-satellite attack, destroying another Pakistani navigation relay. Cloud of wreckage spreads around the equator.*"

"A second one?" I passed the phone to Terek. "I didn't even know Pakistan had satellites."

"Hardcore," Damon said. "Not even low Earth orbit. That was a hit at MEO, sixteen thousand kilometers up. Russia and America are screaming at them to stop, but nobody wants to get involved in a shooting war. They're talking trade sanctions. Like that will do anything."

"MEO?"

"Medium Earth orbit. That's more than two thousand kilometers, but less than geosynchronous. A lot of delta-v to get up there."

"Delta-v?" My tech-speak was levels below Damon. "Change in velocity?"

"Need a lot of it to get out to that orbit."

"They better watch it." Terek handed the phone to Chuck. "Russia is supplying weapons to Pakistan now. Missiles, the whole thing. They're even sending up the first Pakistani astronaut."

"Cosmonaut, you mean," Chuck said. "A nuclear exchange between India and Pakistan—a hundred warheads on each side— would push the planet into a nuclear winter for ten or twenty years. That would stop your global warming. Kind of a solution, if you think of it like that."

"Except for the hundreds of millions dead," Damon replied.

"I'm kidding."

Luke frowned his serious look. "Daddy, what's a nuclear exchange?"

"Uncle Chuck is joking."

"Is he always joking?" Luke asked, his frown deepening.

"And look at this," Chuck added, reading something on Damon's phone. "India is denying they launched the attack."

"Really?"

"But our military has confirmed that the launch came from India's Satish Dhawan Space Centre on Sriharikota Island, near Chennai."

An air horn sounded. Three long blasts. A quiet descended over the tourists. Everyone turned to the gantry in the distance.

I thought about getting Luke down from Terek's shoulders, but before I had the chance, a billowing cloud shot out from the cement test range, a jet of flickering brilliant white against the darkening azure sky. Crickets chirped quietly as the exhaust thunderhead blossomed to dwarf the gantry.

The accompanying silence to the visual violence was surreal. A full three seconds passed before the ground beneath our feet shook in a low rumble, followed by an ear-splitting roar that thundered and engulfed us in its fury.

Luke's eyes went wide as his hands shot to his ears.

Not unimpressed now, huh?

I smiled and stuck my fingers in my ears, too. But I couldn't help wondering: A cloud of debris spreading around the equator?

Chapter 4

A howling bass rhythm propelled me through the saloon doors, the music a living thing that flowed around me on a beer-and-sweat-soaked eddy of air. Together we merged with the swirling humid saltwater breeze outside. I stumbled across the exterior landing, then slid down the stairs and onto the grass.

With one finger stuck in the ear opposite my phone, I said, "Everything is fine!"

Lauren's voice on the other end said, "Isn't it too late for Luke," then cut out for a second. A moment later, I heard: "Up?"

"He's loving it. Dancing in front of the band." I checked my phone. It was 9 p.m. here, so 10 a.m. in Hong Kong. "How's the conference?"

She said something I couldn't understand. Too garbled on her end, or too many whiskeys on mine.

"I'll still be meeting you in Washington next week?" I asked.

That was the plan. I'd fly up with Luke and meet her and her family. Then Lauren and I, together with the kids, would drive back to New York.

She replied, "You've got my flight information?"

"Of course. What about all this stuff with India? What are they saying over there?" I cleared a tangle of people chatting outside and found a quiet spot. "Lauren? Hello?"

I checked my phone's screen. The line had been disconnected.

Chuck had followed me out. "Everything okay?"

"Yeah. Sure. Lauren called, but my reception is bad."

"I got full bars. Want to try mine? I just talked to Susie and Ellarose and Bonham."

I shook my head, no, I didn't need his phone. Lauren had to get to her meeting anyway. I said, "Bonham is talking already?"

"He's four."

"Really?"

"You need to visit more."

"No kidding."

"Where's Luke?" Chuck asked.

"Inside, with Terek. They've taken a shine to each other."

"Take a load off?" Chuck found two wooden Adirondack loungers at the edge of the gravel driveway, a hundred feet from the entrance. Far enough to feel private.

I slumped into the chair next to him. Exhausted. Vacations wore me down.

Chuck said, "Amazing place, huh?"

"New Orleans? I love it."

"I mean *this* place."

I glanced over my shoulder at the clapboard building we had just exited. Blues Night at the 100 Men Hall. It was a thirty-minute drive from the Stennis Space Center further into Mississippi to this unassuming structure. It was little more than a shack in the modest gulf-front town of Bay Saint Louis.

"This is the oldest remaining structure of the Southern Chitlin Circuit," Chuck said. "You know that? The last of its kind."

"Sounds like you."

"That's the plan."

I stretched out and stared up into the sky. Almost completely dark out. No moon, no streetlights. One lamp over the door to the hall, but the bulb was burned out. Nothing but a dense field of stars overhead, which seemed to shift as if there were grains of sand between them.

I rubbed my eyes.

"How did Damon meet Terek?" Chuck asked.

"I thought at MIT, but he said he's working at the dock."

"That kid doing physical labor? A stiff breeze could blow him over."

"You're telling me you didn't do odd jobs when you were a kid?"

"I did whatever it took."

"Exactly."

A pause. Chuck said, "I'm not sure I trust him."

"He flies a drone like nobody's business."

"I'm serious."

"You don't think I should leave Luke with him?" I sat upright.

"That's fine. I mean, not that." Silence for a beat. "There's something about him."

"That he's an immigrant?"

"Don't be an asshole."

"You're suspicious of everybody you don't know."

"Whereas you trust everyone."

That was true. Lauren often had funny feelings about people that turned out to be right, that this person or that shouldn't be trusted, but I almost never had that sensation. It was like I was emotionally tone-deaf.

I blinked and rubbed my eyes again. *Were* those stars moving overhead?

Chuck said, "You see that too?"

There were definitely motes of light floating between the stars.

"The sun set an hour and a half ago, so we're getting a reflection at just the right angle. Those are the satellite nodes of your hero Tyrell Jakob's SatCom constellation. I think there's...what? Ten thousand satellites he's launched. Covers the planet in a web. And he's going to send up double that by next year."

"Triple." Terek appeared from the darkness behind us. "Luke's with Damon, he's got him up on stage with Babet."

That was my boy. Life of the party. "Triple?" I said.

"Goddamn sky pollution, if you ask me," Chuck said. "Astronomers are going nuts. You can't look into a pristine sky anymore. Billionaires, like I said. Can't control them. Can't kill 'em."

"Tyrell plans to have thirty thousand satellites in orbit soon," Terek said. "Three years ago, there were only two thousand operational ones. That was from all the countries in the world, and over a half century of space launches."

"And now one billionaire sticks ten thousand up in a year by himself," Chuck said.

I whistled. "How do they not bump into each other?"

"They have thrusters and fuel. But that's a good worry to have. That's why I came out here, to show this to you guys. There are multiple debris clouds spreading in orbit now."

He handed me his phone. Another article about an anti-satellite attack, but this one featured a headline about Russia demanding that America not intervene in the growing dispute between India and Pakistan.

"Russia backing up India?" I asked. "Aren't they usually on opposite sides?"

"This isn't about the Indian anti-satellite attacks. The Pakistani military retaliated and hit an Indian communication satellite in geosynchronous orbit. Maybe more than one. They're reporting loss of communications with other satellites now."

Chuck and I stayed in the chairs after Terek went back in. We sat in silence and listened to frogs croak in the darkness.

"I don't trust everyone," I said finally. "Look what happened to you. You lost your *hand* because of me. Because I didn't trust what was right in front of my eyes."

When a massive cyberattack had crippled New York in the middle of winter, years before, Chuck and I had hidden with our families on the fifth floor of our apartment building in the Meatpacking District. All communications had gone down, even the internet, and then the power and water.

Eventually, we had to escape the metropolis as it disintegrated around us. We managed to get his old Range Rover out to his cabin in the Blue Ridge Mountains, but that was when the real horror show started.

After I walked to DC and saw Chinese and Russian military units parked there, I thought the US had been invaded. Even though it turned out they were there to help, all I saw were attackers. My mind refused to believe anything else. I returned to the cabin and we spent a month and a half in total isolation, starving and in desperate need of medical supplies. Damon had finally shown up and rescued us.

Our friend Tony had lost his life in a shootout with a gang that wanted to steal supplies from us. Before it was all over, Chuck's left hand had to be amputated. We were lucky, he always said, and he wasn't wrong.

Over seventy thousand people had lost their lives in that disaster.

"It's not your fault," Chuck whispered. A cicada buzzed in the distance. "I know it's been weighing on you, Mike, but you did right."

"No, I didn't."

I never talked about this. Not ever. At the time, we were so happy to be alive, and afterward, I felt ashamed. More than ashamed. I clenched my jaw. Maybe it was the booze, but I wiped away a tear with the back of one hand.

Chuck didn't look at me. He stared straight up and said softly, "You remember those people you saved, when that hospital shut down?"

Images swirled. Freezing darkness. Tunnels of snow. Swinging bags of liquid on IV poles. "I remember."

"And all those people you brought into our apartment? That was you. Saved a lot of lives, Mike, you should be proud. You're setting a good example for Luke."

"I did what I had to do."

"Exactly. You didn't waver. You got on with it."

A wind rustled the treetops.

I said, "Is it happening again? I've got a bad feeling."

This war between India and Pakistan. These things had a way of spreading like a contagion. What was happening up there? I watched the bits of light move between the stars.

"I'm so tired." I wanted to go to sleep right there. Wake up and have everything be back to normal. Maybe it would.

"Whatever comes, Mike, we're going to get through it. Together." Chuck sat upright and looked at me. "Our grandfathers fought in world wars, got out of boats in front of machine guns on beaches like Omaha, but these new disasters that grip the world? These are the wars that we fight now, in this future that our grandparents couldn't even imagine."

"Is this your fight song?"

"Get up, you lazy slug. We got some fishing to do tomorrow."

Chapter 5

I hunted for my prey across the undulating sand.

"See anything?" Damon asked. "Let the tool do its job. Don't overthink."

A flash of sunlight blinded me. Sweat trickled down my back. I paused to get my bearings, the air stagnant and metallic with the smell of cut bait. The weapon tilted left and right. I pulled back to gain some altitude.

Luke yanked at my pant leg. "Dad! Dad! Over there."

"Where?"

"You're too far."

"I'm coming b—" I was halfway through giving in when the display lit up.

An angry red box stutter-flashed around the target in the display of the goggles strapped to my face. I zoomed in for a better look, and there it was: a clear oblong shadow beneath my target's glittering armor.

"I got a lock," Damon said. "I'm bringing the other drone in. Don't do anything—"

"Damn it." The target turned and looked right at me.

With a flick of his tail, the silver king sailed away under the cover of seagrass.

A fat orange sun lounged on the horizon and spit fiery color onto mackerel-striped vapor trails high in the stratosphere. Huge thunderheads threatened on the horizon.

"You suck at drone fishing," Chuck said to me.

"What's that saying?" I asked. "Red sky at night? Sailors' delight?" I eyed the storm clouds warily.

"We best get going in," Grandma Babet said.

"You guys got the drones stowed?" Chuck asked Terek and Damon.

When they both nodded, he sat down in the captain's chair, made sure everyone was secure, then started the boat. He asked for Damon's phone and opened the map app. "Babet, is Bay Dosgris this way or that?"

Even with the GPS, the bayous were a maze inside a puzzle wrapped up in mud.

Grandma Babet stood and began pointing, but Chuck offered her the controls instead. She immediately turned the boat into a different channel.

"We find Lake Five," she explained, "go up Bayou Saint Denis into Cutler and then the Dupre Cut, follow that all the way into the Mississippi herself."

Chuck handed the phone back to Damon. "Your GPS is out."

Damon checked and rechecked his phone. "Maybe busted when I dropped it yesterday?"

"Or got too hot?" Terek said. "You left it out in the sun."

"There's no internet, either."

"Don't you use the SatCom constellation?" Chuck waved his left hand at the sky. "Isn't that supposed to work anywhere on the planet?"

"It was fine this morning."

I sat next to Damon.

"This cloud of debris from the anti-satellite attacks, isn't it dangerous?"

"It's not a good thing, but there's a lot of space up there. And I mean a *lot* of space."

"So we shouldn't be worried?"

"There's a strong possibility the debris might hit other satellites, and from what I've heard, authorities are taking defensive actions. It's not time to panic. And I have to say I'm impressed."

"By the defensive actions?"

"That the Pakistanis were able to hit a satellite in geosynchronous orbit. Nobody's ever done that before. Russians must have supplied the hardware, but even then...targeting something at that distance. Getting into orbit means going hundreds of miles up and moving at eighteen thousand miles per hour, and imagine if all that is this."

Damon illustrated with an inch gap between his left thumb and forefinger.

I said, "Okay," but didn't quite understand.

"Getting up to geosynchronous orbit, compared to that, is like this." He held his right hand a foot above his head. "It's almost like a moon shot. In terms of effect, though, it's better. Less stuff for any wreckage to hit up there. The Pakistanis are retaliating tit-for-tat against the Indians for hitting their first geopositioning satellites. Better than them firing nukes at each other."

The boat slowed.

"I don't normal-wise come out this way." Babet scanned the horizon as though she was trying to get her bearings. "Not sure if that's Wilkinson Bayou or Mud Lake. That GPS still not working?"

"That's definitely north." Chuck pointed helpfully at ninety degrees from the setting sun.

Babet said, "You know how many ways we could get lost out here?"

"I honestly don't want to."

Babet got us back. The boat's engine growled into high gear as we cleared the narrow waterway and pulled into the main channel, with the Mississippi Bridge and the Port of New Orleans visible in the distance. Past 6 p.m. and the sky was overcast. The thunderheads pulled closer from the southwest and obscured the setting sun.

A mountainscape of multicolored containers lined the northern shore of the Mississippi, their blocky peaks silhouetted against the glittering skyline of New Orleans beyond. The jet boat fought the current of the turgid brown river flowing against us. We passed the French Quarter, and Babet pointed out the neon-topped Harrah's Casino.

Dusk. Huge floodlights illuminated the water and docks.

"This is the biggest bulk cargo port in the world," Babet explained. "The Ports of South Louisiana and New Orleans are the biggest in America. Eighty thousand ships come through here ev'ry year. Day and night, it never stops."

Babet swung the nose around to clear a rusted metal platform. "I'm going to park us under the bridge five minutes up river." She deftly navigated our tiny boat between two container ships, their hulls a yawning metal canyon above us. "Everything controlled by GPS these days. The ships, the cranes, the boxes."

Forty years of service at the port had earned her special privileges, like mooring her friends' pleasure craft downtown.

Terek was taking pictures of the port facilities, but now awkwardly clambered to the back and sat next to Luke and Chuck. Luke, of course, still had his nose in the iPad. I thought of taking it away, but then what? He'd bug me till I gave it back.

"Dad?" Luke said. He saw me looking at him. "I'm hungry. I have to pee."

"I've got half a KitKat," Terek said.

Luke took the offered chocolate. "How much longer?"

"Almost there, I promise."

Something didn't feel right, but I wasn't sure what. A tingling sensation crept along my arms. A taste like pennies in the back of my mouth. The air was still, the humidity almost palpable. Was it the storm clouds?

They towered angrily, high into the sky.

I shifted in my seat, turned to inspect the city.

Lights flickered on in the office towers in the sudden gloom. Hovering aircraft dotted the middle distance as they lined up for approach at Louis Armstrong Airport. Everything was normal.

Except.

"Why aren't the port cranes operating?" I asked nobody in particular.

Babet maneuvered the boat between two container transports as she headed for the dock.

The waterway was quiet.

Almost deserted.

None of the buzzing activity of tugboats and barges we had seen every other time we'd been here, and that had been on the weekend. Today was Monday. The work week had just started.

"Babet, is today a holiday?"

"Only for me."

The boat engine whined into a higher gear. We surged forward. The gap between the massive hulls of the two ships we passed between seemed to narrow.

"Why are none of the port cranes operating?" I repeated.

Babet replied in a terse voice: "They always be operating."

I looked behind me. "All those ones there aren't moving."

"Excuse me, Mr. Mitchell, but we got other problems right now." Her voice ratcheted up, became quick and panicked. "Ev'body hang tight to something."

"What's goin—"

We were moving at almost full speed, maybe thirty miles an hour. Not fast in a car, but very quick on water. Chuck grabbed Luke with his left arm and gripped a handhold with his other. I managed a half-turn before Babet threw the boat into reverse.

A clashing screech erupted.

The towering walls of metal above and around us tore one into the other, crushing together around our tiny boat.

With my right arm I tried to grab my seat, but I jerked forward as if a giant had grabbed my neck. I rammed sideways into the console and became airborne, my feet lurching over my head as I flew out into open space over the water.

Chapter 6

Lauren Mitchell hoped her husband wasn't doing anything dumb.

The clock beside her bed read 6:14 a.m. That meant it was—she did a mental calculation—5:14 p.m. back home? That's right. The boys should be off the water by now. Hopefully not *in* it.

Coffee in hand, she got up from sitting on the bed and nervously pulled back the curtains of her hotel room at the Sheraton. Three stories down, at street level, a double-decker tourist bus growled around the corner from Salisbury Street onto Nathan Road, the main thoroughfare through Hong Kong.

The orange blob of the rising sun reflected in the windows of the Peninsula Hotel straight across the street. To her left, the dusky waters of Victoria Bay were visible past the waterfront parks, with the hills of mainland China lining the horizon.

She took a sip of her coffee.

Not that Mike usually did stupid things, but he and Chuck had a way of getting themselves into trouble. Which was fine, Mike was a big boy, but now their troublemaking included her baby boy, Luke, who was out on the fishing trip with them. She sighed and exhaled, counting to five. He wasn't a baby anymore, Luke kept telling her, he was eight.

Eight.

They grew up so fast. A little man now.

She had never been away from her kids for more than a weekend their whole lives. Olivia, her daughter, was five, but already displayed a rebellious independence. Just like her mother. She loved her nana, though, and Lauren's mother doted on her little granddaughter. They spent a lot of time all together now, Lauren and her kids and their nana, more time than she had ever spent with her mother.

It was nice, but sad, too.

Lauren's father had died two years earlier. His death was an immense shock to her tight-knit family. They'd come together, though, and Mike had been great. They moved from their small apartment in Meatpacking to the Upper West Side near Columbia University, into a place with an extra bedroom. The granny quarters, Mike joked. He really had been great.

Maybe that's why he'd suggested she go on this trip. Go out into the world, stretch her wings a little.

When her firm had asked if anyone wanted to go to Hong Kong for this conference, she knew part of it was her uncle—Leo, the senator—pulling strings in the background. Now that her father was gone, Leo took on a little parental responsibility. She felt like he was gently grooming her for a political career, and who knew? America still needed a woman president at some point.

Mike had encouraged her to go. Nana could take Olivia to stay at the family estate outside Washington with Lauren's uncle, he had said, and he would take Luke fishing with Uncle Chuck.

Really, she thought Mike wanted to hang out with Chuck and Damon, but she also knew he wanted to give Luke some experiences he'd never had as a kid, like going off to the outdoors and doing something exciting.

She smiled.

Which was great. She enjoyed coming here, if she was being honest, but that didn't mean she didn't think about her kids every second of every minute she was away from them. Two days she had been gone, and she would be back in five. At least she hoped she would.

Mike and Chuck going fishing wasn't the reason she was nervous.

She sat on the bed. Her TV was tuned to CNN, which was only available in certain hotels over here.

"India is still denying the anti-satellite attacks," said the TV news anchor, a blond woman in a blue suit, "while China and the United States have confirmed yet another launch by India's military against a Pakistani satellite in low Earth orbit. Pakistan has retaliated, saying—"

Lauren picked up her cell phone and dialed Mike's number again. Earlier, it had gone to voicemail, which had made sense, but now it returned a busy signal. *Why is it busy?* By itself, that wouldn't be worrying, but she dialed her mother's number and got the same thing, and her uncle's landline number was busy as well.

Something was going on.

She got up and went back to the window.

Protesters still wandered the streets, weaving between the buses and taxis making their way up Nathan Road. It seemed like there were more now. Were they getting up and heading into the streets this early? In the waterfront park to her left, a row of police with plastic shields and riot gear stood at the ready, joined by men in gray camouflage holding what looked like assault rifles.

She was sure they were using dummy bullets, but those could still maim.

Then again, the police hadn't moved on any of the protestors all night. They were there as a presence, to make sure things didn't get out of hand, and Lauren felt like that was the right thing to do. Which was an interesting confluence of events, as she was here to attend a conference on international relations.

The TV news anchor said in the background, "Russia is warning the United States not to interfere in what Moscow is calling a local conflict, threatening to move its fleets from the Baltic and down into the Mediterranean—"

Lauren still wasn't exactly sure what the protestors were upset about. There were lingering disputes that had been going on for months, but the rumors last night had been about online social media networks being cut off, even the internet itself going dark in some neighborhoods.

Her laptop was open on the work desk by the window, and she checked her email inbox. Nothing since last night. She could still surf the web, but maybe that was because she was staying at the Sheraton.

That morning, she had checked for early return flights. There hadn't been any cancellations of scheduled flights, so things couldn't be too bad—but then how many times in recent years had international flights and borders been closed suddenly?

And she hadn't received a single email in the past ten hours, not from anyone in America, despite sending out a few to her mother and Mike.

Lauren sat back down on the bed and dialed her colleague in the room next door. Evelyn picked up on the first ring. "You going down soon?" she asked.

"Soon," Lauren replied. The conference started at 7:30. "Hey, are you getting any email from back home?"

A pause. "You either?"

"Busy signals when you call?"

"Same here."

Lauren exhaled and counted to five. "Okay. Thanks. I'll see you in a minute." She hung up.

A sharp bang outside in the street.

Lauren got to her feet and approached the window cautiously.

A group of a half dozen young men sprinted up the opposite side of the street. The noise had sounded like a firecracker. The police in riot gear hadn't moved, but the men with the assault rifles had advanced in a line in front of them.

Those were definitely assault rifles. She recognized them as the QBZ-95, a bullpup-style weapon with a signature circular thirty-round cartridge behind the trigger. It made them a more compact weapon while still packing a punch comparable to the AR-15.

Her husband hated guns, but after what happened in New York, Lauren had taken it upon herself to get some training. Her family had a proud military background, but she hadn't served and part of her regretted it. She was trying to make up for it, at least the training part, and she had taken lessons at the local gun range for the past few years, along with self-defense courses. Even tactical training with semiautomatic weapons. Mike disliked it, but it was her choice.

Of course, she didn't have any guns here. Her Glock was locked up in the safe back at the apartment in New York.

She listened to the noise in the street, tried to hear if there was someone yelling, when she noticed something else. Her TV had gone silent.

Lauren found the remote and stood in front of the screen. The TV was on, the channel on CNN, but the screen was blank. She flipped a few channels. Other stations were working, but Fox News was blank as well.

A loud bang from outside. She ducked involuntarily.

That wasn't a firecracker. Her hotel window reverberated with the detonation. The stuttering pop of automatic gunfire erupted beyond the glass.

Chapter 7

I hit the water upside down. Swallowed a screaming mouthful of the Mississippi before I managed to shut my trap. The terrible gnashing of metal was even louder submerged. The sound enveloped me, the vibrations crawling along my skin in steel-rending wails.

I thrashed.

Adrenaline jacked into my bloodstream. An electric jolt flashed up my spine. My arms paddled and legs wheeled as I tried to orient myself. Panic tightened its fist around my brainstem. Then, through the murky brown, I glimpsed light. Somehow my head broke the water.

I gasped for air.

But my lungs wouldn't take anything in.

I slapped the water with the flat of my right hand to try and stay afloat. My head craned back. The hulls of the two ships flattened into each other, the gap between them narrowing with a nails-across-chalkboard squeal. I caught sight of our jetboat—maybe twenty feet?—then gagged and gasped another mouthful of brown muck. Tried to spit it back out.

Went under again.

My hands clawed for the surface.

An arm grabbed my waist and pulled me up. I spewed water as my head cleared the surface. Someone was beside and below me. I grappled with them and fought to get air into my lungs.

"Mike," a voice yelled, "over here!"

Something hit my head and skittered onto the water. Orange. Life jacket. I grabbed it and pulled it under my arms. The metal canyon around us collapsed further in a howling roar.

Our boat was just a few feet away from me. Chuck leaned over the bow. Someone pushed my midsection up.

Terek's face appeared beside me. "Grab...grab his hand," he sputtered through a mouthful of water.

I lifted one shaking hand as high as I could. Chuck's right hand gripped my forearm and hauled me slithering over the gunwale in one shoulder-wrenching motion.

"China has now joined Russia in warning America not to get involved in what they are saying is a local conflict," said the Fox News anchor, a blond woman in a blue suit with her hair in a bun.

After we'd gotten out of the boat at the Port of New Orleans, we'd retrieved our phones—and the dozens of messages on them. A full-blown shooting war had broken out between India and Pakistan. I was shivering and retching up brown water, and Chuck asked me if I wanted to go to the hospital. I said I wanted to get back to the hotel.

We piled into Grandma Babet's Monte Carlo and drove through the French Quarter. Damon and Terek were renting a small apartment for the summer a few blocks away from us, and Babet lived in the Fourth Ward, a few miles further away.

For now, we all stayed together.

Our hotel was the Claiborne Mansion on Dauphine Street, just off Frenchmen Street in the Seventh Ward. Chuck thought it would be more authentic than a Marriott. A bit of New Orleans history in the three-block Faubourg Marigny section, famous for its jazz clubs.

Ours was a two-room suite, with two queens in the bedroom—Chuck on one, me and Luke on the other. Each mattress had its own metal four-poster frame. The furniture throughout was faux Louis XVI, with fourteen-foot ceilings and what appeared to be genuine antique chandeliers overhead. The great-grandfather of the famous fashionista Liz Claiborne had built the house before the Civil War, and the family now rented it out as a nine-bedroom shabby chic hotel.

Chuck, Babet, and I sat together on a couch in the living room of our suite. Luke was on the floor building Lego ships and smashing them into each other, the collisions complete with improvised crashing sounds.

Terek and Damon had cleared the lamps off two side tables, pushed them together, and connected their laptops into a network. I didn't ask what they were doing.

I was too focused on the television.

The Fox News anchor said, "We have announcements of multiple launches from Sriharikota Island and perhaps other locations around India."

I said, "Did she say missile launches? Like *nuclear* missiles?"

"They would say if it was," Chuck replied.

"We now have unconfirmed reports these might have been nuclear missiles," the anchor said.

"*Jesus,*" Chuck whispered under his breath.

The man next to the anchor, an expert of some kind, said, "Our seismology detectors have not registered anything to indicate—"

"Still no GPS?" I asked Damon.

"Nothing on my phone, but Galileo seems to be working."

"Galileo?"

"The European GNSS—global navigation satellite system. That's still up. And online, I'm seeing that the GPS is still working in some places. The signals seem to be getting overwhelmed. Maybe jammed?"

"You can jam GPS signals?"

"See that lightbulb?" Damon pointed at one of the lamps he and Terek had put on the floor. "That is projecting a billion billion times more energy than what we get from one GPS satellite at this distance. They're easy signals to overwhelm."

"Why are they so easy to stop?"

"Because the system was designed back in the day, before anybody thought anyone would try."

"Why *would* someone try?"

"Well, it might not be jammed. But it doesn't make sense, the signals getting dropped like this everywhere. If it's being interfered with—militaries do that before invasions."

"Let's not get carried away."

Damon shrugged. "I didn't say invasions *here*."

"You mean India and Pakistan?" That could make sense.

I grabbed my phone and dialed my wife's number again. It picked up after the fourth ring. "Lauren, are you—"

"Please leave me a message," said her voice on the other end.

I hung up. No sense in leaving a fourth plea to call me back.

Two missed calls from her this morning. I'd texted her, but hadn't gotten any replies. Unusual, but not enough to panic. Not yet. It was still early morning in Hong Kong, but she had to be up, right? Watching the same news I was?

Maybe not.

The television cycle had a way of blowing things out of proportion. Every time there was a snowstorm, the cable channels made it seem like Armageddon. India and Pakistan were a long way from here. Unfortunately, they were also between me and my wife.

"Still nothing?" Chuck asked.

I shook my head and raised my shoulders at the same time.

The internet was working, and the TV service was fine. Lights and power on. But the cell phone networks were jammed. Working, but sporadically.

From too many people accessing them, Damon said. New Orleans, especially the area we were in, was full of tourists. Everyone was calling home at the same time.

Chuck's phone rang. "It's Susie." He got up from the couch and talked to her in a soothing voice as he went into the bedroom.

"Wide areas of the country are now reporting GPS signal outages," said the news anchor.

"That's why the port cranes are not working," Babet said to me. "If the GPS is out, they don't know where containers go, or where things are. Ship navigation is going to be back to the eye. Everything is going to get clogged up. That's maybe why those ships crashed into each other."

Grandma Babet felt responsible. She had said it was her fault a half dozen times. She shouldn't have navigated between the two container transports as a shortcut to the dock, but it was something she'd done a hundred times before. She said boats kept their distance on autopilot, and even then, there were always humans at the controls.

Something had gone wrong, that much was sure.

The two huge ships had collided at their bows, and Babet had managed to reverse course out of harm's way. We wouldn't have been crushed, since the hulls had angled outward above us and left a gap. But I'd hardly had time to think about it as I'd almost drowned. The adrenaline and terror still had me trembling.

Even so, I told Luke it was no big deal. Can't let your kid think you almost died.

I coughed. Hacked up brown sludge.

Chuck returned to the couch.

"How's Susie?" I asked. "The kids?"

"Everybody is fine. I'm heading back to Nashville tomorrow. I'll go get my car from the garage in the morning." He checked his watch and then looked out the window. It was dark, past 8 p.m. "Why don't you come with me?"

"My flight is Wednesday." That was the day after tomorrow. I'd already tried to change it, but I couldn't get through. "You go ahead."

"How are you feeling?"

"I'm never going on a boat again. I swear to God, never again." It had taken Chuck a month to convince me to go on this fishing trip.

The first day out, I'd put on a life jacket, but felt silly when nobody else did. The water in the bayou seemed calm, and we usually kept close to shore. I made sure Luke always kept his on, but by the second day—sweltering in the intense heat—I left mine on the seat.

I coughed again, a hoarse, phlegmy hack.

Chuck inspected my arm. "That's going to be a nasty bruise."

"And that's a nasty cut." I pointed at the bandage covering the cut over his left eye.

"Quite the pair, huh?"

"Switch it to CNN?" I asked.

Chuck gave me a look. He hated CNN as much as I disliked Fox. "Sure." He took the controller and went to the guide.

I got up to see what Damon and Terek were doing.

"I'm trying to contact my friend at the Ares project," Damon said.

"And that is?"

"They track orbital debris at NASA. LEO-to-GEO environmental model. I want to see what info they have on these anti-satellite tests. What they're saying on the TV doesn't make sense. There is no way someone knocked out that many GPS birds. Not this fast."

I pulled a chair next to Terek. "Any luck yet?" He was trying to call his own family. His uncle and aunt.

He pulled back from his laptop and rubbed his eyes. "The internet is working here, but I can't get a message through to Ukraine. No VoIP—voice over IP. No server pings."

"Thanks for today." I coughed again.

Terek had dived into the water after me. Straight away. No hesitation. The young man might have saved my life. It was a brave thing to do.

"Of course."

"I mean it. I owe you."

"You would do the same for me."

A phone rang. I turned, expecting to see Chuck pick up his again, but realized my hand was buzzing. It was my phone. I checked the screen, my heart leaping into my throat. I'd been trying to reach Lauren all afternoon and night, but this was a Washington number I didn't recognize.

"Hello?"

"Mike, is everything okay? This number is our landline."

It was Lauren's uncle. "Luke and I are fine. Did you hear from her?"

"She called this morning, but said she couldn't reach you."

"I had my phone off." Damn it. I shouldn't have let Chuck pressure me into leaving it behind. "How's Olivia?"

"She's fine. I think you should come back to Washington. You and Luke."

"I tried, but I couldn't get—"

"I got you a flight, tomorrow at lunch. You should get an email confirmation. American Airlines at twelve-fifteen. Do you have a pen?"

I scribbled down the information.

"What's happening?" I asked. "Have there really been nuclear launches in India?" The senator would have more information than anyone. This line was a live wire straight into the heart of the government.

"Don't pay attention to the cable news. Nothing like that has happened."

He explained that there had been four launches from India and Pakistan, all of them anti-satellite reprisals. Some of the debris had hit our GPS satellites, but it was a minor disturbance. The Air Force was repositioning them, he said.

I hung up.

Chuck said, "Uncle Leo has a better airline loyalty membership than you, huh?"

What a relief. The tightness in my chest eased. Lauren was good, Olivia was fine. Luke and I had flights to Washington.

"I think I know why you can't reach Lauren." Terek looked up from the online article he was reading. "Turn back to Fox News."

"…reports that Russia and China have shut down their internet connections to the outside world," the news anchor was in the middle of saying when Chuck flipped channels.

"The Great Firewall of China," Damon said. "And Russia too. They have totally disconnected from the rest of the internet."

"And this just in." The news anchor stared at something on her desk. She paused. "The Russians say that their GPS system—the GLONASS global positioning network—has been destroyed. I'm going to repeat that. The Russian global satellite positioning system is reportedly completely disabled, and their military is now on their highest alert status. And there are rumors that some members of the Russian politburo are now blaming America."

Chapter 8

Through the plane's window, streaking whitecaps became visible across the ocean's expanse. Turbulence rocked the cabin, the hum of the turbofans ratcheting up as the aircraft struggled to remain level. Passengers moaned as it hit another patch of rough air and veered to one side. The plane banked toward the mainland.

The engines roared again.

And then silence.

"Oh my God, oh my God." A young man bent over, his face inches from his knees, tears streaking his face. "Please, God, please tell my family—"

The plane bucked to one side and then back.

Out the window, the whitecaps grew. Individual surging waves rose out of the deep blue, the seas roiling and heaving in the storm. No sound of the engines anymore, just the whistling of wind past the airframe and quiet prayers and groans from the passengers.

"Please, oh my God—"

The image switched to the view from a hotel balcony overlooking a beach. Thundering breakers crashed on the shore. A sudden gust whipped palm trees. In the distance, the Sukhoi jet turned in the air. One wingtip caught the water.

It disappeared in a flash of white.

"Turn that off," I said.

Chuck put the iPad screen down and said, "I gotta hit the head."

Luke was still asleep in the bedroom. During the night he'd gotten up to go to the bathroom, and instead of getting back in the bed with me, he had snuggled up with Uncle Chuck. Damon and Terek had gone back to their place for the night, as had Grandma Babet.

Damon was already back. He knocked on our door, a tray of coffees in one hand. The sun was up. I'd set my phone's alarm to wake me, but I hadn't really slept. Our flight to Washington was in a few hours, and I wasn't in the mood for watching an air accident on YouTube.

Even less in the mood for Luke to see it.

I asked, "What happened to that plane?"

"That was four hours ago." Damon closed the door quietly behind him. "An Aeroflot flight from Moscow to Zanzibar. When the GLONASS network went down last night, it sent the Russian aviation system into chaos. Most planes can switch to GPS or Galileo, but those positioning systems went down last night as well."

"Jets don't need GPS to fly," Chuck said as he came out of the bathroom.

"But not having it does slow them down."

"Slow them down?" I said. "Like airspeed? Why?"

"What I mean is, without GPS, airplanes have to be spaced further apart when they're heading into airports. The pilots are still able to fly on analog controls and dead reckoning, but there's more opportunity for error."

"There was a big storm around Zanzibar," Damon said. "That plane was circling for hours before it ran out of fuel."

I glanced at Luke, who was still sleeping in the bed. "Don't let him see that video, okay? Have the cell networks improved?"

Damon offered me a coffee. "Gotten worse, if anything, which is weird."

"Has anyone checked the TV news?" Chuck said.

"Don't turn it on," I said.

I didn't want to wake Luke yet. I had a feeling today would be a long day. He needed all the rest he could get.

"Took me an hour to download that Zanzibar video," Chuck said. "The hotel internet sucks. Forget trying to FaceTime over it."

I checked my cell phone for the hundredth time.

Text messages from friends, but nothing new from Lauren. No overseas phone calls. I tried Skype, WhatsApp. Nothing. Tried calling her number again, but got the busy signal once more. Worse, now my text messages came back with angry red "undelivered" notifications with exclamation points.

As I was putting my phone away, it pinged. A text message from a number I didn't recognize. The contents of the message, however, explained who it was from.

"Damn," I muttered.

My flight was canceled. I showed Chuck.

He said, "Not sure I would get on a plane today. Why don't you and Luke come with me to Nashville? I'm going up to the garage right now."

If flights were being canceled, I doubted I would get a new one. The airport would be pandemonium. "Yeah, I think that might be a good idea." I turned to Damon. "Why is it weird the cell phone networks are worse?"

"Because the volume of calls should have gone down since yesterday. That explains why all the VoIP services are almost unusable this morning. No cell service means everybody is trying to get on them at once."

"You think that's why I can't get Lauren?"

"I think that's something more than simple congestion."

"What about the hotel phone?" I'd tried it the day before, but with no more luck than my cell phone.

"I'm not sure how the hotel phone is routed. It could be VoIP. It could even be going to a mobile network. What we really need is a landline. Something that gets into the phone companies' analog systems."

"Lauren's uncle called from his landline yesterday," I said. He was about the only person I knew who still had one.

"What about a pay phone?" Chuck said.

Damon frowned and looked at the ceiling. "You know, I didn't even—"

"Too young to remember pay phones?" Chuck said. "Twenty years ago there were millions of them, but there must still be some around."

Damon did a search on his laptop. "Look, here's a list of active pay phones in the French Quarter. And their phone numbers."

"In a disaster, pay phones are usually the last things still working." Chuck leaned in to look at the list of addresses on Damon's screen. "A few here close to the garage. I need to go get my Jeep."

"And I need to do some testing," Damon said.

The wrought iron gate squeaked on its hinges. Eight in the morning and the air outside was as sticky as a Café du Monde *beignet*.

"You go ahead," I said to Damon.

He held one of his drones in both hands. Luke ducked under it and shot past him, running shrieking ahead of us past a gnarled live oak sagging with fronds of hanging Spanish moss. We'd decided to walk the two miles from Frenchmen Street to Canal Street along Bourbon to Chuck's garage.

"How far ahead do you want me to go?" Chuck said.

"I'll launch the drone from the middle of the park," Damon replied. "How about we go back to Dauphine Street, and then you go the next block down to Royal?"

Damon's meshnet app was already on all our phones. An updated version of the same technology he'd used six years earlier, when massive storms had hit New York in the dead of winter. The app made it possible for one cell phone to contact another that was within Wi-Fi or Bluetooth range, without needing a connection to the cell network. A point to point network that expanded as more people joined.

Creating the meshnet in New York had saved thousands of lives. Earned him international recognition. Made him something of a cult figure in hacker circles.

Since yesterday, he'd been online and had encouraged masses of people to install his mesh-networking software on their phones. There were already a few hundred with it on their phones in New Orleans.

Now he wanted to take it to the next level.

He stopped past the branches of the first live oak, set the drone down, and then stepped back. It came to life and levitated into the air.

He had attached one of his phones to the bottom of it to use as a mesh-networking relay station, like creating our own cell phone network. He wanted to test it on the walk over to the garage.

The drone rose two hundred feet and became a small dot.

Chuck was already at the other end of the park.

Damon opened his mesh-networking app and selected Chuck's number. A second later: "Hey, it's working!" Chuck's voice came clearly over the speakerphone.

Damon said, "Now walk down the next block and I'll try calling you again."

I waved at Luke. "You going with us, or Uncle Chuck?"

"Chuck," Luke called back.

Doesn't want to be with his old man, huh? "But you stay close to him."

"Deal."

My son ran off after Chuck, who waved and waited.

I turned to follow Damon. "What's happening up there?"

He pointed at the blue sky. "You mean the satellites?"

"I don't mean the pope."

"The Russians claim an anti-satellite weapon hit one of their heavy old birds at an altitude of nineteen thousand kilometers. There was an impact at a closing speed of forty-two thousand kilometers an hour, and the resulting cloud of debris hit their other satellites in the GLONASS constellation."

"What was that news anchor talking about earlier? The Kessler syndrome?"

"An uncontrolled cascade. Hit one satellite and it blows into a million pieces, and then one of those fragments hits another satellite, which blows into more bits, and so on. Before the big SatCom constellation, there were maybe two thousand operational satellites in orbit, ten times that many discarded rocket parts, and other odds and ends big enough to track. Add to that millions of marble-sized fragments that aren't tracked. There's a literal swarm of stuff flying by over our heads at six miles per second."

"Communications with the SatCom network are down as well, right?"

"With customers, yeah, there's no service, but they're still in comms with their fleet. They sent out an email this morning saying they're repositioning their equipment. I guess that makes sense."

"You guess?"

"I tried to contact a friend of mine there to find out more, but I couldn't get through."

"I'm sure they're busy."

We exited Washington Square Park, opened another wrought iron gate, and crossed Frenchmen Street toward Dauphine Street. The roads were deserted. Nobody out, no cars driving along, not even any dogs barking.

It felt a little bit eerie, and struck me with more than a little déjà vu. At least this time it wasn't freezing cold.

With the sun rising in the sky, it felt like it was over a hundred already. Sweat licked down my back.

Damon held one hand up to block out the sun and searched the sky for his drone. He looked back at his phone.

"Did you get in touch with your friends at NASA?" I asked him.

"I did, but they get their data from the DOD's Space Surveillance Network. I'm getting a direct connection."

"Any idea why Russia and China shut down their internet? Is India closed off as well?"

"They didn't shut down, exactly. They cut off outside connections."

"And this has what to do with the space problem?"

"Space and cyberspace are more connected than people realize." Damon looked up into the sky and narrowed his eyes. "When Sputnik launched in 1957, it changed everything. Satellites broke the link between a nation's physical territory and its ability to gather global information and project power. You know what did that next?"

The question was rhetorical, but I answered anyway. "Cyberspace?"

He handed me the phone. "Try calling Chuck."

I opened the mesh-networking app, and was about to ask Damon how to get into the address book when I realized he wanted to see if I could figure it out myself. It took me twenty seconds of fussing around with the app to find Chuck's number. I selected his name. A second later, his phone rang.

Luke answered. "Hey, guys!"

"Taking care of Uncle Chuck over there?"

"You're the one that needs taking care of."

I smiled. "Okay, hang up the phone, buddy."

We reached the corner of Pauger Street and turned left. Another block and we passed Esplanade, and Pauger turned into

Bourbon. The normally boisterous avenue was as empty as Frenchmen Street.

"Space and cyberspace are both entirely technological domains," Damon said. "Without technology, you can't get into either of them. And they were both once seen as global commons, domains that were shared between all nations."

"That doesn't seem to be working anymore."

"We've gone from the World Wide Web to the state-wide web. Not the internet, but the splinternet. And where space used to be the realm of wealthy nations, now we've got wealthy *individuals* sending up thousands of satellites and owning whole chunks of space. It's the Wild West up there."

We passed two of the pay phones on the list Damon had scribbled down, but there were a few or more people in line at each of them. We decided we could wait until we got to the garage.

While we walked straight down Bourbon Street, Chuck veered another two blocks further south. As the drone hovered two hundred feet up, it relayed phone messages from us to Chuck. Damon had four drones in his apartment, and he figured he could set up a local communications network that could cover a few thousand feet if he needed to.

Our optimism dried up the moment we arrived at the garage.

"It's something to do with the computer," the mechanic said. "I would order parts, but I haven't been able to contact my supplier."

"The computer?"

"Something in the ignition sequence." The mechanic shook his head. "It's not like the old days when I could take something apart. I can fix it with a replacement, but you'll have to wait until all this blows over."

A small TV in the corner of the shop had Fox News on. "GPS now appears to be down all across the country," said the news anchor. "For more on this story…"

A woman in cut-off jean shorts and a frilly top was at the pay phone outside the small garage. Two young men stood behind her, hands in their pockets and fidgeting like they were in a hurry. I waited a few feet behind them and listened to Chuck talk with the mechanic.

Luke was down the road on Canal Street, bringing the drone down out of the sky with Damon. Chuck was trying to convince the mechanic to rip out the ignition circuit board and hot-wire it.

The frilly-top woman finished her call, and one of the young men got on the phone. I heard him tell his father there was no way he could get home today. I turned away and tried not to eavesdrop. Two minutes later, he hung up, cursed at the phone, and then said it was all mine.

I pulled the scrap of paper with the senator's number from my pocket, slipped some quarters into the phone, and dialed.

"Do you have any cars I could rent or borrow?" Chuck asked the mechanic.

"They were all taken last night and this morning. I got nothing left."

I held the receiver to my ear.

"What about rental places?"

"There are some up and down Canal," the mechanic said, "but I wouldn't hold much stock in that. I doubt there's cars to rent or steal left anywhere in New Orleans by now. Maybe you heard all flights in and out were canceled this morning."

Someone picked up on the other end.

"Hello?" I said.

"Mike, is that you?"

It was my mother-in-law. "Yes, Susan, this is Michael. Listen, I've got some bad news. Our flight was canceled. I'm not going to be getting to Washington today. I'm going to drive to Nashville with my friend—"

"Did you talk to Lauren?" Her voice was shrill and tense.

"Haven't been able to reach her yesterday or today. Did you talk to her?"

"Mike, she's on a flight."

"What flight?" A creeping fear prickled the hairs on my neck. Down the street, Luke and Damon retrieved the drone. "When did you talk to her?"

"I didn't. I received a courtesy message from American Airlines after the plane had left the ground."

"Left the ground?" I stupidly repeated what she'd said while my brain tried to assimilate and comprehend the meaning of her words.

"Lauren left late yesterday. I mean, last night Hong Kong time, but early morning here. About three hours ago. Direct. With everything happening between India and Pakistan, and the riots breaking out in Hong Kong, she decided to leave early."

That was probably a good idea, but—"To where?"

"Here. To Washington."

"Direct? She got a *direct* flight?"

Was that even possible? She had connected through LA from New York on her way to Hong Kong. If her flight wasn't direct, then what country would she connect through? The floor felt like it disappeared beneath me, the air sucked from my lungs.

On the other end, Susan sounded like she was on the edge of tears. In a strangled voice, she asked, "Do you have the news on?"

"Turn that up," I heard Chuck say from inside. The volume on the TV increased.

"We now have a announcement," I heard a news anchor say, "that the president has ordered the closure of American airspace."

Susan said, "An hour ago, the president shut down our borders, just like after 9/11, just like when the virus hit. Most European countries have shut their borders as well, and so have Russia and China, India, Pakistan—"

I asked in a panicked voice, "Wait, wait...so *where* is my wife?"

Chapter 9

"Ma'am?"

Lauren pulled her eyes away from the airplane's window. As twilight faded to night, she caught glimpses of what looked like patches of snow on the ground forty thousand feet below, but it was hard to tell.

"Another glass of champagne?" asked the flight attendant, an attractive young woman with her red hair pulled back in a bun. Her skin was pale, and she was dressed in blue pants and a matching blazer over an open-necked white shirt. A red-white-and-blue kerchief was tied around her neck.

Lauren twizzled the empty glass flute in her hand and considered it, but finally said, "Thank you, but no."

"Are you sure? I opened a fresh bottle of Dom Pérignon." The flight attendant hovered and smiled.

Was that a nervous smile, or was Lauren projecting?

Lauren handed over the glass. "I'm trying to get the flight tracker working, but it seems to be frozen." She tapped the flat panel in front of her and illustrated the point.

"I'm very sorry, but it's been turned off."

"Turned off?"

The young woman crinkled her nose. "Because it's not working."

"Why isn't it working?"

Now the attendant's eyes widened theatrically. "Technical problems. I'll talk to the captain, how about that?"

Yes, how about that, Lauren thought, but replied, "Thank you."

"Would you like a turndown service? I can make your bed. Fresh sheets and a down comforter? Did you select what pillow you would like?"

Lauren felt guilty. Almost. She'd managed to get maybe the last seat on the direct American Airlines flight that day—a brand new route from Hong Kong to our nation's capital. It had cost Lauren about two months' salary. First class. Not business. First.

Mike would probably yell at her when she got back. Tell her she'd been hysterical, that it had cost a year's tuition for one of the kids. That wasn't fair. He never yelled. He would mope around a bit and do something passive-aggressive, make those faces she always made fun of. Of course he'd want her to get home safely.

Even if this flight cost every penny of her savings, Lauren would have spent it. She needed to be back with her kids.

The protests in Hong Kong had died down under a torrential rainstorm that day, but the news wasn't getting any better. The concierge at the front desk of the hotel had insisted everything was fine, that the internet would be working soon. The conference people had said to wait it out.

Lauren's gut had said otherwise.

Get the hell out of here, her every instinct had screamed.

After maxing out both of her credit cards that morning, she hadn't even bothered checking out of her room, but had walked out the front door after lunch, taken the train from Kowloon out to Lantau Island and the Chek Lap Kok airport, and checked herself into the Flagship Lounge.

Just being in the American Airlines lounge had made her feel like she was closer to home.

"Ma'am?" The flight attendant was still hovering. "Is there anything else I can get for you?"

"I'm fine. I can do the bed thing myself."

"Are you sure?"

"I am."

She watched the flight attendant walk to the next pod behind her and start asking the same questions. Lauren noticed a woman with brown hair staring at her from business class. The flight attendant drew the curtains.

Lauren turned back to the flat screen and the stalled flight tracker. Was the attendant lying? She sensed something was off. The in-flight internet wasn't working either. What were the chances that all these systems weren't working on this nearly new aircraft?

Lauren checked her watch.

It was 11:14 p.m. Hong Kong time. She should switch to New York hours, which would be 10:14 a.m. Right? She found it confusing.

Three hours and twenty minutes in the air, so far. Almost thirteen to go, which would usually be painful, but—she had paid for first class, and she might as well enjoy it. She could get a good night's sleep and be fresh for her little girl when she landed tomorrow.

Lauren looked out the window again.

The sun had gone down in Hong Kong as they'd started boarding. Through the windows of the Flagship Lounge, she had watched the sunset over the green hills of Lantau Island.

Before takeoff, the captain had come on the intercom and described the route. They wouldn't be chasing the sun by heading east—when they took off, they would fly almost due north. Due to high winds in the jet stream, he said, they would be taking a more northerly route, keeping clear of North Korea and passing near the edge of Mongolia. Then up into Russia and Siberia, south of Yakutsk, and out over the Sea of Okhotsk and the northern part of the Kamchatka Peninsula.

The route would take them north of Nome, Alaska, and then through Canada, down the East Coast, and home. A deep twilight persisted well into the night as the plane slid up over the top of the world.

Lauren settled back into her chair and stared at the ceiling. The cabin was dark, the mood lighting shifted from deep purple to black. Everyone else was sleeping, or pretending to be in the way that people did on airplanes. Maybe she would get another glass of champagne, then hit the sack.

How often would she get offered Dom Pérignon? And a down comforter on an aircraft?

She closed her eyes and laughed.

Maybe she wouldn't tell Mike she'd taken first class. She could ask her mother for the money. She usually couldn't wait to hand it over. Mike hated it when she did that, got money from her parents, though less so since her dad had passed.

Her smile fell away.

A rumbling noise.

She opened her eyes. Was that their engines? She glanced out the window and did a double take. What the hell was *that*?

Red lights blinked in the inky blue distance over the faintly curved line of the Earth's horizon. *Not* in the distance, she realized, as she craned toward the window. That was another aircraft, and it was close. And it swung closer.

Passengers on the opposite side of the plane pointed out their windows. The noise level in the cabin grew. The 777 suddenly angled left in a stomach-lurching roll, eliciting a collective gasp in the cabin.

The pilot came over the intercom: "Ah, ladies and gentlemen, I'm very sorry, but we have been ordered to make a change in our flight plan."

Outside Lauren's window, the unmistakable and aggressive lines of a fighter jet materialized from the darkness. A single red star on each of its two tail fins.

Chapter 10

"Somewhere in Siberia, maybe the Arctic," I whispered to Chuck. "A sixteen-and-a-half hour flight almost straight over the North Pole."

"She's in Russia right now?"

I nodded. "Assuming they weren't turned back. Her flight took off more than three hours ago, about when that Aeroflot crash was announced."

"*Jesus*," he muttered under his breath. "What was she thinking about?"

"Getting home. Like us."

Billowing thunderheads crowded the morning sky.

A groaning whine echoed within the nearly deserted canyon of Bourbon Street. We both looked up. A commercial jet headed away from the storm clouds. Another dot moved in the distant sky. And another, and another. Jets circling New Orleans in a holding pattern, each of them waiting for their turn to land.

How much reserve fuel did each of them have?

Luke walked ahead of us, awkwardly holding the large drone that was almost as big as him. He took his job seriously. It kept him occupied. At least he wasn't on his iPad playing games. I hadn't said anything to him yet. What would I tell him? That mom was lost? Somewhere?

"Over a million people in the air at any one moment." Damon watched the jets circle. "Ten thousand planes up there, and they gotta get them all down."

"*Damon*," Chuck whispered urgently.

Our young friend glanced at Chuck, and then me. "Sorry."

With GPS suddenly not working, aircraft were being spaced much further apart for landing sequences when they arrived at airports. Everyone should be able to get on the ground, the TV anchor had said, but then the news had cut to busy airports around the country, detailing how many airplanes were in the sky, how many were unaccounted for, and how many were running low on fuel—and then they cut again. To scenes of the burning wreckage from earlier that morning.

Only one reported crash, the one off Zanzibar.

So far.

What else would happen with GPS down? How many interconnected systems relied on it?

And who the hell still had a map? A real, physical map of highways and roads? When I was a kid, my dad always had one in the car, one of the whole United States. You used to be able to buy them in gas stations. Not anymore. Chuck didn't even have one packed in his bug-out bag. Somehow the thought hadn't occurred to him.

Even in the confines of the French Quarter, I felt lost without the map app on my phone. I knew Frenchmen Street was back along Bourbon, but at some point the streets seemed to zigzag. I could get lost within a few blocks. But with air travel shut down, I would have to somehow make my way by ground transport all the way across the country.

I didn't know where Lauren was, but I couldn't control that situation. I needed to get back to my little girl. I needed to get to Washington.

"We can't take Babet's car," I said to Chuck.

We'd tried two other gas stations and three rental offices on Canal Street, but everyone was out of anything to rent. Cars, SUVs, trucks. Even camper vans. Nothing. We'd called Grandma Babet's landline from the gas station, and she'd volunteered to let us take her Monte Carlo to Nashville if we couldn't find anything. Said we could take it all the way to Washington if we needed.

Damon was less enthusiastic.

That plan would strand his grandmother without a car if there was an emergency. Chuck volunteered to pay for the car, double what it was worth. I sided with Damon. We couldn't take her car. Our current plan was to find a dealership near the highway and buy a used one outright.

"Let's try in there." Damon indicated a coffee shop a half block down on Saint Louis Street.

We needed an internet connection.

Usually the bars were crowded, but now the coffee shops were overflowing. Every table was occupied. Damon found us a spot to perch near the front on the interior ledge of a bay window. Before coming inside, we'd launched the drone high into the sky. It hovered two hundred feet overhead.

Luke went with Chuck to go and get some coffee, while Damon logged in to the café's wireless on his laptop.

"Anything?"

A minute's wait felt like an hour.

"There it is." Damon turned his laptop's screen for me to see.

A flight tracking website. He entered Lauren's flight information, and it showed a dotted line from Hong Kong, up over Russia and the Arctic, then down between Canada and Greenland to the East Coast of America.

The Boeing 777 had taken off at 7:55 p.m. Hong Kong time, which was 6:55 a.m. our time. A little more than three hours ago. The website indicated the sixteen-and-a-half-hour flight was on schedule for an 11:30 p.m. landing at Washington National, except there was no dot on the screen to indicate where the plane was right now.

"What does that mean?" I asked.

Had the plane fallen out of the sky?

"It's probably out of radar contact. At least, civilian radar. There are a few systems onboard that ping location, but they rely on satellites. It could be a GPS malfunction. I'm not sure how this website gets its location data."

"But it's still indicating an on-time arrival?"

He checked the American Airlines website and two other flight trackers. "So far."

"Will it be allowed to land? Isn't American airspace closed?"

"Usually that means they're rerouted to the closest airport."

"So she'll end up in Siberia?"

"I doubt the Russians want an American airliner. Neither do the Chinese. Back on 9/11, almost all the transoceanic planes en route to the States ended up in Canada. Labrador. Places like that."

"Canada?" That didn't seem so bad.

"But this isn't the same as 9/11. We don't have the threat of terrorists in the air actively attacking American targets. This is global. Everybody is walling themselves off because they don't know what's happening. Even Canada is shutting down its borders."

Unusual, but unfortunately not unprecedented. Same thing happened when that virus outbreak started, but not as sudden as this.

"So where will all th—"

My phone pinged. A text from Terek: "*I'm at the hotel. I might have a solution.*"

He'd contacted me through the mesh-network app.

"You see this?" I held my phone up. "Your buddy says he might have a car."

Damon read the message. "Did you turn on location tracking through Wi-Fi?" He opened my settings, shook his head, made a change, and handed my phone back. "Not as accurate as GPS, but if we set a latitude and longitude for our Wi-Fi mesh nodes—"

"Will my regular map app work?"

"Sort of." He nodded. "And look at this." He pointed at his laptop screen. "Two NOAA satellites have gone offline."

"Noah?"

"The National Oceanic and Atmospheric Administration. They're trying to update the track on Hurricane Dolly, but can't get any new imaging. Same thing for the fires in Appalachia and California, and the storms in the Midwest."

"Offline?" Chuck returned with the coffees. "You mean, destroyed?"

"Maybe NOAA is moving them to get out of the way."

"What altitude were they orbiting?"

"About two thousand kilometers."

"So the wreckage is spreading?"

Damon raised his shoulders. "I'll try and contact my friends at NASA, see if they have any more info."

"We found Lauren's flight," I said to Chuck.

He handed me a coffee. "And?" He looked over his shoulder.

Luke watched us carefully. He knew things weren't right. A bottom-of-the-stomach unease was infecting everyone. All around us in the coffee shop, hushed cursing and quiet but urgent conversations.

I leaned toward Chuck and spoke quietly. "The online flight tracker shows that the plane took off, but there's no information on where it actually is. With GPS down, and who knows if satellite tracking—"

"Is something wrong with mom?" Luke frowned.

"She's on her way home," I said.

Luke considered that for a second. "We're going to get her?"

"I promise."

Damon said, "We should get back to the hotel. My grandmother says we need to get over there."

"Who the heck is that?" Chuck said.

Damon and Luke were across the street in Washington Square Park retrieving the drone. Babet's Monte Carlo was parked outside the hotel, so we expected to see her in there. I put the key in the door to our room and opened it, but instead of Babet's slim frame, we discovered a twenty-something woman in a windbreaker rummaging through Chuck's bags by the TV.

"This is my sister, Irena," Terek said. He stood to one side of the bags.

"Mind getting her away from my stuff?" Chuck growled.

Irena held her hands up in mock surrender, a lopsided grin on her face as she backed away. "I'm impressed. I've got my own survival stash in the back of my truck."

"Truck?"

"This is what I was trying to tell you," Terek said to me. "Irena has a truck."

I heard a toilet being flushed, and then water running. "I told them not to touch your stuff," Babet said as she exited the bathroom a second later.

Luke lurched through the door, the huge drone grasped in both his arms.

Damon walked in behind him. "Have you guys met Terek's sister?"

Irena put her hand out. I shook it. "Nice to meet you," I said.

Firm grip.

Her dark brown eyes were expressive and kind, her black hair close cropped but long enough that a curling loop drooped down over her forehead. She was slender, not much more than a hundred and twenty pounds, and stood maybe two inches shorter than Chuck's six feet.

Irena squatted and held out a hand to Luke. "And what's your name?"

He took it and pumped firmly. "Luke."

"Irena."

Luke turned to me, his face beaming. "Dad, just like Gorby's mother. You remember, from the old apartment?"

How could I forget? "Yeah, I remember."

Irena maintained a puzzled smile and stood. "I'm sorry, who do I remind you of?"

"It's your name," I said. "We used to have a neighbor called Irena. A wonderful lady." I remembered the two barrels of a shotgun emerging from the Borodin's apartment, with the eighty-year-old Irena behind it.

"I heard you guys need a lift to Nashville." Irena offered her hand to Chuck.

Chuck hesitated, but then shook. "Yeah, that's right."

The TV was on with the volume low. Luke squeezed past us and deposited the drone on the floor. "Dad, can I use the iPad?"

I nodded, sure.

Irena looked at the drone, her eyebrows raised. Impressed. She pointed out the door past us. "That's my Range Rover right there."

It wasn't new. Rust showed through the fenders. The paint chipped in places.

"I keep it stocked at all times with emergency supplies, too." She nodded at Chuck. "Though I don't have all the equipment you do." She flicked her chin at the bags by the TV. "Night vision goggles. Very cool."

"And you need to go to Nashville?" Chuck said.

"Washington. To Terek's wife. Gotta take care of my little brother, and I should get back up to New England, got my stuff up there—but I figured Nashville could be on the way. Damon has helped us out, so we'd like to return the favor." Her accent was Eastern European, but she spoke like an American.

"You were working on the docks, too?" Chuck said.

Irena's grin widened. "Just finished college. Boston University. Was trying to figure out what to do, and this was an easy way to spend a few months in the Big Easy, you know?" She looked back at the TV. The news anchor was listing the satellites NASA had lost contact with. "But it looks like the holiday is over."

Chuck turned to Damon. "Tell me again how you know these two?"

C huck pulled me and Damon onto the front balcony of the hotel. I left the door ajar so I could see Luke by the TV. Babet sat protectively behind him. I checked my watch. Almost 11:30.

Thunderheads crowded the sky, the midday sun high between them, the air damp and thick. Cicadas whined from the branches of the oaks across the street. I held one hand up to block the sun and watched the dot of an airplane crawl across the bright blue.

"I met Terek online, playing *Slayer*," Damon said.

"What's that?" Chuck wasn't into video games.

"It's a massive multiplayer—"

"I thought you went to school with him at MIT."

I hung back by the door, one eye on Luke and the other on the TV. The news was back to covering the airports. My heart felt like it was stuck in my throat, held up by a trip wire, as I waited for news of another air crash.

Where the hell was Lauren? Had they turned her back?

I checked my phone. Full bars, but no luck when I tried using it on the cell network. It was connected to the hotel Wi-Fi, but no text messages. No messages from Lauren, but then I assumed she was in the air.

I tried calling her mother again, but got a busy signal. It wasn't that the line was busy—the cell networks weren't working. Not connecting.

"I met him while I was at school," Damon said. "What's the big deal? I thought you would be happy. And she's got a truck. Isn't that what you wanted?" He pointed at the aging Range Rover.

"You were playing games with him? And what, you decided to meet up?"

"I met him on the gaming boards, but he's an amazing hacker. That's how we got to know each other."

"A hacker?"

"I mean he can build things, not break into banks. He and his sister came here by themselves after their mother died a few years ago. Immigrated. Irena pretty much raised Terek—I mean, since she was the older one. Their father took off when they were young." Damon stopped at that. It seemed like he was uncomfortable about saying more.

But it quieted Chuck down. He and I had each lost both of our parents early. "You know, Aristotle said that there were three types of friends."

"Aristotle, the old philosopher guy?"

Chuck nodded. "Ones you find useful, ones that give mutual respect and admiration, and ones for pleasure—"

"What are you worrying about? Exactly?"

I heard the TV announcer say that all the airports in New York were closed.

Chuck said, "Do you trust him? Or is he just useful, or fun to hang out with?"

"You mean unlike you?"

"I'll take that as a compliment."

I said, "Chuck, that kid might have saved my life."

Damon said, "I've known him for a year. He's always been straight with me, and he and his sister are hard workers. Honest to a fault. If you don't want to take them up on their offer to drive you to Nashville—"

"I've got eleven hours until Lauren's plane lands." I checked my watch. It was 11:35. To Chuck I said, "I'm going with them, whether you come or not. I need to get to DC as soon as I can."

The chances of Lauren's plane landing in DC were slim. It didn't matter. I needed to be there, no matter what. I needed to get Olivia. Start to get my family back together.

"You decide," Damon said to Chuck. "I gotta go back inside and see if I can get my friend at NASA online." He slipped past us and went in, but left the door open.

Chuck said to me, "We could still take Babet's car."

"We can't take her car. I don't have time to stay here and debate and come up with some other solution. I'm going. If you need to stay and fix the Jeep, I understand, but Luke and I are going with Damon and his friends."

The volume on the TV was low.

The screen showed riot police in Prague. A train had crashed somewhere else. Lineups outside grocery stores in Argentina. A news crawl scrolled along the bottom of the screen, announcing that global stock markets were suspended. The TV shifted to a video of a citizens' militia roadblock in the Midwest.

The last image was of a fire raging in California. The news anchor said that emergency services were crippled by the loss of GPS, and that mobile networks were down across the country.

I logged into the hotel Wi-Fi.

The flight tracker website still listed the same takeoff and landing times for Lauren's plane. Unchanged. It didn't say canceled, which was what often happened when a flight crashed or disappeared.

Sometimes, no news was good news.

At least the flight was still there.

My phone had full bars, so I tried calling Lauren's uncle in Washington. I lifted the receiver to my ear.

Busy signal.

Damon and Terek were on their laptops at one of the side tables. Babet and Irena sat on a couch, while Luke played with his Legos in the bedroom.

Luke called to me, "Dad, can I use the iPad?"

"I think Uncle Chuck is busy with it," I said.

"He's been using it forever." Luke pouted for a bit, but then returned to his Legos.

Chuck was cross-legged on the bed, busy taping together scraps of paper he'd scavenged from the hotel's front desk, our iPad in front of him.

I paced back and forth.

"I thought you said cell service would get better once the initial rush was over," I said to Damon.

Terek answered, "GPS has been spotty since yesterday, and has been completely down since last night."

"I don't need to know where I am, I just need to use my phone."

"What he means," Damon said, "is that GPS isn't only for location services. Timing. Timing is probably even more important than location."

"GPS provides time?"

"To pretty much every mobile network. GPS signals are used to provide universal timestamps. The information sent over the cell networks is digital. It's not analog, like on landlines. When you digitize information, each packet needs to have a timestamp. When those packets arrive on the other end, you can use their timestamps to put the information back in order and re-create the audio or data stream."

"But it worked sometimes last night."

"Cell towers have their own timing mechanisms. Quartz oscillators. When they lose GPS, they can work for a few hours, maybe even a few days. But eventually, if they're not updated by GPS signals, the network loses coherence. Data packets can't be reconstructed. And there are thousands of systems that require those timing signals."

"Systems that are all failing now?"

Damon waved me over. He turned his laptop around. "My friend gave me access to the space debris tracker they're running at NASA."

An animated graphic played over and over. In the center was the blue Earth. An outer circle was labelled GEO, with the circle right around the Earth labelled LEO. A red bloom spread steadily toward LEO.

"So that's the debris?" Chuck said.

"The anti-satellite hits spread maybe millions of fragments into descending orbits."

"How do they get the information?" Chuck asked. "Radar? Or something else?"

"So far, this is purely modeling, based on reports of what's happening up there. The DOD does radar imaging to generate the Space Surveillance Network data, but that takes time and needs objects bigger than most of these fragments. But it doesn't make sense."

"Sure it does," Terek disagreed. "That's taking out the satellites, one by one. Kessler syndrome. They've been warning of this for years."

"Taking out GLONASS? All the Russian geopositioning satellites, in less than a day? That's twenty-four satellites at nineteen-thousand kilometers of altitude. And then GPS?"

"They're both in medium Earth orbits," Terek pointed out.

"Yeah, but GPS orbits a thousand kilometers above GLONASS. And there are thirty-one satellites in the GPS constellation. Twenty-two in the European Union's Galileo. Thirty-five in the Chinese BieDou system. The Indian NavIC system only has three of their seven in geostationary orbit—"

"You said that's coming from NASA? They should know, if anyone."

"That's not imaging. We haven't seen any actual debris yet. It's too small to detect at that distance and speed."

"What else could be causing this?"

"I have no idea. And the Indian military is still denying that it sent up any anti-satellite weapons."

Chuck walked into the living room, holding a folded stack of papers under one arm. "The American, Russian, Chinese, and British militaries have all confirmed that the anti-satellite missiles were launched from the Indian base off Chennai, and the Pakistanis aren't denying their attacks. They confirmed the Indian launches as well."

"I trust our military," I said.

"I trust none of them," Chuck said. "But, in this case, I believe them. Who exactly do you think is lying? Everyone else, or the Indian government? They're trying to cover their asses as this whole mess gets worse and worse. When the space dust settles, someone's going to be paying for this. They don't want to be the ones holding the bag."

"Still better than an all-out nuclear war between India and Pakistan," I said.

"I haven't heard any fat ladies singing yet, have you?"

"Quite the optimist, huh?"

"Pragmatists drink the water whether the glass is half full or half empty." Chuck taped his newly constructed map to the wall by the TV. "I drew this as best I could. From here we go north on I-55. We head up to Nashville and pick up Susie, Bonham, and Ellarose."

"So you're coming with us and Irena?"

"Does the pope—"

"I'm pretty sure the pontiff doesn't defecate in the woods." His go-to joke was getting old. "But I'll take that as a yes."

A not-insubstantial weight flew from my shoulders. My bravado about heading out on the road without Chuck had been sincere, but I was relieved to know he would come with us. "And then I continue on from Nashville with Terek?"

"I'll go to DC, too," Damon said.

"We all go together," Chuck said. "At least as far as my cabin." He stabbed a finger at the midpoint of Interstate 81 on his map, next to the squiggly line of the Appalachians, the backbone of the East Coast. He looked me square in the eye. "We go to the cabin again? Take Susie and the kids there?"

The cabin.

I was hoping he wouldn't say that. Those two words brought back a rush of sensations and images. Of pain. Starvation. And Tony. Our friend Anthony had died protecting Luke at that cabin. I never told Chuck, but I swore I would never go back to that place. I swore there was no way I would ever...

I felt like I wanted to vomit, but instead I said, "Can we leave now?"

It was past noon already.

Eleven hours till Lauren's plane had to land, one way or the other. A sixteen-and-a-half hour flight. I'd checked, and 777s couldn't stay in the air for more than eighteen hours. Modified ones could go up to nineteen at cruising speed, maybe even longer at low speeds and with low cargo. I'd become an expert on 777s in the last twenty minutes.

"No traffic, it's a fifteen-hour drive from here to my cabin." Chuck traced a line across his map. "Once we get there, we secure everyone and everything. I've got my own truck up there. Then we go in both vehicles, and we can take Highway 66 into Washington. Another hour down the road."

An hour's drive in a car, but last time it had taken me a whole day and night to walk down that road, alone, afraid, in the cold and dark and rain—my mind keening on the sharp edge of insanity.

Chuck said, "It might take us more than a day to make the whole drive. There's a lot of confusion out there, but even if we have to head off the main roads, we follow sunrise to the east. As long as we don't cross the Ohio River to the north, eventually we'll get to the edge of the Appalachians. Interstate 81 cuts north to south all the way from New York to the Carolinas. We can't miss it."

Chuck produced a round bauble that looked like it was from a dollar store. A north-south needle floated in the liquid within it. "Even if we have no GPS, we still have these old things called compasses."

"Aren't there fires in there somewhere?" I pointed vaguely at the middle of the map.

"We're going to head up past Kentucky, all those fires are down—"

"Quiet for a second," Damon interrupted.

He grabbed the TV remote and turned up the volume.

The screen filled with an image of clouds and ocean, but from high above. From orbit. Huge solar panel arrays reflected the sun in a glimmering wave as the Earth slowly rotated beneath the space station. It was silent.

"The crew successfully evacuated the station over two hours ago," the CNN news anchor said. "These images are from exterior cameras, and we have reports that…oh…oh my…"

In total silence, part of one of the solar panels seemed to detach and shear away. Shimmering fragments filled the space around it, thousands of tiny mirrors reflecting the sun in a sparkling glitter.

A dark hole appeared in one of the crew compartments, and then another. After a few seconds, black dots littered the station's pressure shell amid a growing haze of debris.

The steady progression of the blue Earth and distant clouds below the station tilted. The viewpoint spun and the crescent edge of the atmosphere became visible.

The field of view became cluttered with wreckage, the entire station coming apart like a toy model dropped two floors onto an invisible pavement.

Luke reached out to hold my hand. I squeezed his.

Chuck said, "Guess that's enough proof the debris field exists." Dumbfounded silence as the space station disintegrated. "That's two hundred billion dollars down the toilet."

"Is there a chance some of that could hit us?" I asked.

"Only the biggest chunks of that would make it to the ground," Damon said.

Somehow that wasn't reassuring. "What about something in the air?"

Chapter 12

Lauren peered out of the 777's window. The pane was frosted over at the bottom. She wondered what that signified, if anything. From the corner of her eye, she thought she saw a flash high up, but it didn't persist.

The sky was bright and cloudless, dark blue straight overhead fading to baby blue at the horizon. The sky merged almost seamlessly with a sheet of white that stretched unbroken from one side of her window to the other.

Not quite unbroken.

If she squinted and concentrated, Lauren could make out cracks in the ice sheet forty-plus thousand feet below her.

It had been four hours since the Russian jets had disappeared. For two hours they had ferried the passenger jet, hugging the wingtips of the Boeing aircraft. They had forced the plane to turn left, which meant...further north?

At first, the captain had said it was a security measure.

That hadn't stopped the passengers from asking what *exactly* was going on. After the fighters left, the captain had finally spoken over the intercom. We would be extending the flight by an hour, he said, but the plane had more than enough fuel. The flight needed to gain altitude to keep a ceiling over Russian bases. He didn't explain why. He only repeated that these were security measures.

Security for what? No answer.

Just another round of drinks served up by the flight attendants. That was three hours ago.

Passengers, Lauren included, kept asking for the flight tracker to be turned back on. She heard requests muttered—some almost yelled—asking where exactly the plane was.

One man in business class, a few rows behind Lauren, got up and belligerently demanded to see the captain. A male flight attendant confronted him after the man shoved one of the female attendants, at which point it became a chest-thumping contest. The male attendant told the man to get back to his seat. *Or what*, the man asked, glowering.

At that point, another passenger got up from his seat. Not threatening, but quiet and swift. He said something to the man, who then sat down. Lauren guessed he was the air marshal. They had guns, didn't they?

The tension in the recycled air became something Lauren could almost taste, like cardboard stuck to her tongue.

After the near-altercation, the captain came back on the intercom, and in a drawling, Southern-accented voice, explained that they couldn't turn the flight tracker back on because they had lost the satellite uplink. The same reason the in-flight internet wasn't working.

This didn't have the calming effect he might have hoped for. Whispers and rumors began circling the cabin.

Lauren heard people saying that a war had broken out, that GPS was lost. That all the satellites were gone. A man behind Lauren grumbled to his wife, saying that this far north over Russia, we were directly over the north magnetic pole. Even a magnetic compass wouldn't work here, but would spin aimlessly.

We're lost, he said.

His wife told him to shut up.

Lauren checked her watch again. For the millionth time.

It was 4 p.m. in New York.

Nine hours in the air so far, give or take.

Eight and a half hours to go, according to the captain.

Even if there was no compass, there was still the sun, right? Except up here, east and west ceased to matter. Only south became a thing.

Still.

If they had turned west, Lauren reasoned, then they would have been following the sun. It would probably have been dark right now if they had followed that path. The bright sunlight meant the plane had gone either north or east, except she hadn't felt the aircraft's wings tip right. So, more northerly, which explained the endless expanse of white.

The purple twilight out her window had never gone away, but had rotated toward the front of the aircraft and grown brighter until three hours ago, when the sun had burst over the horizon. A few people had clapped to see it rise.

When Lauren looked out the windows on the other side of the plane, she could just see the sun. It stayed toward the nose of the plane as it rose into the sky over the next few hours. Which meant they were heading east, right? Toward the sun? And if the sun came up at 1 p.m. East Coast time, what did that mean?

She had no idea.

Her head felt like it was spinning.

"More champagne, miss?"

Lauren turned from the window.

The attractive female flight attendant with the red-white-and-blue kerchief held a bottle of Dom. She lifted it up. "Champagne?" she asked again.

Lauren shook her head and looked toward the window.

"Can I do something else for you? Maybe freshen up your—"

"I'll tell you what you can goddamn do for me." Lauren's voice rose as she turned back to the young woman. "You can tell me what the hell is going on. What's happening out there? Where are we?"

"As the captain said, we are taking a little—"

"Why is there no satellite link? Has a war started?"

"Please, ma'am, why don't I get you someth—"

"I don't want an hors d'oeuvre!" Lauren almost screamed. "I want to know where we are."

The young woman's lower lip quivered. Lauren immediately regretted raising her voice, but it was too late. The flight attendant burst into tears and began sobbing, but bravely kept the bottle of Dom up.

"I'm sorry." Lauren pulled down the small jump seat each first class pod had for guests. "Here. Sit."

"I don't know what's going on," the flight attendant said between sobs. "They're not telling us anything."

She sat, handed the champagne to Lauren, who set it on the floor and put an arm around the girl. "It's okay, it's okay." She patted the young woman's back.

This was bad.

When turbulence hit, the violent stuff that rocked the cabin and terrified Lauren, she would watch the flight attendants calmly chatting and putting the carts away, getting out their magazines while the plane bumped and jumped around. Seeing them so calm helped Lauren rationalize that nothing bad was really happening.

Holding this young girl crying in her lap, Lauren realized how serious this situation had to be. The plane was flying smoothly, but she broke into a cold sweat. Her cheeks flushed.

Lauren looked out the window at the unending sheet of ice.

Where on God's Earth were they?

Chapter 13

"Timing signals? Seriously? That's why our cell phones aren't working?" I leaned over the divider from the back seat to get a look at what Damon was doing.

He had his laptop out, but still wasn't able to get a signal from the SatCom service. It didn't surprise me, but he couldn't understand how the thousands of satellites in the constellation could all be suddenly unresponsive. Even the terrifying images of the space station disintegrating on TV hadn't entirely convinced him of what was happening up there.

Terek sat in the front passenger seat of the Range Rover beside Irena, who drove. Damon and Chuck were in the middle two seats, with Luke and me in the cramped third row pop-ups.

Luke was playing games on the iPad, but complained that he couldn't connect to watch videos. I explained again that it didn't work.

We'd crammed all of Chuck's gear, Terek's stuff, and my bags into the rooftop rack. Covered it as best we could with a tarp and tied it down with cord. The small trunk area held all the twelve-volt batteries that Damon used to charge his drones.

The Range Rover's interior had a lived-in, musty smell, the floor caked with dried mud and littered with empty coffee cups.

"Aircraft transceivers, emergency beacons, Babet's shipping containers down in the port," Terek said from the front seat. "You would be surprised how many digital devices depend on satellites and timing signals from GPS to work. The most critical is the electrical grid."

"Why does the power grid need it?"

"Power stations feed electricity into the grid, and the output is synchronized to 50 or 60 Hz, depending where you are in the world. Very important, though, that everything is synchronized across the whole network, across a whole nation."

"Let me guess. Power stations use GPS timing as a universal clock."

"Bingo. We have a winner."

"So will power go out?"

"Not right away, but I'll bet we'll see blackouts soon."

"There's a common misconception about GPS," Damon said. "It doesn't provide any location information, not by itself."

I let go an audible sigh, but that didn't stop him.

"GPS is entirely and only timing signals. Here I am, here I am, the satellites announce, beaming down a timer. We figure out location using the delay caused by distance due to the speed of light, and very carefully compiled tables of satellite orbits and positions. You need at least four to triangulate—"

"One more word," Chuck said, "and I'm going to make you eat your drone piece by piece, you understand?"

Damon blinked with his mouth half-open, and then muttered under his breath, "I'm not sure that's really possible."

"Hold on a second." Luke looked up from the iPad and scrunched his nose upward. "So, you're telling me that because we don't have time signals coming from satellites up there a thousand miles away, our cell phones don't work? And I can't watch videos?"

"That's right," Damon said.

"That is the dumbest thing I've ever heard." Luke returned to his game.

After lunch, we had said a hasty goodbye to Babet, got into Irena's truck, and drove through the crowded French Quarter of New Orleans. It was surprising to see so many people out, drinking and having what looked like a good time in the middle of what felt like a disaster to me—but then again, what else was there to do? If I didn't have a family, getting drunk on Bourbon Street might seem like a good idea.

The traffic wasn't bad on Canal Street, but as we went north of New Orleans onto Interstate 10 and crossed south of Lake Pontchartrain, it became bumper to bumper.

Irena had filled up the truck before arriving at our hotel, which was a small mercy as the lineups at the gas stations stretched for blocks. We stopped at a small supermarket, but half the shelves were already empty. The clerk said that no new shipments were coming in, that what was there was what they had. We settled on Doritos and beef jerky and a dozen gallon jugs of water.

Chuck said the water was the most important.

At about 3 p.m., as we inched up the side of Lake Pontchartrain, the threatening clouds finally swept over us and unleashed a sleeting rain that made it impossible to see even five feet through the deluge. The already slow traffic ground to a standstill. Red taillights glimmered through the rain in front of us. I passed the time reading a book to Luke.

We kept the radio on the local news channel, which alternated between warnings of heavy thunderstorms and recapping the loss of the space station and the list satellites going offline.

"Surrey Technologies reports loss of communications with two more of their Disaster Monitoring Constellation satellites," listed the radio news announced, "and WorldView 1 and 2 from DigitalGlobe. RapidEye in Germany says it has lost three of their five earth imaging arrays…"

The rain finally let up and we inched past Louis Armstrong Airport as we reached the outskirts of the city. I asked Chuck to roll down his window. The air was foggy and humid, the running lights of an aircraft approaching the runway shining fuzzily through the haze in the distance.

Luke studied me as I watched the plane land. "Are we going to get mommy?" he asked.

Mommy. The way he said it. In some ways he was already growing into a little man, but in others he was still a child.

After two hours of gridlock, we finally reached the turnoff for Interstate 55 north, and Chuck convinced Irena to take the alternate road up. When that was crammed too, he asked her to go onto the shoulder to skip around.

Almost immediately, a State Trooper materialized, as if from nowhere. The trooper didn't even ask for Irena's license, but told us to get back in the traffic. He said there were accidents further up, and that we would have to be patient. Told us to stay off the shoulder, as emergency vehicles might need it.

Chuck cursed under his breath, but I secretly found it reassuring that things were so under control that the traffic was still being policed.

"Welcome to Mississippi," announced a waterlogged road sign. "The Birthplace of American Music."

The steady drumming of the rain against the roof rose to a rhythmic hammering. Out the window, white balls of hail skittered across the pavement and bounced off the car next to us. Seconds later, the hail turned back to rain.

Luke woke up, eyes wide.

I pulled his head into my chest. "Go back to sleep," I whispered to him.

"Can I use your phone?" he asked.

"There's no network."

"I can still play *Marble Mixer.*"

"Why don't you go back to sleep?"

"I'm not sleeping."

"Try. Please."

He put his head back down.

I waited a moment and then whispered to Chuck: "I thought Mississippi was east? You sure we're not going the wrong way?"

Chuck was navigating with his hand-drawn map and a headlamp. The map was spread across his knees, and he crossed off the names of towns as we passed them.

"The great state of Mississippi stretches all the way from Tennessee to the Gulf Coast," he said without looking up. "It cuts across the top of Louisiana."

"What kind of trees are those?" I was bored. "I always thought it was weird how there are evergreen forests in the deep south."

He glanced out the window into the semidarkness. "Loblolly pines. You know they used to make turpentine from them?"

It was exactly the sort of useless-but-interesting trivia I relied on him for.

I checked my watch. Past seven.

Wherever she was, Lauren's plane had four, maybe five, hours of fuel left. Maybe she was already on the ground? That might be a good thing, but then she wouldn't be home. She would be stranded in a foreign country.

The sun was setting somewhere behind a new set of towering thunderheads, but the clouds were so low and dark it had been a murky twilight for hours already.

Irena's truck had a radio scanner in the front, right under the CD deck. Chuck called it a police scanner. Terek insisted it wasn't a police scanner, just a private mobile radio. Like a CB. The same kind used by emergency services, which operated mostly on the 800 megahertz band, Terek said, and the newer systems on 700.

The muffled sounds of two-way radio chatter competed with the steady drum of rain on the hood of the truck. We still had the radio on the local news channel, the volume turned low.

I pressed my face against the glass of the side window and felt the coolness of it. I looked up. The car inched forward. Rivulets of water streamed down the window like tears. I clutched Luke tight beside me. He was back asleep and snoring softly.

I needed to get to my daughter. She was with family, but I needed her close by me. Needed to feel her breathing, the same as I could feel Luke's little chest right now. And we needed to find Lauren. No matter what. No matter where.

"Planes don't need GPS to land," Chuck said, as if he was reading my mind. "Every pilot starts out on a Cessna, starts with the same analog controls and instruments that every single plane always has, even if all the digital systems fail. Every airplane has a magnetic compass floating right there in the middle of the cockpit, no matter how advanced the rest of it is."

"And radar is still working," Damon said. "The weather channel still has all the Doppler radar maps of the storms, even if they don't have satellite images. Planes mostly use radar when they get close to airports."

"Not in the far north," Terek said from the front. "There's no radar coverage up there. But Lauren's plane probably didn't continue north."

It was the first time someone had offered an opinion like this. "Why do you say that?"

"No radar and no navigation markers. Going over the North Pole without GPS would be almost suicide." He paused. "I mean, dangerous. It could be dangerous."

Chuck held up both hands as if he was trying to hold Terek back.

I put a hand on my friend's shoulder. "I thought you said they could navigate with analog controls."

"Yeah, but that high up in the north? If you get over the north magnetic pole—"

"Which is in Russia now," Terek said.

"Straight where Lauren's flight was heading. Over magnetic north, a compass needle spins in circles," Chuck continued. "You get stuck in clouds, or it's dark, or you're over the snowpack without visual markers…" His voice trailed off.

"What?"

"There's a lot of empty space up there."

"Didn't someone think of this?" I said. "That by relying on GPS for timing signals, for position, that everything could eventually go wrong?"

Terek replied, "They didn't think through what would happen if billions of people suddenly lost contact, what all the ramifications might be. More and more devices started using GPS, because the signal is cheap and easy to use."

Damon said, "That's not entirely true. Networks like 5G have timing signals built into them. Or, they should have." He cocked his head to one side. "Implementing timing signals in cables is expensive, and the US hasn't done it. Places like South Korea and Japan might have their mobile networks working right now."

Terek said, "The US government did look at the weaknesses of GPS. There are other ways to provide a timing signal. Antennas, high-altitude balloons, wired connections…"

"I don't think anyone will be getting any other satellites up there soon," Chuck said.

"That might be true." Damon shut his laptop. "If we have a full-scale Kessler syndrome going on over our heads, the debris could take hundreds of years to degrade. Some of it might never come down. No more satellites, no more space travel."

"No moon base?" I'd read about NASA's planned Artemis project, which was meant to put a space station around the moon in the coming years. "No going to Mars…"

"Yeah, forget all of that," Damon said. "Not in our lifetimes. Not even in Luke's."

"That might be a good thing," Chuck said.

"Good?"

"A whole new space race has started. Going to the moon. Going to Mars. China, Russia, America, Japan, and now India and Pakistan? We have a whole mess of things to fix on Earth, down here."

Damon said, "The mess down here is exactly why we need to get up there."

"Not a bad idea to have a plan B," I said. "Maybe we should get to Mars. Sam Maxwell is planning on dying on the Mars colony he plans to build." Maxwell was a competitor to Tyrell Jakob.

"If that's not a billionaire-idiot bucket list wish," Chuck snorted.

I ignored him. "Humans need to be on more than one planet to survive in the long run. What happens if this nuclear war starts? Between India and Pakistan?"

"What the hell are you guys smoking? Are you listening to yourselves?" Chuck said. "We mess up this planet, so we move to the next? The peak of Mount Everest and the deepest reaches of Antarctica are balmy compared to the warmest tropics of Mars."

"Just because there are challenges," Damon said, "doesn't mean we have to give up."

"Exactly! And it sounds like you're giving up on here already."

"You're the one that doesn't believe in global warming."

"I didn't say I didn't believe it. I'm skeptical that people are causing it."

"If that's your logic, then how could we fix it?"

"Exactly what I've been saying."

Butting heads with Chuck was an old game. "Look, even if we're not talking about going to Mars, space-based systems provide communications, GPS, weather imaging and prediction—"

Chuck interjected, "Tang and memory foam, aren't those derived from the space program?"

"They are," Damon said.

"So you're saying Tang is worth an investment of a few billion dollars? Sounds legit. I mean, Tang is a refreshing beverage and all, but—"

"Of course I'm not saying that."

"And what I'm saying, which is exactly what Terek was saying earlier, is that almost all of these things could have been done without needing to go into outer space."

Terek said, "So you think maybe this will be a good thing?"

"Instead of spending trillions of dollars there"—Chuck pointed up—"we could have spent that money solving problems here." He pointed down.

"Looks like your wish is going to come true," Damon said.

"Sometimes reality has a way of rearing its ugly head."

"Speaking of ugly heads." Damon pointed at Chuck's wild hair. "What is—"

"Hey." A thought popped into my head. "Damon, does the military use the same GPS as commercial customers and civilians? Or do they have a separate ones?"

It made more sense if they had their own, didn't it? Could we switch to using theirs?

"The military uses the same satellites, but there is a separate encrypted signal."

"What does the encryption do?"

"So that you can't spoof it. Or, not easily. And it's more accurate. The Air Force has been sending up new Block III GPS birds, and those have directional antennas that make it hard to jam. They also support the L1C international signal, same as BieDou and Galileo. BieDou is the new Chinese system, and it can even get signals underwater, it's been a geo-positioning arms race this—"

"But the location signal is still coming from the same source?"

"If those satellites are pancaked, positioning for everything from drones to aircraft carriers is gone. Seems like they're losing imaging satellites now, too. No more overwatch."

"Maybe," Chuck said quietly.

"Wow," I mouthed silently.

Taillights glowed red in a line and snaked into the distance. Traffic had ground to a halt again. Another accident?

"We could get out and walk faster," Chuck grumbled to nobody and everybody.

The hail started up again with renewed fury.

"Everyone, quiet down for a second." Terek turned up the radio. "They're saying something about Pakistan launching another miss—"

"Turn the radio down," I asked. What was that noise? Something off to the left of the road. "Please, turn it down," I insisted.

Ahead of us, cars and trucks pulled from the road onto the shoulder, some pulling into the grass. Why were they in such a hurry? A commercial about life insurance played as Terek turned down the radio. The announcer's voice was replaced with a low warbling noise from outside. A rising groan.

Not a groan.

A siren.

Why did they have sirens out here?

It sounded like a freight train behind the trees somewhere.

Out my side window, hail pellets the size of golf balls bounced off the pavement. A few hundred feet away, the loblolly pines seemed to stand to attention. And then moved toward us. Branches flailed in a wall of wind. I looked up into a churning black maelstrom.

Chapter 14

"Chuck, what the hell...?"

He looked up from his map and followed my eyes left.

"Holy c—" He stuck his nose closer to the glass, then shoved Irena with his right hand and screamed, "Drive, drive!"

Luke jumped awake in my arms and squealed. He grabbed my shirt and climbed onto me like a baby monkey.

How far away was the churning wall of wind? A football field? Two?

Hail hammered on the hood of the Range Rover. The cars on the opposite side of the highway scattered like cockroaches. Irena tried to pull out of her lane, but almost slammed into the rear of a hatchback in front of us trying to do the same.

"What are you doing?" Chuck hollered. "Get past him. Over there!"

Cars and buses jerked back and forth as their drivers tried to disentangle their vehicles.

Luke's nails dug into my chest. He screeched, "Daddy, what's happening?"

Total darkness lay past the weak glow of the headlights and taillights along the road. Beyond the honking horns, an unmistakable growl shook the ground like a grading machine ripping up the highway.

"Drive into them!" Chuck yelled.

Irena gunned the engine and we heaved forward, crunching into the rear end of the hatchback. In turn, it bounced into the car in front of it. In the gap that opened, we veered to the right and unstuck from the melee. The Range Rover spun into the sand and gravel past the shoulder.

Down the grassy embankment, a wall of pine trees bounced into our headlights.

I craned my neck to look behind us. Nothing but blackness and pouring rain.

The Range Rover jackrabbited up and down as we shot to the bottom of the slope. The tree trunks grew. Irena jammed on the brakes. We slid. I grabbed Luke and braced for a side impact, but she gunned the engine again and the Rover's four-wheel drive dragged us forward and past the first row of pines.

Tires spinning, we fishtailed and rocketed toward a thicket of bushes. The truck burst through, airborne, and slammed into the ground.

My face hit the back of Chuck's seat. Pain exploded in my nose.

"Over there," I heard Chuck say.

I wiped away tears streaming from my eyes. Chuck pointed past Irena's head. A dirt road loomed in the darkness. Skidding left and right, she managed to straighten and then turn onto it. A sign bordered by checkered red-and-black squares announced, "Pine County Speedway."

The sign was fixed to a chain-link fence. We were going too fast to stop.

"Hit it," Chuck said.

I wrapped my arms around Luke and hunched over him. Irena accelerated. We blew into and through the barrier with a jolt and a crack. Four-story-high bleachers loomed in the headlights. We spun onto a sand track ringing the main raceway.

"Over there." Chuck pointed ahead.

A single-story building appeared through the driving rain. White walls ringed with a checkerboard pattern under the roof.

Irena hit the brakes. We skidded to a stop. Rain spattered against the windshield. A howling whistle was followed by a blinding flash of light and the bone-deep crack of an echoing thunderclap.

My hands were wet. The rain?

Damp, cold air rushed past me. Chuck was already outside the truck, his door open. He pushed his seat forward for Luke and me to get out behind him from the third row. I grabbed my backpack. The rain was horizontal in the gusting wind.

"Come on." He offered a hand.

I lifted Luke's arms from around my neck and handed him through the door to Chuck. Irena and Terek were already at the door to the structure. It had cinder block walls, I saw now, and a corrugated tin roof.

Irena hammered at the door handle with something.

I stepped through the car door and out into the rain. Another building was about a hundred feet down the track. Doubled over, I followed Chuck to the door. Another bright flash and thundering roar. The wind whipped leaves and branches past our feet. Irena picked up a rock and slammed it against the padlock securing the door.

A squealing yelp.

Was that Luke? I reached Chuck on the side of the building away from the wind.

"Are you okay?" I asked Luke, as calmly as I could.

He nodded mutely. Another squealing yelp, but it wasn't my son.

"Dad," Luke said. "Over there."

It was a small dog, maybe ten feet away. It yapped at us furiously.

"Is that Gorby?" Luke asked.

He meant the Borodin's dog, from our old apartment in New York.

"That's not Gorby," I replied.

With a final heaving blow, Irena snapped off the lock.

"Where's Damon?" I yelled.

The truck was empty, but the lights were still on inside the cabin.

Irena was halfway through removing the chain from the door handle when Chuck said, "We need to go. This isn't solid enough."

In a howling gust, the corrugated roof of the structure rattled. On closer inspection, it wasn't more than a shack. Maybe a ticket office? A bathroom?

Chuck pointed at the next building. "That's two stories," he shouted in my ear. He said something to Irena and Terek. They both nodded.

"I need to get some stuff from the truck," he said to me. He handed Luke over.

My son's arms gripped tight around my neck. Doubling over, I ran back out into the screaming wind. Rain bit into my face. The ground was soaked, and I stumbled in the wet sand. The little dog followed at our heels.

We arrived at the next building with Irena and Terek. The little dog yapped at us from a distance. With a single blow, Irena snapped the padlock from the door. She flung it open, the wind hurling it against the brickwork of the wall.

I stumbled inside with Luke.

Irena and Terek came in behind us. I fumbled in my pocket with my right hand, my left still around Luke, and found my phone. Shaking, I clicked on the flashlight.

Terek closed the door. It slammed shut.

In front of us were benches and a wall of lockers. A set of stairs led up to the second floor. The wind beat against the walls outside, its fury muted now, but I could still hear the dog yelping.

I held Luke away from me so I could inspect him in the light from my phone. He was spattered in something black. Not black. Red. Bright red.

"You're bleeding," Terek said.

My heart skipped a beat, then settled down. With the back of my hand, I felt my face. My nose throbbed. I'd smashed it into the back of the front seat, I remembered. It was streaming blood.

"We should get under the stairs," Irena said.

She opened a wooden door underneath them. I expected to see steps going down, but instead the space was filled with mops and stacks of bottles. Terek joined his sister and they grabbed what they could to empty the closet.

The exterior door opened behind us, and the wind roared in. Chuck appeared, loaded down with bags. Damon came in right behind him, balancing his four drones, one on top of the other.

He deposited them gingerly on the floor. "They're my babies," he said sheepishly.

The wind slammed the door shut behind them.

"You okay?" Chuck had his flashlight on too. He advanced toward me and checked out my face.

"A bloody nose." My hands trembled.

"Sit down." Chuck indicated the bench. "What, you never seen a tornado before?"

Shaking my head, I sat.

Chuck cracked a grin. "Me either. Terrifying, huh?"

Luke slipped from my arms. "Dad, you okay?"

"I'm fine." Throbbing pain in my face and nose filled the gap left when the rush of adrenaline subsided.

From outside, we heard the yelping dog over the thrumming wind.

"We can't leave him," Luke said.

"I tried to grab it on my way in," Chuck said. "But the thing ran away from me."

Terek and Irena had finished emptying out the cupboard under the stairs.

"You really think we need to get under there?" I turned to Chuck.

"Sounded like pennies in a giant garburator when that thing got close. All I hear now is wind, but might be a whole string of thunderstorms with tornadoes."

"I'll get the dog," Irena said.

"It's not our problem." Chuck walked the closet. He examined the staircase. "He doesn't want to come in. I tried."

Another boom of thunder shook the ground. A howl outside.

"I can't leave it out there," Irena said.

She walked over to the exterior door and opened it a foot. She stuck her head out, then turned on her cell phone's flashlight and held it out. The wind sucked in and scattered leaves and pine needles across the floor.

Chuck said, "Mike, why don't you bring Luke over here?"

My son was transfixed as he watched Irena lean out the door. She glanced back at him, smiled, and said, "I'll be back in a second." She disappeared. The wind pressure walloped the door shut behind her.

Terek looked at me, then back at Chuck, and said, "I need to go with her."

He ran to the door and opened it. Squeezed through. It slammed shut again.

Damon and Chuck and I looked at each other, then at the door. The sound of the yelping dog stopped a few seconds later.

We all waited for the door to reopen. Five seconds. Ten. Nothing.

I walked over, opened it, and stuck my head out. Rain pelted me. Beyond the weak ten-foot beam of light from my phone, everything was dark. I hollered as loud as I could, "Terek! Irena!"

No response.

"Can't see them." My head was already soaked.

I retreated and let the door close.

"They're probably chasing the dog," Damon said. "I'm going to find the circuit box."

Chuck did his what-the-hell shrug, an expression between irritation and perplexion on his face. "It's their funeral," he said, and then in a softer voice, to Luke: "Hey, buddy, why don't you come over here?"

He held one of his bags awkwardly in his left hand, and pulled out a blanket and offered it to my son. When he saw me looking at his hand he said, "I plugged in my phone and your iPad, but forgot to recharge my prosthetic. Damn thing is like a block of wood now."

I followed Chuck over to the corner, picked Luke up, and then sat both of us down in the closet under the stairs. I wrapped him up in my arms under the blanket. Damon must have found the circuit box, because the lights blinked on for a few minutes in a comforting glow—but then clicked off.

"Power lines must've been downed by branches," Chuck said. "Looks like I'll have a cold hand for the night."

He pulled out another blanket, put his phone down flashlight-side up, and took a seat under the staircase next to me and Luke.

"Can I play on the iPad?" Luke asked.

"I think I'll join you," I replied and fished it from my backpack.

Three hours since Terek and Irena had gone out.

We'd opened the door and yelled their names a dozen times, but with no response. Chuck even scooted out to the truck, but it was locked. He came back and asked who locked it. Damon said it wasn't him, and I knew it wasn't me. There was no way to get into it, and Terek and Irena had disappeared.

And everything from on top of the truck was gone, too.

Chuck paced like a caged possum in front of the lockers, fussing with his prosthetic. "Where are they? If they don't come back, we're going to be stranded in the middle of nowhere."

"They might be hurt," Damon said. "Should we go out and find them?"

"Not till it gets light. It'll be impossible to find them out there now."

I held Luke tight in my arms and didn't say anything.

It was past 11:30 p.m.

Lauren's plane was supposed to be on the ground by now. Chuck was so obsessed with Terek and Irena, I didn't even want to speak about Lauren, didn't want to bring it up. I was afraid to even talk about it. I was concerned about Terek and Irena, but there was only one person I really needed to know was safe.

Where was she?

Chapter 15

The cabin lights were low.

"I'm pregnant," Emily whispered to Lauren.

The flight attendant sat in the nook of Lauren's first class pod. Their heads were almost touching. They held each other's hands.

Over the past seven hours, since Emily had burst into tears, the two of them had become fast friends. Lauren had even gotten up to tell the other passengers to stop asking Emily for things, to go into the galley and get whatever they needed.

Of course, Emily protested that it wasn't necessary, but Lauren's scowling mamma-bear looks ensured that people were starting to get things themselves.

Having someone else to look after felt good. It was what Lauren was used to, protecting her kids. Emily was someone to talk with. About Luke and Olivia. Mike. They had shared their lives in the past seven hours.

"I haven't told anyone else yet," Emily added. "Not even my boyfriend. I mean"—she leaned closer and lowered her voice—"I wasn't even sure I was going to keep it."

Emily wasn't the only one who had decided it was time for confession.

Murmured prayers and quiet weeping filled the cabin. Wrappers and papers were strewn through the aisles. The space smelled like a nest, as if they were nomads who had been wandering through the skies for weeks.

"You need to keep the baby," Lauren said. "I felt the way you did once, and I was so wrong. I would never have met Olivia."

She squeezed Emily's hands between hers. The young woman was only twenty-five, but then again, Lauren was only thirty-eight.

"Everything is going to be okay," Lauren promised.

She said it, but her hands trembled. She held back her own tears only because she wanted to be strong for Emily. It was good to have someone to take care of.

That magnetic pull tugged at her again. Lauren had taken off her watch and stowed it in a drawer beside her chair. She had kept looking at it every minute and that had started to drive her crazy, so she'd taken it off, but now she had to keep taking it out to check the time.

She didn't want to look, but it pulled at her. She took it out.

It was 12:40 a.m. in New York.

Lauren didn't need to do mental calculations. Every minute felt like an eternity. Almost eighteen hours in the air, on a scheduled sixteen-and-a-half-hour flight. How much longer could they stay airborne?

At 9 p.m., Lauren had watched as the sun finally went down on the opposite side of the aircraft. Which meant they were flying south at that point. It stayed light long enough for her to see the ice below break into fragments and then, finally, to see open blue water. They passed over land for an hour, but then headed back out to sea. Twilight had come and gone, and then darkness swallowed them again.

No moon. No stars that she could see. Nothing but a black abyss outside her window for the past three hours.

The pilots had locked themselves in the flight deck. Nobody in or out, not even other cabin crew, Emily said. Why wouldn't the crew give their location to the passengers? Two hours ago, the pilot had tersely announced that they would be landing in America. This had earned raucous applause, but there had been nothing further since then.

Sunset at 9 p.m.? At the start of September? How far north were they, really?

"Everything is going to be okay." Emily squeezed Lauren's hands tighter.

"You just take care of that baby." Lauren squeezed back. "We're going to be fine. My husband's friend, Chuck, he's taken flying lessons, and you know what's the number one rule for pilots?"

"What?"

"Aviate, navigate, and only then, communicate. The pilots are busy getting us where we need to go, that's why they're not saying anything."

She should never have come on this trip. Why had she left her children?

Something flickered in her peripheral vision. She looked out her window. It was the moon, rising over the horizon. And something else. Below.

She leaned into the window to get a better look.

Glittering waves.

Close.

Not thousands of feet away, but hundreds. All the way to the horizon, nothing but waves and black water.

The intercom crackled. "Ah, folks, we're lowering our altitude to conserve fuel, bringing the speed of the aircraft down. We're...ah...that's all for now. Please remain in your seats, and make sure you are buckled in tight."

Chapter 16

"Hello?"

I opened one eye.

"Hello?" asked the voice again.

Something warm and wet brushed up against my fingers. I opened my other eye. A small white dog busily licked my hand.

"What happened to you guys?" Chuck asked.

The exterior door was open. Terek waved at me. Irena stood facing Chuck, a backpack over her shoulder.

"We chased the mutt across the street, and then decided to take refuge in another building. We figured it was safer to wait it out there."

"We were worried." Chuck didn't specify about what.

"That's why we stayed where we were."

"Everything got ripped off the roof of the truck."

"Noticed that. I don't know what to say. Wasn't expecting a tornado. We went and looked this morning, all the way back to the road. Nothing."

"But you got your pack?" Chuck indicated Irena's shoulder.

"It was inside the car."

Luke woke up in my arms. We were still in the closet under the stairs. He and I had stayed there the whole night. My face was still painful, even though Chuck had done his best to fix me up the night before. No more blood, at least, but I had to breathe through my mouth.

"What's it like out there?" I asked.

I disentangled from Luke and left him on the floor to play with the dog.

"Blue skies," Irena said. "Beautiful day. A little hot."

I stepped into the sunshine and walked over to join them. Clear skies at dawn, with not a cloud in sight. A little hot? She wasn't kidding.

Chuck stood beside me. "It's hotter than a glassblower's arseh—"

"Okay, okay," I said.

"Sorry. We should get some food. I think there's a small town up the road. Magnolia?"

Irena said, "Let's take the truck. See if we can find some of the stuff that blew off it."

We spent an hour searching before we went into the town.

The wind's fury must have taken the bags off the top, or maybe it'd flown off when we'd slammed through the bushes and trees on the side of the highway.

Damon remembered that he had left his wallet and ID in his bag, and they were gone. Completely missing. Chuck couldn't understand how someone wouldn't keep their wallet in their jeans, but the two of them were cut from different cloth.

We backtracked, but as Irena and Terek had said, we couldn't find anything. The highway was almost empty. One or two cars passed us while we searched.

On the other side, we found unmistakable proof of the tornado. A swath of trees had been knocked down, with huge branches strewn across part of the Interstate and onto the grassy divider.

Everyone was hungry. That was one thing we all agreed on when Damon brought it up, so we decided to abandon the search for the moment and head into the small town.

We went back down the road next to the speedway, and then turned left. There was a church a few hundred yards up the road. Calvary Baptist, according to the small sign. A knot of people were outside talking. One of them—the pastor, I assumed, from the way he seemed to be directing everyone—was helping a man who limped toward the entrance.

Irena slowed the truck and rolled down her window. "You need some help?"

"All we can get. One of you a doctor?"

"I was a medic in the army," she replied.

On hearing this, Chuck looked at me over the seat divider. He raised his eyebrows. We pulled over and parked. Irena went over to the limping man, and the pastor waved us inside.

Terek had fashioned a leash for the dog from some string, and Luke got out ahead of me holding it. The dog, predictably, started barking.

"Look familiar?" I asked the pastor. "We found him last night."

The priest shook his head. "You guys want some coffee?"

Chuck said, "Does the pope—"

I elbowed him in the ribs. "That would be great."

My backside was already soaked with sweat.

It felt great to get out of the sun and inside the wood-paneled interior of the church. There was a coffee urn on a foldout table, with some Styrofoam cups next to it. I walked over and filled two.

Terek came in behind us, but instead of going for the coffee, he went to the front row of the church and sat down at a pew. He bowed his head and began to pray.

"Did that tornado come through here?" Chuck took a coffee from me while he spoke with the pastor.

The pastor nodded. "Further up the highway, it caught some cars. Turned them over. A terrible mess. We're trying to do what we can. We set up beds downstairs. There've been some bad injuries."

"You haven't been able to get in touch with any paramedics?"

"Magnolia's sheriff looks after four other towns. We haven't been able to get in touch with anyone."

"No emergency services?"

"Nothing yet."

"There are eighteen thousand police agencies in America, almost a million officers, and not one of them is here?"

The pastor shrugged. "It's still early morning. I'm hopeful. I'm sure there's a lot going on out there."

Chuck added, "You know that we have more police in this country than the total standing army of Russia?"

"Have you heard anything else on the news?" I asked, ignoring Chuck.

The pastor frowned. "Mean all that satellite stuff?"

"You have a TV somewhere in the church?"

"Our cable service stopped working yesterday, even before the storm. Our telephones as well."

"Landlines?"

"Everything. Completely cut off from the outside world. Our local radio comes from Stephentown, across the way, but they stopped broadcasting last night. Must've been the storm."

"Where's the closest hospital?"

"Well now, that is the problem. Beacham Memorial closed down last year. That was the only one we had in town. Gotta go to Southeast Regional, twenty miles south."

It was definitely much cooler inside the church. I felt a breeze on my cheek and looked left. An air conditioner was running. The lights were on. "But you have power?"

"Afraid not. Not exactly." He followed my eyes. "You hear that sound? That's the generator running out back. All the power to the town went out last night in the storm."

I heard it now, the low growl of a diesel engine, outside, over the sound of the AC unit blowing cool air.

"You got some water for my dog?" Luke asked.

"It's not your dog," I said.

"Sure, I'll get you some water," the pastor said.

Luke tugged my leg. "Can I play on the iPad?"

"Why don't you play with your dog?"

"Dad, come on, please?"

I relented. "Stay inside, though, okay?"

"Can I use your generator to recharge some batteries?" Damon asked the pastor. "They're big ones," he added.

When the pastor said it wasn't a problem, Damon said, "I'll get the drones out of the truck. I think we need to get a bird's eye view of what's going on."

"I'm going to charge up my hand," Chuck said, his prosthetic raised. He already had a USB cable out.

"And I'm going to show some of these people how to install the mesh-network app," Terek said. "At least that way we will get some communications going."

From five hundred feet up, it looked like a giant had scrubbed the forest floor. The slender trunks of the pines were flattened to the ground like strands of spaghetti, while the green trees to either side were seemingly untouched. About a half mile from the church, near the Interstate, Damon hovered the drone over three cars scattered there, and then followed the tornado's path east.

Most tornadoes moved southwest to northeast, Chuck observed, and this one was no different.

Chuck and the pastor and his wife stood beside Damon, fascinated, and watched as he navigated the drone with the VR goggles on. The video feed from it played on his laptop.

I sat next to him and kept an eye on Luke, who petted the dog while it lapped water from a bowl. The poor thing must have been dying of thirst. Terek sat at a desk near the front of the church, installing the mesh-network app on the phones of several locals. Irena joined him and helped out.

The image on Damon's screen swept over the pine forest bordering the Interstate and then over a road.

"That's Carmont," the pastor said. "We're just down the street."

Damon followed the path of ruined trees. A few hundred feet further along, the drone crossed a dirt road. The remains of an above-ground pool came into view, one side crushed. It was surrounded by scattered white debris. Then the crumpled remains of a trailer. And of another.

Someone walking on the ground looked up.

And waved.

"Do you know him?" Chuck asked.

"That's Louis," the pastor replied. "My goodness, the whole neighborhood was hit."

From behind us Irena asked, "Has anyone been over there?"

"We should get going," Chuck said.

I said, "You want to leave them?"

Chuck had pulled me to one side of the coffee stand. "I'm not saying that."

"Then what are you saying?"

"You remember what happened last time we tried to help people?"

"You told me at that blues bar a few days ago about how proud you were of that."

"I am, I'm...look, they have a few people with cars. They can go to the hospital."

"I doubt they'll be able to take all the injured people at once. The Range Rover has a lot of space."

"Then they do a few trips."

"And they don't have drones. They don't have someone like Damon."

"The last time we did this, we ended up getting attacked ourselves."

"This isn't like last time."

"It kinda is. What I'm saying…" Chuck glanced at the pastor and his wife. He kept his voice low. "We do our best to help, but we make it clear we need to get going as soon as we can. We have no idea what's happening out there."

He didn't need to remind me.

One way or another, Lauren's plane had come down by now. There wasn't any use in worrying about the worst that could have happened, so I was trying to stay positive. I needed to get to Washington as soon as I could, but at the same time—

"We make one trip down," I said. "Twenty miles back, and then we continue north. We leave Damon and Terek here to help them with the mesh app and use the drone to see if there are any other people in trouble. They don't have anyone else."

"One trip? We make that clear?"

From behind us, the pastor asked, "Louis? Are you okay?"

He spoke through Damon's cell phone, the voice and video relayed over the drone. The man, Louis, cried on the other end, and said that they had to hurry.

Irena gave in and let Chuck drive the Range Rover. Damon kept one of the drones hovering high to use as a communications relay. He directed us to the first set of wrecked trailers. In five minutes we were at Louis's place. What had been a home was now a pile of splintered timber and folded metal.

His wife, Sonia, sat in a picnic chair holding her head. Her blond hair was matted black with dried blood. Irena got her first aid kit from the truck, while Chuck and I went to the trailer next door. Only a hundred feet away, yet it was untouched.

Two cars followed us from the church. They fanned out down the street.

We emptied out the back of the Rover and improvised beds using blankets from the church, then helped Sonia to one of them after Irena had attended to her. A few cuts, she said, but the woman had a deep bruise on one side and might have internal injuries.

I left Luke back at the church with Damon, at least while we went out to try and find injured people, for fear of what we might find. He was happy playing games on the iPad and chasing the dog.

My worries were justified at the next trailer Damon guided us to. Inside what had looked like a crushed tin can from the air, we found a young woman. Lifeless. Pinned underneath a refrigerator.

It was past 6 p.m. by the time we approached the Southeast Regional Medical Center. The skies had been clear all day, though we checked fearfully for any rising thunderheads. We collected Luke at the church and made as much space in the Range Rover as we could for the three injured people we ferried to the hospital. Irena and Chuck remained behind, doing their best to help anyone else who arrived.

By the end of the day, almost the whole town had shown up at the church, and we organized a convoy out to take the more seriously hurt. We debated whether we should go, but it was already late in the day, and I wanted to get back to civilization to try and find a phone. Damon wanted the internet.

"It's going to be the same in any rural area," Damon said from the front seat.

Terek drove. I sat behind him with Luke on my lap.

A young man named Brandon sat in the seat beside me, his arm bound in a makeshift splint Irena had fashioned for his broken arm. We'd laid the two seats in the third row flat to make beds for two badly hurt people. One was Sonia, and the other was an elderly lady named Yolanda, who reminded Luke of Grandma Babet.

"Lack of communications?"

"Most rural areas don't use wire line anymore. Upkeep is too expensive. Even if the cable to a home looks like a landline, the connection to the network is by mobile or satellite further down. TV as well. That's why their cable went out."

I checked my phone. Still no GPS, although it had been fully charged through the USB cable attached to the Range Rover. Having a charged phone still felt comforting, even if the thing was now a glorified camera. It was a constant battle for everyone to keep their devices charged from the limited options in the truck.

"You think the internet is still working?" I asked Damon.

"No reason it shouldn't be, if we can get somewhere connected to fiber optic. Pretty much any city bigger than a few thousand people should be connected."

The hospital would have analog phone lines, Chuck had promised me. He'd asked me to call Susie and tell her everything was okay, but that we'd had to stop for a day to help some people.

"It's here," Brandon said. "Take this exit."

The young man knew the way, and the rest of our convoy followed. Just in case, Chuck had asked the pastor to pinpoint it on another hand-drawn map.

We pulled off the highway. The sun was low in the sky.

Two blocks later, the six-story structure of the medical center appeared over a row of trees. The street outside jammed with cars. Terek parked as close as he could, while Damon and I went inside to find someone to come out with stretchers. Inside was chaotic, but we found a police officer and explained the situation. He found people to send out to help us.

Chaotic, but not out of control.

The first chance I got, I excused myself and asked the information counter where the telephones were. Chuck was right. They had pay phones, but I had to wait twenty minutes in line. I pulled out the scrap of paper with the senator's phone number on it, and dialed.

It picked up on the other end.

I said, "Hello? Senator Seymour?"

"Please leave a message after the tone…" The line beeped.

Damn it. "Ah, this is Michael. I'm wondering if you've heard from Lauren." I left Chuck's number in Nashville, then explained that I was driving to DC and would be there in the next day or so.

I hung up and let the next person in line take the phone.

"Dad." Luke pulled on my hand.

In my mind, I saw that plane off Zanzibar, pirouetting as it hit the waves, the aircraft coming away into fragments in a flash of white.

"Everything's going to be okay," Luke said. "Mom's going to be fine. Did you check the internet?"

"Did I…"

"On your phone. There's Wi-Fi here. Uncle Damon is online. Why didn't you just use Zoom or FaceTime to call them over the WiFi?" He took my hand and led me down the hall. "Let's go to the cafeteria," my son said. "You should eat. And Uncle Damon is there."

I'd been so focused on getting to a phone I hadn't thought about it. While we walked, I connected to the hospital's network and brought up the flight tracker.

It felt like the floor opened up beneath me.

I stopped.

"What?" Luke pulled my hand and tried to move me forward.

"Nothing," I lied.

The app said that Lauren's flight had been canceled. No arrival time. Nothing at all. It gave no other information.

"Luke, I need to call the airline."

My phone pinged. Messages arrived on my phone now it was connected. I scanned them and opened one from Lauren's mother. My scalp tingled as I opened the message.

My stomach dropped.

No sign of Lauren, her mother wrote. No calls from her. No messages. *Nothing from the airline.* They were trying to find out what had happened to the flight. The senator had his people on it and would contact me later in the day.

Contact me? How, exactly? When we were on the road, there was no mobile service. I would have to wait until I got to somewhere with internet and Wi-Fi.

I wrote back and asked her to send me an email when they heard anything new. I said I would be driving to Nashville and then to Washington. I said my phone didn't work, that there were no communications in the countryside.

It was already dark out.

Almost twenty-four hours since Lauren's plane would have run out of fuel.

Luke said, "Dad, what do you want?"

We'd reached the entrance to the cafeteria. The smell of cooked meat and vegetable soup wafted by. Damon waved from a table under an enclosed glass veranda. He and Terek had their laptops connected on a table.

"I'm not hungry."

"I'll get you a granola bar and a coffee," Luke said.

When I didn't respond, he let go of my hand and said he'd meet me at the table. In a daze, I let my feet walk me over to Damon.

"Look at this," he said.

He indicated his laptop screen. An image of the Earth hovered in the middle of the screen, crisscrossed by angry red lines and a glowing orange haze. It didn't look good. "I logged into the NASA space debris tracking center."

"Is this the Ares model?" That was what he'd shown me last time.

"This is real data from the DOD," Damon said. "I have security clearance. They're asking me and some colleagues from MIT to do an analysis. Hundreds of satellites went offline in the past day. Destroyed. They're getting actual radar bounces from multiple expanding wreckage fields."

"Isn't this what they expected?"

"The Russians are now blaming the Americans and Indians for the loss of their GLONASS constellation. Things are getting ugly."

A TV was on by the entrance, tuned to CNN. I heard the news anchor say, "NASA is now saying we may not be able to have any satellites in Earth orbit for perhaps a hundred years—"

"Dad!" Luke yelled.

I spun around.

My son ran toward me. He held one hand above his head.

Chapter 17

We drove north as the sun climbed into the sky. A furnace of a day. The mercury topped a hundred before the clock hit noon.

Irena had barely slept, and Chuck tended to be restless and unhappy when he wasn't commanding, so he drove while Irena slept in the front passenger seat with a new hand-drawn map draped across her knees. Luke and I took our spots in the jump seat in the back, with Damon and Terek in the middle seats.

Damon and Terek had their laptops wired together again. The two of them were almost glued at the hip, like conjoined hackers. They were analyzing the data they had downloaded from the space debris system the day before. Every now and then, they exclaimed as they watched a satellite collision or shared some insight.

The rest of us half-listened.

Luke smiled a goofy, gummy grin at me. He held up his prize in his left hand and showed me. His left incisor.

Both front teeth were missing now.

He'd run at me in the cafeteria with his other front tooth above his head. He said it'd come loose in the crazy car when the tornado was chasing us, said he would keep it in his pocket until we got home.

So the tooth fairy could find us, he said.

His grin widened to expose the tiny button teeth in his gums. I laughed despite myself as I realized my son wasn't just humoring me. He was trying to cheer me up. I did my best to smile.

The night before, we had left the hospital and driven back up to the Calvary Baptist Church. Irena worked well into the night, doing her best to help the injured people who came in from the darkness.

When I awoke at daybreak, Chuck had already done a round of the area. The dog's owner had shown up. We returned him. A joyous reunion.

We woke Irena at about 7 a.m., about the time she had only just gotten to sleep. The pastor bundled some snacks for the road, which we tried to refuse, but he insisted. By 8 a.m., we were back on the road and heading north.

Not more than eight hours to Nashville, Chuck said. But that's what he'd said two days ago.

The traffic was light.

I mostly watched the pine forests sweep past and wondered where Lauren was. I watched the blue skies for planes, but where the air had been full of them when we left New Orleans, now there were only birds. No white contrails, no distant specks crossing the blue.

No airplanes up there at all.

When we passed rest stations, we stopped for a few minutes. I tried the pay phones, but none of them worked. Damon explained, again, that communications in rural areas, even rest stations like this, worked off mobile networks. Between the big cities, no wireless, no mobile, no TV.

Everything cut off.

The truck stops seemed like they had been hit by bombs. Shelves cleared, even of junk food. Trucks were still rolling on the highways, but Damon wasn't sure how much longer that would last.

"Two days GPS has been down," Damon said.

A huge eighteen-wheeler switched gears and pulled out behind us. The engine roared as the trucker accelerated. Luke leaned to the window, made a fist, and pulled down twice. The truck's air horn sounded off in two blasts.

Luke smiled and waved.

"These guys are all still pulling the loads they started with before this all started," Damon continued. "Another day or two and supply chains will start to break down."

"Computers are still working, aren't they?" I said.

"Sort of, but those systems don't have position-tracking data anymore. They don't know where their fleets of trucks or containers are."

"Can't they do it by hand?"

"To a point, but these networks have been optimized to work with GPS. A few days without a connection, and things can bend. Like the mobile phone networks. But more than a few days, and they'll break."

"These guys won't get lost," Chuck said from the driver's seat. He waved at the trucker too. "They know where they're going."

"I think you might be surprised."

"And I think you're not giving them enough credit."

"Getting from point to point isn't the problem. It's downstream, literally. At the port where Grandma Babet works, the containers aren't getting off ships. And the ships are stacking up, taking longer to find their way in from the ocean."

"The captains aren't going to get lost either," Chuck said. "Like all those airplanes didn't get lost." He glanced back at me. "Everyone got down safely, as much as the cable news was predicting Armageddon."

Damon looked at me as well.

He didn't say it, but not everyone had gotten down safely. There were reports of another air crash. One in China. Possibly others, but the media was overwhelmed with conflicting stories of riots and protests in a world spasmed by the loss of normal communications.

"Terek," Chuck said, "tell them what you told me, about the government turning off GPS last year? On purpose? When was that?"

"Fall of 2019, the American Air Force turned off GPS in Nevada."

Damon said, "They do their regular Red Flag exercises every year. That's not new. They train pilots to execute strike missions without GPS. They don't turn it off as much as block it locally."

"Hundreds of flights going over Arizona to Nevada lost signal," Chuck said. "That's not nothing."

"Nothing compared to the actual switching off of GPS in the summer of 2019 and the winter of 2020." This time Terek looked up from his laptop at Damon. "Those were widespread outages. Complete signal loss."

Damon didn't reply, but nodded his agreement.

"They never admitted it," Terek said. "But the US government must have been testing what would happen to the civilian infrastructure with an unannounced GPS failure, including the loss of timing signals."

"So they knew this might happen," I said.

"Or maybe they're the ones doing it," Chuck countered.

"You seriously think *our own government* has shut off GPS and crippled the country?"

"They did it before."

"As a test."

"Maybe this is a bigger test."

"People have lost their lives."

Chuck weighed the point. "I agree that's a long bridge to cross, but…" He paused. "If we can switch off our own GPS, what's stopping the bad guys from doing it? Damon, you said that any capability we have ourselves, an adversary can steal?"

"I meant any information," Damon replied. "Any piece of information we have on a computer, you have to assume an attacker could find it."

"But doesn't that apply to anything controlled by a computer system?"

"Yes and no."

Chuck said, "I heard that our own nuclear codes are still controlled by floppy disks and computer technology from the eighties."

"That's actually a defensive posture now," Damon replied. "Means you can't access them via the internet and modern protocols. Which makes stuff very difficult to get to."

"And that's a good thing?"

"I would say so."

"The Russians," Terek said.

"What about the Russians? They've lost their global navigation system as well."

"So they say," Terek said. "Russians have been attacking the global navigation systems for the past decade."

"Blocking it?" I asked.

"Spoofing."

"Spoofing?"

"Not removing the signal entirely, but changing it so the receiver doesn't know the difference. Back in 2013, in the Black Sea by Ukraine, my home country, dozens of ships got lost when anomalous GPS signals were received over a few days. The International Space Station has been tracking suspected GPS spoofing incidents at ten global locations over the past decade. Over ten thousand of them."

Chuck said, "They were using the space station to track that? The space station that was just destroyed in orbit?"

"Again," Damon said. "Not blocking, but spoofing."

"That's right. Thousands of ships and aircraft have been fed the wrong positional data in hundreds of incidents over the years."

"I've heard of this," Chuck said.

"There was a high correlation between those incidents and the movement of Russian politicians," Damon said. "It was defensive."

"You're defending the Russians?" Terek looked up from his laptop again.

"If anyone, maybe the Chinese. I haven't heard anything about their Baidu system lately. It seems like it might be the only geopositioning system still intact. Does anyone have a Chinese phone?"

Everyone in the car shrugged. We all had Apple devices.

"Spoofing?" Chuck slowed the car. "That sounds like a cyberattack."

I leaned forward to get a look at the road to see why he was braking. A line of cars and trucks snaked up the next hillside. What looked like police cars lined the road to each side, their lights flashing. A line of olive-green trucks bordered the cops.

"You're right," Damon replied to Chuck. "It is a kind of cyberattack. The problem is nobody knows how to respond. There hasn't been any real space-cyberspace power theory put forward."

I said, "Nobody knows how to respond to an attack like that?"

"This is why we're in this mess. When someone attacks your ship, standard military power theory is that you respond by attacking one of their ships."

"An eye for an eye," Chuck said.

"Proportionality. Or super-proportionality. If they hit one of your ships, you sink ten of theirs."

"Deterrence."

"Problem is, in this case, India hit one of Pakistan's satellites. So they responded in kind, and within a day, we had a cascade of unintended consequences that affected the entire planet."

"Like a cyberweapon," I said.

"Right. Congestion is a problem in both space and cyberspace. In cyber, we have malware and spam and bots that clog up the bandwidth, but in space, the equivalent is orbiting garbage and debris. What's happening now, it's not like a conventional bomb. They don't have any idea what the blast radius of unleashing attacks like this might be. Cyber and outer space are similar in a lot of ways."

"There's one big difference," Chuck said.

He nudged Irena awake as we edged forward in the traffic. There was a roadblock ahead. State Troopers were pulling people over. Not only State Troopers, but other men and women in camouflage holding automatic weapons.

"The big difference," Chuck continued, "is that with cyber, you can't tell who attacked you, which means you can't even figure out who to retaliate against. But with space stuff, you know whose rocket that was. They can track where a missile came from. India and Pakistan, they launched these."

"India is still denying it."

"Like Iran tried to deny shooting down that airliner a few years ago. Because they didn't want their own people blaming them. The Russians, Chinese, British, and Americans all confirmed those missile launches. Who are you going to believe? Them, or the Indian government?"

"Like I've been saying," I said, "better them shooting down satellites than launching nuclear weapons at each other."

"I hope you're right," Chuck said.

"There's another big difference," Damon said.

Chuck rolled down his window. We didn't have a chance to hear what Damon's next point was.

"Good day, officer," Chuck said. "What can we do for you?"

The State Trooper had on a tan shirt with khaki pockets, which matched the slightly too-tight pants he wore over scuffed black boots. He was a thick-set young man with corn-fed cheeks.

He leaned down to bring his face level with Chuck's. The officer's eyes scanned Irena—who had shorts on, and whose bare legs were stretched up on the dash—paused on Terek and Damon, and stopped to nod at Luke, who waved.

"We need to do an inspection."

"What are you looking for?"

"Please, sir, pull over."

The car in front of us had pulled to the side. A camouflage-wearing soldier with an automatic weapon slung over his back popped the trunk. Chuck followed the officer's hand signals and parked the Range Rover.

The young officer inspected the front of our truck and pulled a branch from the grill. He ran one hand over the dented and chipped hood, then leaned in to inspect the windshield.

"Stuck in a hailstorm coming out of Louisiana," Chuck explained, his window still down.

"Got you good."

"You should see the other guy."

The officer didn't even crack a smile.

"Everyone, please step out of the vehicle," the officer said.

Damon and Terek stowed their laptops, and the officer indicated that they should leave them in the car. The back doors opened. I squeezed out to follow Damon onto the grass of the divider. Over the honking cars and shouted instructions, cicadas hummed in the distance. Going out into the heat felt like stepping into a steel foundry.

"You okay?" I asked Luke.

His face was red and puffy from sleep. He nodded.

The officer smiled at him, then said to Irena, "Ma'am, please leave everything inside the car."

She had her backpack halfway out. "Everything?"

"Everything."

She tossed the bag back in.

Four soldiers approached, two men and two women, head-to-toe in camouflage and all holding automatic weapons on harnesses. The officer nodded to them. One of them, a young man, smiled at Luke, then slung his weapon around his shoulder onto his back and opened the driver's side door. The other three opened other doors.

"National Guard?" Chuck asked the officer.

"They've been called out all over the country. There were riots in Detroit and Los Angeles last night."

"Over what?"

"Local governments instituted curfews over looting. Emergency services are..." The officer's face pinched. "Some people are taking advantage."

"Is that what these roadblocks are about?"

The officer's face returned to impassive. "Can't say what this is about, sir."

"Is there anything else happening out there?" I asked.

"Anything else, sir?"

He was standoffish, but polite.

"We've been off-grid since last night."

"Everyone is off-grid now, sir."

"I mean, any new developments since last night? On the news?"

"War broke out between India and Pakistan."

That wasn't exactly news. "I knew that, the anti-satellite—"

"I mean, war has *really* broken out."

"How do you mean?"

One of the soldiers ducked her head out of the car and gave a signal.

"Are any of you armed?" the officer asked.

Chuck said, "I've got a Glock. Full disclosure, it's loaded. Another magazine is in the truck, in my bag in the back." He produced the weapon from the holster under his shirt. "I've got a license." He produced his wallet.

"In my handbag," Irena said. "A SIG Sauer. Also loaded."

I didn't know she had a gun. Chuck and I exchanged a quick glance. Then again, we hadn't asked.

"Nine millimeter," Irena added. "My papers are in the glove box."

"Are you all American citizens?"

"We are." I brought Luke next to me. Chuck raised his hand and nodded, as did Damon.

"My brother and I are Ukrainian," Irena said. "Our passports are also in the glove box, together with our immigration docs. As I said."

The officer nodded at the young Guardswoman who was searching the passenger area. She opened the glove compartment and nodded back.

"Ukrainian?" the officer asked. "Isn't that like Russian?"

"This is very different than Russian," Terek said.

Chuck said, "It's okay, the officer doesn't mean anything by—"

The officer cut him off. "Sir, please do not presume to know what I mean and do not mean."

Chuck blinked. He closed his mouth, paused, and then said, "Yes, sir."

"How are y'all traveling together?"

"We—"

"I go to school with them," Damon interrupted Chuck. "In Boston. I go to MIT."

"The Massachusetts Institute of Technology?" The young officer's eyebrows raised, the edges of his mouth angling down. "How long have you known each other?"

"A few years."

Chuck gave Damon a look, but didn't say anything.

The Range Rover's doors closed one at a time. The young soldiers each waved an all-clear signal to the officer, then moved on to the next stopped car.

"Please get back in the vehicle and go on your way," the officer instructed, his gaze already forward. "You have a nice day," he said to Irena as she passed by him. "And y'all should stay off the roads if you can. There's a lot of roadblocks. Not all of them are us. You be careful. And be careful with those weapons."

I waited until Chuck had pulled back onto the Interstate before asking, "Not all of the roadblocks are *us*? Who is 'us'? And who would 'them' be?"

Chapter 18

Damon slouched in the backseat and eyed Chuck at the wheel. Irena had been doing great driving, and this was her truck. Why did he need to get behind the wheel? He always needed to be large and in charge.

If the guy wasn't disabled, Damon might tell him off more. That wasn't true. Damon hated confrontation, and truth be told, he was a bit handicapped himself. He suspected he might be diagnosed as slightly autistic if he was ever tested.

But he didn't like the way Chuck dominated every situation. On the other hand, you learned to either accept your friends the way they were or go your own way, and Chuck had become a big part of Damon's life in the past six years.

That didn't mean that Chuck couldn't be an asshole from time to time.

What was really gnawing at him? There was something in the look Chuck had given Damon when he tried to cover for Terek and Irena.

What was the harm in telling something that didn't even amount to a white lie? He said he was going to school with Terek and Irena. That was true. Irena had been going to Boston University while he was at MIT.

Damon saw it coming a mile away.

The way that cop had looked at Terek when he said he was Ukrainian. *Is that Russian?* That's what the cop said, as if he was an alien, which was exactly how America termed anyone from outside—resident aliens.

Terek had told Damon the stories, about how he had tried to apply for jobs, but nobody wanted to hire an immigrant. He and Irena had been struggling to figure out what to do when she graduated last semester. When Irena said she always wanted to see New Orleans, and that she always wanted a job outside, Damon called Grandma Babet and convinced her to get them jobs at the port.

Damon had been wanting to get back to New Orleans, anyway. Babet had raised him after his mother passed, which was another thing that brought him and Terek together.

Last winter, after a late session of playing *Slayer* online—before Damon had met Terek in person—Terek said he needed a break. Damon joked and prodded, until Terek finally told him that it was the day his mother had passed and he needed some time off.

Terek and Irena's mother had died of a drug overdose six years before, like Damon's mother more than twenty years ago. Also like Damon, Terek and Irena knew about quiet fear and shame and anger and desperation. Their father had taken off when they were young, too. They needed help, and Damon was in a position to provide it.

For the past eight months, Damon and Terek had been almost inseparable. Damon was serious about getting Terek into MIT. The kid was the smartest person he had ever met.

Already it felt like Damon had known Terek his whole life, like the guy was a part of him. Damon and Terek would riff off each other's programming in the way other people might finish sentences for each other. Like a dance. Adding and improving, tweaking and moving. They shared a hidden depth and elegance in thought that nobody else in this car would ever, or could ever, understand.

"You see that?" Terek said.

Damon's laptop pinged with a message. Their laptops were almost always connected via a USB. They had no outside network connection, but two computers connected, that was a network, right? A network of two.

He opened the message. A screen of numbers of figures that he guessed would look like nonsense to anyone else.

"You see that?" Terek repeated.

Damon did see it. A pattern emerged from the jumble. "The debris almost looks like it's self-organizing. Is that gravitational?"

"I don't know. If that's right, it just took out the Copernicus Sentinel-5P."

That was a satellite launched a few years ago by the European Space Agency to monitor air pollution levels across the globe. Not a critical asset, but not insubstantial, and now it was probably gone.

Damon wiped his eyes, patted Terek on the back and agreed with his analysis, then shifted in his seat to look back at Mike and Luke.

Helping people, that was Mike's thing. Chuck's too, despite his abrasiveness. When that cop questioned Irena and Terek, Damon imagined it escalating. Damon needed to maintain control, to alter the future path before it veered, so he told the cop a slightly stretched version of reality and things came back into line.

Control the future. It was Damon's new obsession.

The truth was, Irena and Terek's papers were about to expire, maybe already had. Damon didn't ask because he didn't want to know. When Terek made the surprise announcement, right before coming to New Orleans, that he had gotten married, Damon congratulated him, but didn't pry. Was it a marriage of convenience? For papers? Terek didn't talk much about Katerina, his wife, but he called her every day. He almost never went out, and sent all his money to her.

What was the harm in covering for Terek? Just a little?

But that look Chuck had given him.

"You okay back there?" Chuck asked. He swiveled the rearview so he could see Damon. "You look like you're brooding again."

There it was again.

That look. As if Chuck was saying, "What the hell's wrong with you? Why are you always attached to that computer? Get some fresh air." Damon had never had a father in his life, apart from the string of his mother's abusive boyfriends early on, before she died. Maybe that was it. An aggressive male in authority rubbed Damon the wrong way.

"I got a game for you," Damon said and sat up. Closed his laptop.

"Lay it on me." Chuck returned his eyes to the road.

"Let's say a self-driving car is speeding down a two-lane road and its brakes fail. Should it stay in its lane and hit a pregnant woman, a doctor, and a criminal on a crosswalk? Or swerve and hit a barrier between the lanes, which would kill a family of four, including two children?"

Chuck glanced in the mirror again. "Easy. Stay in my lane, protect my family."

"I'm not saying it's *your* family. In fact, let's say it's *not* your family. Just a family. Any family of four."

"This is a stupid game."

"But it's a real one. We're designing automated vehicles, and they will have to make decisions like this, in split seconds. Same as real drivers."

"Still stupid."

"Humor me."

Chuck sighed long and hard enough that everyone heard him. "Okay, if those are all the options and info I have? I go straight, take out the pregnant woman, doctor, and criminal."

"Why?"

"A criminal counts less, the doctor is a person who dedicated their lives to saving other people, and the pregnant lady, that's a tough one, but she counts the same as the mother and one kid in the car."

Damon said, "Mike, what about you?"

"I would swerve the car," Luke said. He put down his iPad and leaned forward from the third row. "It's our car. We're the ones going for a drive, right?"

Damon nodded. "Sort of. You're not in the car." Luke was a smart kid.

"But the people in the car, they wanted to go for a drive, so it's their responsibility. If they didn't go for the drive, those other people would be fine. And the doctor, don't they count for more? If she dies, she might not be able to save someone else later in the day."

Mike smiled at his son. "I agree with Luke."

"He does make a good point," Chuck said from the front.

"Okay," Damon said to Chuck, "what if it was you and me in the car, and a doctor and a criminal on the road. Would you swerve? Kill us and save them?"

"If I knew which one was the criminal?"

"I guess."

"Then I'd do my best to swerve and hit the criminal." Chuck caught Damon's eye in the rearview and smiled.

"Watch the road," Mike said from the back.

Damon asked, "But it wouldn't matter what law the criminal broke?"

"A criminal is a criminal," Chuck replied, his eyes straight ahead.

"A criminal," Terek said, closing his laptop, "is whoever the state decides is a criminal."

"Exactly," Damon said. "One day you go to jail for ten years for a gram of weed, the next day it's legal. You would opt to kill the person who the law says was a criminal one day but not the next? The day after weed is legal, you wouldn't kill a guy smoking it, but you would the day before?"

"Hold on, now we're getting into a lot of hypotheticals."

"Sure, but it demonstrates a state of mind."

"What's the point of this?"

I've just demonstrated it."

"I think we could all agree," Mike said from the back, "that we would be willing to sacrifice ourselves if it really came down to it."

Chuck snorted, "I'm not sure that's true."

"Terek jumped in the water to get me."

"The point is," Damon said, "that we all make different life and death decisions based on our own moral and societal compasses. At school, we played this game online with people around the world to get an idea of how we should program autonomous vehicles. Overall, people preferred to spare humans over animals."

"That's reassuring." Chuck laughed.

"Younger over older, in general as well, except for Confucianist cultural groups in Asia who showed little preference for those with high status or low."

"Good to know."

"The ones people spared the least were dogs, followed by criminals, then cats," Damon said.

"So people killed criminals before their cats?" Luke said.

"That's what the results said," Damon replied.

Luke scrunched his face up and declared, "That's *dumb*. That's wrong."

"But it seems to be what people think."

"Okay, okay," Mike said, holding a hand out. "That's enough. New topic. I think we get the point."

"Actually, I don't think we've reached the point at all," Chuck said.

The car went quiet. Only the sound of the wheels on the road and wind thrumming past.

"And what point is that?" Damon asked.

"The point is," Chuck said, "that guys like you get to decide who lives and dies in the future. Isn't that what you're trying to say?

You ask me what I think, but then you take that power from my hands, literally."

He lifted his hands off the wheel.

"Hey, stop playing around," Mike said.

Chuck put his hands back down. "What I'm saying is that Damon is making the point that he's taking power away from people like me, and putting it into his signals and systems. Our lives in the future are going to be in the hands of god-like algorithms that provide food, and decide who gets medicine and who lives and dies on the road. And Damon and Terek are the ones behind the curtain controlling the great and powerful Wizard of Oz. Isn't that what you're trying to say, Damon?"

Chapter 19

T he entrance barrier to the Cool Springs Estate creaked open.

It was a gated estate, Chuck joked, but more to keep the kids in than to keep anyone out. He left his driver's side window down as he leaned back in from the keypad. The air outside had cooled down to tolerable from the swelter of daytime.

"You guys are going to love Susie," he said to Irena.

He seemed almost gleeful that we hadn't been able to call ahead, that she wasn't going to get any warning of our arrival. He loved surprise birthday parties, but I knew Susie hated them. She would be up and waiting anyway. She'd been waiting for almost three days. On the same bed of nails I felt I was on.

At least her painful wait would be over.

Chuck swept the Range Rover around the estate roads a little too fast, but it was almost midnight. There wouldn't be any children out. In fact, there wasn't anyone out.

The traffic outside of Memphis had slowed to a crawl, and we'd been stuck in two more roadblocks. The seven-hour drive had stretched to fifteen.

After we passed the first roadblock, I sensed a tension between Chuck and Damon, which culminated in the debate about the morals of who to save and who to kill, if it came down to choice. The discussion had wound down, become civil, and eventually devolved into games of *I Spy*.

We'd had to stop once for gas between Memphis and Nashville, and the gas station attendant had told us cash only. Credit card machines weren't working anymore.

The second our headlights lit up their cul-de-sac, the door to Chuck's place swung open. It was a large two-story brick house with manicured bushes out front lit by spotlights. We didn't need to honk the horn or even get close to knocking on the door.

Susie spilled out the door, ran barefoot across the grass, and jumped into Chuck's arms as he got out of the truck. "Oh, baby, thank God you're okay!"

"I love you, too," Chuck managed to say around mouthfuls of kisses.

Damon lifted the back seat forward.

I put Luke out ahead of me and he ran to Chuck and Susie. She knelt to wrap him in her arms and smother him in her long brown hair. She was crying now.

I wiped my face, too. I couldn't help it. Mine was a happy tear, but one infused with fear. Seeing her drove another spike into my gut. Where was my own wife right now?

"Ah, Susie, this is Irena"—Chuck pointed to her—"and Terek, her younger brother."

Susie took Luke in her arms and stood. She grunted and whispered, "Boy, Luke, you're getting heavy." She stretched out a hand to shake hands with the Ukrainians. "Thank you so much for bringing Chuck home to us. Irena? That's your name?"

Irena shook her hand and smiled. "I know. Like your old friend from Manhattan. I heard good things about her."

Ellarose, six now, and Bonham, four, wandered out through the open front door of the house. They were both in their pajamas and half-asleep. Ellarose's little face lit up when she saw me. A teddy bear in one hand, she screeched, "Uncle Mike!" and ran across the lawn to me.

I bent and scooped her up. Two years younger than Luke, but less than half his weight. Still a waif. I squeezed her. "How are you doing?"

"I'm good. And Uncle Damon!"

She extended one arm to include Damon in the hug.

Bonham wandered across the grass. More lackadaisical. He waved at his dad and me and smiled. Chuck introduced the kids to Irena and Terek, and Susie put down Luke to give Damon a big hug.

She left me for last.

"Mike." She raised one hand to her mouth.

"I guess you haven't heard anything?"

"Not yet." She burst into tears and opened her arms.

I squeezed her tight, as much for her as me.

———

"Multiple widespread power failures are reported around the country," said the Fox News anchor, a thirty-something woman with blond hair.

"Are these related to the loss of satellites?" asked a commentator.

The consensus around the table was that nobody knew, but everyone assumed it was. The first stage of a cyberattack, said a rotund, sweaty man in a badly fitting suit. This time not only the East Coast, he said.

It's the whole country.

The entire world.

"I always said the CyberStorm wasn't an accident," Chuck said.

"You did not," I said.

"Yeah, I did."

"India and Pakistan didn't mean to trigger a full-blown Kessler syndrome. They didn't intentionally wreck all the satellites in orbit."

"So, all of this is down to more coincidences?"

"Not all the satellites are gone yet," Damon said.

He and Terek had set up their laptops on the dining room table the instant we walked in the door. He was already logged into the NASA space debris server. Irena and Susie went into the kitchen to get some coffee. I heard them talking, heard Susie laugh.

Chuck had turned on Fox almost as fast as Damon had gotten out his laptop.

"You still think all of this is accidental?" Chuck said to me.

"If not accidental, then unintended."

"Isn't that the definition of accidental?"

"You know what I mean." I settled into a chair, took the TV controller from him, and prepared for another round of whodunnit. "Who thinks it's the Russians?"

"That would not surprise me," Terek said from the kitchen table.

He'd only been in the gang a few days, but he was getting into the orbit of Chuck's circling mind.

"They've been hit as bad as we have," I said. "Or worse."

Chuck said, "Maybe the Chinese? Their Baidu geopositioning satellites haven't been wiped out yet."

"That's who we blamed last time," I said. "Remember? Washington filled with emergency supplies? We thought it was an invasion?"

"*You* thought." Chuck smiled as he corrected me. He scratched his chin with his prosthetic hand, and I felt another twinge of guilt. "And we're—"

"Oh, sorry, Chuck, hold on." I held up one hand while I turned up the volume.

The TV screen filled with images of airplanes stacked nose-to-nose down a runway.

"This is Heathrow," said the Fox news anchor. "England has been forced to take in hundreds of international flights as Eastern European countries close their airspaces." The image switched to a wind-blown, grassy expanse bordered by craggy rock. "And this is Goose Bay, Labrador, in Canada."

"I bet you she's there," Chuck said.

Susie shushed him as she and Irena came in from the kitchen.

"However, Canada closed its own airspace soon after the United States," the anchor continued. "There are more rumors of aircraft lost at sea, but in the confusion, these may have landed and not been able to report in. With China, India, Russia, and a dozen other countries shutting down their physical and digital borders, little information is getting through…"

Susie deposited a coffee carefully on the table in front of me. "I'm sure Lauren is fine," she said quietly.

"Sure you're right," I replied without enthusiasm.

"Your friend Irena is wonderful, and so is her brother. She was telling me about the fishing trip, I didn't know—"

"Hold on a sec."

I turned up the volume again. "The passengers from any aircraft that has landed are being quarantined," said the anchor. "Planes are being directed to central airports, with all passengers being held in Heathrow and Atlanta. These are the only two locations we can confirm."

"See? Planes landed in America. I'm sure she's stuck in all that, somewhere," Susie said. "You want something to eat?"

I shook my head.

"Why would they quarantine passengers from airplanes?" Terek said from the table.

The word 'quarantine' had very negative imagery. It hadn't been that long since the world had recovered from that pandemic. As if answering him, one of the talking heads on the TV said, "Officials could be worried about a terrorist threat, possibly chemical weapons."

"Viral?"

"Nobody is saying that—"

I switched to CNN.

A bright red banner emblazoned with the words "Terror Alert" rolled across the screen. "We have raised the terrorist threat alert to the highest level," said an announcer in the background.

"The CNN terror alert," Chuck snorted. He waved his hands in the air and got up to go to the kitchen. "Scary."

The image shifted to shaky handheld videos of fires. "Blazes have spread rapidly in California, engulfing the entire San Fernando Valley." The picture changed to a view from a drone or an airplane. "And fires are out of control in Virginia as well. There have been stories circulating of bright lights in the sky before the new blazes started." A man in a baseball cap and jeans, pointing at a green hillside, began recounting what he had seen.

"Holy cow." Chuck returned and sat down. "Where, exactly?"

"Not sure."

Susie brought out more coffee and some sandwiches. "Irena told me you guys saw a tornado."

"Yeah, it was close," I said.

"Not that close," Chuck countered. "And it wasn't that big."

"Not that *big*?" I said incredulously.

Luke grabbed one of the sandwiches and began stuffing his face. The kid had a good appetite. Like his old man. Susie ruffled Luke's hair and sat down next to me.

Irena joined us and squeezed in beside me. "How big do you need things to be in America? You even need tornadoes to be huge?" She turned to Chuck. "I don't remember you yawning through it. In fact, I recall you—"

"I'm saying it wasn't like *Twister* or something."

"No emergency services," I said. "Nobody showed up at all. Irena did first aid, and we ferried people to the hospital."

Susie said, "What about the fire departments? The police? Losing imaging satellites must be making oversight on natural disasters tougher, and having cell phones stop working…"

"There are eighteen thousand US police agencies. That's city police, county sheriffs, state and federal agencies," Chuck said. "They'll get their act together. This has just knocked them off their feet for a bit."

I said, "Don't police and emergency services still have VHF radio and line-of-sight radio? Person-to-person and digital mobile radio networks with base stations? All that should keep working, right?"

"Yeah, but having cell networks go down would eliminate their informal networks," Damon said from the dining table. "And then their private systems become overwhelmed when 'public' cell comms go down."

"But they would keep working to some degree, wouldn't they?"

Damon shrugged. "But in rural areas, with no TV even? No landline, no mobile. Makes it very difficult to know what's going on."

"So no emergency services at all?"

"People have always got each other, but official channels have been caught flat footed with the speed of this. Either in the dark or overwhelmed."

The TV shifted to images of rioting in streets. The announcer explained these were happening in Detroit after a huge power blackout. Images of empty store shelves.

"At least we're not in the Big Apple this time," Chuck said. "Better to be here." He turned to Susie and said, "Let's get the kids' things packed up."

"What about the fires?"

"We can drive around them. I promised Mike we'd get him to DC."

The TV shifted to videos of roadblocks, but not manned by National Guardsmen or State Troopers. "Local militia groups have taken control of towns throughout the Midwest," said an announcer.

"That must be what the cop was talking about," I said. "You sure you want to drive through that?"

"The Seventh Fleet has been recalled to bases in the Philippines," said the announcer on CNN. "With disrupted satellite comms, the navy is on high alert for possible attacks, and sporadic contact with nuclear submarines has left—"

The news anchor paused, then said, "We have a report from the Russian authorities that their bases in Tajikistan have detected high levels of airborne radioactivity, signaling possible evidence of nuclear detonations in the Kashmir region."

"See? The further away we are from civilization, the better. We're going," Chuck said to me. He stood, then turned and said, "Damon, come with me."

The garage smelled of rubber and gasoline. Naked neon tubes twenty feet overhead bathed the cement floor in stark light. The only car was a Mini Cooper parked in the far bay. Susie's car, Chuck said before I could ask. He led us down the wooden stairs to a refrigerator and pulled out three beers. He opened them and handed one each to me and Damon.

"Cheers," he said.

We clinked bottles.

I said, "What's up?"

He had obviously led us out there for some privacy.

"What in the heck is going on?" Chuck asked.

"I mean, the internet is still working, and the mobile networks are still up in South Korea," Damon said. "Most of the BieDou GNSS satellites and the QZSS from Japan seem to be working—"

"I don't mean out there." Chuck jabbed a finger at Damon. "I mean you. What the *hell* are you doing?"

"Ah…" Damon was confused.

"You told that State Trooper you were going to school with Terek and Irena. Said you'd known them for years."

"Technically, that's not a lie. I've known Terek for about a year, and Irena was going to Boston University, so we were going to school together in Boston."

"She's finished."

"I mean last year—"

"And Terek is not in school with you."

"He should be. I'm getting him into MIT next year. He's smarter than—"

"You don't lie to the police. Not at a checkpoint, especially when they're *looking* for something. Are you insane? If they had questioned you, we might all be in some lockup getting our colons inspected."

I stood between them. "Hey, it's okay. He wasn't lying. He was stretching the truth."

"Did you hear that hick trooper?" Damon said. "*Isn't Ukrainian the same as Russian?* You know what southern cops do to immigrants? I didn't want them stuck in some detention center."

"Southern?" Chuck replied. "That's bordering on an insult, friend. And that wouldn't have happened." He said it somewhat unconvincingly, though.

"Have you seen the news? It's *already* happening."

I said, "Did you see the way Irena helped those people in that town in Mississippi? Are we really going back to what happened last time? And Terek? The kid—"

"I know, I know. He saved your life." Chuck's expression softened. He eyed Damon in a way I'd seen a hundred times before. He grinned. "Do you have a thing for his sister? Because, I mean…"

"Do you?"

Chuck's smile widened. "I *was* impressed by her SIG Sauer." He leaned over and entered a code into a keypad on a gun safe. The lock chimed. He pulled a three-foot-long weapon from inside. "Nothing compared to Black Beauty, though."

Guns made me nervous, something Chuck knew only too well, which made him enjoy showing them to me even more. He'd told me about his AR-15, had been talking about it on the way here as if it were his third child.

"Is that loaded?" I asked.

"Course not. But what I really mean"—his smile became a naughty grin—"is not *yet*."

Chapter 20

Lauren pressed her face against the airplane window and did her best to look straight down. Black water glittered in the moonlight, the ocean waves rolling under a starless sky. The pane of carbonite plastic was cool against her burning cheeks.

She clutched her purse tight in white-knuckled fists.

The cabin lights were low. The man in the pod across from her recited the Lord's Prayer, his head bowed. A male flight attendant pulled out the jump seat in the galley beyond the bulkhead. The man's arms gripped the waist of another attendant as he slid to sit down. He sobbed and burst into tears.

Her hands trembling, Lauren took a picture of Luke and Olivia from her purse. "I love you so much," she whispered. Tears streamed down her face.

Outside the window, the waves edged closer. Ghosts rolled and rolled in the swells.

"Mike, I'm so sorry, I should never—"

The familiar background vibration and noise of the cabin changed in pitch. Like something settling. The engines had stopped. Silence. Whistling wind. Moans of terror. The plane dropped.

"Brace, brace, brace," came the captain's terse instructions.

Lauren glanced once more out the window at the endless black water, then at picture of Luke and Olivia clutched in her fingers. She ducked her head down to her knees.

A flash of white—

I awoke from the dream in a lurch, almost jumping from the bed.

It took me a few seconds, bedsheets clutched in my balled fists, to remember that I was in Chuck and Susie's spare bedroom. The blinds were down, a thin gray light weakly illuminating a work desk scattered with papers. On the wall at the foot of the bed was that picture of dogs playing poker, which Susie hated but Chuck could never let go of.

But the nightmare wasn't over.

My wife.

Still breathing hard, I took a few lungfuls to calm my heart. And where was Luke? On the floor was a blowup mattress, but no sign of him. Outside in the hallway, a shriek, but then a laugh and little footsteps racing away.

I gripped the railing on the stairs to make sure I wouldn't slip on the hardwood in my socks. Still unsteady and bleary-eyed, the dream of Lauren crashing wrapped tight around my awakening brain.

Tired. Beyond exhausted.

I hadn't slept more than three hours. Maybe not even one. I made my way carefully down the stairs.

Chuck and Susie's house was a sprawling two-level, with an open atrium in the center at least twenty feet high. The guest rooms were on the second level with the kids' rooms and playroom.

Chuck was already up—had never gone to sleep?—and was in the kitchen at the far end of the open atrium cooking something on the gas range. Luke was chasing Bonham, who shrieked and ducked around the kitchen island. Ellarose ran after them both.

"Flapjacks and bacon?" Chuck asked as he saw me coming down.

"Coffee first," I replied. He poured me a cup. "Nothing from Lauren?"

He shook his head.

Their landline was still working, so I had tried the Seymour residence a few times last night, but hadn't managed to get through. Emails and the internet were still working, so I'd sent messages. No responses so far.

"Don't any of you sleep?" I said to nobody in particular.

Susie and Irena were on the couch in front of the TV, curled up together and chatting under a blanket. Chuck liked to set the air conditioning to arctic. Damon and Terek, predictably, were on their laptops, connected together on the kitchen table.

"The American and European militaries are unable to confirm the radioactive readings coming from the Russians," a blond reporter said on the TV set above the fireplace. "But imaging from one Russian satellite seems to indicate that…"

I took a sip of hot coffee and luxuriated for a moment in the sensation of it hitting my throat, the warmth of it seeping into me. Sighing, I went to the side table in the hallway and picked up the handset from the cradle, then opened my phone to find the number. I dialed the Seymours' number in DC. It was 8 a.m. there, one hour behind us.

"Hello?"

"This is the Seymour residence…"

I gently put down the receiver and considered calling again, but turned and went to the couches by the TV. I sat on the one opposite Susie and Irena.

I asked, "Anything new I should know about?"

"The Russians managed to launch a new global positioning satellite overnight," Susie said. "It passed the debris field into an orbit higher up. They were recalibrating it to provide a signal, they said, but then they lost it almost right away."

"They're offering to provide location data to the American military," Irena added.

"Fat chance we'll take them up on that," Chuck said from the kitchen. "Pancakes?" He waved a plate.

I wasn't sure when I'd last eaten. My stomach growled. "Sounds great." I got up from the couch.

Terek came to join me on a stool at the kitchen island. Damon mumbled something and went into the hallway. I heard him pick up the phone.

Luke ran up and wrapped his arms around my waist. "You okay, dad?"

"I'm fine," I said.

When had he become the one taking care of me? "You had breakfast?"

He held up two fingers. "That many pancakes."

Chuck deposited some flapjacks and bacon on plates in front of Terek and me. "Sleep okay?"

"As can be expected."

"Maple syrup?" Chuck asked.

"Does the pope?"

"I figured." He retrieved a bottle from the fridge. "Terek, I saw you praying at the church in Mississippi." Chuck took a stool next to us. "You're Christian?"

"Faith is very important to us," Terek said around his first mouthful of pancake.

"Us too," Chuck said. "We go every Sunday, to a big evangelical mission around the corner."

"My sister makes me go each Sunday as well." Terek smiled at Irena.

"He makes me sound like a monster," she said in response.

"No, I like it," Terek said. "My grandmother, she always, I mean, after our mother…" His voice faded.

"I heard," Chuck said, his voice softer. "I'm sorry."

Terek put his fork down. He shrugged. "It seems another lifetime, but then also like yesterday. Irena took care of me after our mother passed. She had just gotten out of the army."

"I lost both my parents," Chuck said. "Car accident."

"I am sorry to hear this."

"It was a long time ago."

Terek nodded, picked up his fork. Prodded the pancakes.

"What denomination are you?" Chuck asked.

"Eastern Orthodox. Wait, but is that a denomination? I don't know."

"I get it."

The voice of the TV news announcer: "Russia is now offering to send aid to the United States as power outages continue rolling across the country. This has shades of six years ago, when the CyberStorm…"

Terek pushed at a chunk of pancake. "The Russians, the Soviets, tried to take away our religion. My grandmother was forced to stop attending the church, many years before. They boarded it up." He waved a fork at the TV. "You should not trust them."

"That's terrible," Chuck said. "And I don't."

In the hallway, Damon was talking to someone on the phone.

The image on the TV shifted to a view of the New York harbor. "Ships coming into port are being held up," the news anchor said. "The entire logistics network has ground to a halt. Shipping companies have lost track of containers and shipments."

Damon reappeared. "Same thing Grandma Babet is saying."

"You talked to her?" I asked.

"Just now."

"And?"

"She says that the Port of Louisiana is in total chaos. They can't track anything. They're unloading ships and opening everything up. They're trying to get perishables in first. Almost back to pencil and paper."

"Things will still get through?"

Damon sat back down at his laptop. "They'll adapt, I'm sure, but it might take months."

I finished my pancakes, then grabbed the remote and switched to CNN. The screen filled with images of burning forests.

"The Daniel Boone wilderness is now ablaze," said a TV anchor, a black-haired woman with dark skin. "Fire crews and emergency response teams are hampered by the lack of satellite imaging and loss of communications. They are now flying over affected areas and taking pictures with their cell phones, then physically taking those phones down to the ground and explaining where the photos were taken. As you can imagine, this is a chaotic process. Witnesses are reporting multiple new blazes, possibly caused by what some are referring to as fire falling from the sky. The flames have now spread from the Pennington Gap…"

"That's the tristate," Chuck said. He walked in front of the TV with a pad of paper in his hand. "The Daniel Boone Wilderness Trail runs through Tennessee, Kentucky, and Virginia."

"Is that near your cabin?" I asked.

"Five hundred miles from it, but not more than a hundred miles from here."

"Explains the haze outside." The air had been thick the night before, and not only with humidity.

"But we better take a more northerly route to be safe," Chuck said. "Up around Lexington."

"Are you sure you still want to go?"

"Stuff like this is what I keep that cabin for. Besides, we gotta get you to Washington. I bet Lauren will be waiting for you."

"Chuck," Susie whispered under her breath.

"What?"

"Don't say things like that." She glanced around to see where Luke was.

"It's what I think," Chuck said. "Glass half full. Optimism. It doesn't hurt."

"Now you're the optimist?"

"He might be right," Damon said from in front of his laptop. "A lot of the international flights over open water were redirected into national airports, even after airspaces were closed. Maybe she's in Canada, though."

"I'd take Canada."

"Everyone, finish up your breakfast. We have a busy day. We need to go to my restaurants and collect some food for the trip."

"Are we leaving today?"

"Get loaded up today. They've declared curfew in Nashville at night."

"Damon," Susie said. "Can I ask what you're doing? You've been stuck on your laptop all night."

"Analyzing data from NASA."

"And why would NASA need you?"

"I worked with them on my PhD project about satellite constellations."

I noticed he didn't mention he was working with the DOD.

Damon continued, "Semiautonomous drones in space, that sort of thing. They're already planning on launching new GPS satellites, but need all the help they can get figuring out where the debris is spreading."

"And Terek's helping you?"

"We're good friends. I'm getting him into MIT next year."

"And how's it looking? I mean, up there?" Susie pointed at the ceiling.

"A lot of satellites lost or offline. They're trying to move them out of the way. But it still doesn't make sense."

"What doesn't?"

"The whole thing." He turned to me. "That conversation we were having yesterday? The big difference between outer space and cyberspace?"

I nodded. It was a rhetorical question. He was already halfway to developing his professor skills for what I suspected would be an academic career when all this was over.

"The biggest one is still money. Getting into cyber costs very little. Hackers cause havoc for pennies on the ruble. Whereas getting into outer space is incredibly expensive. I still don't understand how Pakistan could have afforded the system that carried out their end of these attacks."

I asked, "That's the only big difference?" It seemed like there would be more.

"Attribution is the other one. Like Chuck said. In cyber, it's hard to know with certainty who's attacking you, whereas with the space system—I mean, missiles and rockets—you know where they come from. But it still doesn't make sense."

Chuck said, "I believe *you* are the guy to make sense of it. So figure it out. We're going shopping."

"I really respect what you did for those people back there," Chuck said.

Irena was in the front seat beside him, with me squished in the back of the Range Rover. We'd thought of taking the Mini into the city, but Irena had insisted we take her truck. More space to load food and supplies, she'd said, and we couldn't disagree.

"I did what anyone would do," Irena replied.

"Well, yes and no. You really put in extra time and effort."

We pulled off the highway at Exit 37. Chuck had opened two Tex-Mex restaurants in Nashville after selling the ones in New York to move here.

As we pulled around the off-ramp, we saw that cars were lined up ahead of us. Another roadblock manned by the National Guard, but this one wasn't stopping and searching. Only acting as security.

A thick haze hung to the east in the morning sky, obscuring the sun in an orange blanket. The smell of fire in the air, even from a hundred miles away. There was a stiff easterly breeze that morning. Dry and blistering hot. The worst possible combination.

"Terek's a good kid," Chuck said.

Irena replied, "He is."

"Must have been tough, basically becoming his parent."

"This is why we came to America. For a new start."

"It's very courageous. I mean, I had a hard time moving from New York to Nashville, and I came from here originally. But going to a whole new country? Where you don't know anyone?"

We pulled into the parking lot of his restaurant.

"You didn't have family here when you came here, did you? Friends?" Chuck asked. He looked low through the windshield and inspected the building.

"Nobody," Irena replied.

"I gave everyone time off when this started, three days ago." Chuck completed his sweep of the parking lot and windows. "Place still looks intact."

We had stopped at a Krogers supermarket on the way in. With the news channels and internet warning of impending Armageddon and the shutting down of logistics and shipping, the supermarket had looked like it had been hit by a zombie apocalypse.

There had still been flowers in plastic wrap and magazines and gum by the checkout, but most of the shelves were stripped clean, except for stuff like ketchup and the straggling remains of greens in the vegetable aisles.

No signs of looting, though. Not in Franklin or Nashville, as far as we had heard or seen, but the situation was worse in big cities. New York was remaining calm, from what I'd read on the internet.

We exited the Range Rover.

The restaurant was in a strip mall. The parking lot empty apart from us. The dry cleaner beside Chuck's restaurant was closed. All the other shops shuttered. Same as a few years ago during the virus outbreak, and years before that in the cyberattack.

Chuck saw me looking. "Those blackouts and service interruptions they're reporting? Doesn't mean it has to be a cyberattack or even caused by GPS loss. Power companies need power stations, and power stations need people to operate them. Everyone goes home, all the services will stop."

He unlocked the doors and checked the back. Nobody had been in. He directed us to the freezer and each of us filled a box with meat, then another with cans he selected from the shelves.

A powerful sense of déjà vu overcame me.

"I know," Chuck said. He didn't need to say what. He closed up and we ventured back into the sweltering heat.

Chuck keyed in the access code for his gate. A part of me waited for the electronics to stop working, for everything to suddenly shut off.

It felt weird that some things were working, but some weren't. We had the internet, but no cell phones. We still had TV, but no long-range weather forecasts. We'd only been on the road for an hour, and already I felt the itch.

What had happened while we'd been gone?

"You really got a license for that SIG?" Chuck asked Irena.

"I said I did. You want to see it?"

"Just curious," he said.

"It's right there in the glove box." She was driving. She nodded at the compartment in front of Chuck.

We rounded the corner to Chuck's house, and before he could decide whether to look at the license, we saw Susie on the lawn. She waved her arms above her head and ran at us.

She was crying.

"What's wrong?" Chuck rolled down his window. "Something with the kids? What happened?"

"It's not the kids." She held a hand to her mouth. "It's Lauren."

Chapter 21

The excitement of not dying was beginning to wear thin.

"Welcome to the Naval Air Station Oceana," announced a hand-painted sign on brown packing paper stuck to the cement block wall across from Lauren's cot.

She had been staring at it for more than a day now.

Welcome indeed.

With the waves of the Atlantic Ocean almost touching the 777's wingtips, at what had seemed like the last instant before a disaster, solid ground had materialized below the aircraft. Wailing prayers had transformed to gasping cries, and for vertigo-inducing seconds, houses had appeared below them—but then landing strips and lights.

Just before 1 a.m. on September 8, American Airlines flight 1265 had touched down on runway L25 of the Naval Air Station Oceana. Pandemonium had erupted in the cabin, shouting and hoots of laughter and tears when the wheels had squealed against the tarmac.

"Ladies and gentlemen," the pilot had announced. "Welcome to Virginia Beach. It is now 1:04 a.m. local time, East Coast, United States. We apologize for the inconvenience."

That was perhaps the most understated address Lauren had ever heard. She could have kissed the pilot at that moment.

They had left Hong Kong at sunset on September 6th, arrived in Virginia on the morning of September 8th, and Lauren was never going to leave her kids ever again. When they opened the cabin doors, the fresh sea air, humid and hot as it was, was sweet relief—somehow it had even *smelled* like America.

Polite young men in camouflage had escorted them off the plane. Lauren had been amazed to see more commercial jets than she could count stacked along the edge of the runway and between the metal hangars. They'd herded the passengers along and divided them up, and Lauren had ended up here. In a gymnasium at the far end of the Naval Station.

Emily wouldn't leave her side. The young men asked crew members to go with them separately, but she said she wanted to stay with Lauren. They were in this together.

When they'd offered Lauren a cot and said she had to stay here for now, Lauren couldn't have been happier. A tiny metal cot with polyester sheets in an open gymnasium with a thousand other people had seemed like a godsend, and she'd hit the covers and slept like a dead person until the morning.

That was two days ago. Since then, no luggage. No shower.

She had been in these clothes for how long? It was September 10th now, her watch said. Her cell phone was out of power, but she'd heard that didn't matter, because there wasn't any coverage. No bars. Four days now she had been in these same clothes. Not even a change of underwear. Stinky didn't even begin to cover it.

"I'm going to keep the baby." Emily was lying down in the cot next to Lauren. The flight attendant's beautiful red hair was a shambles. She had a glow to her, though. She couldn't care less. "I'm going to tell Paul as soon as we get out of here."

Lauren replied, "That's great, honey."

Enough was enough. She stood and gently took the arm of a young man in uniform who was delivering sandwiches to anyone who wanted one.

"Excuse me," Lauren said. "But when are we getting out of here?"

"Ma'am, I don't have an answer for that."

The young man's green eyes were a lot like Luke's. The thought elicited what felt like an ice pick stabbing into her stomach. She hadn't even been able to call her family, to tell them she was safe. They had to be beyond worried. She hadn't talked to Mike in five days, the longest time they'd gone without contact since the day they'd met at Harvard, over a decade ago.

"Can I use a phone?"

"Ma'am, as I'm sure you have heard, telephones are not working."

"I need my family to know I'm safe."

"There are people working on that. We sent out all the passenger information to the DHS as soon as we processed it, but you have to understand"—he lowered his voice—"we got forty-plus passenger aircraft dumped on our heads in the middle of the night. There are more than four thousand civilians from every nation on Earth in here. They got the gates locked up, and won't let anyone out till the DHS processes everyone. And right now, it is a mess out there. They shut down the borders."

"I'm American. I have my passport. What's the problem?" In a lower voice she asked, "It's not biological, is it? Viral?"

"No ma'am, it's not that. If it was up to me, I'd let you walk right out of here, ma'am."

"Can I get my luggage?"

He shrugged. "That is above my pay grade."

Lauren let go of his arm. "Thank you," she said, "and thank you for your service."

The young man continued on his way.

Lauren sat down on the squeaking cot and sighed.

"Ma'am?"

She looked up. It was the young man, but this time he was with someone else. A man in a suit with dark sunglasses.

"I think this is your ticket out, ma'am."

The man in the dark suit asked, "Mrs. Lauren Mitchell?"

"That's me."

"I've been sent by your uncle, Senator Seymour. Please follow me."

"Can I come?" Emily stood up from her cot.

"I'm sorry, I'm only authorized to bring Mrs. Mitchell."

Emily looked at Lauren. "Please? I need to get out of here too. I need to talk to Paul."

Chapter 22

"Daddy!" Luke ran at me with a paper in his hand. "Daddy, they found mom." He jumped up and down in his socks. Ellarose joined in and Bonham ran in circles around me.

I still had my arms around a cardboard crate from Chuck's. Kicking off my shoes, I crossed into the dining room to put it down, then turned to pick up my son. "I know, I know."

My scalp was still tingling from the fear, and then the rush of excitement, when Susie had cried out Lauren's name in the yard and said they found her.

Found her wasn't quite accurate.

Lauren wasn't home yet, from what I understood. The Seymours had gotten a note from the airline that she had landed. I dialed their Washington number. It picked up on the first ring.

"Michael," answered a familiar voice.

"Senator Seymour, yes, I mean, it's me. It's Michael."

"You heard the good news?"

"Do you have her yet?"

"She's in a receiving center in Virginia. We sent a car to get her an hour ago. You're at the Mumford residence?"

Luke stared up at me, smiling his gap-toothed grin. I grinned back and held up a finger for him to give me a minute. "That's right. In Nashville. We got hung up on the roads coming in. We'll be leaving for Washington tomorrow morning."

"I'll call you the second Lauren gets here."

"How is Susan holding up?"

"Do you want to speak to her?"

Luke pulled on my pant leg. "Can I talk to mom? Can't we do a FaceTime?"

I whispered to him, "She's not there yet," and then said to the senator, "Ah, no, that's okay. Just want to know she's okay. That everyone's okay."

"We're more worried about you."

"Me?"

A pause. "Mike, be careful on the roads." Another pause. "There is some indication that this all might not be an accident. These space attacks."

"Did India launch a nuclear strike?"

"We think that's false information, but we're not one hundred percent sure."

"About what?"

"About anything, to be honest. Be careful. And get here as soon as you can." He hung up.

How could he not be sure? He was in the epicenter of those-in-the-know.

Chuck stood in the doorway behind me, Irena beside him, both of them laden with boxes. He asked, "What did he say?"

"That they sent a car to get her."

"Did I hear him say this wasn't an accident?"

"He said there was an indication." I wasn't sure what he'd meant.

"I am so happy, Mike. This is amazing. I told you." Chuck penguin-walked through the entrance with his awkward load. "I'm going to start loading the cars. We head out at first light tomorrow. I'll get you home. Get you back to Lauren and Olivia."

Irena followed him. "We'll come too," she said.

"What's that in your hand?" I asked Luke.

"A paper airplane," Ellarose answered. She was still jumping up and down. "We've been building them."

Luke showed me the airplane he had made. "Like mom's. Want to see it fly?"

"Sure."

Luke and Ellarose shot past me and thumped up the wooden staircase to the catwalk landing a story up, which ran through the atrium. Bonham followed behind them.

"Watch this," Luke exclaimed.

He stretched a rubber band out on one thumb. His airplane shot forward, spun in a tight circle before it flattened out, then sailed smoothly forward until it hit the wall of the atrium thirty feet away.

"Cool!" Ellarose shrieked.

"Guys, guys, can you hold it down?"

Damon waved his hands at Ellarose and Luke. He wanted them to be quiet. He obviously wasn't used to kids, not the way I'd become used to them. Quiet wasn't one of their settings.

I hadn't noticed Damon and Terek by the kitchen table. Still on their laptops, but now they were standing in front of them instead of their usual slouching. I picked up my box from the restaurant and took it into the kitchen.

Luke came thumping down the stairs. "What did you get me?"

"Frozen turkey, I think."

"Yuck."

"You wouldn't say that if you hadn't eaten in two days."

"Why wouldn't I eat in two days?"

It was meant as a joke, referencing the disaster in our apartment in New York, but of course he didn't remember it. It wasn't the sort of joke I should be telling. Whatever was happening now, we were still in the middle of it.

"I'm only kidding."

"Guys, please," Damon urged as I got closer.

He wasn't just noodling on his laptop. Someone else was on the screen, and not only one. A video conference with a half dozen people.

I opened the freezer door and said, "Sorry, I'll keep it down." Then I whispered to Luke, "Buddy, Uncle Damon needs us to be quiet. Why don't you show Ellarose and Bonham how to make another plane?"

My boy frowned his serious look. "Okay, I'll take care of them. You're right."

Only one year older than Ellarose, but to him it meant he was the little man of the house. In a low voice, he explained to them. They nodded and all glanced at Damon. I did as well, and I tried to be as silent as possible while I stuffed the freezer.

"You can buy a signal booster from any electronics store," I heard Damon say. He stood up straight in front of his laptop and held up a device in his hand. "I'm sending you the modified mesh-networking app. You can use it to send pictures, even do voice calls. Do you have any drones?"

"Who's he talking to?" I whispered to Terek, who stood to one side as Damon gesticulated to illustrate something.

"The first responders in Virginia are trying to deal with that fire."

"How did he start talking to them?"

It didn't really surprise me. Damon had a way of becoming the center of attention in almost any online space.

"We've been installing his mesh-networking app on as many phones as we can," Terek explained. "Like he did New York. With you guys. He's kinda famous."

"Kinda?" I was being sarcastic. I'd been there when people asked for his autograph.

Four years ago, through a campaign led by Senator Seymour, Damon had been awarded a Congressional Gold Medal in recognition of his work saving perhaps thousands of lives by encouraging people to install his mesh app during the disaster. He had gone out of his way, and sometimes into harm's way, back then, and now people were looking to him again.

"His DamonNet website has dozens of requests from groups. He's explaining how to use a phone attached to a drone as a relay to give wide area voice coverage."

"Maybe we should leave him here?" The work seemed important.

"It's all set up now," Terek said. "He's created auto-responders on his email, bots that can answer questions."

"Still…"

Terek said, "No way he's not coming with you. You're his family."

Damon's dad had taken off when he was a baby, same as what happened to my brothers and me. It was another thing that had bonded us. Damon felt like a kid brother. He always stayed in touch. Sent stuff to the kids for their birthdays, came to visit us on the holidays.

I suddenly felt very proud of him.

"He's a good man," I said.

"The best. He's been a very wonderful friend to me."

We watched him finish his presentation. The moment he said goodbye, he immediately clicked a button on his laptop and started another discussion group.

I asked Terek, "Can you get your laptop?"

He mumbled, sure, without asking what I needed it for. He brought it over to the granite kitchen countertop, out of sight of Damon's presentation.

Luke had Ellarose and Bonham busy building with Lego. The leader. Grown up beyond his years.

Terek turned his computer on, then spent a minute shuffling folders before offering it to me. I pulled up a web browser with a map of the Virginia area.

"There are sixteen airports near Virginia Beach," I said. "That's where they said Lauren landed."

"They didn't give an exact airport?" Chuck asked from over my shoulder.

He'd gone into the garage carrying the boxes from the restaurant, but had returned holding his AR-15 and another gun I didn't recognize. He laid them out on the dining room table. I glanced at the kids to see if they noticed anything. I had more than mixed feelings about guns. In New York, it wasn't common for anyone to have one, not in my circle of friends, but further south they were sometimes a point of pride.

"They're not loaded. I need to clean and get them ready."

"For what?"

"In case we need them. What's he doing?"

He pointed at Damon, who was waving his arms in the air in front of his laptop. I explained that he was presenting to the first responders. Chuck was suitably impressed.

"I've seen pictures online of detention areas in Virginia," Terek said.

"You think they put Lauren into detention?"

"Maybe this is not the right word. Processing centers. When they closed airspace, hundreds of planes had nowhere to go, so they had to open airports and make exceptions—otherwise they would have run out of fuel. Messy and improvised."

He opened another tab on the browser and showed me some articles online.

Chuck had disassembled part of his AR-15. "Why are they detaining people from airplanes?" he said. "That doesn't make any sense. Unless they're looking for someone."

"Or something," Terek said.

Lots of conspiracy websites were already freaking people out with talk of viruses, but I didn't see the police or anyone else wearing masks.

"Same as the National Guard we ran into," Chuck said. "What are they looking for?"

I didn't have an answer. I found a pen, took some paper from a printer by the window, and began scribbling down the names of roads in the Virginia Beach area and all the locations of the airports.

"I thought you said they sent someone to get her," Terek said.

"She's not home yet," I replied.

"We'll have you in Washington by tomorrow night," Chuck said. "We get up at five and leave at first light. Eleven hours of driving."

"Do we need to go to your cabin?" I was still nervous about going back to that place, as irrational as the feeling was.

"Susie wants me to drop her there. And I want to get The Wolf."

That was the Range Rover we'd used to escape from New York. "You still have that?"

"It's been upgraded a little. Can I turn the TV on?"

Damon had finished his presentation and was fiddling with something else. The guy never stopped. Without turning around, he said, "Sure, but keep it down?"

Chuck found the remote on the kitchen counter. The screen opened right onto Fox News—and an aerial view of a nuclear submarine.

"Russia is again claiming that there is radioactive dust in the air near Kashmir," said a blond news anchor in a corner box, "with Pakistan saying it is uncertain if a nuclear device was detonated or not. India is still denying—"

Susie came out from the garage. "Do we have to have that going all the time?"

"Honey, how else are we going to find out what's going on?" Chuck returned to taking his gun apart.

"Our nuclear fleet is still able to receive messages via VLF array," the blond announcer said. "But it is one-way communication. VLF, or very low frequency, waves bounce off the ionosphere and can be received anywhere on the planet. Ships are also equipped with shortwave gear, which can send and receive from almost anywhere on the globe, the same as ham radio operators."

"But from what I understand, isn't that analog voice?" a brunette talking head asked. "Analog is 'in the clear,' isn't it? Meaning anyone listening can listen in? Without timing signals from GPS, security of communications from ships have been degraded."

"Degraded but not gone," said a man with close-cropped blond hair in what looked like a military uniform. "Even extremely low frequency comms that go through seawater are encrypted. There is no way the military is sending any unencrypted messages to our boats. Nothing important, anyway."

"Even so, the navy has recalled the Seventh Fleet to Yokosuka in Japan, where the Japanese QZSS satellites—"

"Q what?" asked another talking head.

"The Japanese have two specialized geopositioning satellites in what are called highly elliptical orbits, higher than geostationary orbits, and these are still providing position signal. The Japanese authorities are providing this signal to anyone in the Asia-Pacific region—"

"Everyone. Please," the main anchor interrupted. "We now have...the US military has raised its threat level to a global DEFCON 2. This is the first time in our nation's history."

We were still trying to absorb what was on the TV when Damon stood in front of it. "And those fires? I talked to first responders all up and down the East Coast." He paused.

"What about the fires?" I asked.

"They're not only in the Daniel Boone wilderness. People are describing flashes in the sky. Blazes appearing everywhere, and nobody knows why or how."

Chapter 23

"I'm not sure this is a good idea," I said.

How many times had I repeated this already? More than I could count. Enough that nobody responded anymore.

High noon, and the sun beat down directly overhead. Not a cloud up there, but the Kentucky sky was the color of whiskey, like a keg of bourbon had been poured across the heavens to hide the blue beyond. The flat plains around Lexington gave way to the low rolling foothills of Appalachia, and the haze grew thicker the further north and east we headed.

We hadn't seen any fires, not yet, but where there was smoke…

Six hours on the road.

Chuck and Susie and their two kids led the way in the Mini Cooper, with Irena, Terek, myself, Luke, and Damon pulling up the rear in the Range Rover. No way Chuck wasn't going to lead the charge, even stuffed into the Mini. He was back with his family, which made me want to be back together with mine—whole—that much more.

I'd called the Seymour residence when the sky had lightened on the horizon, about 4 a.m., and the senator had answered but said, no, they hadn't heard anything. The men they'd sent said they were still trying to find Lauren in one of the collection areas, but there was some confusion. It was a mess over there, he said. They hadn't found her yet. He said not to worry.

I did.

The traffic all morning had been sparse. A few trucks, and hardly any going in the direction we were headed.

We had left at first light.

Leaving the protective safety of Chuck's house felt like we were exposing ourselves, like going outside naked when you had a full set of clothes inside. It seemed wrong, and I told Chuck and Susie how I felt.

They wouldn't listen.

They needed to get to their cabin in the mountains, they said, to which I responded, the same mountains that were on fire? Chuck had a plan, like always. We'd head north up Interstate 40, past Bowling Green, and go on to Lexington. We would skirt the worst of the fires, which had started in the Daniel Boone Wilderness, but were spreading north.

Chuck still maintained that the fires were five hundred miles from his cabin, no fire spread that fast, and anyway, if there was a fire coming, he needed to cut a break so his home wouldn't burn down.

His plan was to go north until we hit the Ohio River where it branched off the Mississippi. The Ohio wound east. If we stuck close to it, Chuck explained, then even if we did get trapped by fires, we could always take refuge in the river. But we wouldn't get close to any fires. We would keep going north.

When disaster had struck before, we had stuck together, and there was no way I was going to convince Chuck to leave me with two strangers, as nice and brave as they were, to get to Washington by myself.

Not quite by myself.

"Damon, what the hell are you eating?" I asked.

Chuck had been busy all-night cooking what we'd taken from the restaurant. We packed it all in coolers and stuffed them into the back of the Range Rover. There was more space now, without Chuck in here with us, but Luke and I stayed in the third row, with

Damon in the middle. He was busy eating something that looked like milky dog food. Smelled like it, too.

"Psychobiotics," he replied.

"You mean, probiotics?"

"Psycho." He took out a spoonful and offered it. "One level up. Did you know that single-celled organisms have control over your mind?"

"Single-track thoughts have control of Chuck's."

"I'm serious. All those microbes in your gut, they don't just make you healthier if you have the right ones. They make you happier. They actually affect your moods and thoughts. I'm trying to keep any edge I can."

Luke put down his Lego to inspect what Uncle Damon was eating.

"Legook, you want some?" Damon asked.

"That looks gross," Luke replied.

"I gotta ask. Why do you call him Legook?" I asked Damon.

They exchanged a look, and Damon replied, "It's a secret."

I rolled my eyes, but didn't press. "You got some turkey sandwiches in that cooler?"

Damon nodded. I held his psychobiotic cup of goo while he found one for me and one for Luke.

"Could you turn up the radio?" I asked Irena, who was driving.

Terek had the police scanner on as well. Nothing unusual in the past half an hour. When there was a roadblock ahead, there would usually be chatter on one of the frequencies as the police coordinated. The FM channels were blank, none of the usual soft rock or classical, as many stations had gone offline. What was left were news reports and discussions, more than half of which felt like conspiracy rants.

"DEFCON 1 means that nuclear war has already started," said a male voice on the radio. "And we are one level below that."

"DEFCON 1 does not necessarily mean nuclear war has started," said another voice, this one female. "It means it is imminent."

"We have never been at DEFCON 2," countered the male.

"We were at DEFCON 2 in the Cuban missile crisis in '62," the female said, "and again with the Gulf War in '91, and during CyberStorm six years ago."

"But those were all local. This is the first time we are at *global* DEFCON 2," countered the man.

The female acknowledged his point.

I hadn't even known there was a difference.

The female began talking about how the grocery store shelves in Lexington were empty, that nothing more was coming in, and what was the government doing about it? This was a problem created by the elites, she said, with their reliance on technology and their greed, and now the price was being paid by the average American.

"Can you turn it off?" I asked.

We exited the highway and headed north, to the Ohio River.

This was a slow-motion disaster.

Quiet but relentless.

We couldn't see the destruction of the satellites overhead. There were no fireworks or explosions. An orange haze engulfed us. Everywhere but nowhere and suffocating at the same time.

Years ago, when I was a kid, we'd had an ice storm in upstate New York when we were on a skiing trip. It sounds dramatic, and the effects were astounding, but it had been gradual.

The temperature hung right around freezing, and it drizzled for a week straight from gray indistinct clouds. No wind. No actual storm. Damp and cold—but exactly the wrong combination of conditions.

Day by day, a layer of clear ice accumulated. First on the sidewalks, and then on the bare trees. Branches slender as a pinky finger became sheathed with coatings of clear ice thick as a thumb, and then the next day as fat as sausages. It was beautiful in a way— entire forests, everything outdoors, all of it entombed in a crystalline covering.

Fascinating, until the weight of it started collapsing the branches.

Then whole trees.

Telephone lines had come down. Then power lines. Even the massive structures that held up the power cables had collapsed. The electricity went out for weeks in some places. Communications cut off in whole regions.

But the whole time, it had been quiet and peaceful.

This disaster we were now living through felt eerily and dismally familiar, the same as others that seemed to happen every few years now. It started with things like toilet paper going empty on shelves. Lines at grocery stores.

On TV, they said that between what people kept at home and what was in the shops, there was about a week of food for everyone. The last of the delivery vans were now making their rounds. There were almost no trucks on the highways.

Chaos was digging its heels in.

Borders were closed. Again.

Air travel stopped.

But it wasn't like it hadn't happened before. Not exactly.

When that virus had hit a few years before, almost all air travel had ceased. The markets had halted a few times. Uncertainty and panic had set in, but after a difficult few months, scientists and authorities found ways to slow down and stop it. A year or so later, life was back to normal.

How long would it take this time?

A big difference now, was that the military was affected and partly immobilized. During the pandemic, cell phones and communications had functioned. For the most part, those luxuries were now gone.

This time there was also a general call to action for all branches of the military, including the reserves. All local, state, and federal law enforcement agencies were mobilized to maintain law and order. But in rural areas, what did that mean, exactly?

With real information overwhelmed by misinformation, it was hard to tell people to stay calm.

Communications between Russia and China and America and India and other nations were mostly shut off from each other. A world that had talked as one was now fractured into parts. Conspiracy theories raged on the internet and radio. Emergency services crippled. Long-range weather forecasting gone. The world's militaries waiting for threats to emerge from the dangerous fog we found ourselves in.

And all the while, if you stood outside on the lawn of your house, it was quiet. A disaster unfolding peacefully, but I had an uneasy feeling the serenity wouldn't last much longer.

We had turned off the main highway a half hour out of Lexington, then taken a smaller road up to the edge of the Ohio River, following Chuck's plan. This was a smaller road, two lanes, and we passed farms and silos that dotted the low hills and green forests. Up ahead, in the orange haze, appeared a collection of pickup trucks on a field and in the road.

"What's that?" I pointed.

Luke was halfway through his sandwich. "It looks like another roadblock. Is it a roadblock?"

It did look like one. "Terek, anything on the police scanner?"

He shook his head.

I dialed Chuck's number on my phone, using the mesh app. He picked up right away. "Doesn't look like the National Guard," he said. "No police cars either."

Irena slowed the Range Rover.

As we neared, we saw an improvised barricade of wooden pallets stacked across half of the road. A line of Ford pickups stretched to a low stone fence that demarcated the border between two farms. A green-and-yellow John Deere tractor blocked the way. Chuck and the Mini were a few hundred feet ahead of us, and they pulled to a stop.

Heads appeared over the pallet barricades. Not just heads. Rifle muzzles.

Two groups of four men in beige camouflage fatigues walked from behind the first line of pickup trucks. They split up, one group heading toward us, as Irena slowed to a stop as well.

"Stay on the line," Chuck said.

I turned my phone to speaker mode and put it on the seat between me and Luke.

Irena rolled down her window.

The first group of four men had already encircled Chuck's Mini and were talking to him. Their voices came through low and garbled over my phone. Nothing angry, though. Talking, but about what, I couldn't make out.

Two of the men advancing toward us stopped about twenty feet in front of the Range Rover. They wore fatigues and boots, but weren't army—at least not in whatever capacity this was. It wasn't only the mismatched uniforms, but the way they slouched. They held semiautomatic weapons to their chests in casual yet threatening poses.

Chuck's voice was still calm over the phone.

A blond man advanced to Irena's window. "How y'all doing?" he said.

"We're okay," Irena replied.

"Where you headed?"

"DC."

"Why you going there?"

"We have family."

"My wife," I said from the back. "My wife and children are there."

The blond man squinted and lowered his head. "Can you roll down the back windows?" he asked Irena. "I need to look through your truck."

"What for?" I asked.

Irena rolled the windows down.

"Not what," he replied. "It's a 'who' we looking for." He squinted and surveyed the back of the Range Rover. "What the hell is that?"

"Our drones," Damon answered.

"Those look military."

"They're not. Well, not really."

"Do all y'all have some identification?"

The voices on my phone became louder. I heard Chuck swear. The driver's side door of the Mini opened and my friend uncoiled from the tiny car. One of the camouflaged men put a hand under Chuck's arm as he got out of the car, and Chuck flicked him away. The man staggered back. Two more advanced on Chuck, pointing guns and yelling.

The voices echoed on my phone.

"What's that noise?" the blond man asked. He glanced behind him at Chuck, who now had his arms up.

"My cell phone. I was talking to my friend over there."

"You have working cell phones?" The blond man took Irena and Terek's passports as she offered them through the window.

"It's a mesh app," Damon explained.

"A what?"

"So your cell phones can talk to each other."

"I need to see your identification."

"I'll help you install it on your phones," Damon offered. He slid over to the side and started to open the door. "And I lost my wallet in a storm a few days ago. We had everything ripped from the roof of the car."

The blond man backed away, his hand going to the gun on his hip. He had just taken Terek and Irena's passports. "Please stay in the car, sir," he said.

But Damon was already stepping out his side door, his hands up. "I can help you." He reached into his backpack.

I groaned as I saw him do it.

One of the men standing guard in front of the truck, a short, squat guy with a shaved head, had advanced to stand next to the blond man. He took two steps toward Damon to try and get him back into the car, but the second Damon reached into his backpack, the reaction was swift. He brought his rifle butt up.

Damon started to say, "I got this th—"

He spat his air out as the butt of the gun caught his midsection. He doubled over to the ground.

"Hey, hey, hey." I squeezed through the back seat, my hands up. "There's no need for that. What are you doing?"

"Stay back, sir," the blond one said to me.

Damon was on the pavement, curled into a fetal ball and sucking air.

The shaved-head guy who had hit him kicked away his backpack, then picked it up and gingerly looked inside. "Please get up, and keep your hands where we can see them," he said to Damon.

"I was...trying to help." Damon got to one knee.

I stumbled out the side door but kept my hands held high. "Who are you guys? What do you want?"

"Mike!" Chuck called from a hundred feet away. All four of them were out of the car, their hands up as well. "You guys okay?"

"We're fine," I yelled back.

Chuck had his hands high now as well. The four men around his car all had their weapons up and aimed.

"He looks Chinese or Asian or something," the shaved-head guy said to the blond man. He pointed at Damon, who was still on one knee. "I thought he might be reaching for a gun."

"What is this?" The blond man held up Irena and Terek's passports. "Ukrainian? Isn't that like Russian?"

"We are not Russian," Terek said.

The blond man backed up two paces and brought his weapon up. "Out of the car. You're coming with us." He aimed his chin at Damon. "You too."

I held my hands up, palms out. My pulse quickened. "Where are you taking them? Who are you?"

"We're the Vanceburg regiment of the Lexington Rifles," the blond man said. "We're taking your friends and those drones there."

"Lexington Rifles?"

"Kentucky militia."

Militia? "You have no right." I stood in front of Damon. "You can't—"

"Do you know what day it is today?" the blond man said to me.

I was at a loss. Something to do with Kentucky independence? Veteran's Day? He looked at me as if I was an idiot. "I don't know."

"Have you not been listening to the radio?"

"We had it on. What exactly should I—"

"Today is September 11th. Does that ring any bells?"

I hadn't even noticed the date. My mind had been elsewhere. That made some sense. They were jumpy. Worked up. "You can't just abduct people," I said.

"Have you not heard who did this?" He pointed up at the orange sky. "The Islamic Brigade, they claimed responsibility. Now they're saying they're loose across the country."

"Who's loose?" This sounded like another wild conspiracy theory, but there was something about the way he said it. The specific detail. "Responsible for what?"

"All this."

"I don't know what you're talking about, but this is kidnap—"

"She's armed!" I heard someone yell.

Irena had opened her door and stepped out behind me.

The shaved-head guy jumped at me. The last thing I saw was the butt of his rifle rushing at my face.

Chapter 24

Lauren luxuriated in the hot water needling her skin. She turned the shower temperature up even higher and let the scorching torrent hammer against her neck and shoulders. Good water pressure was grossly underappreciated, she thought, and smiled. She couldn't remember the last time she hadn't had a shower in four days. She had been able to smell her own stink, when she'd stepped in and gotten the water going.

This was her second shower since arriving. She would probably take another one in a few hours, it felt so good. She let the steaming water ease away the stress. It was almost perfect.

Almost.

If she had actually gotten home to her family, it would be.

Lauren turned the shower off, took a deep breath of the humid air, and stepped out, grabbing a towel. She exited the bathroom, but almost jumped back inside in fright. "Excuse me?"

One of the young men who had collected her from the naval station the day before, the one with a tattoo of a rose on the side of his neck, stood in the middle of her bedroom with a bag in his hand.

"Oh, darn it, excuse me, ma'am. I knocked, but you didn't answer. I got some fresh clothes for you. These might fit better."

Lauren cinched the towel tightly around her naked body and retreated halfway behind the bathroom door. "You can leave them on the bed. Thank you."

"Yes, ma'am." He dropped the bag onto the covers. "My name's Billy, by the way. William, but everyone calls me Billy."

He glanced at Lauren, then hovered a little too long for her comfort. She asked, "Is there anything else?"

"We're working on getting a line through to your family. So you can talk to them."

"I don't understand what the problem is."

"It's complicated, ma'am. Telephones don't work anymore."

They had explained about the satellites and GPS last night. "Not even for the military?"

"Maybe some, but not us. We're not military. Not exactly. We're private contractors, of a sort. Your uncle hired us, like I said."

She stayed put behind the door. She didn't like being half-naked in front of a man she didn't know, especially one with a gun, but the young man didn't quite seem to get it. He didn't turn away, but kept looking at her and smiling.

"Thank you," Lauren said.

She waited until he left and closed her bedroom door, but then opened it a crack. "Will we be able to go into DC today?"

Her room was on the mezzanine of what seemed to be a beach house by the water, not even a mile drive from the naval station. When they'd picked her and Emily up the day before, she had assumed they would be going straight to her uncle's house in Virginia, but they hadn't.

Something had happened.

She heard voices over the radios saying there had been some kind of terrorist attack, and they'd been diverted here in the Humvee convoy that had picked her up.

The fact that today was September 11th wasn't lost on her.

Lauren guessed this place might be her uncle's beach house—she had never been there, but had heard about it—but the team of people already here seemed to be using it as some kind of base.

A blue house by the water, with bright blue awnings. At least a dozen young men were here, more than was needed to pick her up.

And one woman. As Lauren stood by the door and waited for Billy to answer her question, she spotted a woman with brown hair disappearing around a corner.

Was this place a safe house?

She was confused, but then, this was a confusing time.

At least she was clean and had fresh clothes and a comfortable bed and a good night's sleep protected by a lot of armed men.

Billy was a few paces down the hallway when he turned and shook his head. "I don't think we can drive in today. The security situation has changed. It's not safe."

"Can you at least find out if my husband is with my children?"

"I'll get right on that, ma'am. Don't worry. Everything is going to be fine."

How many times had Lauren heard that in the last few days?

"I'm going to go out on the beach with Emily," Lauren said. "It looks like a nice day. Is that okay?"

Billy took in a sharp breath through his teeth. "We would prefer not, ma'am. We don't know the security situation, and your uncle told us to take care of you."

"Can I at least see her?"

Now his expression changed to confused. "She's already gone. She didn't say goodbye?"

"She left? I thought you said it wasn't safe."

"For you. I mean, for her, she's not a senator's niece we were sent to protect. We found her a ride. She needed to go talk to Paul." He shrugged.

"Thank you. And please tell me when I can talk to my family."

"Of course, ma'am."

Lauren closed the door and went to the window. It was narrow, not more than a foot high, and three feet long, and too high up to look straight out of. Strange design for a beach house. She opened it two inches, which was as much as it would go, and enjoyed the fresh sea air.

Why had Emily left all of a sudden? Without saying goodbye?

Lauren guessed it was because she had been in the shower. It made sense. The young lady had been in a hurry. She had a whole new life ahead of her.

Chapter 25

"Y ou okay, son?"

An elderly man with a shock of white hair and iron-gray stubble across his chin and cheeks held a cool rag to my head. Rivulets of water streamed from it across my forehead and into my eyes. I wiped the drops away with the back of one shaky hand. I was laid out flat on a bench by a dark wood wall.

"My name's Joe," the old man said, his voice calm. "Everybody calls me Farmer Joe. Sorry 'bout the boys, they got a little skittish on account of the news." He inspected my face. "You're gonna have one beauty of a shiner around that eye."

I took the rag from him. My nose was still sore from two days before. I felt like I'd gone a round with Foreman. "Thanks."

"Luke, you okay?" I heard him whispering.

"Go on," I heard Chuck say.

My son appeared from my right and wrapped his arms around my neck. "I thought you were dead," he whimpered.

"I'm fine," I said, but I wasn't.

I remembered the rifle butt coming at me, Chuck yelling, someone else screaming about a gun. My memory after that was patchy, my head pounding, my vision still swimming. And what was that smell?

Manure? Hay?

Both of those. And shoe polish. And smoke. *The fires.* The air felt heavier, denser.

I lifted my right arm to hug Luke, then used it to prop myself up. Hay was strewn across a cement floor. Chuck sat on a matching bench on the other side of the stall. There were bars across an exterior window with the hazy orange sky beyond, and bars on the opposite wall. It took me a beat or two to piece together the high arching ceiling and figure it out.

"Is this your barn?" I asked Farmer Joe, who perched on the bottom edge of my bench.

"That's right." He was dressed in a red plaid shirt and faded, stained dungarees. His long, bony fingers were calloused and knotted thick as braided rope.

Luke wiped away snot with his shirt sleeve. I whispered to him that I was okay and to go back with Uncle Chuck on the other side. I needed air, and while I wanted my boy close, having his arms pincered around my neck wasn't helping right now.

I inspected the polished woodwork of the walls. "Nice."

"Not built for working animals. Made this for my wife, God rest her soul. She liked horses. I do too. Not as much as she did. Had to sell them when she passed. So now it's an empty barn. And empty house."

"Sorry to hear that."

"Mike, you okay?" Chuck took Luke back between his arms. "You took a hell of a shot to the head." He glanced out past the bars of the door.

I could see the shaved-head guy. Standing guard, I assumed.

Farmer Joe stood to give me room to swing my legs down and sit up. A wave of nausea doubled me over.

"You want some water?" Joe asked.

For the first time, I noticed a small white dog. He barked. Saying hello. I nodded back.

"That's Roosevelt," Joe said.

"Where are Susie and the kids?" I asked Chuck.

"In the farmhouse," Joe replied. "Not to worry, I got them taken care of. You'd be up there too, except your friend here...well, it was a bit of a Mexican standoff when you went down."

I said, "You didn't shoot anybody, did you, Chuck?"

"Almost." He looked over at the guy with the shaved head again.

I gritted my teeth and tried to will the headache away. I scrunched my eyes closed for a second, took a deep breath, and sat upright. "Is everybody okay? Damon? Terek and Irena? Did *she* shoot anyone?" I remembered she had a loaded gun as well.

"They're in the farmhouse with the others," Joe said. "They've been, well, I guess they've been asking them questions. They're not too happy."

"They?"

"The boys."

"You mean the Kentucky militia?"

"They're good men, like I said."

"You know this is illegal."

"Vanceburg is a home rule class city."

"Which means you can abduct and assault people?"

"Well, basically we can make our own local laws. Like an independent state within Kentucky. And with all this happening, sheriff being gone, and that news of the terrorist attack today, we instituted the Vanceburg Rifles militia to protect ourselves."

"You can't band together vigilantes to—"

"Easy, son. I'm the head of the Rifles. Careful what you say next."

"Damon lied to them," Chuck said. "Or, stretched the truth, like you said. He told them he went to school with Terek and Irena, that he'd known them for years."

"How did they find out he lied to them?"

"Because I didn't lie. I told them the truth."

"Chuck…"

"Damon *doesn't* know them that well. That's the truth. Look, it makes sense now. All those roadblocks? Why they routed those passenger planes into holding areas? The government knew this whole thing was caused by terrorists. It's no accident. They're saying that there are terrorists loose in America."

That's right.

My memory clicked disordered bits of recollection together. "The Islamic Brigade? So that's true? That's a real thing?"

"As near as we can tell," Joe said. "We only got one radio station, and some say they heard it on shortwave channels, too. From the hams."

"It's a Chechen terrorist group. They're Russian, and Muslim," Chuck said. "The news is that they mounted a cyberattack against GenCorp and your hero, Tyrell Jakob, and hijacked the SatCom network of thousands of satellites. They used the fight between India and Pakistan as cover when they launched their attack, so they could cause maximum damage before anyone figured it out. They're using the satellites as projectiles to knock out everything else up there."

This sounded like it made too much sense to be fabrication. "For what purpose?" But did terrorists really need a purpose? Inciting terror, wasn't that their main goal? Mission accomplished, then.

"They're demanding the release of Muslim terrorists being held by America," Joe said. "And Chechen prisoners of war. And independence."

"We have Chechen prisoners?" I asked.

"Not us. The Russians."

"In exchange for what? Haven't they already destroyed everything up there?"

"Not yet," Chuck said. "But they will in the next few days, if they don't get what they want."

"So this *is* a terrorist attack? Not an accident?"

Chuck said, "I've been saying that all along."

I sighed long and hard, then felt at the tender spot on my face. My fingers came away bloody. Where was that smell of shoe polish coming from?

I looked down. Joe's dungarees were stained and frayed, but his boots shone like he had just cleaned them. "You were in the armed forces?" I asked him.

"Army. Vietnam. 101st Airborne."

"Tip of the spear. Screaming Eagles." Chuck whistled. "Thank you for your service, Joe."

"Yeah," I said. "Thank you for your service." I took a moment to gather myself. "Mr. Joe? Or, Mr. Farmer Joe? Can you explain to your guys that we're not the enemy?"

"You going to have to convince them of that yourself, I'm afraid."

"Are you serious?"

"You didn't do yourselves any favors. Coming up a side road with a load of foreigners and guns and what looks like military hardware. Trying to pass through a mysterious firestorm encircling DC to get into our capital on September 11th, right at the moment our government puts out the word that terrorists are attacking our nation again."

That did paint a picture. Everybody was more than a little tense, and the terrorists must have picked this date to make their announcement. Maximum impact.

"I have family in Washington," I said. "My little girl, my wife. Can you—"

"They're good men, and they mean right," Joe said. "Vanceburg has been most-wise cut off the past week. No TV. No internet. No house telephones. No mobile phones. Just the one radio station."

"I understand," Chuck said. "They're protecting their families. Same thing I was doing when your boys stopped me."

"I understand that, too," Joe said. "And that's why I'm down here, trying to make sure y'all are okay. I'm sure this will all be cleared up soon enough."

"We need to get going," I said. "I need to get to Washington."

"Not sure you'll be going anywhere soon. Not through those fires."

Chuck stood and looked out the window. "How far?"

"Hard to say, but the smoke is getting thicker. Not far over the ridgeline, I'd wager, and the wind is blowing this way."

I held one hand to the back of my neck and stood to look out through the bars. Thick golden fields rolled in a wind under the blood-orange sky. The sun low to the horizon.

"You better cut a fire break in those fields," Chuck said. "Is that corn? That's going to go up like a torch."

"I have considered that eventuality."

The deadpan way the farmer said it would have sounded like sarcasm if not for his measured tone and steady eyes. He wasn't trying to be clever, he was telling it like it was. But he wasn't volunteering any information, either.

Chuck waited, then asked, "So what's stopping you?"

"Four thousand acres, a broken axle, and some goddamn terrorists, as near as I can tell."

"You mean us?"

"I do not mean you."

"Can't you get some bulldozers? Tractors? Get out there and start cutting a break in those fields? Get some help?"

"Help is exactly the problem," Farmer Joe said calmly. "We're the only farm left this side of Vanceburg. Thousands of acres, five miles a side into those hills. We took up the Dillan family, the Avilas—"

"What about people in the town?" Chuck interrupted.

Farmer Joe blinked slowly, like a lizard. It was obvious he didn't appreciate being interrupted, and he didn't seem to like people in a hurry, either. "They're good people, but they're scared, and they're not farmers. As I said, we've been cut off for most of a week. No phones. No TV. Just the radio. Sheriff Coolidge left three days ago, and that's the last we heard from anyone we could call the government."

"But we could do this ourselves," Chuck said. "You must have a lot of equipment, a farm this size. I can drive a tractor. Get some of your Kentucky militia boys on it. We can do this."

"I appreciate the sentiment, son, but we don't know where those fires are out there. Not only that, but there are lights in the skies some nights. New fires seem to spring up from nowhere."

"What kind of lights?" I asked.

"Doesn't matter. What matters is that these fires could be all around us already. They're coming in fast, and we have no communications. No idea where the blazes are, and visibility is low. It's dangerous and probably futile, even if we did have the equipment."

Chuck said, "I still don't understand. Why no equipment?"

Joe let out a long, slow sigh. "No GPS," he said. "I got one corn head harvester I can drive, and that's got a busted axle. A replacement was supposed to be shipped this week, but that's not happening anymore. The other four corn heads and tractors are all guided. They can follow my main rig, but usually they're automated. Operate by GPS. My son's idea. Only way to run a farm at a profit these days is to automate."

Chuck paced the length of the stall. "Okay, but we could still go out and flatten the crop. We have cars, trucks. You must have some older tractors?"

"Flatten it? Those stalks will bounce back up unless we strip them. We'd need a lot of hands. Hundreds of them. I would put the call out, but the phones are down. This new fire front only started coming this way yesterday and the mess on the radio only made things worse. We rounded up the militia to protect the town. How else can I explain this?"

"It's chaos," I said. That word was getting used a lot.

"About sums it up. Anyway, if I don't harvest this crop, my farm is as good as gone. Spent everything we had to automate."

"Do all farms need GPS?" I asked Joe.

"Not all equipment needs it, not on smaller farms, but almost everything on a farm is helped by it these days. No GPS means no farming, the way we do it now. And it's harvest season. Don't get that GPS up, going to lose a lot of crops."

Chuck sat down and pulled Luke onto his knee. "All shipping stopped, all deliveries on hold. No food coming in. No farms working. And that's all across America, all at the same time."

"All around the world, I reckon." Farmer Joe nodded. "Going to be a lot of hungry people out there soon."

"We need to find a way to harvest your crop," Chuck said. "We can't let that go to waste. But if you don't cut a fire break, you'll lose more than the farm."

"Probably the whole town. Everyone is packing up to leave."

"They'd leave before trying to defend their town?"

"With these mystery fires and lights in the sky, then this news of the terrorists? Phone services go down? No TV? Orange skies? This has the feeling of the end of days. Like I said, we don't even know where those fires are. I'd say we are up a creek, son. Unless you have a way to fix the GPS."

I stood up, my head still pounding. "I just might."

Chapter 26

A door slammed. Footsteps across the cement beyond our holding pen. A familiar voice said, "Hey, I can walk by myself."

"Damon," I called out, "you okay?"

Our door slid open.

"Get your goddamn hands off me." Damon shrugged free of the blond guy who had stopped us. "You want me in there?" He pointed into our stall.

"That's why we opened the door," the blond guy said.

"Go easy, Ken," Joe said.

Chuck stood from the bench, gently set Luke aside, and extended his hand. "Ken? My name's Chuck Mumford. I think we got off on the wrong foot here."

Ken took a long look at Chuck's outstretched hand, then glanced at Farmer Joe, who nodded. He took Chuck's hand and pumped it. "Ken Logan," he said. "And this is Oscar." He motioned at the shaved-head guy, the one who had hit me.

I stuck my hand out as well. "Mike Mitchell, and this is my son Luke."

"Look, I'm sorry about all this." Ken shook my hand. "The only information we get from the outside is KLMB radio, and when they made that announcement yesterday...it didn't help when you pulled those guns. And all that drone hardware and the Ukrainians and the two eggheads babbling about satellite debris."

"Let's put that behind us." I grimaced and held my head.

"I know you guys must think I'm a dumb hick," Ken said. "Joe and me forming up a local militia. But what choice do we have? We have laws here for exactly this. Sheriff Coolidge took off three days ago, we're seeing weird flashes of light in the mountains and fires spreading everywhere. No help's coming, and after that news about the attacks..."

"We don't think that," Chuck said.

"I got an engineering degree from Virginia Tech," Ken said. "Mechanical. I live in Pittsburgh, but came here to my family when this got going to hell."

"Me too. I came down from Pittsburg with Ken," Oscar said from beyond the stall. "Gotta protect my family."

"Which is what we're trying to do," Chuck said.

"I'm from Pittsburgh," I said. "I've still got two brothers there."

It was a few hours up the road from here, and not far from the path we planned to take into Washington. I had talked to Chuck about maybe stopping in on my brothers, but we wouldn't have had time. Now even less.

Ken nodded. Part of the tension evaporated. "Now what's this about? You asked us to bring your friend down here to talk about something. He says he's in touch with NASA? He's tracking the space debris? Is this for real? I know you think we're full of—"

"Damon," I said. "Tell Joe here about your PhD."

Damon looked perplexed. "What? Drone constellations?"

"That's right, and—"

"Before we get into it," Ken said. "Are you guys going to vouch for him? He has no ID and he talks a lot of technical stuff, but—"

"This man," I said, "was awarded a Congressional Medal. Is that good enough?"

Ken frowned and said to Damon, "So you're a hero?"

"I'm not sure I'd say that."

"I would," Chuck said.

Ken said, "And your other friends? The Ukrainians? Are you going to vouch for them? Because Congressional Medal here already lied about how he knew them."

"I was trying to protect them," Damon said.

"Those passports look fake," Ken said. "And that gun license for the SIG? I'm not sure foreign nationals are allowed gun licenses, and I'm not being a dumb hick. I'd go and look up the rules, but our internet is out. Something is weird about this."

Farmer Joe snorted. "Kenneth, how would you know what a Ukrainian passport looks like?"

"You need to let us go," I said. "I need to get past those fires and get to DC. I need to get to my family. My wife's uncle is a senator in Washington, we can—"

"Hold on a second." Oscar still held his rifle in both hands. "What's this senator's name?"

"Seymour."

"The one always going on about the Russians?"

"That's right."

I eyed his hands on the weapon. Were his knuckles white? Some far right-wing groups had a strange affinity for Russians. Had he taken offense? I held one hand to Luke. Edged protectively toward him.

"And your name is Mitchell? Mike Mitchell?"

Oscar started laughing in big guffawing hoots. Even Farmer Joe's eyes went wide.

"Holy mother in heaven," Oscar said. "You got a brother in Pittsburgh?"

I nodded slowly.

"You're Terry Mitchell's little brother, aren't you? And Booker? He's your other brother?"

"You know Terry?" It didn't exactly surprise me. Terry knew everybody in Pittsburgh around our age. In some ways, it was a small town. Which meant I knew what circles Oscar orbited in. My brothers had both been in jail.

"Oh. My. God." Oscar wiped a tear from his eye with the back of one hand. "Do I know Terry? Cripes, everybody in Dirty 'Burgh knows your brother. He owns that town. I keep hearing stories about how his little brother is married to a girl whose uncle is a senator." The smile dropped from his face. "Oh my gosh, I'm sorry I hit you. I didn't know. Terry is a badass, he's gonna kill me!"

"Don't worry. I'll talk to him when this is all over. We'll all have a beer together and laugh about it."

"I hope so. Man, you gotta tell him it was an accident." Oscar's eyes skittered left and right.

I paused. "I'll vouch for them," I said to Ken. "For the Ukrainians. Irena and Terek are good people. I've only known them a week, but Terek might have saved my life. And Irena helped a whole bunch of people in Mississippi after a storm."

Ken said, "So that's true? She told us that."

"That's true."

Oscar said, "Damn, Kenny, if Terry Mitchell's brother is going to vouch for them…"

Silence for a few beats.

"Okay then," Ken finally said. "We'll send you on your way. We're evacuating the whole town, you gotta go back—"

"I can't go back," I said. "I need to get to Washington. Something happened to my wife. And my little girl is there."

"I don't see you have a lot of options, unless you want to risk getting trapped by fires up in those hills."

"Damon," I said. "Farmer Joe here has eight tractors that drive autonomously using GPS."

"Four corn heads, four tractors," Joe corrected.

"That sounds a lot like a drone constellation to me," I said. "Am I right?"

Damon nodded. "You're not wrong."

I continued, "Joe can't control them now, as GPS is gone. And we don't know where the fires are. No airplanes or satellites to give us images."

"We can help with that." Damon saw where I was going.

"And we can't send people out into the haze to look for the fires, because we have no cell phones, no GPS and no emergency services. It's too dangerous, and they're too scared."

"We're not scared," Ken said, "as much as we're not stupid. We need to protect our families. Those fires have been spreading for weeks, no matter what anyone out there has been doing. And not just spreading—I've heard people talk about seeing lights at night. Fires springing up out of nowhere. All I know is they're coming this way. Without outside help, we best get out of their way."

Farmer Joe fixed me with a steady gaze. "Son, it sounds like you have a plan. Why don't you tell us what it is? 'Cause we don't have much time to waste."

"Luke," Damon said. "Can you hand me that knife?"

My son looked at me with his arms tight to his chest, in that hesitant way he had when he wasn't sure if he should be doing something. "It's okay," I said.

Luke gingerly picked up the box cutter from the toolbox and gave it to Damon. I thought he would have preferred to stay with Bonham, Ellarose, and Susie in the air-conditioned farmhouse, but my little man had refused to leave my side. I had to admit, having him close somehow made me feel a little safer, too. Was he trying to protect his old man? Of course he was.

"At least we still have power," I said.

High-wattage LED floodlights lit up the shed. Beyond the lights, the night was pitch-black. About 10 p.m., I figured.

"The shed" was what Joe called this building. "Hangar" would have been more accurate. The outbuilding holding the corn heads and tractors was about three hundred feet down a gravel road from the main farmhouse. One side of the forty-foot-tall building was completely open to the air, with the first ten feet of the walls made of cinder block. The rest was corrugated metal, with the open side's roof held up by thirty-foot steel I-beams painted red. The floor was smooth cement, cracked and stained in patches.

A giant garage for the massive machines it housed. It smelled equal parts engine oil and manure.

I had only just learned what a "corn head" was. A thirty-foot-wide contraption with a dozen conical spikes in a horizontal row and a circulating blade behind them, like the auger of a snow blower—except instead of collecting snow, this collected corn. The whole assembly was fixed to the front of each self-driving, four-wheeled behemoth. There were four of these automated GPS corn heads in the shed, along with four smaller, more multi-purpose, self-driving tractors.

To Damon, they were huge drones.

We sat to one side of the big green machines. Damon on a stool, Luke and I on a wooden bench beside him.

"This isn't like the last time," I said to Damon. "Gotta say, I prefer it hot and with lights to being frozen in the dark."

I tried to make conversation, but my thoughts kept circling back to Lauren. Where was she? What happened? Was she at her uncle's place already?

Damon had the side control panel of the corn-head-drone open and was splicing wires. He didn't have the right USB plug, he said, but he could cut open the cables and connect everything together.

"Is it true?" Luke squinted to get a better look at what Uncle Damon was doing. "Are there terrorists crashing satellites in the sky?"

"Makes sense," Damon said without looking up. "That's why the NASA models didn't match. It's not just wreckage. They're using the ten thousand birds in the SatCom network as five-hundred-pound bullets to take out everything else up there."

He stopped for a second. "They're clever. I said earlier that the biggest difference between outer space and cyberspace is cost. Outer space is extremely expensive, but cyberspace is cheap. They found a loophole. Use a cyberattack to gain access to the assets in outer space. Brilliant, really."

Luke went inside to get a sandwich. Damon and I worked for another half an hour in silence.

Finally, I asked, "Can you share the secret yet?"

"Secret?"

"Legook."

Damon laughed and checked over his shoulder. No sign of Luke returning. "It's not Legook, it's *Leguke*." He spelled it.

"That's not making things clearer."

"It's a form of gibberish."

"No kidding."

"Seriously. There's a whole class of language modification called gibberish. It's simple encryption. I'm trying to get him interested in the kind of stuff I do. Math. Encryption. That sort of thing."

"Still clear as mud."

"You never used pig latin when you were a kid?"

I had heard of that. "So that's what it is?"

"Pig latin is a form of gibberish too, but the one Luke and I use is Egglish."

"English?"

"*Egg*-lish."

"What are the rules?"

"Simple. You add 'eg' after the first letter of each syllable, unless it starts with a vowel, in which case you stick the 'eg' first. Simple encryption."

I thought about it for a second. "Leguke. That's Luke in Egglish."

"Exactly."

We went through a few more examples, until we heard my son coming down the path. He waved as he approached.

I switched topics. "Can't the government do anything about it? The satellites, I mean?"

Luke sat back down on the bench next to me.

"They must be trying," Damon replied. "Satellites contain propellants so they can change orbit and maneuver. Most of them use things called Hall thrusters, which use xenon and krypton gas and electricity. So I'd guess that now they know this isn't passive— not only random debris, but an active attack—NASA and everyone else must be moving whatever they've got left up there."

"Can't they regain control of the SatCom satellites? I mean, wouldn't they have sent a SEAL team to the HQ? Like the instant they heard that announcement? Maybe even before? Our military can't be that degraded."

"Yeah, they would've. Maybe the attackers only announced it when they lost control of the satellites. Maybe the gig is already up."

That sounded more hopeful than anything else.

Damon added, "There's still a huge expanding debris field up there."

I mulled that over. "Any idea how the attackers might have gotten into the SatCom network to begin with?"

"They must have broken the encryption on the TTC—the telemetry, track, and command—of the communications system. Ground stations. I don't know."

"So, they mounted a cyberattack to take over the satellites?"

"Space systems are an indistinguishable part of cyberspace. Doesn't make any difference if you're attacking a desktop computer or a hunk of electronics flying at six miles a second a hundred miles up. Space is *in* cyberspace from a computer's point of view."

"Fat chance they're going to get their prisoners released. They're incurring God's holy wrath, not just from us, but the Russians as well. From everybody. Won't be an inch of this planet they can hide on afterward."

"They've certainly made a statement. Exposed a soft underbelly."

On some levels, it made sense, but on others, it didn't. Then again, how much sense did it make to blow yourself up wearing an explosive vest? I needed to focus on the here and now.

"You really think you can rewire one of these?" I slapped the metal sheathing of the hulking machine.

"I don't need to 'rewire' it, but more reprogram how it accepts commands. If I had a transmitter, I might be able to locally spoof some GPS."

"This thing is like a tank."

Even the tires were ten feet high.

"More like a big self-driving car," Damon said. "It's got sensors for avoiding poles and people. A better analogy would be a robotic vacuum. Except this one sucks up corn instead of dirt."

Luke said, "It could suck up *people*."

I laughed. "I bet it could." I certainly wouldn't want to get in the way of one on a rampage.

"Why did those men push us into the barn?" Luke asked. "They made Ellarose cry. She was scared."

"Those men were scared, too," I replied. "They're doing what they thought was right. We're the outsiders here."

"When people get cut off, they tend to go back to their roots," Damon said. "The old Kentucky militias are famous. In the secession crisis of 1861, there were pro-Union, pro-Southern, heck, even pro-neutral militias. This was ground zero of militia country."

Damon was something of a Civil War buff, a passion he shared with Chuck.

"What's a secession?" Luke asked.

"When parts of a country want to separate from the other parts."

He nodded seriously. "Right. Got it."

"Which is the reason for all this mess," Damon said.

"The Civil War?"

"Wanting autonomy. These Chechen terrorists—from their point of view, they're freedom fighters." He turned to Luke. "But what they are doing is very, very wrong. You understand?"

My son nodded.

The wind was hot and dry and dusty. I coughed. The smoke thicker. A gust brought a flurry of black snow through the floodlights.

"Dad, what's that?"

A spinning mote settled in my hand. I squinted into darkness. Flickering lights played in the distance.

"Ash, I think." To Damon I said, "Whatever you're doing, hurry. Are you going to have time to rewire all eight?"

"Just one. An hour of straight running, it can cut a swath all the way across the east side of the farm, I think."

"You think that will be enough?"

"These don't even slice away the corn stalks. They strip and flatten it down. We would need a silage harvester to cut." Damon spliced together two more wires. "Firewalls in a network I understand, but fire breaks in the physical world? The wider the area of dirt the better, is my understanding. Don't worry, Mike. It's a good plan."

A good plan. My plan.

Back at the barn earlier, I'd asked Damon if he could rewire the GPS tractors, operate them like he did his drones. He'd said he could. Then I explained how we could have Ken's militia go door to door tonight, before everyone left the town, and take Terek to help install the mesh-networking app on everyone's phones. That way we could coordinate.

And ask everyone who had something that could move dirt to come.

So tonight, Terek and Irena went out with Ken and Oscar and their guys to canvas the town and tell them the plan. See if we could get enough people on board.

Damon flew one of the drones up five hundred feet to act as a base station for the mesh-network. Joe, Chuck, and Susie were in the farmhouse fielding calls. Before sunset, we flew a drone to its limits, about a mile out and a thousand feet up. No fires were that close.

So we had time.

The next morning, we would use the drones to provide an aerial view, keep in communication with everyone, and use the corn-head-drones to plow a path through the fields—harvesting it at the same time—and hopefully save the town and the farm.

That was the plan. My plan.

It had seemed clever at the time—and maybe I'd been trying to get us out of that stable pen—but it was *my* idea, and we were about to risk a lot of people's lives, put them in harm's way, when they were all about to leave for safety.

My mouth was so dry it felt full of corn dust.

Damon fiddled the last wires together. He twisted tape around them and plugged the end of the newly constructed USB cable into the laptop on his knees.

He paused.

"What?" I asked.

"The Range Rover is right there," he said. "The keys are in it. I checked."

"Why did you check?"

"Why do you think? We could just leave," Damon said. "Get right back on the road. We're ahead of those fires, I think. Those militia guys are gone. Chuck and Susie are in the farmhouse. Joe wouldn't stop us."

It wasn't like I hadn't thought of it.

Past two oak trees, the Range Rover was visible in the light spilling out of the farmhouse windows and onto the lawn.

"I'll leave a drone here. It's easy to operate from a cell phone with the app installed. Ken's a smart guy. I'll leave instructions. I'll even leave them this laptop with instructions on how to drive this corn head. We don't owe them anything. In fact, we owe them less than nothing."

"We can't leave Terek and Irena," I said.

"I can call Terek right now." He held up his cell.

If Ken and his militia hadn't stopped us, we might be in Washington by now. Or at least Chuck's cabin. Of course, we might have been stopped by the fires. Even trapped by them. It was impossible to tell their extent without flying above the mountains to see what was happening.

Could we have made it?

"Mike," Damon said. "Maybe we should go. I'm serious."

"I...uh…"

Before I could answer, Terek appeared from the darkness beyond the floodlights. "Guys, I can maybe stop them."

"Why are you back already?"

"I got a message. Maybe we can stop them."

I said, "Who? Ken? The Kentucky guys? Because we don't—"

"The Islamic Brigade. We might be able to stop what they're doing."

Damon was still staring at me.

"Mike, what do *you* want to do?" he asked again.

Chapter 27

A t first light, we drove in a two-pickup convoy ten miles east and south, and then launched the drones up into the sky, into the amber haze. The machines followed us as we drove back, hovering at a thousand feet and as far to the east as reception allowed. The fires were heading our way, but we still had time to save the town.

I almost wished the flames were closer, wished that someone said it was too late.

But it wasn't.

Not yet.

Black leaves whipped in a dust devil. A gust sucked a suffocating wave of smoke behind it, which roiled across the field. Through the mud-streaked window, an orange-gray sky shimmered with flecks of black.

"Mike, you guys okay?" Damon's voice barely audible over the roar of the old tractor's engine. My cell phone was taped to the dashboard of the tractor. I had it set to speakerphone.

"We're good," I yelled back.

A buzzing mechanical insect hovered in the orange haze. One of the drones doing overwatch, coordinating the operation, and keeping an eye on the fires.

"Nothing near you," came Damon's voice over the phone.

"Ten-four." Wasn't quite sure what that meant, but it seemed like the right thing to say.

Three hundred feet ahead, the hulking corn head cut a swath through the swaying field, spitting a stream of kernels into an open trailer. It left a mess of husks and stalks in its wake.

It was unnerving to see the huge machine navigating unmanned, but it wasn't self-driving. Damon controlled it remotely from the central command he'd assembled in the dining room of the farmhouse.

"You say something?" came another crackling voice.

It was Oscar, the shaved-head guy who'd cracked me in the face. His voice came from a walkie-talkie I had on the dash, next to the phone. He'd apologized profusely, and was now acting like he wanted to be best friends. I think he feared whatever he thought my big brother Terry might do, whenever he got back to Pittsburgh.

He should be.

Even I was scared of my big brother.

I thumbed the transmit button. "All good. Talking to Damon on the phone."

Oscar's tractor was a hundred feet in front of me. His big green John Deere had a factory-made snowplow on its front. He drove right behind the corn head and swept aside the husks and leaves, while I followed in an older rig and did cleanup.

Luke coughed.

My son rode shotgun beside me.

He'd refused to stay with the other kids. He hadn't screamed like a baby but had steadfastly made the point that I might need him. I sensed a desperation beneath his stoicism. We still hadn't found a way to contact the Seymour residence from here. Still didn't know where Lauren was. He wasn't about to let the only parent he had left out of his sight.

And Luke was the reason we remained.

When Damon had asked me what I wanted to do, Luke had answered for me. We needed to stay and help these people, he said. I was proud and worried at the same time, but then, what else could I say?

I ruffled Luke's hair. Like father, like son.

Riding shotgun wasn't exactly dangerous. We could jump off and walk faster than the corn head was grinding forward. Maybe five miles per hour?

Oscar's tractor edged further away from me.

I jammed my foot down on the tractor's clutch. The gearbox squealed. I attempted to switch into a higher gear. It took me two tries to force it into place. The corn head and Oscar's vehicle slipped another fifty feet ahead and turned.

To my left, the field stretched a few hundred yards to the road. The farmhouse was about a mile away. A green forest of oaks and firs to my immediate right. We had already made a first cut, maybe twenty feet wide. This was a second pass.

Luke coughed again.

"Keep the rag wet," I said.

We both had bandanas tied around our faces. Mine was blue and red, but he'd gotten one from Oscar that had the lower half of a skull imprinted on it. Luke tried to splash water from a plastic bottle onto his hand and then onto his face, but it was empty. With one hand on the tractor wheel, I reached into a cardboard box with water containers.

"Take this." I handed one to my son.

We might have enough time for one more pass down the eastern flank of the farm. Would a forty- or sixty-foot fire break be enough?

I'd never seen a fire up close like this. With the wind gusting, the burning embers could jump hundreds of feet, Farmer Joe had told us. While we were cutting the break, two dozen people from the town assembled fire teams to put out any patches that might catch.

The tractor's engine coughed and sputtered.

The thing was almost as old as I was. I didn't even know Ford made tractors. This was an '85, and looked more like what I thought farm equipment should look like than the spaceship-looking lines of the self-driving corn head. The tractor's cracked and knobby back tires were taller than me, their rims hand-painted red. Rust showed through the paint.

Joe had welded steel I-beams onto the chassis, then rigged up a contraption to strap a snowplow a neighbor had brought over onto the front. There was no way to raise it, except by hand. We used a chain attached to a welded crossbeam to lift it up, which took three people and a steel bar.

The whole thing rattled and shook on the loose edge of coming apart as we rolled over the field rows.

The plow slammed into something.

Luke flew forward into the dash. I grabbed the back of his T-shirt, but he had his hands out to catch himself. He righted and clambered back to perch on the seat next to me.

We jolted up and down.

"Dad, be careful."

"I'm trying." I wiped away sweat streaming down my face, stinging my eyes. It was hard to keep focus.

The field was dry and dusty.

It hadn't rained in two weeks, Joe had said. What we would give for a thunderstorm or two from down south. My back slick with sweat, my shirt and shorts soaked like I'd been swimming.

Swimming.

I was so hot, even the memory of being thrown headfirst into the Mississippi seemed delicious. Even drowning seemed secondary to the idea of cool depths of water.

Light flickered through smoke cascading down the rolling Kentucky hills that climbed to meet West Virginia. The sun rose blood-red over the Appalachians as a hot wind blew in from the southeast. The air sweltering and acrid. Burned my nostrils even through the soaked bandana across my face.

Not more than a mile away, flames licked the treetops.

The sky was literally falling. Spacecraft burning up in the atmosphere.

A slow-motion disaster was grinding mercilessly across America. Across the entire planet. All at the same time. Soon people would be going hungry. Natural disasters going unchecked, power failing, food supplies running out. The world's militaries on the trigger edge of disaster.

We had one long shot to maybe stop it all, to save everyone, and here I was driving a broken old tractor across a dusty corn field through the eye of a firestorm.

With the weight of it all on my beaten-down shoulders.

Damon's talk about the morality of the self-driving car the other day was more than academic. Who do you save in a disaster?

No matter which way you turn, someone will be hurt.

The immediate gut-punch reaction was to save the people close to you. Friends. Family. Loved ones.

My gut screamed for me to run, to find my wife. But my mind rationalized that she was safe. She landed in Virginia. She might already be sitting back on their country estate, sipping a gin and tonic.

And if I could have asked her, I knew what she would say.

Stay. Help these people. Same thing Luke had said.

"Dad!" Luke yelled. "Look out!"

He pointed.

I barely swerved around a stump at the edge of the field. Wiped more stinging dust and sweat from my eyes with the back of one hand. "Good work, Luke. You keep that eye out."

The plow bounced and ground its way over the dusty hard pack. My teeth rattled in their sockets.

And what about Terek?

The young Ukrainian had burst into the shed last night and babbled about how he could maybe stop the Chechen terrorists.

As Terek had spread the meshnet through the town, explaining to people how to install it and asking them to go and spread the word, the area had slowly become reconnected. By the early morning, some of those connection points had tapped into an outside mesh node.

A few messages made it through to the wider network.

Damon got a text from Grandma Babet.

And Terek received from an out-of-the-blue message from a Russian hacker collective he had contact with. Sometimes he worked with them, he said. Just friends.

And I thought he didn't like Russians.

The hackers said they had compromised the GenCorp network—but months ago, far ahead of all this happening. They said they had a backdoor into the system, but that they didn't want to contact the Russian or American authorities for fear of exposure, or legal action. Or worse.

They'd seen Damon on video broadcasts, pushing the mesh-network, and had seen Terek in the background. Damon was famous, and he was a fellow hacker. He was the kind of guy that inspired trust.

Terek explained the technical details of his idea to Damon, who said it was a long shot, but it was something. It seemed fanciful, maybe even dangerous. They said they needed to get somewhere with a high-bandwidth connection to explore the idea, to see if there was anything to it.

And this begged the question: Where were the people at GenCorp?

Now the Chechens had revealed their hand, every government person from the NSA to the CIA and every other three-letter agency here and in Russia and China had to be trying to disable those satellites.

So why did these Russian hackers think they had an upper hand?

Because they were in beforehand, Terek said. They were already *inside* the network. They left a secret backdoor they could open, which was inside the perimeter of the security the Chechen group had installed when they'd taken over GenCorp's networks.

They didn't want to open it themselves, because they were in Russia. Which was where the Chechens were. The hackers didn't fear the Russian police—they probably paid them—but Chechens were another story.

"Dad." Luke grabbed my shirt. "Hey, look."

He pointed into the haze. The smoke from the fires was getting thicker. A hundred feet in front of us, Oscar's tractor growled behind the corn head, the two vehicles kicking up a choking cloud of dust that flowed into the swirling smoke. We needed to go in soon.

I wiped the sweat away from my eyes.

A white blur raced across the dirt, halfway between us and Oscar.

I took my foot off the gas.

"That's Roosevelt!" Luke pulled on my shirt more urgently. "That's Joe's dog."

We slowed. Oscar's tractor pulled away from us. We had driven into a bend in the field, a small divot that turned into the hills and forest.

"Dad!"

"I see him. I see him."

That was definitely Roosevelt. The little dog barked at us. I put my foot back on the gas.

"Luke," I said, "this is his place. His home. We don't need to stop for him."

"He wants something."

"I'm not—"

My arms slammed into my body. Face smacked into the windshield. A screech of metal. The tractor bucked sideways into the air. My stomach in the steering wheel, I grabbed wildly for Luke. The tractor catapulted and I fell sideways, half out of the open cabin.

Luke grabbed my right hand. His face scrunched together with effort, he hauled me back as hard as he could. I scrambled into the seat and wiped my face with the back of my hand.

It came away bloody. Again. "What the hell was that?"

The tractor was at an angle. The plow gone.

"You hit a stump," Luke said matter-of-factly. "I told you to—"

"Yeah, yeah."

"Roosevelt is still barking at us."

"Stay here."

I climbed out of the tractor to inspect. Found the plow. Ripped off and lodged between the front and back wheels on the left side. That's what had rocketed us into the air.

"Dad, Roosevelt wants something," I heard Luke say from the cabin.

"Don't move, don't—"

I was on one knee, inspecting the damage. Two short legs appeared on the other side of the tractor.

"I'm going to see what he wants." Luke ran off after the dog.

"Damn it, Luke, what did I say?"

I took one step into the cabin to get the cell phone, but it had ripped loose. No sign of it. Luke disappeared into the trees to the side of the tractor. Roosevelt kept barking. What the hell was it with this kid and dogs?

I grabbed the walkie-talkie, clambered down, and ran after my son.

Chapter 28

Lauren couldn't shake the feeling.

Everyone here was being nice. Almost too nice. They called her Mrs. Mitchell and apologized and offered her food and asked if she wanted anything to drink. It reminded her of Emily, which took her back to wondering why the young woman hadn't said goodbye. More than that, though, being here made her feel the way she had on the airplane.

Trapped.

Politely but firmly, the young men in black ballistic vests would tell her it wasn't safe for her to leave the room. That there were things going on they couldn't control. That she would have to be patient.

It was the middle of the afternoon. She'd been in the house for over a day already. She desperately wanted to go out for a walk on the beach. Above all, she needed to get to her family. At least know they were safe.

Yesterday, Billy, the young man with the rose tattoo on his neck, had helpfully provided a few books, said he'd enjoyed one of the thrillers. She tried to keep still and read it, but that nagging sensation wouldn't go away.

The door to her room opened. "Lunch?"

A young man she hadn't seen before offered a tray with a sandwich and a bottle of water.

Lauren got up to take it. "Thank you."

Past the young man, on the ground floor of the house, she saw that more equipment and computers were being set up. She glimpsed a young woman with brown hair dart past without looking up. She looked familiar.

"Can I talk to Billy?" Lauren asked.

"Sure, give me a minute." The young man smiled ingratiatingly and closed the door. Politely. But firmly.

That was the last straw.

Lauren picked up a chair and took it over to the window, which she found she could open, though it was too high to see out of. She stood on the chair and got up on her toes. Just high enough to see the beach and the backyard. A man in camouflage pants, a khaki shirt, and a black ballistic vest was dragging trash bags over to the back fence near the seawall.

He tossed them onto a growing pile.

The blood drained from Lauren's face.

In the middle of the pile of garbage bags was a tangle of red. Not leaves. Not garbage. Hair. Red hair. A head. The man glanced behind him. Lauren dropped off the chair and put her back to the wall, her heart thumping through her chest.

Had she just seen what she thought she'd seen?

The door to her room opened. Billy's smiling face appeared. "Is there something I can help you with, Mrs. Mitchell? I swear to God, we're getting moving tonight. And I have news."

"News?" All Lauren could think about was the red hair in the pile of trash, curls spilling from the bag.

"Are you okay?"

"What news?"

"Your husband. He's in Virginia with your uncle and mother. We got word. They're all at the house in McLean by the Potomac. I told you not to worry."

Lauren sat down on the chair. "I know we don't have a phone line, but aren't there computers? What about an email? Skype?

VoIP?" She had left her laptop in her checked luggage. Hadn't been able to recover it. Not that it would have helped.

Billy said, "You're right. I can get you a computer so you can send an email, but we can't do voice calls. But anyhow, we'll be gone soon. Is that all for now?"

He gave her his best smile.

Practiced. Forced. Nice. Too nice.

Lauren's skin crawled.

"Where's that accent from, Billy?"

"Pittsburgh."

"You're from Dirty 'Burgh? That's where my husband is from."

"You don't say."

"But there's something else there."

He nodded, his perfect smile never wavering. "You got me. My mom's from Texas."

"Texas?"

"And my dad, he was Ukrainian. Maybe that's what you hear."

"Maybe."

"Okay, I gotta get back. We're going to leave soon."

He closed the door.

Lauren waited. Pittsburgh? He thought that accent sounded Pittsburghese? He was from where Mike was from? It was too much of a coincidence. And they had computers and email, but no Skype? No VoIP? No direct communications, even with all that gear?

That neck tattoo didn't look new. Visible tattoos like that were definitely against military regulations. Maybe he was a private contractor now, but what exactly did that mean?

And that woman downstairs.

The one with the brown hair.

Lauren was good with faces. She was sure she'd seen that woman before. Her mind clicked another puzzle piece into place.

That was it.

The plane.

The woman with the brown hair, Lauren saw in business class. Before Emily had closed the curtains. The image clear in her mind.

Lauren got back up on the chair and looked out the window. The pile of garbage bags was still there, but no red hair. Maybe she was seeing things. She scanned the yard. Mike always said stress would make you see conspiracies around every—

Across the sand, something red-white-and-blue.

A kerchief fluttered away in the wind.

Chapter 29

Damon Indigo took the offered cup of hot coffee.

"Thank you," he said.

The woman handing it to him let her hand linger. Their fingers touched.

"No, thank you," she replied in a lilting southern accent, then smiled a bewitching grin. "My name's Pauline."

"I'm—"

"I know who you are." Pauline let her fingers slide away. "I can't tell you how much we appreciate you and your friends helping our town like this."

"It's...I..."

Damon was at a loss for words. Freckles were sprinkled across her nose under clear blue eyes. Her hair was in a long blond braid and she wore cut-off jean shorts and cowboy boots.

"Pauline," she repeated. "You remember that."

She sauntered into the dining room. Damon couldn't not watch her go.

"Wow," Terek said. "She's pretty."

"Yeah...ah..."

It had been a long time since a woman had caught him off guard like that. Damon had immersed himself in his work these past years. He told himself he didn't have time for relationships.

If he was being honest, though, his fiancée's death still haunted him. The memory pulled forever at the dark edges of his mind, digging its sharp claws deeper and deeper. Wasn't time supposed to heal all wounds? Not this one. Work was the only thing that kept him from sinking completely.

Pauline glanced over her shoulder as she went around the corner.

"I think she likes you." Terek poked him in the ribs.

Damon blinked and shook his head. This wasn't the time for whatever *that* was. Then again, he couldn't stop staring at the spot where she had disappeared. He felt an unfamiliar wave of heat in his face.

Shaking his head at himself, he returned his attention to his laptop.

The corn head tractor wasn't self-driving today. He was in control of it. They didn't have GPS, but that morning he had flown one of the drones down the eastern edge of the farm near the forest and logged the data points he was able to map.

His laptop screen showed the view from the camera mounted on the front of the corn head. The tractor followed a set of grid points now under his control, the instructions relayed from a drone that hovered near the middle of the fields. It followed a set path, but he turned off the auto-avoidance controls.

He monitored and adjusted.

They used two drones for communication, each fitted with a phone with extra memory and a signal booster, which provided coverage to everyone on the meshnet in direct line-of-sight and signal distance.

They needed two, because the drones could only stay airborne for about an hour at a time. One recharged while the other flew.

Damon managed the overall operation, but two of the town's teenagers oversaw the launching, recovery, and recharging.

Terek had gone earlier out with his sister and Ken and Oscar to talk to the townspeople, asking them to install the mesh app on their phones and explaining how to use it. It didn't take long for them to figure it out, and Ken and Oscar continued the process, encouraging people to spread the word.

While they did that, Damon finished reprogramming the corn head and set up a command center in the kitchen of the farmhouse. It was a cheerful space with sagging wooden beams, whitewashed walls, and handmade furniture.

As soon as Terek got back, they set themselves up on the large pine table in the middle of the kitchen. They took the forty-inch flat screen TV from the living room and installed it in front of the raised fireplace by the pantry.

Terek was in charge of the second set of drones. These patrolled the periphery of the farm, watching for any advancing spurts of fire. Terek used the VR goggles to fly them, but he projected the image onto the big screen so everyone else could keep an eye out for things he might miss.

Another team watched these videos, did upkeep on the flying machines, and coordinated fire crews as they dispersed with vehicles and sand and water.

Most of the time, Terek hovered the reconnaissance drone near Mike and Oscar as they drove two tractors behind the corn head Damon controlled, which plowed down the corn.

Damon's phone pinged.

A message from Grandma Babet. *"Port is a mess. Something strange is going on."*

He typed back: Something strange? Explain?

As they installed the meshnet on the townspeople's phones, and some of the people started traveling south and east, small dribbles of network data began to arrive. He was glad to hear his grandma was okay. She was a tough nut. He didn't need worry about her.

But of course, he did.

The message was odd, though.

And it might take hours, or even days, to get a response.

Voice calls worked locally over the meshnet, connecting one phone directly to another, or through a relay like he'd set up on the communications drone. Getting any data further across the ad hoc network required both luck and the goodwill of the people connecting to it.

Luck, because it required one phone to pass the message and data to others. This spread randomly through the network, patching to the internet when an open connection was found. The system's protocol searched for the unique address of the person who would receive the data.

Only once a path through had been found, would a connection be established and the data passed. Which might require a pass-through of dozens of individual phones all the way from Kentucky to Louisiana.

The average data rate was measured in bits per hour for a distance like that. Enough for simple text messages, but never for a phone call.

And it required goodwill, because each person in the network needed to authorize their phone and individual meshnet to pass information from others through it, and because people near internet connections had to open their networks.

But it was better than nothing.

Terek was sitting next to him, controlling the overflight drone. The image from the drone's camera played on the large screen they'd put in front of the kitchen fireplace. Two townspeople, Richard and Liz, scribbled notes and asked Terek to back up or go forward. They then made calls to direct the people moving in the fields.

"Message from Babet?" Terek glanced at Damon's phone.

"Yeah," Damon replied. "Something's strange, she said."

"Strange?"

"That's what she said. At the port."

"Did she say what?"

"I sent a message to ask." Damon tapped his keyboard and edged the corn head to the right. It was driving too deep into the field. "Did you hear back from your Russian friends?"

"Not yet."

"How well do you know these people?"

"Not very. Never met in person. Only by reputation."

"How?"

"Online message boards. That sort of thing. I think they were more interested in you than me."

It was a vague answer, but it made some sense. Damon often visited message boards that were frequented by less than reputable characters. The seedy edges of the web were the most interesting, but also the most dangerous.

"It doesn't surprise me," Damon said.

"My Russian friends hacking GenCorp?"

"Yeah. Or anyone. I went to GenCorp last year, and sent an email afterward to their security team. No answer, of course."

"What were you asking them about?"

"I wasn't asking, I was telling."

"Let me guess. Their security sucked?"

"It's not just information security that's important, it's physical security, too. I mean, you get to their headquarters, and it's more like visiting a fancy nightclub than a secure facility. The parking lot attendant makes sure you're on a list, but they don't really check your ID. There's a velvet rope you stand behind outside, and then a guy that looks like a bouncer calls people in."

"That does sound like a nightclub," Terek said. "And I never get into them."

Damon laughed. Terek barely looked old enough to enter a bar. Six years younger than Damon, but he seemed even more. The way he always deferred, asked for his opinion. Mike felt like an older brother, but Terek was like the younger one he never had.

"Then when they ask you in, there's no biometrics. No picture taken. They didn't even do a body search or take my phone. They should have mantraps at the doors, monitoring to prevent piggybacking. All the standard physical security."

"They didn't take your phone?"

"And didn't search me. I could have had a Shark Jack, a USBdriveby, anything on me. I could have owned that place inside of an hour. It doesn't surprise me they got hacked."

"It's all about endpoint security," Terek said. "Physical and digital."

"Exactly."

"Doesn't matter how good the encryption algorithm is, if your endpoints aren't implemented securely, you're going to leak data. All a smart attacker needs is an entry point."

Damon swung the corn head a bit to the left. The track it followed led it toward the edge of the field and away from the corn. He glanced at the big screen. Terek took the drone up to a thousand feet so they could get a view of the mountains to the east, but from that height, all they could see was brown haze. Visibility was down to a few hundred feet.

"There's got to be a backdoor to those satellites," Terek said. "Even if their networks have been owned, there must be a fail-safe."

They had talked it through a dozen times. The cyber kill chain to start an attack on a place like GenCorp didn't need to be anything special, but the problem began the moment they realized what you were up to.

Any network admin, the second they knew they were hacked, would commence shutting down their own systems. At worst, they could "brick" their equipment, turn their servers into useless hunks of wrecked metal. The process had to be the same for satellites.

But you couldn't physically interact with the birds, not once you launched them. Unless you sent another drone satellite into space to cozy up to it, which was the real topic of Damon's contract with the DOD.

He didn't know for sure, but he suspected that military satellites would probably have self-destruct sequences if they were ever owned by an attacker.

But commercial satellites?

They must have fail-safe backdoors. There had to be a way to shut them down, render them useless, in the event of an attack. That, or reset to factory mode, or something.

When all this started, when they were in New Orleans, Damon had emailed his friend at GenCorp, asking about their constellation. Back at the hospital, when he retrieved messages, he got a vague reply. His friend said the situation was under control, that they were moving their satellites around to avoid the debris.

He hadn't said anything about getting hacked, but disclosing network breaches was against confidentiality for any corporation. The bigger question now—why weren't they shutting them down yet?

"I gotta admit," Damon said. "Using the SatCom birds as weapons is a genius idea. Perfect for the job. Have you seen them? Pack a hundred to a rocket by building them wide and flat. Which also makes them great kinetic weapons. Turn sideways to the direction of travel and you have a nice big area to collide with."

"I never thought of that," Terek said.

"You didn't?" Damon got up. "Come on."

Terek shrugged. "Not the way I think."

"I need to go to the boys' room. Back in a sec."

Damon hit *stop* on the corn head controller. He waited. Watched Terek bring the overwatch drone down. The corn head and the tractor following came into view. Everyone could use a break. Satisfied, he got up and walked into the next room.

His eyes automatically searched for Pauline. He found her, humming as she cleared dishes from a coffee table. She waved and gave him that smile. His cheeks tingled.

He didn't really need to go to the bathroom.

He flushed the toilet for appearances, turned the water on and off, wiped his hands, and walked back through the living room. Something was bothering him, something he'd just seen on the TV. Were there flames in the distance?

Pauline grinned at him again. He returned her smile and felt his face go hot.

Something else filled his mind.

There was a big problem with satellite communications that had never been properly solved: What were the security postures of their ground systems and the data links that controlled them?

In 2018, JPL had been hacked. The attackers took control of such a large portion of their system that they'd disconnected the Deep Space Network, which had been communicating with NASA probes billions of kilometers into space.

The attackers could have wrecked tens of billions of dollars' worth of equipment with only a few keystrokes, but luckily, whoever they were, they weren't malicious. Then again, maybe they were simply testing JPL's defenses.

That was the very first element of the cyber kill chain.

Terek's idea was a desperate one, but working with criminals could sometimes be a way for the good guys to beat the really bad guys. Damon thought of Frank Abagnale, who eluded the FBI and Interpol for years, forging checks and stealing money, until he was apprehended—and eventually hired by the same agencies that once chased him.

Damon rounded the corner into the kitchen and was about to tell Terek to message his Russian friends back, but he stopped, his mouth halfway open.

Terek slipped a USB key from the side of Damon's laptop.

Damon was sure he'd caught Terek's eye as he walked around the corner, but now Terek looked steadfastly away. The USB key disappeared into his friend's pocket. Something was up. Terek was trying to fake not looking back at Damon. Why would he do that? What was he up to?

Had he snuck something onto Damon's laptop?

Damon paused and was about to ask about it, when the first thing that was bothering him resurfaced. That itch in the back of his head he couldn't quite scratch. The sudden realization settled like a brick into the bottom of his stomach.

"Hey, can you turn the drone around to see the corn head?"

"One sec," Terek said.

"*Now*, please. Right away."

Terek gave him a look, but the image on the big screen swiveled. In the distance, the hulk of the corn head loomed through the smoke screen, as did the one tractor beside it—which was already pulling away and driving into the cornfield, like it was escaping from something.

One tractor. Where was the other one?

Damon said, "Where's Mike?"

Behind the corn head, the trees in the hazy distance seemed to shimmer. They burst into leaping flames.

Damon took control of the overflight drone. Using the visual on the TV, he lowered the drone and skimmed the cornfield.

He dialed Oscar's number. "What happened to Mike? Where is he?"

"I don't know," came the noisy reply.

"We better keep cutting the break," Terek said quietly. "Should I get the corn head moving?"

"Sure," Damon replied.

A crowd gathered in the kitchen. Pauline glanced at Damon, but he barely acknowledged her. He focused on backtracking the drone along the path at the edge of the forest. Smoke poured out between the trees. Flames danced through the underbrush.

Something appeared in the haze. He pulled back to get a little altitude.

And there was the other tractor.

Mike's Ford and plow were surrounded by flames that lit up the corn stalks and the leaves on the dirt. A fallen fir tree fueled the growing conflagration.

Chapter 30

"**L**uke, *goddamn* it, don't run off like that."

I rarely swore at my son, but I was scared. I wasn't sure how long I'd been running after him and the dog, but I was heaving. I stopped to lean against the chipped bark of an oak to get my lungs under control.

My son was barely even breathing hard.

"Dad, he wants us to follow him," he said again.

Roosevelt, the little Jack Russell, turned and barked at me as if to confirm the point.

Letting go of my support tree, I bent to pick up the dog, but he skittered away from me and ran up the slope. "*Goddamn it,*" I muttered under my breath.

How far had we come? A few hundred feet? Any further and we risked getting turned around. The smoke roiled in thick blankets and stung my eyes. My frustration jolted into fear.

"Luke, leave the d—"

"Dad, you hear that?"

I slowed my breathing. What was that? A crackling sound. The fire. It was close. But something else.

"Help," came a faint cry.

Luke was already running toward the voice. I stumbled behind him. There, fifty feet further up the slope of the woods, were two people. One of them lay on the ground, while the other, a small young woman, knelt beside him.

"He twisted his ankle," she said as soon as she saw me. "Thank God you came." She was crying, her face streaked with mud and tears. "I can't...he's too heavy for me."

"What are you doing out here?"

She pointed. I saw we were on a trail. Two packs rested in the middle of it a hundred feet back. "We were hiking the Appalachian and down through Carter Caves when we saw the fires. We were running, trying to get away, when…"

"It's okay." I knelt and pulled one of the man's arms around me.

He was six-six and probably two-fifty. No wonder she couldn't move him. I grunted under the load. Got him upright. "Mike," I said through gritted teeth.

"Steve." He grimaced in pain.

"Brandie," said the girl.

Luke introduced himself while I scanned the woods.

I turned to go back the way we'd come, but orange flames appeared through the smoke in the distance between the trees. Back along the trail, flickering red tongues. Ahead of us, the noxious smog was too thick to see through. I coughed as I tried to get a clean lungful.

"Which way?" I asked.

Roosevelt barked to make sure he got my attention, and then rocketed away down the slope ahead of us.

"You are one crazy sonofabitch, you know that?"

Chuck's lopsided grin stretched from ear to ear. He hopped through the underbrush like a kid in a schoolyard and bent down to take Steve's other arm. They said their introductions, and Brandie said hello.

I released Steve with a merciful groan. I had to get back in the gym when all this was over. I seemed to say that every time there was a disaster, which seemed to be every few years.

"Trust me, this wasn't my idea," I replied.

Roosevelt ran straight at Irena when he saw her and leapt up into her arms. Dogs loved this woman. She held him up and he licked her face. She cooed and laughed.

"Michael," she said, "you certainly seem to know how to get into trouble."

"Like I said."

We crossed from the forest to the field and stepped onto dry dirt. Irena dropped Roosevelt and went to help Chuck with Steve. Luke was making sure Brandie was okay. The Range Rover was parked at the edge of the corn, a good sixty feet from the edge of the trees.

Overhead, the drone whirred and circled. When the six-motored machine had appeared through the smoke, we'd yelled and waved. That's when I knew we were going to be safe. Whoever was guiding it buzzed it ahead of us for the last two hundred feet, but Roosevelt knew the way anyway.

I stopped, bent over double, and hacked and coughed. My lungs felt like they were full of burnt popcorn.

To the left of me, not a hundred feet away, yellow flames zipped up a fir. Orange patches dotted the dirt in the fire break where embers fell.

"We better hurry." Chuck passed me with Steve.

"Coffee first," I said.

A ragtag gang of well-wishers gave us a round of applause as we disembarked from the Range Rover. Damon held open the farmhouse door.

"You had us worried for a second," he said.

"You're not the only ones."

Irena followed me in, helping limping Steve. She took him into the living room to see what she could do about his ankle. Luke joined me, Chuck, and Damon in the improvised command center in the kitchen. I slumped into a ladderback chair.

The drone's video feed played on a big-screen TV mounted in front of the kitchen's fireplace. From a hundred feet up, I watched a team of people dump dirt on patches of fire and stamp on embers. Terek guided the drone higher and inspected the fire, then made a call to another team out on the farm and directed them to a different spot.

A mug of coffee clumped down on the table in front of me.

"Good job, son." Farmer Joe clapped me on the back.

A puff of dust and soot erupted from my shirt.

I picked up the cup and took a sip. "I can't really take credit. It was this guy here." Luke attached himself to my leg. I tousled his hair. "He's the one that found them."

Luke's face was smudged with soot and dirt. Ragamuffin came to mind. "It was Roosevelt, he was barking, and then I heard them calling for help, and then I ran over, and then there they were." He jumped up and down but didn't let go of my leg.

Joe knelt and held out a hand. "You, sir, deserve a medal."

Luke shook with one hand and saluted with the other.

"Seems your boy has inherited your savior complex," Chuck said from across the kitchen. "Good job, Luke."

"I need to head back out." Joe groaned as he stood.

"Thank you." I held up my coffee.

"No, son. Thank *you*. I cannot tell you how much—" The old man's face creased up. He pulled off his cap. Wiped a calloused hand across his eyes. "I have to say my belief in angels is renewed after some time of doubt. We've been through some tough years, lately."

"You're welcome." I lowered my head. Tired.

"Everyone, can we please come together for a moment?" Farmer Joe held his hands out and motioned for everyone from the living room to join us in the kitchen. "For a second, and then we'll get back to it. Can we all stand?"

I stood. Terek set the drone to hover and said something into his phone. A dozen people whose names I couldn't remember filtered in until the kitchen was shoulder to shoulder. When Farmer Joe spoke, his voice was low, but everyone listened.

"Hold hands, please," he commanded gently.

Terek, Damon, and Irena held hands, with Damon in the middle, until a young blond woman in cut-off jean shorts inserted herself between Irena and Damon. Irena released his hand and the new woman took it and smiled at Damon. He smiled back. His cheeks flushed.

Chuck took one of my hands firmly, and Luke took the other. The whole group formed a circle around the kitchen table.

"God, thank you for bringing these people into our lives today," Joe said.

Everyone bowed their heads and closed their eyes. I did too.

"And please give us the strength and your good blessing to save our town and keep everyone safe. In your name, amen."

"Amen," mumbled everyone around the table but me.

We all released hands, and a few people said quiet thanks to Joe. Everyone went back to what they were doing.

Everyone let go of hands, except Damon and the new girl.

"That's Pauline," Chuck whispered into my ear. "You see the way she pushed Irena away?"

I picked up my coffee and took another sip. "I did."

"Two beautiful women fighting over Damon."

"Do I detect jealousy?" I held my cup up to obscure my mouth.

Damon and Pauline weren't more than ten feet away, and *still* held each other's hands. They turned away from us to watch the big screen.

"I'm a happily married man," Chuck said.

"You can live vicariously," I said.

"That I can, that I can."

Chuck mentioning his wife made me think of Lauren. We needed to get going.

"I noticed you weren't into the prayer circle," Chuck said.

"Just don't like holding your hand."

But he was right. Chuck knew me. Holding hands and praying made me feel vaguely uneasy, like I was doing something I didn't believe in. Did I believe? The jury was out, so to speak.

Now that we were back in the farmhouse, my phone had a better connection to the meshnet. More bandwidth, as I was connected to a lot of other phones. I picked it up to look for messages.

The kitchen's side door flung open. Oscar's shaved head appeared. "Holy God in heaven, son," he said, his face beaming. "I was worried."

He took two big loping steps and wrapped me up in a bear hug, lifting my feet from the floor.

"Thanks," I grunted.

Ken followed in behind him. He took off his cap. A white line from where it had covered his forehead and blond hair. His face dark with soot and grime. "I think we got this thing beat. It'll burn down to the Ohio, but that's a thousand foot across. This here is where the buck stops."

Whoops and cheers from the living room.

Oscar returned me gently to the floor and whispered, "You'll tell Terry I done you right?"

I laughed. "I'll say you pistol-whipped me in good fun."

His eyes went wide. "That weren't no pistol, and I didn't mean—"

"I'm kidding."

I picked up my phone again, and my heart fell to my feet. The stink of fumes and soot suddenly made me want to retch.

"What is it?" Oscar asked.

A message from Senator Seymour. They still hadn't found Lauren. She had been processed in the Virginia holding encampment and held there for a day, but she had been released two days ago. There was no record of where she was now. Senator Seymour's staff had been looking for her, but they were returning to the Capitol because of the mess going on. They didn't know what to do.

"My wife...Lauren, they can't find her."

Chuck took my phone and read the text. He handed it to Damon.

"It's not even noon," Chuck said. "We get in the cars. We can be in Washington before dark."

"We're not getting through that." Damon pointed out the window at the inferno in the treetops a half mile away.

"What about bridges?" Chuck said.

"There's the Harsha Bridge a half hour back," Oscar said. "But that's been closed since the ice damage last year."

"You'd need to go all the way back to Combs-Hehl in Cincinnati," Ken said. "That's an hour and half along the Ohio. But who knows if you can get through the fires, if they've gotten all the way to the river back there."

Chuck said, "You might need to cut a fire break on the other side of town."

"That's what we're doing next."

"I need to get to DC. Right now," I said.

"And I need to get to Washington to get to some big data pipes," Damon said. "Terek's idea might have a snowball's chance. We need to at least test out what these Russian hackers have. See if it's something. Then find some authorities. No better place for that than Washington. And I bet we can get the senator's resources on our side, if we need."

"Going back to Cincinnati," Chuck said, "will add hours to the trip. That's assuming we can get past any fires."

"So, what?" I held my arms wide. "We wait for the fires to burn out?"

Silence.

Oscar and Chuck talked quietly, head to head, for a minute.

"I got an idea," Oscar said.

Chuck looked at me, barely containing a grin. "And you are *not* going to like it."

Burning embers shot into the sky from licking flames along the banks of the Ohio. Even a few hundred feet away, the heat scorched my face. An ash storm of blackened leaf fragments settled onto the undulating water.

I held tight to my life vest.

"Don't go too close," I said.

Oscar gunned the outboard's engine as we fought against the current. "We gotta stay to the east side," he yelled. "This corner is the Twin Creek sandbar. It's always moving. We'll get hung up in the middle of the river if we don't stay well clear."

The thought of being trapped in the center of a fast-moving river while fires raged around us made me feel like spiders crawled under my shirt and out my collar. Luke squeezed my hand.

Irena and Terek sat in the front of the open twenty-foot aluminum boat, with Damon, Chuck, Ellarose, and Bonham behind them. All our gear was piled in the middle. Luke and I were on a back bench next to Oscar and Susie.

"We gotta get around this point," Oscar said. "And we should see Huntington on the other side. My cousin Rickie will get us all set straight. He said the Sandy River is blocking the fire to the south of them. We need to get past the meeting of the two rivers a mile up."

"Let's just get going," I said.

The engine coughed and sputtered and went dead. Oscar cursed. Our forward momentum stopped. An eddy caught us, and we floated backward and then sideways—toward the rising flames.

"Gosh darn it." Oscar stood and pumped the hand starter.

We spun toward the searing wall of flame.

Chapter 31

T hird pull on the starter, the engine roared back to life. Hurling profanities at the fire, the water, the engine, and everything else within sight, Oscar turned the boat back into the current. For a stomach-lurching instant we tipped to one side, but the boat wobbled back to stability and we sped away from the flames.

True to his word, Oscar dropped us off in Huntington, the next town down the Ohio River. We met his cousin Rickie, a hefty man wearing a Pirates baseball cap and a cut-off T-shirt over his barrel chest and potbelly. He loaned us his old Escalade. Said he'd been trying to sell it after he got his new one, so we could borrow it for a while.

Oscar told him I was Terry's brother, and that seemed to be more than enough reason to hand over the keys. I honestly didn't know my brother was *this* notorious.

Chuck promised we would return the Escalade unscratched. Or, at least not more scratched. It had seen better years. Oscar said that he and Ken would drive the Mini Cooper and Irena's Range Rover to the cabin once the fires died down and it was safe, and then they would return in the Escalade.

Handshakes and hugs all around, like we were the best of friends, as if we hadn't been hijacked by Oscar at gunpoint a day ago.

The most interesting goodbye, however, had been when we'd gotten on the boat back in Vanceburg. Pauline hadn't only hugged Damon, she'd given him a kiss. Right on the lips. Surprised him as much as anyone else. He had nearly fallen off the dock and into the water.

The roads coming out of Huntington were almost empty. Even Interstate 81, the backbone of the East Coast, usually stacked with traffic going up and down the country, was quiet. We only saw two cars the whole hour we were on it, and one of those was a police cruiser.

I sat in the front passenger seat. Chuck drove, Susie and Irena sat in the middle row with all three kids, and Damon and Terek squeezed in the back, their laptops wired together, doing whatever they always did.

"Ain't it beautiful?" Chuck said.

Indeed, it was a sight to behold.

An ink-blue sky greeted us as we topped the Shenandoah section of the Blue Ridge Mountains. We'd pulled off Interstate 81 and onto the 66 before turning to Chuck's exit.

Behind us, an angry orange sunset was obscured by a thick haze of smoke to the horizon, but with the wind blowing west, the miasma wasn't infiltrating this side of the range. We hadn't seen clear skies in the best part of a week, and the clean air felt like drinking in a cool mountain stream.

I was still coughing up black goo.

My elation over the fresh air couldn't quite cover my deep anxiety about returning to the cabin. The same house where we had holed up before. Where our friend Tony had died. Where we'd almost died ourselves. I hadn't been back since, had sworn I never wanted to return, but we were just around the corner now. Like going back to the scene of a crime I still tried to forget.

Luke had been there, but he didn't remember. I hoped he didn't. The pain and fear, the starvation. To him, we were heading into the woods. The adventure continued, the sky was blue, and we were free and on our way to meet mom.

I hadn't told him they hadn't found her yet. I couldn't bring myself. I even tried to hide it from myself.

Chuck said, "Hey, did I ever tell you the story about my friend, Doug?"

"Doug?" I frowned and searched my memory banks but came up blank. Shook my head.

"Sad story."

"Go on."

"He got up one morning, going to work as usual. In a hurry, though, he didn't bother to say goodbye to his wife and kids. Grabbed a granola bar and coffee and scooted out of the house."

I had a feeling this was going to have a less than happy ending. "What happened?"

"First intersection, he T-bones a truck that runs a red light. Doug didn't put on a seatbelt, in too much of a hurry. He went straight through the windshield headfirst. The paramedics said he'd snapped his neck and was dead before he hit the pavement."

"Why are you telling me this now?" I looked back to make sure Luke was still wearing his seatbelt.

"It makes me think."

"Me too." I rechecked my own seatbelt.

"Life is short. Do you think Doug wishes he told his wife and kids that he loved them before he left the house?"

"Of course he does," I said. What was the last thing I said to Lauren? I was sure I said I loved her. What did she say to me? I couldn't remember.

"Do you think he even knows he died?" Chuck asked. "I mean, sudden like that?"

"He knows."

"But how?"

"I don't know."

Chuck's face went from sad to suspiciously gleeful. "Explain to me exactly how you know he wishes he'd told his kids he loved them."

That look on his face. "Doug's not a real person, is he?"

"Answer the question."

"If he loved them, then of course he wishes he told them before he died."

"But he's dead. If you're dead, you don't wish for anything. Isn't that what you believe? That it's like a switch going off? Just darkness afterward?"

It didn't take long for Chuck to switch gears and get into his combative mode. I laughed. "Seriously?"

"See, Mike Mitchell, you believe in an afterlife. Whether you believe in God or not, you *do* believe in an afterlife, where we have wishes and fears. If there's an afterlife, what is it? What are we talking about here, Mr. Smarty-Pants?"

I didn't have an answer for him.

When I didn't have an answer, it was because he was winning the argument. The longer I stayed silent, the bigger his smile became.

We pulled off the main road onto a gravel one. The smile on my face slid away. The lines of the cabin became visible through the trees. In the distance, in the twilight, clouds amassed in the foothills.

He pulled the Escalade up to the cabin and outdoor lights automatically winked on.

"Motion detectors," he said. "Done a lot of upgrades. Can't wait to show you. It's not like last time."

A deep-seated dread tightened like an invisible straitjacket. He might have renovated the cottage, but the basement was still there. Where we'd hidden that afternoon when someone had attacked us. Where Tony had died. Last I knew, he was still buried up here.

Chuck turned the engine off. "I know. A lot of memories, right?"

I nodded. None of them good.

"I can't tell you how important it is to have a real landline," Chuck said. He pointed proudly at a red plastic phone on the kitchen counter. "Don't get that VoIP garbage. It's not a real line."

"Phone companies maintain their own power." Damon nodded in agreement. "There's a five-volt signal that comes over the phone line to power everything."

"So even when there is a power blackout, you still get a dial tone. Landlines are the last thing to go out in an emergency."

"I'm going to call the senator," I said.

"Of course."

Chuck led Irena and Terek away to give me some privacy. As I dialed, I heard him telling them how he'd rebuilt the whole place, that the walls were concrete up to ten feet, and that the place was built like a bunker. He was explaining the solar cells and battery storage when someone picked up on the other end.

"Mike," said a deep, mellow voice.

"Senator Seymour."

"You can call me Leo. Mike, where are you now?"

"Virginia. Chuck's cabin. We had a hard time getting around the fires. I got your messages. Did you get mine?"

"We've been worried. I've been getting news about the fires, but they've been sporadic. The whole country is in convulsions. It's good you're safe."

"Any news on Lauren?"

"I was required to bring my staff back."

"You couldn't send anyone else out."

"I'm sorry, Mike. All senior staff were recalled to Washington. It's hard to explain what's going on. We need all hands on deck. I haven't been back to the house in days."

"But you have someone with Susan and Olivia?"

"My best guy. When are you getting here?"

"How's Olivia?"

"She's great. Perfect. Susan doesn't let the little one out of her sight. Everything is calm on the estate, but Washington is a shambles. The Russians managed to get a few geopositioning birds up, offered even their encrypted signals, maybe that will help. How long till you can be here?"

"Tonight. We're coming now." His house was only an hour away. "Are the streetlights still on?"

"For now. Power has been going out all over the country."

"What's happening in space?"

"I can't say a lot over the phone, Mike. But you heard about the Islamic Brigade?"

"I did."

"The Russians flattened Chechnya. The Russkies are saying the Islamic Brigade is associated with a faction called the Black Army in Ukraine. This is in high gear now. The Red Army is sending tanks into southern Ukraine tonight."

"My God. And India and Pakistan?"

"I'm heading into a Senate Armed Services meeting right now. We've had India's ambassador in the Capitol all week. They're still denying everything, the idiots, but we're going to get some more visibility today with the pressure the president is putting on them.

We're going to throw them to the wolves if we don't get more detail."

"You can't get imaging? I mean, can't you see what's going on over there?"

"What satellites are left are being moved, and without reliable GPS, even tracking where the damn things are has become a problem. Do you have the internet where you are?"

"I do." Chuck had just finished telling us how much it had cost him to get a fiber-optic line rolled all the way in here.

"I'm going to send you a pass from my office. It should get you through the checkpoints."

I thought of telling him about Damon and Terek, about the Russian hackers, but I wasn't sure if that would go anywhere.

"Mike," the senator asked again, "when can you get here?"

Chuck led all of us into the two-car garage across the gravel driveway.

I said, "Don't tell me you still have The Wolf?"

If I had any positive memories of that time, they were of the old but tough-as-bricks Range Rover we used to escape from New York, starting with Tarzan-swinging it off a three-story parking garage.

Not quite all of us came into the garage. Susie rolled her eyes when Chuck said he wanted to go out there, as in, you boys have your fun. Irena was with us, but I thought I sensed her keeping a slight distance from Damon.

Luke also joined us, along with Bonham and Ellarose. The kids bubbled with anticipation, squealing and making little faces at each other. Chuck's kids knew what was under the blue tarp. One of them must have told Luke. He made silly eyes at me.

The floodlights came on. Chuck grabbed one corner of the tarp and smiled. He waited a beat.

"Ta-da!" He pulled the cover back with a flourish.

"Holy…" was all I could get out.

It wasn't The Wolf. It was—a twenty-foot slab of stainless steel and black glass with huge knobby tires.

Chuck slid his hand gently along the hood. "The new BullyBoy truck. Ordered her online the moment they were announced. Full specs."

The BullyBoy was from another megacorporation owned by a rival to Jakob, Sam Maxwell, building everything from robots to space rovers. They had their own satellite constellation in the works, as well.

"I thought you hated billionaires."

"I didn't like SatCom cluttering up the sky, and was I wrong?" Still running his hand along the hood, he gloated visibly. If Chuck loved anything in this world, it was being right.

"You dislike billionaires, but still buy stuff from them?"

"That's how they become rich. Great products. I believe I said I'm a practical optimist. How could I resist? Cold rolled stainless steel body, bulletproof armored glass, quad motor with a thousand horsepower, and its own integrated solar panels. All electric and watertight. Doesn't need a snorkel in deep water because the engine doesn't need air."

It was impressive.

Damon wasn't quite as moved. "You know how easy these things are to hack? This has the full self-driving option?"

Chuck nodded.

"Last Black Hat conference in Vegas, a team got into one of these remotely. Took over the whole thing. Brakes. Accelerator. Turned it into a remote-control drone."

"When the only tool you have is a hammer," Chuck said. "Everything is a drone to you, isn't it? Even us?"

"I'm just saying. I could own this thing inside of five minutes."

"Lucky there's not a lot of guys like you, then. I'm taking us into Virginia in this tonight," Chuck said.

"Will we fit?"

"I'm staying here," Susie said.

She came into the garage, pulled some boxes from the wall, and then cleared a hockey net and sticks from the front of a metal locker.

"Why don't you come?" I asked.

"Into DC? No thanks. Why do you think we built this place? For situations exactly like this. I'll stay here with the kids. You guys go find Lauren. Leave the Escalade for me. Oscar and Ken will bring up the cars from Huntington, and we'll bring the Range Rover to Irena in the next few days. You'll be staying with Terek's wife?"

Irena nodded. "That's fine. Perfect."

"Are you sure you'll be—"

"You think Chuck is the only one who's prepared?" Susie swung open the locker door. The inside was stacked with firearms.

The lights of Washington glimmered on the horizon. Sixty miles as the crow flies. About the limit of how far my feet had been able to take me a few years before.

Storm clouds massed to the south in the glow of a full moon. We sat a hundred feet behind the cabin on a huge stone outcropping that provided a view down through the woods from our perch in the Blue Ridge Mountains.

At three and a half thousand feet, the air was clear and cool. Sweet relief from the oppressive heat and smoke of the past days.

"I can take the Escalade in," I said. "You should stay with your family."

"Ain't gonna happen, Mike. Not going to leave you to do this on your own, and Susie wouldn't let me anyway."

Here Chuck had reached his safe place, together with his loved ones, yet he refused to stay until Lauren was found. I almost wanted to cry. In fact, I did want to cry, but I held it back. I cried at all the emotional bits of movies. Even though I knew Lauren found it sweet, I wasn't going to let a tear loose in front of Chuck.

"Fires won't get all the way up past the top of the Blue Ridge, that's more than four thousand feet. Wind's blowing the wrong way. And those clouds, I bet that's rain."

"Are the Baylors still here?" I asked.

The next cabin over. The scene of the disaster that had started the last time we'd been here, when Tony had been shot.

"They put it up for sale after all that. I bought it."

"You did?"

"Use it as a guest house. I dug a tunnel between the two places. Well, a ditch, and covered it up. Works as a tunnel. I didn't show anyone else. It's a secret. Only telling you."

"You seriously dug a tunnel?"

"You know how much snow we get up here in winter?"

No idea. Thinking of the snow made me think of something else. "Is Tony still buried up here?"

Chuck took a deep breath. "Yeah. Right where we left him, down by the stream. His family comes up, stays at the guest cottage sometimes. We made a nice headstone. It's a beautiful spot."

"It is."

"What about the Borodins?" Chuck asked. "The old Russian couple? When Irena, she came into the room with that rifle…" He laughed.

"Aleksandr died," I said.

He stopped laughing.

"It's okay. The guy was almost a hundred. Irena went to live with her family in Florida. That's the last I heard before we moved out of the apartment."

"And Gorby? Their dog?"

"He went with Irena. Luke's always wanted one."

"That kid. You know he saved those hikers' lives. You should be proud."

I was. More than proud.

We turned the TV on when we got back inside.

The satellite service wasn't working, but Chuck had his fiber-optic cable, so we streamed Fox News and CNN. The debris field from the shattered satellites was still spreading, but the authorities were also trying to track the thousands of rogue SatCom satellites now controlled by the Chechen attackers.

And it was as the senator had said.

Russia was reported to be moving tanks into Ukraine in response to the threat. They were offering their help with geopositioning data, as well as sending aid into Western Europe. China was offering to help as well. They didn't seem as badly hit by this as the United States.

America was in spasms as supply lines shut down. Power blackouts.

A full week into the event now.

Conflicting and heated debates online about the global situation. There were civil disturbances, rioting, but coverage was spotty. Only China had part of its positioning network operational, which left most of the world's militaries blind, and fueled even more speculation who might really be behind all of this.

On top of that, there was an almost total loss of emergency services across the globe, as we had suspected. Massive fires and tornadoes in America, a cyclone battering islands in the Pacific, the tail end of brutal heat wave in Europe, and an earthquake in Peru. Mobile comms wiped out; satellite imaging gone. The death toll mounted with grim statistics.

Nobody talked about the farms, though. Not one word on the TV channels about that. Not yet.

It was a hidden danger that nobody seemed to get, that a big part of the food production in America would be shut down. Countries that were less automated wouldn't have this problem.

We'd gone with full automation to optimize yields and save money, but when the machines stopped working, where did that leave our American farmers?

I couldn't worry about all that. I went back outside with Chuck.

It was surreal, knowing all that was happening out there. In the mountains, it was quiet and calm. The lights of DC glittered in silence.

Something tickled my cheek.

A light rain began.

I said, "It's almost midnight. We should be able to get there in an hour, right?" It sounded too good to be true. Too easy. The last time we'd ventured into Washington from here, it had almost killed me.

Chuck seemed able to read my thoughts. "Don't worry. This time we're driving in a bulletproof tank. And we're not going all the way to DC."

Chapter 32

The drive from Chuck's cabin to the senator's compound in McLean, Virginia took us less than fifty minutes. After everything we'd been through so far, it seemed like one skip of a heartbeat from the moment I stepped into Chuck's gleaming new stainless-steel machine to when we turned onto the leafy suburban end of Potomac River Road.

We found our way with more hand-drawn maps. Carefully double-checked the street names in the driving downpour.

When we pulled up to the ten-foot-tall brick walls and hedges, we weren't even sure we were at the right place—but the wrought iron front gates slid open when I spoke into the intercom on the wall outside.

Chuck pulled through and navigated his BullyBoy around the circular cobblestoned driveway.

"Who's my baby girl?"

Olivia raced at me with a My Little Pony held high in one hand.

She didn't waddle anymore, not in the cute way I'd gotten used to when she was two and three. Now she was five, her baby fat melted away. Green pajamas with white leggings. Her brown hair done in pigtails. Her legs pumped up and down like a soccer player heading for a score. She leapt into my arms.

I wrapped mine all the way around her and squeezed.

She smelled like syrup and hay, the same way she always did, even after bath time. I buried my face into the top of her head and took in another lungful of sweet goodness.

I wondered what I smelled like to her? Daddy, I guessed. She squealed with delight. Pure joy.

"Livia!" Luke yelled and pulled at his little sister.

She jumped down from my arms and hugged her brother as hard as her little arms would let her.

We stood in the entranceway of Senator Seymour's house. Or was it a portico? Two sets of neo-gothic columns rose on either side of the raised brick platform before the two massive wooden doors that stood open.

Damon and Chuck stood behind me, while Terek and Irena were still getting out of the BullyBoy's third row.

Through the doors, I saw Senator Seymour coming down a curved oak staircase with wrought iron bannisters. He was wearing a visibly rumpled blue suit and half-done-up red tie. His hair was full and white, his eyes blue.

"Mike," he said. "Thank God. Come in, come in."

"Excuse me, sir." This was addressed to me by a thick-set man in a perfectly pressed black suit and tie as I walked in through the door.

He seemed to have materialized from the humid Virginian air to stand between me and the senator, who'd made it to the bottom of the stairs. "I'll need to see some identification."

"Secret Service," the senator apologized. "I'm president pro tem of the Senate now, so technically, third in line for the throne."

I fumbled for my wallet and held it out for the man to inspect. I guessed he knew who I was and was following the rules, but then times like this demanded a little of that.

I had met Lauren's uncle very briefly only twice before, and I'd forgotten he'd been awarded this position. What was the proper way to talk to him? I wasn't big on protocol. Lauren always elbowed me at fancy dinners when I used the wrong fork.

"Senator." I extended my hand.

"Please, call me Leo." He shook it firmly, almost crushing my fingers.

His features seemed chiseled from a block of Potomac bluestone, hewn of the official rock of DC, like he was part of the same foundation rock of the White House, the Capitol Building, and the Washington Monument.

Mrs. Seymour—Susan—was halfway down the sweeping staircase behind him. Usually I saw her done up for an evening out, in a gown and coiffed, but now she was in velour sweatpants and a matching top. She looked ashen. She hadn't been the same since her husband, Lauren's father, had passed from a heart attack two years before. She stayed with her brother quite a lot these days.

Susan stopped where she was.

I shook my head, as though asking, nothing yet? She shook hers in response, almost imperceptibly. Her face creased. Lower lip trembled.

Chuck and the senator shook hands warmly. They had met once before, back in New York.

I walked past Leo and the Secret Service guy and took three steps up. Susan took one down. She wrapped her arms around me. She smelled of strong soap, but under that were faint hints of mothballs and sweat. Her body felt frail, her bones thin and her skin loose under the voluminous sweatshirt.

She let out a sob.

I hugged her gently and whispered, "I'm going to find her. Don't you worry."

"They don't know where she is," she said. "They came back without her."

"I promise you, I won't come back without her. No matter what."

"Sir, sir, I need to see some identification," I heard in a stern voice behind me.

I turned to see the Secret Service agent facing Damon. Olivia had wrapped herself around one of his legs and was trying to crawl up him. Luke shook hands with the senator.

Terek and Irena stood awkwardly to one side in the polished marble foyer, their hair soaked and their clothing leaving drips on the floor. It was pouring cats and dogs and chickens and every other animal out there.

Two more Secret Service agents appeared from the darkness outside and approached our group. These guys weren't taking any chances.

"I don't have any ID," Damon said to the Secret Service agent. "We got stuck in a st—"

"Benjamin, Ben." The senator intervened and stood beside Damon. "This is the young man I awarded a Congressional Medal to not two years ago. Don't you recognize him?"

"That's not the point, sir, I—"

"I'm vouching for him," the senator said.

"Thank you, Senat—"

"Leo." He turned and took Damon's hand. "Please, everyone, call me Leo."

The two other Secret Service agents were busy looking at Terek and Irena's passports. Chuck had already provided his ID.

Leo said to Damon, "These people are with you? You trust them?" He pointed at Terek and Irena.

"With my life."

"Boys, it's fine. Let them in. Come on, let's dry you all off and get something warm into you. Maybe something with bourbon?"

———

The marble countertop in the kitchen was laid out with sandwiches and snacks, as if they expected two dozen people for a party. A full bar service was to one side, and a woman—Leo introduced her as Barbara, the housekeeper—offered to make us something.

Chuck took a Bulleit Bourbon old fashioned, while I asked for a glass of water and picked up a ham sandwich. The kids each got a pop and took a platter of snacks to the TV room in the basement, where Olivia promised Luke they had the coolest-ever gaming system.

One of the Secret Service agents went with them.

The rest of us retired to a sitting room adjoining the kitchen, a thirty-by-thirty room with a polished oak floor, twelve-foot ceilings, and wall-to-wall windows that provided a view of floodlit trees. It smelled of pine cleaner and new leather.

"No trouble getting in?" Leo sat in the middle of a twelve-foot black leather couch.

"The pass you gave us worked like magic." I sat opposite him on a matching sofa.

Between us was a ten-foot glass table with swivel chairs at either end in the same leather as the couches. Damon sat on one side of me, Terek on the other. Susan and Chuck sat next to Leo. The two agents remained standing and at attention. One beside us, and another out of sight.

Irena stood next to the one near us.

"When I saw that steel truck coming up the driveway, I thought we were being invaded." Leo laughed. "Makes sense it's you, Chuck."

"Makes sense?" Chuck took a sip of his drink. "Mike, what have you been saying about me?" He sat up straight and seemed buoyed by the idea of a senator having an opinion about him.

"Only good things."

"Ben," Leo said to the Secret Service agent standing beside us. "I want to get government ID documents, congressional staffers, for everyone here. Can you get on that?"

The agent hesitated, but then nodded. He stepped back a pace and spoke into his wrist.

"Will be easier to get you through checkpoints if I say you're on a congressional fact-finding mission, and you'll need ID." He glanced at Damon, then stood to lean over the table and slap his knee. "Especially for this kid." The senator's well-practiced smile was warm enough to reveal he had a soft spot for Damon. Leo sat back down.

Our tech wunderkind, smiling at the compliment, opened up his laptop. He had already plugged into the house's Wi-Fi, and he snapped another black cable into the back of his computer. He brought up an online map of the Virginia Beach area and magically projected it on the wall of the room. I looked up at a projector in the ceiling by the chandelier.

"Chuck, you want to make notes?" Damon said.

"There are sixteen airports on the Virginia Beach peninsula. Hampton Roads Executive, Chesapeake Regional, Virginia Beach local, Norfolk Airport, and Norfolk International. And then there are three air force bases, each with three runway complexes, and finally the Armada-Hoffler and Lynnhaven heliports. When the GPS went down and the borders were closed, the Virginia Beach area was designated as a collecting zone."

Leo said, "Two hundred and twenty-six flights coming into the US were diverted there. The US Naval Air Stations operate three NDBs—"

"NDBs?"

Damon explained, "Non-directional beacons. They emit a wavelength that reflects off the atmosphere so it can be detected at long distances."

Leo continued, "Any planes coming over the ocean out of radar contact were redirected to military NDBs to make sure they stayed on courses that got them home. Lauren's 777 was directed to the Naval Air Station Oceana, and the civilians were held in the air passenger terminal and gymnasium there. Ben, Agent Coleman, why don't you tell them what happened?"

"We went there two days ago to retrieve her," Agent Coleman said. He'd finished relaying his instructions to whoever he'd been speaking to. "The morning of September 11th, however, to speak bluntly…"

"Go ahead," said Leo.

"All heck broke loose that morning, when the Islamic Brigade announced that it had attacked us."

"Us?" I said. "They attacked pretty much the entire planet. They wrecked the Russian satellites first."

"The decision to use September 11th to make such an announcement indicates a certain directed intent," Agent Coleman said in a deadpan voice. "In all cases, the biggest holding areas are at the Norfolk International airport and the Naval Air Station Oceana. When we arrived at Oceana, we found that Mrs. Mitchell had been removed from the holding area by military transport."

"How did you know this?"

"There was a written entry in a log book." He held up his phone. "I took a picture of the entry."

"Where was she moved?"

"It did not say. She may have been taken to one of the other two civilian holding areas—"

"There are still people being held there?"

"Not many. Almost all civilians have been released at this point. We stayed for the day and into the night, but given the level of alert, and that DEFCON 2 had been instituted, we were recalled to our duties here."

"So where should we go?" Chuck asked.

"Start with the Norfolk Airport and Naval Air Station."

Terek was now busy on his laptop. "Mike," he said, "could you send me a few pictures of Lauren?"

I didn't ask why. I'd already connected to the Wi-Fi, so I went through my photos and selected a few.

"And these new IDs you're giving us, they'll get us onto an air force base? Don't they require background checks?"

"These are your background checks."

I squeezed Susan's hand. She squeezed back. "Mike, you need to go back out there and find her. Please, you—"

"I'm going, don't worry."

"I am worried."

Wind whipped rain against the ten-foot windows. It howled.

"I'm going with him," Chuck said. "In that steel truck outside. We'll be okay."

"I'll go with you," Irena offered.

"What about Terek's wife?"

"She's fine. She's with friends in Georgetown."

I had heard Terek on the Seymour's landline right after we got in. It was nice of Terek and Irena to come with us from Vanceburg and trust the Kentucky militia boys to return her Range Rover to Chuck's cabin. They could have waited a day or two for the fires to pass, but there was an urgency there, for Terek to get to his new wife. They had only been married a few months, he'd said. I heard Senator Seymour offering one of his cars, but Terek said no, they would stay here.

Something else was bothering me.

I wandered off from the group and opened my phone, then looked up the name Irena. To me it sounded about as Russian as the Bolshoi Ballet and Red Square rolled up into one shining Red Star. It was actually more of a Slavic name in origin—Polish, Czech, Slovak—but then Russians were ethnically Slavic, as far as I understood it. It was a common name in Ukraine.

My fingers hovered. I paused for a beat.

Then I typed in Terek's name. The search popped up: *Places in (1) China (2) Kyrgyzstan (3) Russia.* A red line drew an image of the Terek River, a major river in the northern Caucasus that ran from Georgia through Russia and into the Caspian Sea. I zoomed in. A name popped up on the screen: Chechnya. Part of the Terek River ran right through Chechnya. Then again, it was a place in China, too.

Chapter 33

I walked back into the war room in time to hear Damon say, "Senator, there's a chance we might be able to hack this Chechen group."

"Please. Call me Leo."

"We could have a way to get into the SatCom network. If not, maybe some new SIGINT."

Signals intelligence. I'd watched enough movies to know the term.

The senator's mouth opened as he processed. "Every egghead from the Hill and down through Langley is working that. If you weren't who you are, I'd stop you there. A lot of bull-poop circling right now."

"All I need is to talk to someone at GenCorp. Top level. I've met Tyrell. Get me a line in."

The senator's face went blank in a practiced way.

I asked Damon, "But don't you have friends there?"

He nodded. "There's one guy, Gunther, who I know pretty well. I've emailed him the past week, but I get these really short responses. I figured he was busy. Soon as we got here, I checked my mail again. One message from him. He said they have everything under control now, but I don't see how that's possible. I'm beginning to suspect..."

"What?"

"I mean, if their networks have been hacked, it's not impossible. Maybe they're spoofing my friend. I checked his social media, but nothing on there. Tried his personal email, but didn't get an answer. So what I need, senator, is a direct connection to someone high up. Don't you have a team over there? You must have sent a team in the second the Islamic Brigade made their announcement?"

The senator steepled his fingers. "This stays between these four walls?"

"Of course," I said.

Damon and Terek agreed.

"Over the last thirty hours, we have been in touch with the top levels of GenCorp. Tyrell assured us that he had taken back command of his SatCom network from the attackers. Our tactical cyber team confirmed with them. We thought we were back in control."

"And?"

"They had us for a little while. Smart bastards. They compromised the GenCorp communications servers. Someone pretended to be Tyrell and other top execs, in fact, every damn person there. Someone, or more accurately, probably some*thing*. Whenever we send an email to GenCorp servers now, we think a sophisticated chatbot AI is generating responses. That's the latest."

I asked, "So how long since you *know* you talked to someone there?"

"Four, maybe five days. We have a SEAL team going in as we speak. We'll know more in a few hours."

The information took a few brain cycles to sink in.

"Why don't you take whatever you're doing into Langley?" Leo said to Damon. "I can send you in right now. We're literally around the corner from the FBI, the CIA...all those guys are gunning for the same thing. Why don't you tell them your slant on this?"

Damon nodded his head in silence, but then began shaking it. "Because our angle involves some unsavory characters who aren't fans of law enforcement. If we walk into the CIA, they'll probably know it, one way or the other, and might shut down talking to us."

"You have a high-bandwidth connection here?" Terek asked.

"A secure T1 straight into my office on the Hill."

"Can we work here?"

"Only if you keep me updated on exactly what you're doing. And I mean every, single, thing."

Damon sat up straight. "Of course, Senator."

Terek nodded as well.

Damon asked, "Can you give us any more details?"

The senator began pacing. "The Russians are pissed off, the Chinese just as mad. And don't even get me started about the mood at the Pentagon. The Chinese still have three BieDou up there, but that's not enough for position tracking, and the Russians managed to get two launches—God knows how they did it so quickly—with GLONASS on board, but one of them was taken out by debris."

Leo laughed grimly.

I asked, "What's funny?"

"If you told me two weeks ago I'd be an expert on global positioning, I'd have ridden you out of town."

"Are we putting up any new GPS satellites?" I said.

"What I can tell you, is that we still have birds up there."

"So they're moving them around?" Damon asked.

"I can't say more than that at this time."

Damon said, "The new Block III GPS birds have directional antennas. Any of them left?"

"As I said." The senator pursed his lips. "Some good news I can share, is that regional branches of the army, air force, and the National Guard are starting set up of local GPS transmitters on towers in cities, onto drones, anything that gets a device up high."

Damon's eyebrows raised. "Already?"

"It'll take weeks, maybe months, but we'll get there."

"What about the power blackouts?" I asked.

"The utilities are scrambling as hard as everyone else. It's hard to say what's going to happen short term as effects cascade down. It's going to get worse before better."

"And India?" I asked.

"We've had their ambassador and a dozen diplomatic staff with their feet to the coals the past week. The best we've been able to get is that maybe—*maybe*—a rogue element of their military ordered the release of the missiles. It's been made more difficult as the Pakistani military has all but obliterated the launch site now."

I was more concerned about nuclear weapons. They would affect the entire planet. "What about radiation? The Russians said there were traces in the air?"

"Both the Pakistanis and Indians are denying any nuclear strikes. That was easier to verify after we got our initial SIGINT snafus under control. No nuclear war. Not yet, anyway, but the two sides aren't far from it."

"So what was the radiation from?"

"The Russians are saying it might have been a downed satellite. Traces of radioactive isotopes high in the atmosphere. They're still livid, and they're as blind as we are with all the comms and satellites going down. The Red Army is in overdrive. We just learned they sent troops into Latvia last night."

"Why?" I asked. "We let them do that?"

"Let them? How exactly *how* would we stop them right now?"

Leo leaned toward me and gazed straight into my eyes, as if he was asking me what to do. "They claim exceptional circumstances due to these attacks, and most of our Congress is with them. We've declared a new war on terror and are aligning with the Russians."

I said, "Most of Congress?" The way Leo said it, he didn't seem to approve.

"This is a knee-jerk reaction. Somebody has definitely attacked us, and the Russians were the quickest to help—"

"You don't think it's this Islamic Brigade?"

"I think we need more time to evaluate."

"With respect, sir," Chuck said. "When the poop flies into the spinning stuff, it's often better to make any decision than sit still and get hit."

It was a serious moment, but I couldn't help wondering why so many of Chuck's sayings seemed to involve the word "poop". I didn't have the balls to contradict a sitting member of Congress, but Chuck, well, this was the moment he'd been preparing for his whole life.

The senator smiled. "You're not wrong, son. The Russians might be helping, but they might not be."

I watched Terek and Irena's faces as Leo announced that Russia had just stormed their home country. Their expressions didn't change. Not a twitch. Terek went right back to whatever he was doing on his laptop. I'd heard Ukrainians were more stoic than we were, but there was a steely calm beneath it, like something explosive was lurking just below.

"It's about a three-hour drive," Chuck said.

"I'm going to come with you," Agent Coleman said.

"You don't need to do that," Irena said. "I'm ex-army. Ukrainian Tenth Division. I can handle myself."

"You're armed?"

She nodded and said to Agent Coleman, "Aren't you needed here?"

Terek looked up from his computer. "Irena, it is a good idea. I would feel safer if he was with you."

"You don't need to come," I said to Irena. "You should stay with your brother."

She laughed. "Here? I think he's safe here."

"Three hours," Chuck continued, "down to the Virginia Beach area. I suggest we get at least a couple hours sleep to recharge before—"

"I found her," Terek said.

"Who?"

He turned his laptop around to me. "Your wife. Lauren. I found her."

Chapter 34

L auren raised her voice over the sound of the shower. "I'll
be out in a minute!"

"We need to get going soon," a voice called back. "You
sure you're okay? You've been in there a while."

"I'm fine. Just need a minute."

She pulled back the shower curtain to make sure the door was
locked, for whatever good that would do. It was Billy out there. At
least his voice sounded like he was in the hallway and not in her
room.

He said, "Five minutes and we're wheels up."

"I'll be ready."

Five minutes was all Lauren needed. She moved the shower
curtain back into place, just in case.

For the past day, she had been as sweet as pecan pie, Uncle
Leo's favorite. She had no doubt he had people out looking for her,
no matter what was going on. She needed to buy time, do
something to tip the balance.

Lauren told Billy that she understood the delays. That she was
so glad her husband was back with the children and that she
couldn't be more comfortable. Made no fuss. She did everything
she could to make them think she was perfectly happy.

Through the tiny frosted window of the bathroom, the sun was
already up.

All yesterday, she'd kept opening the narrow window in her room, and every time someone came in to check on her, they would close it. They said it was hot out, that it pushed the air conditioning too much. They said it needed to be closed. She insisted she needed air. Eventually they gave up. She kept a watch out the window, and saw people walking on the beach. Neighbors? She thought of screaming at them, yelling for help, but there was always one of the men outside.

Thank God for the wind during the night.

It had made enough noise that they didn't hear her breaking that damn window. It was only a foot high and three long, but it was big enough for her to squeeze through. A guard came by every two minutes. She waited till the man passing underneath moved away, then she cracked the glass by covering it with a pillowcase and smacking with her elbow. Picked out the shards and hid them under her bed, then covered the bottom ledge with some of the clothes they'd brought her.

She could have left that minute, but she wanted to wait for the light.

Lauren had an edge right now. With this storm coming, some of the people from the beach, if they were neighbors, had to be packing up, getting ready to leave. At first light, she stood a better chance of finding someone out there to help her.

She decided she needed a weapon.

Lauren's fingernails bled as she worked out the last screw holding the shower curtain rod to the wall. She had been working them out, one by one, with a dime she'd found in the nightstand drawer.

It wasn't much, but it was something.

There was no way she was going anywhere with Billy, or whatever the hell his name really was.

Chapter 35

D awn colored the sky gold and red and violet over the Potomac. Damon sat next to Terek at the round glass table in the kitchen nook, glass patio doors to three sides of them. A brief lull in the rainstorm brought fleeting glimpses of the sun between fast moving clouds.

With the first light, Damon watched the backyard emerge from the darkness. Leafy beech trees and oaks surrounded the house. The back of the kitchen opened onto a steep slope of green grass dotted with Virginia bluebells. The hill led down to jagged rocks with churning white water just past them. Damon allowed himself a few moments of daydreaming of Paulina as he watched the water and finished off his fifth—or sixth?—coffee of the night.

While Mike and Chuck and Irena slept, Damon and Terek had been hard at work.

Terek tried to track down more images of Lauren.

He used a tool on the dark web to pattern match that picture to other images from webcams, map databases, and social media sites. He managed to get a high probability hit on the background in the image to a street near Virginia Beach, along a row of vacation homes next to the water.

There was another woman with Lauren in the photo, a flight attendant named Emily Simmons. No other posts from her since that picture was put up.

Damon got to work on the satellites.

He couldn't believe he had been taken in by a chatbot. He reviewed the messages from his friend at GenCorp. They were short, and devoid of meaningful details. Enough for it to seem plausible they were from someone in a hurry, but nothing specific or identifiable.

Finding out he'd been tricked pushed his mind into a laser-like focus. Damon didn't like being fooled.

He logged back into the Space Surveillance Network, or tried to. His credentials had been revoked. He sent an email to the administrator. In short order, they verified his identity and renewed his access.

Things had changed in the system.

Now the rogue SatCom satellites were highlighted in angry red dots, and clusters of the best estimates of the clouds of debris fields in orange. All US military satellites had been removed from the data display, not only the secret-rated ones.

Any satellites that were still operational were using their thrusters to stay far out of the way of any SatCom birds. A slow-motion game of cat-and-mouse was being played out high overhead.

While the satellites themselves were moving at six miles per second, the speed with which they could change their orbits was like they were being tugged by snails. It was a slow chase, as the Hall effect thrusters now used on most spacecraft had tiny delta-v capabilities.

Tiny thrust parameters, but extremely efficient. Damon did some back-of-the-napkin calculations.

The SatCom satellite's Hall effect krypton-gas thrusters worked off the electric potential applied to them. The normal operation range was from 0.5 to 1.5 kilowatts, with up to 3.5 kW in maximum thrust, which provided 30 to 160 millinewtons of force. The thrusters were rated at 100 hours of continuous maximum thrust, but he couldn't find the total size of the reservoir. The satellites were small, at just five hundred pounds each.

He wrote down equations. Force equals mass times acceleration. Position is a half of acceleration multiplied by the time in seconds squared.

So, with maximum thrust applied over 100 hours, one of these satellites could be moved about 4,500 km vertically. That was over four days of time. At that point, its delta-v would be 25 meters per second, or 2,200 km a day as it coasted up. So how were these used to attack the geopositioning satellites at 20,000 km of altitude? It would have taken ten days to move one of them that far.

It was one of many things that didn't add up.

The SatCom constellation normally operated at about 550 km of altitude and 53 degrees of inclination in twenty-four orbital planes. There were six thrusters on each satellite, one for each degree of freedom, but even if two of them fired and doubled the acceleration, it would take—he scribbled down more equations— at minimum a week, and even then they would have to slow down and attempt to track the targets.

That was no small task.

Space was an awfully big—*big*—place.

On the other hand, the hacker-attackers had the advantage of numbers. They could use dozens or even hundreds of satellites out of the thousands in the constellation to mount an attack, but they would have needed to start doing that weeks before this mess.

Damon did a search online.

GenCorp had reported malfunctions and loss of communications with a few dozen of its constellation in the weeks running up to the event. This wasn't entirely unusual for a fleet of that size. It was September 4th when the first anti-satellite weapons had been launched, and then a week to September 11th, when the Islamic Brigade had announced that they owned the GenCorp assets and had been using them as weapons.

Attacking satellites in low Earth orbit was a much simpler game. A thruster set for twenty minutes could shift a SatCom bird's delta-v by a tenth of a meter per second, which sounded small, but applied within its orbital plane, that would shift its location by four kilometers over a day.

Satellites typically had no automated defenses against incoming threats. It was a gentlemen's agreement, where everyone knew the orbital paths of everyone else's hardware, and if things got in the way, one or the other would move out of the way. Nobody had ever planned for a contingency where someone would maliciously set one satellite in the way of another.

Except for the SatCom constellation. They were the first with automated avoidance systems, but those must have been turned off.

At 3 a.m. Chuck had woken the others, and they'd left in the big silver BullyBoy. Damon gave them the estimated location of the place in the background of the picture of Lauren. The picture showed Lauren talking to the woman, Emily, with red hair. Neither of them look stressed or upset. They stood next to a Humvee parked in front of a row of beach houses.

Mike took Damon aside and told him about Terek's name, how it was the name of a river in Chechnya, but Damon said it meant nothing. It was a Chinese name too, and Damon was half Asian.

Before Chuck left, Damon demonstrated how he could hack into the BullyBoy. While Chuck was sleeping, Damon uploaded code from the Black Hat event he'd been at. As Chuck walked to the truck that morning, Damon turned it on and made it honk and flash its lights.

The look on Chuck's face had been worth it.

Once the others had left, they decided to test the Russian connection.

Terek used a clean boot disk on a USB drive on Damon's older laptop that only ran UNIX. He ran the connection through Tor, for what little good that might do. Running this connection on the senator's T1 line, connected straight through the US government's networks, made him nervous that the hackers on the other end wouldn't reply.

They did, though, within seconds of the first message.

After some haggling, the Russian hackers sent login credentials to the backdoor into GenCorp. They wanted money, of course, but Damon impressed the seriousness of the situation. In the end, he sent them a few thousand dollars from his own accounts.

Damon downloaded the SatCom satellite protocols from a secure government server he had access to. They didn't need the frequency bands and channel information, since they would be going through whatever base station was still active—but they did need the proper protocols.

There was no guarantee the Russian hack was even still active, but at about 4 a.m. he sent a ping, and the GenCorp network pinged back.

Damon had to be careful.

The first rule of any cyberattack chain was that once you got inside, all you did was collect information and do your best not to let them know you were there. In this case, he was hacking the hackers, and if they sensed someone had broken their perimeter, his access might get shut down. *Would* get shut down, Damon corrected himself. These were sophisticated operators.

And they would surely be on high alert.

Every three-letter agency on the planet must be trying to get inside GenCorp's systems and hack back these satellites. That made Damon suspicious that anything this Russian outfit could give them would be useful.

But it was worth a try.

And there was that ping again.

Damon decided to take a chance and send a command to the satellites, requesting a reading on the fuel reserves. No action, he wanted to see if he could exfiltrate a small amount of data. He wasn't sure if his access node could address all the satellites, or only a subset, or even one.

No response. Not yet. Which brought up another point of discussion.

"How many ground stations does GenCorp run?" Damon asked.

"I have no idea," Terek replied.

Damon wasn't an expert on satellites, but he knew more than a thing or two about the antennas he used on his drones. Satellites were similar.

They had a payload—in the SatCom case, the antennas that were pointed at the Earth to provide data services for mobile devices. Then there was the "bus," which was what the payload was riding on. The bus typically used a single global antenna pointed at the ground to communicate with ground stations.

At geosynchronous altitudes, a single global antenna could see the entire planet. Only one ground station was needed. But at five hundred kilometers of altitude, and circling the Earth every ninety minutes, how many ground stations might the SatCom network require?

The attackers might have taken over the GenCorp networks, but once they knew they were owned, the GenCorp sys admins would have ripped their servers apart.

Which meant that, logically, the attackers wouldn't have access to sending up signals to the satellites via the GenCorp ground stations. They would need their own.

It would take dozens of ground stations around the world to maintain continuous contact with that massive fleet of birds, and even then, it would be intermittent. If the attackers had only one or two ground stations, then it might take hours before Damon's query was returned.

A moment later, a message popped up on his screen. Satellites 128 to 256. Readings on their remaining fuel reserves.

Damon sent another request for readings on battery life. He expanded the request to satellites 0 to 1024. He paused before he pushed send. Exfiltrating data like this was usually the last process in a cyber kill chain. He was skipping a few steps, but he didn't have time.

Was it really a connection?

He clicked enter.

"I can use it as usual?" Senator Seymour asked.

He came around the corner into the kitchen from the living room. He was dressed in a fresh suit and tie and looked like he'd just gotten out of the shower.

Terek said, "Once you're connected to the meshnet of people nearby, you need to use that app. Voice calls for anyone directly connected, text messages to more distant nodes. You want me to get everyone on your staff connected?"

"Right away," the senator said. "And everyone on the Hill. This might be Washington, but the mobile networks aren't working here either."

"I'll get right on it, sir," Terek said.

One of the Secret Service agents had put on a new pot of java. The aroma of it filled the space. Damon needed another cup. His fifth? Maybe sixth. Probably seventh.

The senator headed for the coffee and poured himself one. "You boys ever going to sleep?"

Damon stared out the window at the rushing water below. He was tired.

"Beautiful, isn't it?" Senator Seymour mused. "That's the start of the Calico Rapids. You don't want to fall in there, but if you did, you know what you do?"

"Swim for shore?"

"Keep your toes up, keep them downriver of you."

"Excuse me, sir?"

"If you fall into rushing white water," the senator explained. "You get your feet up so they don't get trapped underwater. Eyes focused downstream and navigate. That's a good analogy for life." He laughed and slapped his leg.

"That is good advice, sir."

Damon didn't let on, but he remembered hearing the senator tell Mike the same thing earlier. He suspected this was a canned bit of folksy wisdom used on everyone who came to visit. Then again, it might be good advice for anyone who went for a walk out back. That was a steep slope.

The senator said, "Terek told me you got into GenCorp's systems. Is that true?"

"That is a very big 'maybe.' We have pingbacks from their servers, and we had one data request come back from a satellite, but it's too soon to say if we have actual access. They might be ghosting the signal, or spoofing a return, faking it like they did with those messages earlier to make it seem like things are normal."

"I'll connect you with some DOD people and you can compare notes, maybe talk to my team leaders." The senator put his coffee down. "This massive loss of orbital assets had sent the whole war machine into a tailspin. We're fighting fires on top of dumpster blazes in the middle of a chemical spill, if that's not too many metaphors. Our resources are stretched to breaking."

The mention of fires made Damon think of that young woman, Pauline. She kept creeping back into his thoughts when he should be thinking of more critical things.

"But that's not to say we don't have solutions," the senator said. "Work the problem, don't let the problem work you. We have a lot of smart people out there. The navy and army still have maps, and most systems are designed to work without GPS using inertial guidance, but everyone is scrambling. It's only been a bit more than a week we've been dealing with this, and two days since this announcement by the Islamic Brigade about the hijacking of the GenCorp assets."

"But someone at the DOD must have suspected?" Damon said.

"It was a hell of a smoke screen these bastards put up."

"Diversion, you mean?"

It was the same tactic someone would use in a cyberattack. Mount a denial-of-service attack on the server front end, keep the defensive team busy, then sneak a payload in through a covert channel on the back end.

Damon said, "Didn't anyone on your teams find a fail-safe on these things? Can't we shoot them down?"

"That would make the debris fields worse," Terek said.

"They're already doing something," the senator said. "This is the US military we're talking about."

"Brute force?" Damon said. "Jamming the hell out of them? Overwhelm the signal-to-noise ratio coming at their global antennas? Even if you can't get into the network, you can stop any communications."

"They've tried that. Doesn't seem to work." The senator paused as though considering whether to say anything more. He then added, "This is borderline classified, but we are already using directed energy weapons to take out the rogue birds. No debris. Turns them into orbiting slag."

"Lasers?"

"They picked off quite a few already. Listen, you boys have any more success on this, getting into those satellites, and there'll be Congressional Medals in it." He clapped Damon's shoulder. "We'll get you a Presidential one this time. I'll be back in a few hours. I'm leaving one of the Secret Service detail, George"—he nodded at the guy who had filled the coffee machine—"here. He'll take care of you. Susan is upstairs with the kids. Anything else you need?"

Seven a.m. and still nothing from the second request to the satellites.

The fact that Damon was getting pings seemed to indicate he had access to the GenCorp telemetry servers, which begged another question.

"Why wouldn't they have bricked all their servers?" Damon said to Terek. "I mean, the second you know you're hacked, that someone else has control of your servers—the first thing you do is deny access. Worst case, you unplug everything."

"Bricking" something, in hacker talk, meant turning it literally into a useless hunk of metal, an inert brick. Smashing with a hammer often accomplished the trick, but there were more subtle ways.

"You don't have physical access to satellites," Terek said. "Not once they're up there. Can't reach up and flick a physical switch to turn them off. But isn't that your super-secret project?" Terek yawned. "I think I'm going to hit the sack. Just for an hour."

Damon noticed Terek's hand going to his pocket.

Damon got up and went to the coffee pot. "I'll stay up, wait to hear from Mike and Chuck."

He turned to Terek, and without letting it look like he meant it, slopped hot coffee right onto Terek's midsection.

Terek yowled. "Oh my G—!" He hopped up and down.

Coffee spattered onto the marble floor. George, the Secret Service guy, offered to get napkins. Damon shook his head, apologized profusely to Terek, and attempted to sponge his jeans down with a tea cloth from the counter.

"You better go change," Damon said. "I'm sorry, I'm in a daze."

Terek shook his head, then walked off. Damon waited for him to leave before he looked in his hand. At the USB drive he'd stolen from Terek's pocket.

Chuck and Mike had to be at Virginia Beach by now.

He eyed the USB drive. Something else might be more critical right now.

Chapter 36

Water.

I hated the water.

A howling wind blew riffling waves across puddles on the road.

It was 9 a.m., but almost dark. The sun obscured behind a barrier of angry clouds stacked up like a churning cement wall over the North Atlantic. We parked the BullyBoy on South Atlantic Avenue, at the address Terek had sent us. Three- and four-story vacation homes on stilts, with garages on the ground floors, lined a street of broken pavement.

I said, "Sure we should park here?"

Chuck stopped us on a sandy stretch of sidewalk bordered by orange signs that warned there was no parking. That wasn't what I was worried about. To our right, over the public access bridge, surging gray waves thrashed the beach, pounding spray high into the air that the wind sucked over us in a salty mist.

I checked my phone. No messages. Which meant no data connection.

It was supposed to be a three-hour drive in from the senator's house, but we'd been stopped twice on the way around DC. We also made a stop at the entrance to the Naval Air Station Oceana and asked about civilians. The young man at the guard desk said that all civilians from air passenger aircraft had been discharged the day before.

I told him Lauren's name and asked if he could run it through the system, but he said there was no system to run it through. There was a mountain of papers, he said, but we would need authorization. Which would take time.

I asked if she could have been taken somewhere else.

The young man only said that we better get somewhere safe, because he thought a big storm was coming. He didn't have any more information than that.

He wasn't kidding.

A pounding roar as a wave hit the beach. Foamy spray catapulted into the air. On the last bridge crossing onto the barrier island of Virginia Beach itself, a few cars had been going the opposite direction, but none had been going the way we were. One car flashed their lights at us: *Are you crazy?*

"You sure this is the place?" Irena asked from the back.

Chuck replied, "Aqua Lane and Atlantic Avenue, right? Sound watery enough for you?"

Twisting and turning the last few blocks without access to GPS on our cell phones had been maddening. How many Atlantic Avenues were out here? I would have wagered a few dozen.

I held up my phone. On it was the image Terek found, the one with Lauren. A three-story house on stilts with white balconies in the background. It could have been almost any along this road. In all of Virginia Beach, to be honest.

Terek had found the image on the social media page of this woman named Emily Simmons. A quick look through other pictures on her profile and we found pictures of her in Hong Kong. She worked for American Airlines as a flight attendant. Made sense that she might have been on the same flight as Lauren.

Terek said he had set up a background process to look for facial recognition hits on Lauren, on the chance something was posted with her in it. He and Damon had collaborated on getting the process set up, but they didn't really expect it to work.

Until it did.

We tried calling Emily Simmons at a number Terek dug up, but no one answered. We checked her social media page again and again, but there were no new posts. We had no idea why she had taken a picture of herself with Lauren.

"Let's get out and have a look around," Agent Coleman said from the back.

I think he just wanted to get out of the back seat. He was a big man.

The gull-wing doors of the BullyBoy opened and I was greeted by a pelting rain that attacked horizontally. I stepped out of the truck.

Into ankle-deep water.

In the two minutes we'd sat in the car after Chuck parked it, an advancing front of water had streamed down the street from the south. The water surged across the road and into the lawns and thrashing palmettos of the houses across the street.

Red-brown clouds scudded overhead. The wind almost picked me up as I left the car.

"Which way?" I shouted to Chuck.

Agent Coleman stepped out behind me and leaned into the gale. Irena got out of the opposite side and held onto the door for balance.

"That way," Chuck called back over the wind. "Six-fifty to eight hundred Atlantic."

The range of addresses Terek had given us, his best estimate from the background of the picture of Lauren. In the middle of the row was a tall house with bright blue awnings over the windows. A grassy embankment ran up both sides to the first floor. Two-car garage on the bottom level.

"We go door to door?" I asked Agent Coleman.

"That is the plan."

He didn't seem optimistic. He kept glancing at the pounding surf. I couldn't stop watching it either. Another wave front rolled down the street and slopped against my ankles.

The wind picked up, and then, as if it was hitting its stride, really threw itself into gear. A fresh squall thundered into us. I stumbled back. Agent Coleman caught me.

"We go in pairs," he said. "One team to each side."

Bent almost double to stay stable in the wind, Chuck made his way toward me. "Look at that."

The tower of clouds moved in menacing slow-motion and rotated to the right as far as we could see into the rain-soaked distance. The gusting wind brought fat raindrops, pelting us like watery bullets. I shielded my face.

Chuck almost yelled in my ear, "Two weeks ago it was down in the West Indies. Ten miles per hour. Two weeks. That's got to be it."

"What's got to be what?" The water was at my ankles now.

The churning wall loomed. The sheer scale and lurking power the most awesome and terrifying thing I'd ever seen. Bits of paper and plastic blew past and ripped skyward. Lightning flashed in the foggy distance over the Atlantic.

Water streamed past as though we stood in a river, already as deep as the tops of my ankles. The crashing waves over the sand break crested ever higher. They seemed to be ten feet above me.

"We better hurry," I said breathlessly.

We crossed to the other side of the street to get out of the worst of the wind's fury. If Lauren had been here, there was no way she would stay, not looking at what we were looking at.

We hadn't received any warnings from Leo's staff or seen anything on TV, but then, nobody knew it was coming. Like when the big one hit Galveston a hundred years ago—nobody had any warning at all.

Chuck grabbed my shoulder. "You're not kidding, come on—"

"Hey," I said.

He shielded his eyes and tried to follow my hand as I pointed at a figure running from a house three doors down.

The three-story structure with bright blue awnings had a dish on top of it, like one of those old satellite receivers—but bigger, like the ones nobody used anymore that rusted on the top of sports bars. Except this one looked brand new, and very out of place.

The running figure glanced at our truck, then splashed away through the water toward a car parked under an awning. The hair. That awkward loping gait as the woman tried to break into a run. I'd know her anywhere.

Two men ran out of the house after her.

Lauren.

Chapter 37

D amon watched the bluebells dance back and forth. The brief calm of the early hours had shifted. The sun was up somewhere behind the clouds, and a fresh morning wind whipped the oaks and beeches, stripping away leaves in gusts that bent their branches.

A storm was coming.

His laptop pinged. It was a return response from the GenCorp systems.

Damon checked his clock. 9:14 a.m.

More than three hours since he'd sent the request. He was relieved he'd gotten a pingback, that the heart of data connection was still beating, no matter how slowly—but he was also confused and wary. Why was it so slow? What did it mean?

He opened the data packet attached to the message. Might as well have been opening a bomb. He cringed as he clicked. The key depressed and rebounded.

No explosion. Not even a beep.

But then that's exactly what would happen, even if he'd been compromised. He was running a clean UNIX shell that was sandboxed off from the rest of his system, memory, and processes, so he would wipe it clean—but still, with an adversary as sophisticated as one that could pull off the attack on GenCorp, anything was possible.

Expect the unexpected.

He opened a plain text file. A list of numbers from 0 to 128, with the corresponding percentages of remaining fuel for each of six thrusters. Several on the list returned with a logical fail, which meant, he guessed, that they weren't in contact. Destroyed or otherwise. Most of them were intact.

Could he send them commands? Not just data requests? He'd requested data from satellites 0 to 1024. Why had he only received data up to 128? And why had it taken so long?

He was sure it was related to the ground stations.

There was no way the attackers were using GenCorp's ground stations, which meant they must have their own. He couldn't imagine a bunch of hackers setting up a global network of physical ground stations, so there was...at least one? Maybe two or three?

With the satellites orbiting every ninety minutes, and the Earth rotating underneath them every twenty-four hours, and with ten thousand satellites, there would always be one overhead somewhere.

Sending commands to all those birds from one base station would take days or weeks. An idea flashed through his mind: But not if they were using satellite-to-satellite communications, and flying the constellation using only one or two points to relay commands to the rest of the fleet.

The SatCom network was one of the first to use lasers to communicate directly between birds, flying in formations. If you extended the formation to all ten thousand, then you'd only need to communicate with one of them. That would explain why trying to overwhelm the antennas with radio jamming didn't seem to affect their ability to operate, if they were talking to each other optically.

The constellation was operating semiautonomously. Exactly his specialty. But what to do?

And where the hell was Mike?

Damon sent another message to them, passing a high-priority request into the meshnet. A second later, a return message appeared from Mike: *We just arrived and parked.*

Good. At least they were safe.

The meshnet had found a path to connect them, but the bandwidth was sketchy. He checked the connection. Someone had left their Wi-Fi connection open, without a password. A home somewhere on Atlantic Avenue.

He flexed his fingers over the keyboard.

Usually a hack like this required moving with slug-like pace, but that wasn't in the cards if he wanted to win the hand. Not only win the hand, but take the pot. Part of him wanted to contact the senator, but to say what, exactly? Bring in the cavalry, horns blaring and guns blazing?

That might trigger some other set of uncontrolled responses, which would spook the Russian team that had provided the hack in the first place. They were more terrified of the Chechens than anything else. The connection to the hackers was already tenuous.

He balled his fists.

Another ping on his computer. This one had a different alarm. "Sonofa—"

A window popped up on his screen, a newly spawned UNIX shell and command line. Text began scrolling across his screen, but it wasn't Damon typing. It was Terek, who was supposed to be sleeping upstairs.

Obviously, he wasn't.

Unless he sleep-typed.

When Damon had spilled the coffee on Terek, he slipped a hand into his friend's pocket to extract the suspicious USB stick he'd seen Terek using from time to time. Terek was fumbling with it, and when Damon splashed the scalding hot joe on him, Terek's hand shot out of his pocket, predictably.

Damon patted him down, pretending to help him dry his pants, and took the USB key.

No matter how good your cyber perimeter might be, there was always the danger of a physical attack, like someone stealing something. Like a trusted friend spilling coffee on you and lifting something from your pocket when you were half-asleep. Damon had checked the USB stick as soon as Terek had gone upstairs.

It was a boot disk. Not really suspicious by itself.

It wasn't unusual for someone like them to use a "live CD" image of a fresh operating system on a memory key, which was what was on it. It was a common way to log into networks anonymously, going from there into a Tor router from a public network access point. The thing that troubled Damon was the way that Terek seemed to keep it hidden.

So Damon installed a lightweight keystroke logger called Asciinema.

Then he left the USB stick on the floor under Terek's chair. His friend came downstairs in a fresh set of jeans, made like he was coming to get some more coffee, and leaned over and picked up the USB stick. He glanced at Damon as he did it, but Damon had ignored him.

Damon watched the stream of terminal commands and waited. Everything was being recorded. Terek logged off after a few seconds. Damon went to work. Using Terek's credentials, he opened a link to the dark site his friend had just been in. It was an HDFS interface, a common big data file system.

He had to be quick.

Damon scanned through a few tabs, clicked a link, and downloaded a data file. He logged off, then opened the file in a new instance of UNIX he started up, in case something malicious was in there.

A text file spread across his screen. Damon frowned and tried to decipher it. It looked like phone calls. Text messages. Data from a telco?

His stomach turned over in a lurch.

Not a telco.

This was data siphoned from Damon's meshnet app. Not Damon's own data, but a random snippet of data from any of the thousands of people who had connected using the app Damon had made available, or more accurately, that Terek had been making available on Damon's behalf.

The room felt like it was sinking around him.

Data sent over the meshnet was encrypted end-to-end, but as one of the administrators of the new system, Terek had access to the keys. He had set up what looked like a backup, which was really siphoning data out.

Was this why his friend was so connected to the Russian hackers? Was Terek part of the hacker collective? That was forgivable, depending on the nature of what the group was up to, but why wouldn't his friend have told him? Why the subterfuge?

But then there was another possibility.

Something tickled the back of his mind. That painful but disturbing feeling when he knew he'd missed something but didn't know what it was. What...was…?

He shut down all the UNIX terminals, started his PC, and then opened his email to look at the picture of Lauren Terek had found.

Was Terek connected to the woman who'd taken the photo of Lauren, a flight attendant named Emily Simmons? The lady had beautiful red hair and a red-white-and-blue kerchief around her neck. In the picture, behind Lauren and Emily, was a blue building with bright blue awnings.

He looked closer. There. A satellite dish just visible on the roof.

What the hell—

"Everything okay?"

Terek sat down beside him.

Damon blinked. "Yeah, um, I'm...I'm looking at that picture of Lauren."

"Have you heard from them?"

"Did you get a good sleep?"

"Like a log."

Little footsteps pounded downstairs in a flurry, and a second later Luke came rocketing into the kitchen and launched himself into Terek's lap. The Ukrainian tousled his hair.

"What?" Terek said to Damon. "You look like you've seen a ghost." He glanced behind himself, then rotated his eyes up in their sockets. "Is there something in my hair?"

Luke squirmed out of Terek's arms and gave Damon a high five.

A voice began talking in monotone in the next room. Someone had turned on the TV. Damon heard snippets about food lines and fighting in the metro DC area.

"Hi boys, I just wanted to tell you we're going out," said a woman's voice. Mrs. Seymour appeared, with Olivia in her arms. "Going to take the kids for a walk before the rain starts."

"That's a good idea," Damon said. "Take the Secret Service guy with you?" He still couldn't remember their names. He was terrible with them. Worse when he was under stress.

"Name's Dunbar, but you can call me George," the man said from around the corner.

Mrs. Seymour said, "You think we need to?"

Damon looked at Terek and then back at her. "I think you should."

Chapter 38

Lauren splashed across the street through the calf-deep water, the shower curtain rod in her hand. She didn't have much of a lead. She glanced behind her.

Someone opened the door of the blue house. A man came onto the patio and yelled. It was Billy, who told her to come back, his voice muted by the blasting wind shaking the palmettos. Another man came out and ran straight down the stairs.

She almost stopped in her tracks.

But it wasn't her pursuers that gave her pause.

A colossal wall of clouds rotated high overhead. It engulfed the sky from horizon to horizon. A blast of wind staggered her. She turned.

And ran.

Or tried to.

Wedges and slacks weren't the best outdoors escape outfit, not in driving rain and gale force winds. Bending over, she hopped from one foot to the other in the water. She pulled off her shoes and held them in the hand not gripping the metal rod.

Barefoot would be faster.

She stole another look behind her. The two men were already in the water. They both turned to gawk at the clouds.

"Help," she called to anyone that might hear, and waved her wedges over her head.

Both men turned toward her.

The pelting rain intensified into a sleeting downpour.

She turned and danced through the water as fast as she could. She scanned the street, hoping someone would be out here, someone driving down the street, maybe packing their car—but realized that everyone with any sense would be gone by now.

Maybe not everybody.

Two hundred feet to her left was a huge steel truck. She thought of making for it, but she didn't see anyone near it. It didn't look like the kind of thing someone would leave the keys in. And going that way that would take her across the path of the men behind her.

In the parking area of the stilt-house across the street was an old sedan. Maybe there were people still in the house? Maybe there were keys in the car?

High-stepping through the water, she sprinted fifty feet and splashed to a stop, slamming into the side of the car. Switching her shoes to the hand holding the metal bar, she tried the driver's side. Locked. Passenger side handle. Nothing.

Damn it.

She took two loping, sloshing steps over the water-covered cement to the downstairs door of the house. It was locked as well. She banged on the door. She heard splashing. Someone running toward her. She dropped her shoes, gripped the shower rod like a baseball bat, leaned her back against the wall, and gritted her teeth.

A head appeared.

She swung.

"Lauren!" I hollered as I rounded the corner.

Something flickered in my vision. I automatically leaned back and away. A long, thin bar grazed my temple and whacked into the aluminum siding of the vacation home's wall behind me.

The glancing blow and my attempt to get out of the way toppled me sideways. I splayed face-first into water not quite deep enough to absorb the impact of my forty-something body as I slammed into the concrete slab of the parking garage. I felt my ankle turn, thudded awkwardly onto an elbow, and grazed the skin off my right palm.

But I didn't feel a thing.

Seeing my wife's face uncorked a surge of adrenaline into my bloodstream that felt like fireworks being set off in my veins. Even if she was trying to smash my head in. I rebounded off the concrete like rubber and spun around to face her.

There she stood, legs planted apart and knees bent, just like I'd told her to do when she wanted to crack a softball hard as possible. The index finger of her bottom hand slightly apart from the other fingers, her knuckles in line with the bar.

Perfect form.

She was beautiful. Her long hair was soaked in strands and whipping in the wind, her silk blouse stuck to her body. She was in gray slacks. A cork-soled wedge shoe floated by in front of her.

"Where are the kids?" Lauren took a step toward me, the metal bar still cocked.

I love you too. "They're...I stopped at..." I limped and staggered like a drunk in the buffeting wind. "They're fine. Safe. What the hell are you doing here?"

"You look terrible. What happened to your face?"

"It's a long story. We don't have time."

"Are you alone?"

The wind gusted again and pushed me sideways. It whipped tiny waves across the water pooling in the parking structure. At least we were protected from the hammering downpour. A palmetto frond skittered by and stuck to me. "I'm with Chuck."

She lowered the metal bar. "There are men, they took me. Mike, they're coming." She pointed behind her. "Do you have a gun?"

I shook my head.

Her look of incredulity momentarily eclipsed the growing roar of the hurricane. "You're with *Chuck* and you don't have a *gun?*"

"You know how I feel about guns."

She threw her hands up in disbelief. "But Mike, there are times…"

Were we really about to have an argument right now? My phone pinged in my pocket. "Look, I'm sorry, but we need to go," I said. "That's our—"

"Do not move," said a voice, loud enough to be heard over the wind.

A man stood twenty feet behind Lauren, his feet apart, his arms up, and his handgun leveled at us. He stepped through a waterfall of rain slicking down from the side of the building and into the parking structure. He had short black hair and a tattoo of a rose on his neck, small ears that stood out, and was dressed in tight-fitting camouflage top and bottom. He was slim. No taller than five-six.

I stepped by Lauren. Stood between her and the man. I held my hands out, palms toward him. "What do you want?"

He kept his gun trained on my chest and walked toward me. "Get down on your knees, hands in the air."

Another man, much bulkier, splashed through the deluge twenty feet behind him. The wind howled.

I shouted again, "What do you want?"

"Get down, or I will—"

"Hey," yelled someone to my left.

The rose-tattoo-neck guy kept his gun trained on me, but looked right. Chuck crouched over the hood of the car Lauren had tried to get into, a gun pointed at the guy. A deafening crack echoed.

The small man staggered sideways.

Another crack and glass shattered. The bigger man came splashing through the rain, his gun out. He fired again.

I roared, put my head down, and charged at the smaller guy with the tattoo.

I had never been a fighter, and probably couldn't punch my way out of a paper bag, but when someone pointed a gun at my wife? I slammed into the guy as hard as I could, making sure to stay low and away from the gun in his hand. We fell together onto the cement, the water pancaking away from us.

What was my plan?

I had no plan.

Only blind rage.

I took him by surprise, but he spun with panther-like reflexes and slid his legs around my torso as I tried to jam my hands in his face. His legs gripped my midsection and he used the leverage to slam the butt of the gun against the side of my head. The blow stunned me. I slumped sideways, my fingers grappling at the slick, tight fabric of his camouflage top.

Didn't Chuck just shoot this guy?

Two more gunshots. The cracks echoed in the closed space of the garage.

"Get the hell off my husband!" Lauren screamed.

She swung the metal bar, and must have caught him because his grip on me went slack. But only for an instant. I saw him bring his gun up.

I used the only move I knew.

The one Chuck had taught me.

I punched the guy as hard as I could, straight in the throat, and directed every ounce of fury I had at the man who had kidnapped the mother of my children. The effect was satisfyingly immediate.

His eyes went wide. Hands flew to his neck.

Lauren fell on top of him, pinning the hand with the gun to the floor. I rotated back on top of him as well and pushed his face sideways and down, under six inches of water. A savage thought surfaced—we just had to lie on top of his head and we could drown the bastard.

"Billy, you goddamn asshole, she was pregnant!" Lauren yelled.

"Billy?" I strained to hold his head down. "Who's pregnant? You?"

Lauren shoved her elbow into the side of his head while she kept her knee on the arm holding the gun. "Not me," she grunted.

I threw my weight on top of him.

Another gunshot rang out. Then another.

I ducked involuntarily and looked up from our squirming, gagging prey to see the big guy that had come behind this one. He staggered back, then crumpled to one knee. He fired his gun again, but the shot went wild and hit the ceiling of the parking structure.

Chuck stood twenty feet to my left, his weapon out and steady and trained on the guy.

"Put it down," said another voice.

My excitement drained into the water around my knees. Two more burly men with short-cropped hair, dressed entirely in camouflage, stepped in from the rain. They didn't have handguns, but bigger, meaner-looking weapons they held against their shoulders.

"Not so fast."

A fresh surge of adrenaline hit my veins with renewed enthusiasm. Agent Coleman appeared through the downpour behind the two men, his own semiautomatic weapon raised and pointed chest high. The men quick-checked behind themselves, looked at us, and then back at Agent Coleman. He shook his head, *don't try it*, the small but unmistakable gesture communicated.

They began to raise their arms, and had them halfway up just as two more figures emerged from the driving rain.

One of them was Irena, her hands held high.

A man in black had one forearm wrapped around her neck. The other hand held a gun point-blank against her temple.

Chapter 39

T he wind outside the kitchen patio doors whistled.

Damon blinked and looked away from Terek. "You want another coffee?"

"I'll think I'll get it myself."

"You sure?" *Don't gawk, close your mouth*, Damon instructed himself. *Act normal.* Damon grinned. Or did his best to.

Terek went to the coffee pot on the marble kitchen counter. He reached for a cup, which was right next to a large wooden block of knives. Damon's eyes followed his friend's hand as it passed the blades and picked up the cup, then filled it from the pot.

"Looks like we're here all alone." Terek smiled and took a sip.

Was that a friendly smile, or a menacing one? Wind howled beyond the glass. The house suddenly felt massive and empty.

What did Terek go upstairs to get?

Damon scanned the pockets of his friend's jeans, looked for anything that might be a gun or weapon. Did he know yet? That Damon knew he knew about him? But what exactly did he know?

What was going on?

The skin on Damon's exposed arms prickled as his friend took another sip of his coffee and smiled.

That lopsided grin, the big mop of unruly brown hair, the puppy dog eyes, the constant mimicking and questioning. Like the younger brother Damon never had. But were the boyish looks a sheep's cloak, concealing a predator?

Damon needed to get in touch with Mike and Chuck. Tell them something wasn't right with Terek. What about Irena? Was she involved? Damon didn't know more than that Terek was stealing data from the meshnet app—but that meant he was also monitoring the messages on it.

Or could be.

Probably was.

If he was, he would certainly be monitoring any messages from Damon to his friends.

Terek asked, "You okay?"

He sat down across the table, at his usual spot.

Damon eyed the cable connecting their computers, the umbilical cord between twins that he'd become so used to. He wanted to rip it out, guts attached, but he said lightly, "How's your wife? Not going to call her?"

"She's fine. I just messaged her from my other laptop. Did you get a pingback from the GenCorp satellites?"

Quiet for two heartbeats.

"Yeah, I did."

"You going to share?"

"Gimme a second."

Terek asked casually, "Do you have the latest data from the Space Surveillance Network?"

"Not yet."

Damon glanced at that cable again. Blood could flow both ways through an umbilical cord.

He angled his screen away from Terek and opened a new sandboxed UNIX terminal. If Terek knew already, then it wouldn't matter, but if he didn't—Damon didn't have much time.

Damon's fingers danced over the keyboard, their quick drumming earning his friend's curiosity.

Terek's eyebrows raised. "Writing me a novel?"

"Finishing an email. I'll send you the data file we got back from the GenCorp satellite."

The hack was quick and dirty but should do the trick. He attached a small payload exploit to the text file, which he'd converted to PDF. His finger hovered over the send button.

He looked up at Terek.

This was too obvious.

Why would the text file arrive in a PDF? That would raise flags to anyone, even if they were absolutely trusted. Stupid idea.

If Terek was up to something, he would be on alert for anything unusual, and the USB "accidentally" falling onto the floor already qualified. He needed to get something onto Terek's machine in a way that wouldn't be suspicious, dangle something of value that he would take apart. This wasn't good enough.

Damon deleted the file, attached the uncorrupted text file, and pushed send.

Terek's machine pinged.

"It's strange how there's such a long delay," Damon said.

What was Terek up to? Damon needed to buy some time. Why would his friend be doing this?

When he asked about Terek's wife, did Damon detect tension? Had something happened to her? Was somebody coercing him into this?

He couldn't imagine Terek betraying him.

Damon wasn't sure if his friend—if he could still call him that—was just being an inveterate hacker, unable to resist the opportunity to smash and grab data. He realized he really didn't know this person. Chuck was right. Damon had barely questioned how and why Terek had connections to a Russian hacking group that had access to the GenCorp network.

"You have any theories?" Terek took another sip of his coffee. "About what?"

"How they're controlling the satellites."

Damon stopped typing and sat up in his chair. "I do, actually."

Terek put down his coffee with his right hand. "I'm listening."

"I think they disconnected the entire constellation from ground control, and then rewired them so they're using the satellite-to-satellite laser link."

"All ten thousand?"

"I think they made it one big cluster."

Damon watched Terek's eyes.

His friend glanced up and left. Neurolinguistic programming theories of the mind said that when right-handed people looked up and right when they thought about something, it was an unconscious reaction as they searched for a constructed memory. A lie, in other words.

But up and left?

That was something remembered.

Terek looked up and left. "Interesting. Go on."

"That's why they can't overload the signal-to-noise ratio and disable those satellites by jamming them. There's only one, or maybe a few, that still communicate to the ground. And I bet they added a new control condition for security, a specific ground coordinate."

His friend looked up and left again, and grabbed his coffee with his right hand.

Then again, the latest update Damon had read said that neurolinguistic programming might be a load of garbage. What did his instincts tell him? That painful knot twisting in the pit of his gut?

Then another thought.

Gibberish.

Terek was monitoring the meshnet, and there was no quick way to block him without raising suspicion. Damon could switch encryption keys, but this might make Terek take some other unknown defensive action.

If Damon wanted to keep any kind of advantage, he needed to communicate in the clear with Mike—with the full knowledge that an adversary was reading the messages.

A voice broke the silence. "Reports coming in now that Hurricane Dolly has made landfall on the Virginia coast."

Wind lashed the palm trees and heaved foaming brown waves against a cement seawall. The images were vertical, the videos taken on someone's cell phone and then uploaded over the internet. With no satellites and no mobile, the networks weren't able to get a camera crew out there.

The CNN announcer said, "The weather services lost track of the storm as it headed out over the Atlantic more than a week ago. They believed that Dolly had played itself out."

"Did you get in touch with them?" Terek asked.

"Just that they arrived," Damon replied.

"Nothing since then?"

Damon shook his head. No, nothing since then. Was it the storm, or had something else happened?

Terek had found the picture of Lauren, and then matched it to images of that area. At the time, it had seemed ingenious, but now it seemed a little too clever. Too quick. Had he fabricated the images? Was that possible? Had he sent Mike and Chuck out to the coast? Did he know the storm was coming?

A 3D computer-generated view of the East Coast appeared on the screen, with a TV presenter standing in the middle of a swirling mass offshore. "Doppler radar has been tracking the storm front as it approached the coast, but only in the past few hours has the magnitude become apparent. Hurricane Hunter aircraft were dispatched from Tampa early this morning and are now returning—"

"I hope they're okay," Terek said.

"Me too," Damon mumbled.

"With eyewall wind speeds approaching 180 miles per hour and 880 millibars of pressure, this hurricane has been fueled by the unusually hot temperatures through September that have also fed the fires in Appalachia," the announcer said. "A complete evacuation of the Virginia and Maryland coast has been ordered, but without much warning and without mobile emergency alert systems, there's not much that can be done to get people—"

"Unbelievable," Terek said.

Damon stared at the person he'd thought was his friend. It was unbelievable. What about that big dish in the picture of Lauren? Could that be used as a ground station? How many coincidences before the unbelievable became believable?

The CNN announcer said, "The hurricane is making landfall now. As this coincides with high tide, meteorologists are predicting a fourteen-foot storm surge."

"Nothing we can do," Terek said. "We better get back to it." He turned and headed to the kitchen.

Nothing we can do? It seemed an odd turn of phrase when you had just sent your sister into the teeth of a monster storm.

Damon checked his phone. No more return messages from Mike since the one saying they'd arrived, despite two more that Damon had sent out.

The TV switched to another image, this one grainy and filled with confused, jumbled waves crashing into each other. "Here we have a webcam on the Virginia Pier," the announcer said.

Damon turned on his heel and followed Terek.

Webcam.

He reached the kitchen table and turned his laptop screen away from Terek, then opened a trace on the meshnet app. He found the router in the house near Atlantic Avenue. He logged in.

Damon stared at his screen.

"Did you hear from them? Mike? Chuck?" Terek asked again.

"No," Damon replied.

He hadn't heard from them, but that didn't mean he didn't know what was happening.

On Damon's screen. A pixelated image. Rain sluiced across a glass pane. The picture was from the BullyBoy's dash cam. In the distance he could make out a group of people walking through knee-deep water.

Damon looked up from his laptop at Terek—to make sure he didn't get up—but he appeared to be lost in work on his own screen. Damon looked back at the image.

Two women with their arms held out in front of them, bending their bodies into the wind. A group of men behind them. The image was grainy, but he would recognize those guys anywhere—Mike and Chuck.

With four other men behind them, holding assault rifles.

"*Damn it*," Damon whispered.

"What?"

"Nothing."

What could he do? Nothing from here.

But there *was* something he could do.

Hundreds of millions of people might suffer, maybe even starve, if they couldn't stop the destruction in orbit.

He eyed the cable connecting him to Terek.

"I just got the Space Surveillance Network data," Damon said.

"Why did you say *damn it*, then? Isn't that a good thing? Send it over."

"It's encrypted. Classified."

Terek sat up. "Oh yeah? Why?"

"Has military satellite locations on it. I can't share it."

"Send me a copy? Maybe scrub it?"

"I better not. This is classified. My eyes only. I'm secret-rated."

"Seriously? At a time like this? What am I going to do with it?"

"We're in a senator's house. They send people to jail for disclosing stuff like this."

In the image in the video, the short man behind Mike shoved him with his rifle muzzle. *Asshole*. Another of the men started wading through the water toward the truck.

Damon had to hurry, whatever he was going to do.

There was still a spotty connection to Mike's phone, even if his friend wasn't able to answer it. Which meant he had access to more than only this camera and microphone.

His earlier idea resurfaced. He hoped Mike would remember. Mike *better* remember. Who could forget Egglish?

Chapter 40

I gritted my teeth and leaned into the onslaught.

The churning wall of cloud had enveloped the coast and submerged the streets into a boiling twilight.

The teeth of the raging animal closed around us. The frenzy transformed from something simply atmospheric into a wild beast that ripped at my face and skin and spat spray in blinding sheets as we were force-marched through the knee-deep water.

Waves rolled over the sand embankment. Foam spilled into the street.

I held one hand out and squinted to battle the stinging spray.

"Lauren," I shouted, "are you okay?" I staggered back in a blast but felt the sharp jab of a rifle muzzle in my back.

"Keep moving," said the neck-tattoo guy Lauren had called Billy. He kept step behind us.

"Hey," he shouted to one of his men, "someone go get into that truck they came in."

The man asked, "Are there any more of them?"

Tattoo-Billy shook his head.

My wife waved a hand at me and held it out.

I tried to grab it but fell forward. I'd twisted my ankle in that scuffle, and more than that, I had pain in my ribs, my elbow, and my face, where Tattoo-Billy had punched me after I'd gotten up off him. My face was numb where he'd hit me, my mind off-kilter, my senses wobbly.

Climbing a set of stairs at work usually got me out of breath, but a dragged-out fistfight followed by fighting a hurricane? Despite the wind hammering me, it felt like nothing came into my lungs. I sucked air, my chest burning, my eyes stinging. Five more minutes of this and they would have to carry me feet-first through the door.

More likely, they would let me drift off into the raging surf. I made sure to keep my balance and planted one foot in front of the other.

Every now and then, I glanced behind me.

Tattoo-Billy might have been small, but the guy looked unperturbed by the roaring squalls that almost tipped me over. His eyes straight ahead, grim, his face streaked with blood from the head wound Lauren had inflicted.

With a clattering squeak, bits of aluminum siding ripped free from the house next door. The strips of metal cartwheeled in the air, joined by shingles and palm fronds and anything else the wind could dislodge or pick up and turn into projectiles.

Chuck and Agent Coleman made better progress. They were fifty feet ahead, at the edge of the two-car garage. On the next street, I now saw an eighteen-wheeler semi-truck with its back doors open. Men were stacking boxes inside it and closing the doors. The deep growl of the truck's engine was audible over the wind's howl.

"Did they hurt you?" I yelled to Lauren.

"How did you get here?"

"Came to rescue you."

Despite the lashing wind and the men at our backs with guns, she managed a grim smile. "I assume there's a cavalry coming?"

The rifle muzzle poked my ribs again. "No speaking," Tattoo-Billy said.

That accent. Was it Chechen? It sounded Russian, but then Chechens were Russians, right? My mind tried to follow a thread as it was beaten by merciless hammering wind. Why on Earth would satellite-attacking Chechen terrorists want anything to do with my family?

Satellites.

The only connection was through Damon, but it was a solid one. His secret project at MIT involved the military. Drone satellites or something. He never seemed able to be more specific and I never asked him to be.

What did they want with him? And how were they getting it? I answered my own question: They were using Terek to gain access to Damon's networks. Maybe the satellite position data?

Which meant they had been planning this a long time.

I glanced over my shoulder at Irena, who brought up the rear. The right side of her face was swollen from the blow she'd taken to her face. She kept her hands up. Another man walked behind her with a gun.

We advanced up the driveway and out of the water.

The doors of the large two-car garage were now open. One Humvee in each bay. A procession of men in camo loaded black crates into the backs.

I heard snippets of words, things I thought were in another language. The men talking saw me looking at them, and one hissed, "English," under his breath, too low for him to have assumed I could hear it.

They kept talking, this time in a language an American could understand, about how the wind had ruined the operation. No, said, another, they just needed another location, that it shortened up the timeline.

Behind me, Tattoo-Billy gave me another poke in the ribs.

"Shut up," he said to the two men, and indicated a staircase for me to climb.

The wind screamed up another notch.

Sopping wet, the five of us stood in the middle of the forty-by-forty open main room of the vacation rental. Lauren was next to me, Chuck and Agent Coleman ten feet away with their hands behind their heads. A beaten-looking Irena held a blood-red towel to her swollen face.

I was sure whoever was renting this place out wouldn't be thrilled about twenty Chechen freedom fighters as guests. That was about how many men I counted. Airbnb had restrictions on parties, but from now on, military operations should be added as a banned activity as well.

These guys were definitely not getting their insurance deposit back. They had drilled holes into the faux-old wooden floors across the open area for their computer racks, which they were now in the process of dismantling.

My phone pinged in my pocket, but with my hands up, I wasn't about to try and retrieve it. These guys seemed trigger-itchy already. It had to be Damon, asking us where we were.

A blast of wind buffeted the structure. I was sure the roof would suddenly rip off and reveal a maelstrom beyond.

The ceiling was twenty feet high and sloped with the roof to the apex. There were no windows, except skylights and high slits at the tops of the walls. Perfect if you didn't want to let people see in. There was a second-floor mezzanine with three open doors. Men were moving equipment out of them. The rooms looked like they would make perfect offices. A command center.

"Billy, we need to move, right now," said a man coming down the stairs. He held stacks of papers.

Lauren said, "What's your real name?"

"Tie them up," Billy instructed.

Why did they keep speaking English to each other?

"What do you want?" Agent Coleman growled. "You're not getting away with this. You're not getting any of those prisoners you asked for. You think our government negotiates with terrorists? You think we're bad? Wait till the Russians catch up to you, then you'll be—"

Billy jabbed him in the kidney with the butt of his rifle. "Millions of you pigs will die, then," he said, as if reciting lines from a bad movie.

He took Agent Coleman's wallet from his jacket pocket. "This is the one that is Secret Service. We don't need to tie him. Shoot him now."

Agent Coleman cringed, but said, "Screw you."

I held my hands up. "Seriously, no, no, what do you want?"

My phone pinged again in my pocket. I almost wanted to yell, not now, Damon.

"We only need you and you." Billy pointed his rifle at Lauren, then me. "Maybe her"—he pointed at Irena—"and the other one. Bring her in."

The other one?

The two men behind Chuck and Agent Coleman moved them toward a wall. Chuck looked like he was ready to jump on them, hell be damned. I shook my head, saying, no, don't do it. He shrugged: What the heck else should we do?

Why didn't they seem surprised we had a Secret Service agent with us?

"There are more of him coming," I said, pointing at Agent Coleman. "They know everything about this. We were coming to try and stop any bloodshed."

Billy laughed. "So we're surrounded? That's what you're saying? You think this is a movie?"

"My uncle is a United States Senator on the Armed Services Committee. He knows where we came. I guarantee we got a couple of Ospreys headed this way."

"We know all about your senator. The 'president pro tem' of the Senate, yes? A very important man. I believe he is your wife's uncle?" Billy laughed. "And yes, that college kid who found our location? He is very smart and good, no? Very clever, I agree."

The way he said it made my heart sink.

His accent had changed from something American to something else. A painful hole tore right through me as I realized that it had been way too easy to find Lauren. Terek's sleuthing had seemed brilliant at the time, but he was obviously with them, somehow, for some reason. I glanced at his sister, bloodied and bruised.

This had been a trap from start to finish. But why? Why us?

The big man who had gone downstairs, the one urging Billy to hurry up, reappeared from the basement. "It took them longer to get here than we planned. We need to hurry. Get ahead of the storm if we're going to get out of here."

It took us longer than they thought? So they'd been waiting for us. And the other thing he'd said—*ahead* of the storm?

I glanced out the window at a palm tree bending sideways. This wasn't as bad as it would get?

Through the kitchen patio doors, the only glass I could see through at this level, a gray wave slid by and water seeped through the bottom of the closed door. We were one floor up. The waves were already breaching the seawalls.

The big man picked up the last crate. "The truck is leaving now. The water is already three feet in the street. The Humvees need to go as well." Outside, I heard the revving of the semi-truck's engine over the battering wind.

My phone pinged again and again and again.

"Get off me!" A woman shrieked and struggled as two men forced her down the stairs from one of the offices.

"Katerina?" Irena said immediately. "Is that you?"

"Irena," the woman said. "Oh my God. Why?"

"Did they hurt you?"

Katerina answered, "I'm fine. Is Terek here? What is happening?"

I stood, openmouthed for a second. "That's Terek's wife?"

"The four of them, downstairs." Billy pointed at me, Lauren, Irena, and then Katerina. "We head into Washington"—he looked at me— "and we use your senator's special documents to get through checkpoints. Yes? You have them?"

"I don't know where I—"

"But you do know where your children are, correct?"

A gut-sinking realization drained the blood from my limbs.

Lauren said, "Mike, where are the kids?"

Terek. At the senator's house. How many other people did they have? There was security there, the Secret Service. Wasn't much comfort. These guys seemed to know everything.

"You will be as creative as you need to be," Billy said. "But you will get us to Senator Seymour's residence, and through all the security checks, with that pass you have."

"And you expect to waltz into a high-security compound?" I asked.

"You let me worry about that." Billy pointed at Chuck and Agent Coleman. "Those two, shoot them. We don't have room or time."

They shoved Chuck and Agent Coleman away from us, toward the front wall. Chuck's face twisted in something between fear and rage. My phone pinged again and again.

Billy picked it from the pocket of my jeans, checked it, then held it up to me. "What does 'getet ega wegay' mean?"

I stared at my cell phone's screen. Gibberish filled one text message after another. *Gibberish.* My old brain struggled to remember the new trick.

The whole message read, "Geget ega wegy fregom wegall."

Egglish.

Remove "eg" from the first syllables of each word, or before vowels of words that started with them.

Geget—*Get.*

Ega wegay—*Away.*

Fregom—*From.*

Wegall—*Wall.*

Billy had never used pig latin in English as a child, apparently. Then again, Billy never spoke English as a kid in Chechnya, I would have wagered.

"I have no idea," I replied. "It's nonsense."

Geget ega wegy fregom wegall. Geget ega wegy fregom wegall. The gibberish-encoded text messages scrolled down my phone's screen.

Which wall? Get away from which wall? There were four of them around us. Was a SWAT team about to come swinging in through the skylights?

Billy crouched. Realized I'd lied. His eyes followed mine.

From the corner of my eye, I saw a flash of light. I held my hand in front of Lauren.

Chapter 41

Damon stuck his wireless earbuds in, whistled a Green Day tune, and tried to act like nothing was happening. His heart pounded in his ears. From the corner of his eye, he watched Terek munch on a banana muffin and take another gulp of his coffee.

Staying out of sight of the house Mike had been taken into, Damon navigated the BullyBoy up an embankment three houses down onto a sandy outcropping being pounded by swells coming in from the roaring Atlantic. The seven-thousand-pound truck almost lifted into the air as it went sideways to the gale. He drove it through bumps and dips in the dunes of seagrass already foaming with water.

He focused most of his attention on three other screens. He had activated the cameras in Mike, Chuck, and Irena's phones through the meshnet connected to the Wi-Fi he found. The images coming in from the three cameras were dark. All still in pockets, but nobody had smashed them yet.

He patched the microphones through to his earbuds.

A lot of noise, but he clearly heard Mike say, "…are more of them coming."

Another voice, unfamiliar, said, "…other two, shoot them…"

If these attackers wanted to kill all of them, they would have done it. Which meant they wanted some of them—Mike? Lauren?—for something. This gave Damon a small window.

He needed to get an idea of who was where. He had already pulled an old map app image of the area from the web and isolated the house. He found the vacation rental page for it and scanned the interior pictures. A main room, about forty by forty, with a mezzanine. A stairwell down to the garage by the kitchen patio door.

The patio door looked like the best point of entry. The sandy embankment led straight into it.

Someone, please, pick up your damn phone. Even if only to throw it on the ground.

He pushed send on the message to Mike. Then sent it again. And again. He heard the pinging noise through the microphones. That must be getting someone's attention.

Mike's camera image came to life.

A face. A man with a tattoo on his neck. The image swept in a circle and faced Mike, whose lips began moving, mouthing the letters of the message.

Damon paused the image recording, checked that Terek was still busy on his laptop, and then expanded the picture until it filled the screen. He scrolled back in slow motion.

Three men by the wall with guns. That was Irena in front of them, her hands up. Two more men behind the tattoo guy. Lauren was behind and to the side of Mike. Chuck and the secret service guy behind them. Two more men in the middle of the room with guns.

He closed his eyes.

Time slowed down.

He visualized the room in three dimensions. The future. He just needed to control a small part of this future.

The easiest path forward was straight through the middle. That would hit the two men in the middle of the room and put a barricade between his friends and the other men with guns.

His fingers were already sweeping across his touchpad, controlling the truck. He opened his eyes, managed a last fix on the light coming through the patio door, and accelerated the truck at a forty-degree angle to the wall. As soon as it hit, he slammed on the brakes and set the right-side door to open.

The truck was a beast.

Even at four tons, the thing could go zero to sixty in four seconds.

The truck crashed through the wall. In his earphones, he heard muted pops and cracks, which he initially mistook for interference, until he understood it was gunfire.

They were firing at the truck, right?

The attackers didn't know there wasn't anyone inside—or anyone else coming from outside, for that matter. That should give his friends a few seconds edge.

His heart came up into his throat.

He caught a glimpse of Mike, and then the screen went blank.

Terek was up and out of his seat. His face blank, eyes wide. As if he was terrified. His mouth opened and closed, but Damon couldn't hear him.

He took out his noise-canceling earbuds.

"What's wrong?" Damon asked.

Had Terek just witnessed the same thing he had, but from a different camera? Were they fighting on opposite sides of the skirmish? Was that why he was up out of his chair? Damon looked for a knife, a gun. He crouched and got ready to spring.

"My wife, Katerina," Terek said.

"Your wife?"

Damon hadn't forgotten about her, but part of him suspected that Katerina was a fictional construct, something Terek had made up to get them to come to Washington. To justify what he was doing.

The look on his face was abject terror, though.

"She's been taken. My friends in Georgetown say they went out on the street to get into a food line, now they heard about the hurricane, the city is going even more crazy…"

His voice trailed off.

Damon looked back at his screen. The image from the dash cam was blank. Nothing from any of the phones. Everything blank. Had Terek cut off the video feed? Had he seen what Damon had been doing? More likely, Damon had smashed through and destroyed whatever network hardware had been supplying the data link.

"I need to go," Terek said.

"You want to leave?"

"I don't want to. I *need* to."

Should Damon let him leave?

If he didn't, he'd have to stop him. Then what? Tie him up? He'd need to incapacitate him first. Damon wasn't much of a fighter, and he wondered if Terek was. If this guy was a trained assassin, or something. He checked out Terek's lanky frame. This guy wasn't a cage fighter.

But stopping him wasn't a good idea.

Because it might reveal Damon's new gambit. This game needed some sleight of hand.

"Why don't you take one of the senator's cars?" Damon pointed at the rack of keys over the dishwasher. "He said we could take a vehicle if we needed it. Take the Jeep, that's a solid car."

Getting him out of here would reduce Damon's stress as well. He needed to think. Try and find ways to help his friends, if he could.

Terek said, "Can you come with me?"

Damon still had his earbuds in his hands.

He put them down.

That look on Terek's face—either the kid was going to win an Oscar or his heart had been ripped out. A second ago Damon was sure Terek was about to stab him, but now the kid needed his help. That old feeling of him being Damon's little brother seeped in.

When Damon discovered Terek had hacked his meshnet, his thought was that he might have been coerced. Or that it might have something to do with his wife. It seemed like a lot of wives were suddenly going missing.

Maybe Damon *should* go with him?

"I can't," Damon finally replied. "There might be millions of people counting on us."

"Please."

"You go. I'll be here. Call me if you need help."

Terek hesitated a beat, but then said, "I'll be back in an hour or two."

He grabbed the keys to the Jeep, ran two steps, but then returned to his laptop. He was about to unplug the cord connecting his to Damon's when he said, "Can you give me that space surveillance file? Give it to me raw? I swear I won't show it to anyone."

"Your wife is gone and you want space surveillance data?"

"You said it yourself. Millions of people. I might have time."

"I need to deconstruct the file," Damon said. "Take out the classified stuff."

Terek paused, mumbled something, grabbed his computer and bag, and disappeared around the corner. Damon waited until he heard the Jeep's engine fire up. He watched it drive through the gates and down the street before he sat back down at his computer.

He had at least an hour, maybe two. Damon better make this good.

First things first.

He tried to log back into the Wi-Fi router he had accessed to run the BullyBoy, but it didn't respond. He did a search for any meshnet node along the Virginia coast, but it came up blank. Not a single person in the meshnet. Not a webcam working anywhere.

A voice from the next room. "Hurricane Dolly is the first category five to make a direct hit on the Virginia coast. Experts are predicting tens of billions in damages, and hundreds or perhaps thousands of lives lost—"

No wonder he wasn't getting any network connections out there. There might not even be any houses left standing on that shoreline. He said a little prayer. He desperately hoped his friends were okay, but it was out of his hands.

Terek's little act had fooled him for a while, right up until he'd asked for the space surveillance data before he left.

Damon cracked his knuckles over his keyboard and brought up the space surveillance data he had retrieved that morning. It was real enough, except it didn't include any military satellite data.

That part had been a lie.

If you want to go fishing, his Grandma Babet would always tell him, you needed something that the fish wanted to eat. Not what you might *think* they want, but something they're in the mood for, given the time and day.

And it had to look real.

That was the most important thing. Fish were much smarter than we gave them credit for, especially the ones that were hunters themselves. Trout, marlin, barracuda, these were all fearsome predators, and predators knew a lot about hunting. When you were hunting a predator, you needed the prey to look perfect.

It had to look alive, it had to move the right way. Damon's fingers flittered over the keys.

He looked up a list of military satellites and began creating bogus orbital tables. There were hundreds. This was going to take a lot of time, something he didn't have much of.

One last thing. He opened the protocol files from the SatCom satellites. He needed something simple. Something foolproof.

He scrolled through the list.

And there it was.

Chapter 42

In a splintering explosion of wood and steel and glass, the BullyBoy burst through the wall of the house and crashed sideways through the metal staircase leading to the mezzanine. A man on the stairs sailed into the air, along with the crate he carried, which flew open and scattered papers. The man thudded face-first into the steel roof of the truck.

I flung my arms around Lauren, shielded her with my body. Pulled her to the floor. My momentum carried us backward into Billy's feet. He tripped and danced but maintained his footing.

I scrambled forward as we hit the deck. Terrified the truck was going to drive straight through the house, right over us, and out the other side.

But its knobby black tires locked.

It squealed to a stop on the pinewood floor, splinters and aluminum siding and the wreckage of half the wall dragged along with it.

The truck sideswiped Irena and Katerina and flung them into a mess of chairs and boxes to my left. Drove straight into the two men guarding Chuck and Agent Coleman, right over one of them, ricocheted the other like a beaten piñata into the front wall.

In the fraction of a second before the truck hit the wall, as its LED headlamps sliced through the rain outside, I realized what was happening. Damon was in control of the truck and was about to use it as a battering ram.

The first thought that surfaced as I clutched at Lauren was: It's bulletproof. Then: We need to get inside the damn thing.

The Chechens didn't have the same insight.

They had to be wondering if attackers were coming in behind this tank thing. Would it explode? Would someone jump out of it? I'd told them the cavalry was coming. That the Secret Service had them surrounded.

Billy backed toward the front wall and swung his assault rifle around.

I was up on one knee.

A metallic taste in my mouth. I'd hit the floor with my mouth but had hardly noticed. My face numb. An assault rifle skittered across the floor to my feet.

The man pinned under the truck screamed.

A thundering wind tore through the wrecked kitchen wall in a swirling whirlwind of paper.

Stuttering fire of an automatic weapon. Flashes as bullets dented the hood of the BullyBoy and impacted its windshield. Billy fired straight at it, not ten feet from us. The right gull-wing door began to swing open.

With one hand, I grabbed Lauren's shirt and dragged her up. I fumbled with the other for the assault rifle. Lauren grabbed it and got to her knees. We crouched and ran to the side of the truck.

Someone yelled above us.

A man appeared on the mezzanine, his rifle out ahead of him. Two men from the stairs leading to the garage, also yelling, and not in English. Russian? Chechen?

A burst of gunfire.

Where was Chuck?

Agent Coleman was on his knees by the back wheel of the BullyBoy. He wrenched the gun from the hands of the screaming man beneath. Agent Coleman spun around in one clean motion and unleashed a burst into the mezzanine.

The man up there staggered back.

Billy retreated to the far wall and shielded himself behind a couch, the muzzle of his rifle visible. The two men coming up the stairs had their rifles out and scanned the room, up and down and side to side.

Irena and Katerina were on the floor.

The man guarding them sat on his haunches, his rifle up, but turned away from us, watching the blown-open entranceway.

The wind boomed and swirled the mess of papers.

"Get down!" Agent Coleman screamed at me.

Where was Chuck? A growling rumble overpowered the shrieking wind. A gray-brown wall of water exploded at head height through the shattered opening in the kitchen wall.

The foaming mountain poured down onto the screaming men in the stairwell, extinguishing their yells. The swell heaved into the room. Picked up everything like matchsticks. Chairs and tables and people. Irena and Katerina got to their feet, then were swept away.

A quick flutter like a bird flew past my face. Bullets. Close.

Staccato pops of automatic gunfire.

Someone yanked me by the neck of my T-shirt and I fell onto my ass. Lauren. She crouched in the cover of the BullyBoy's front fender with the assault rifle balanced over it. Let go a stuttering burst low into the front wall where Billy hid.

Water sloshed around my midsection.

"Mike!" Chuck yelled. "Get in the goddamn truck!"

He was in the driver's seat, tapping on a large touch screen in the center console while cursing at me to hurry up.

Another burst of gunfire.

Then another.

Muzzle flashes all around us.

How many of their men had been up here? Bullets ricocheted off the truck's stainless hull. Chuck yelped as I scrambled on all fours past Agent Coleman, who stood and swept left and right as he fired a suppressing round.

Another thundering reverberation as a second wave gushed through the opening.

"Get in, get in!" Chuck's voice forced. Choked.

"Wait!" Irena screamed from the other side of the room.

I grabbed my wife's right arm and pulled.

She resisted for an instant so she could get off one more round, but then followed me into the futuristic interior of the BullyBoy. An acrid stink of cordite mixed with fresh car plastic. I slid in, squeaking on the leather of the back seats. Water rushed through the open door.

Bullets clanged and punched white dots into the dark glass.

"Hurry!" Agent Coleman shouted across the room.

Lauren jumped into the back seat with me, her assault rifle in hand. I grabbed the muzzle to push it away, howled, and let it go. It was red hot.

"Hurry, hurry, hurry," Chuck said in a pained voice. He keyed something into the flat panel on the dashboard.

I was blind to the outside now. Couldn't see anything beyond the truck's dark windows except for Agent Coleman, who leaned against the open gull wing. No more single bursts of gunfire. A steady chattering barrage over the clamor of the waves and wind.

"Leave them!" I shouted.

Agent Coleman stumbled back.

A surprised look on his face as rounds caught him square in the chest. Knocked him off his feet. Lauren didn't hesitate. She launched back out through the door, gun in one hand.

"We must leave quickly," said Irena. She squirmed through the water toward the opening of the door, with Katerina close behind.

I swiveled in my chair to see my wife hauling Agent Coleman into the back seat as Chuck leaned his forward. Lauren held the big Secret Service agent under both armpits and pulled.

Grabbing the back of the seat in front of me, I leveraged myself up as if I was about to give Irena a hand.

I gripped the seat.

And straight-kicked her as hard as I could, flat in the nose. She screamed. Blood exploded from her face. I kicked at her hands and pulled myself into the front seat.

"Close the door!" I screamed at Chuck.

He stared at me with wide eyes. Blinked. Tapped the screen. Blood spatters on his face. Dark splotches on his shirt.

Irena slipped backward, her hands grabbing the bottom edge of the door. She screamed as she tried to hang on.

A flurry of bullets clanged off the metal and thudded into the side window and windscreen. The glass was bulletproof, but that only meant it didn't let them through. The windows were shattered and crazed. I wasn't sure how many more hits it could take before the glass would collapse under the incoming onslaught.

"Go, go, go!" Lauren yelled.

Chuck didn't need convincing.

The wheels of the BullyBoy spun. A whirring vibration filled the cockpit. The door almost but not quite closed, I saw Irena stand up, a hand to her face. A man in camouflage appeared ten feet away, running, his weapon out. He swung its muzzle at us.

A deafening burst of gunfire echoed in the cabin.

Lauren fired her rifle as she leaned back with Agent Coleman on top of her. A spray of bullets from outside clanged off the stainless steel. Hissing pops inside the cabin.

It felt like a rocket engine had been lit.

My forehead slammed into the dashboard. I slid into Chuck, almost knocked him out the still half-open door. The truck spun. Chuck hauled himself back to the steering wheel.

Gunned the accelerator again.

The truck squealed. Three men stood and fired straight at us through the mostly wrecked windshield. We flashed past them.

Another crunching impact and thudding boom. We hit the mangled kitchen wall. A lurching burst of speed. The truck launched through, spun weightless for an instant.

Slammed broadside into churning water.

I cracked my head against the door. Agent Coleman and Lauren flew forward and bashed into the front seats.

"Chuck, Chuck!" I shouted. "The door! Get the goddam—"

"I know, I know!" He gripped the steering wheel and tapped the big screen.

Gray water flooded in from the almost-closed door. A wave tumbled the truck sideways. I yelled. Lauren screamed. Chuck cursed. The door finally closed.

We were back upright in a tangled mess, water sloshing all around us.

The truck surged forward on a wave, and in the moment of comparative calm Chuck leaned back to the console and keyed something. A whine and a hum and I heard the wheels get going again. But no acceleration.

The truck almost tumbled over again before being pulled back by a swell. Through the dark crazed glass, the house and the streetlights faded from view. We were being sucked backward and out onto the beach—but there was no beach anymore. We were being pulled into the Atlantic, into the middle of the raging hurricane.

Another wave. The force and volume of it submerged the truck. We pinwheeled over and over, blood and water and bodies churning one into the other.

No fear, though, and no pain. Only one thought in the tumbling darkness.

They have my children.

Chapter 43

For two hours, Damon tried to find a connection to somewhere, anywhere, along the Virginia coast, but there was nothing.

He tried dialing the senator's meshnet number, but there was no answer. He sent a text message, left the address of the house on the Virginia coast, said that Mike was in trouble and needed help.

Damon had a feeling his messages weren't getting through.

He tried the landline, which still worked, but he only managed to get as far as one of the senator's aides, who said the senator was in a classified briefing and there was no way to reach him. Damon said it was an emergency. They said everything today was one.

Damon needed to be careful how much he said. He knew they were listening.

Whoever "they" were.

The attackers were probably aware that Damon knew something was wrong. Damon had sent a flurry of messages, and he was sure they would be able to decode them in a few minutes. He was a sitting duck.

And that's what he wanted them to think.

Because Terek had given him two whole hours to think.

Damon set his target file down behind a set of carefully constructed firewalls. He set up an intrusion detection system and laid out an almost impenetrable perimeter. Almost no way in or out.

"Almost" being the crucial word.

He made another cup of coffee and watched the rain. It fell in huge gob-droplets that quickly overflowed the gutters and spilled onto the paved back deck, then ran in streams down the grassy incline to the Potomac. The Calico rapids were engorged.

Damon took a sip of coffee and looked at his computer.

Silent for the past half hour.

No messages. No nothing.

Maybe he was wrong.

Terek looked terrified when he left. Maybe Damon should have gone with him. His mind flip-flopped. How could he decide what to do? What had happened to his friends?

It felt like a hundred-pound weight pressed down on his chest.

He looked at his watch. Almost noon.

He had sent a meshnet message and told Mrs. Seymour to take her time. He knew Terek or the attackers would see the message. With this rain, he couldn't imagine Mrs. Seymour going for much of a walk, and he doubted they would go near the city center given the looting and riots. What was she doing?

He was all alone.

The tension sucked the air from his lungs.

Damon had already given away a lot, but he might confuse his attackers by staying still. He assumed Terek had planted a man-in-the-middle attack within the home's routers. As much as Damon wanted to run and scream and punch something, he needed to stay calm.

Sometimes a predator had to lay quietly.

A twinge twisted in his gut.

Maybe he was like the big tarpon they'd hunted. Maybe there was something hovering over Damon right now, something he couldn't see and didn't understand. Had he miscalculated?

The TV in the next room detailed the ferocity of Hurricane Dolly as it lashed the shoreline. "Our experts believe the storm managed at least a sixteen-foot storm surge, but without satellite data or ground stations it's only possible for them to have a rough idea. Two Hurricane Hunter aircraft are circling the storm as we speak, and Doppler radar indicates it is losing intensity as it comes inland."

There was one call Damon could make on the landline that wouldn't arouse any suspicion. He picked up the receiver and dialed a number by heart. Just about the only number he'd always known.

It picked up on the first ring.

"Is that my little Demon?" asked a gravelly down-home Cajun voice.

"Yeah, it's me, Grandma."

Damon felt a warm current of calm run through his scalp and down his spine. She was okay. They'd exchanged text messages, but it was nice to hear her voice. Mike and Chuck had their families, and he loved them too. Would do anything to protect his friends. But his own, real family? All he had was Grandma Babet.

"You staying safe?" Babet asked.

"Yes, Grandma."

"You helping people?"

"Much as I can." He didn't want to worry her. Nobody wanted to worry their mom, which was what she'd always been to him.

A pause on the other end. "You meet any girls?"

It was a question she asked him every time they spoke, no matter the circumstance. "Actually, yeah. How are things in New Orleans?"

"Store shelves are empty. Some people shooting each other in the streets, but that's not unusual. Not much police. I guess they're going to fix this mess given time. I'm keeping to myself. Social distancing. Like last time."

She'd been through a disaster or three, his grandma. Katrina. Corona. Now this. She was cool as a bayou sunset, though.

"You have food?"

"If I need to, I go fishing. Now what about this girl? Not that Irena? I hope not, I mean, she's real pretty and all…"

"I met a farm girl named Pauline, up in Kentucky."

"Farm girl? I'm liking the sound of that."

Damon closed his eyes. Sunk into this tiny oasis of normality outside of the tilt-o-whirl. But there was another reason he'd called.

"You said there was something unusual at the port. Something to do with Irena or Terek, some containers they were involved in moving around? Or something like that?"

A pause. "Some big trucks came in, no paperwork, and took 'em. Just the containers they signed in. And I heard they took 'em up to that Tyrell's place. Uncle Louis, you know, the cook? He was walking his dog—"

His grandma told him a story about how some people said, rumors mind you, that they had been out to the GenCorp headquarters. Something strange was going on. Damon told her to stay clear, because men with guns were on their way there, if they weren't there already.

Outside the kitchen window, it was almost black as night now. The clouds thick and low. Rain came down like a river.

Mrs. Seymour should be back soon. What would Damon tell her? He would wait another half an hour and see if the bait would be taken. If it hadn't been by then, he was wrong. Or they were onto him. Which wouldn't be surprising.

He sat back and listened to Babet.

What had happened to Chuck and Mike? Not hearing something—anything—at this point was a bad sign. Damon's computer pinged.

A message.

"Uh, one second, Grandma."

He checked his machine. The message was from Terek. Despite the tension, a thrill of excitement tickled his neck and scalp.

The game was on.

"Grandma, can I call you back?"

"You always be saying that, but you never—"

"I promise."

"You call that Pauline girl?"

"I will."

"And say hello to Michael and Charles. They're good people."

His machine pinged again. "I really gotta go." He hung up.

He sat down at the kitchen table. The thought of Chuck and Mike and Lauren out there made Damon's stomach flip over. Made him wonder again where Mrs. Seymour and the kids had gone.

Right now, though, the game was afoot.

Damon opened the email from Terek. It contained a modified version of the GenCorp satellite data, along with Terek's opinion of why the ground station relays were taking so long to respond. He said that maybe it was a phased array, but that didn't add up.

Damon wasn't interested.

He wasn't playing that game anymore.

There was an attachment to Terek's email. A file converted into a PDF. Damon shook his head. So messy. *Terek, I thought better of you.* And then he thought: *Much better, as a matter of fact.* Damon opened the attachment.

In another UNIX shell, Damon ran software that monitored his intrusion detection system and firewalls. One after the other, he watched with satisfaction as the worm from Terek's email spawned and then instantiated itself again and again. The exploit went to work, inserting itself into Damon's memory and network file systems.

The fish was going after the juicy worm.

Now Damon just had to make sure the prey was hooked so tight that it couldn't get loose. The attackers had to swallow this whole, deep into their guts.

His fingers worked the keyboard.

He had to make sure the bait looked alive, wriggling and squirming to survive the determined predator. Swim, little fish, *swim.*

Chapter 44

"I can't swim!" I yelled into the darkness.

"Don't be so dramatic," Chuck said calmly. "You can't swim very *well*."

"Dramatic?"

"This thing's amphibious. Like a boat."

"I hate boats. You know I hate boats! I can't—"

"Honey, calm down." Lauren's soothing voice in the darkness. Her hand against my cheek.

My breathing came in and out in heaving gulps. My heart hammered like it was going to burst out of my chest. Out of the frying pan and into the what? The goddamn Atlantic?

"Mike, snap out of it." Chuck grunted. "Get in the game."

A light came on. His cell phone.

The four of us were in a heaped mess. Chuck on top of me in the passenger seat. Lauren and Agent Coleman in the back seat. The truck had flipped over in one of the bucking waves, tumbled, then righted itself. The interior stank of sweat and sulfur, a bit of leather and a whiff of vomit.

I wiped my mouth with the back of one hand as we rolled. I almost threw up. Again.

My kids. Luke. Olivia. They needed me. My fear subsided into a rising anger.

Chuck wriggled to get off me. He held out the phone with the light on. I slid forward and almost floated in the water sloshing two feet deep in the cabin. I took the phone from Chuck.

And got knocked over again by a hammering wave.

I turned and grabbed the seat for balance.

"He's still breathing," Lauren said.

She was on her knees on the back seat, up to her waist in water. Putting one hand under Agent Coleman's head, she lifted him up. "He got hit, but his vest took most of it. I think."

Chuck groaned. He tried to sit up but slipped back. I held the light to the water. Fresh blood swirled with the puke.

"I think I took one," Chuck said. "Damn left arm again."

I said, "What can I do?"

"For a start, get us the hell out of here."

The noise deafening as we rolled and thrashed in the waves.

I tried to form a plan. We had to be out in the Atlantic, in the bay beyond the pier, being driven by the wind and waves. The pounding motion made me think we were floating. It sure didn't feel like we were on anything solid.

My stomach came up. I strained to resist retching.

Water sluiced down the walls. Everything leaked. The windows. The cracks between the doors. Sprays of water shot in rivulets from the battered glass around the pockmarks left by bullets. Water in the cabin already deeper.

We were sinking.

I gasped, "Should I open the doors?"

We needed to get out of this death trap. If I opened the doors, I'd drown for sure, but maybe Lauren could make it. Take Chuck with her, grab Agent Coleman. She was a strong swimmer.

"No, you *idiot*." Chuck leaned up against one window. "Get us the hell back to shore. We can't be far."

"Tell me how."

"The console." He pointed at the flat screen in the middle of the dashboard. "Make sure we're in drive mode. Grab the steering wheel, and push down the accelerator."

"You do realize we're in the ocean?"

"I told you, this thing is amphibious. Get the wheels going at high speed and they'll churn the water like a paddle wheel, even if we're submerged."

"That'll work?" My mind was one step behind the words.

"You have a better idea?"

"Chuck, help me with Coleman's head." Lauren braced herself. "I'll help. Give me the light."

Chuck slithered into the back. He hardly needed to get up as he floated most of the way. I splashed into the driver's seat and gave my wife the cell phone, then tapped the console screen. It came to life.

"At the bottom," Chuck said. "Hit the ignition. I got the keys in my pocket, so it should…"

I tapped, held onto the steering wheel, and jammed the accelerator down as far as I could. A whine filled the cabin. Over the bellowing wind and waves, I heard the wheels churn in an instant thrumming rumble.

A map appeared on the console.

No GPS signal, a flashing light warned. No kidding.

"How the hell will I know where to go?" I yelled.

I could be driving us further out into the ocean, for all I knew.

Chuck cackled, something between a laugh and a sob, and pointed. "Use that."

I followed his finger. In the middle of the dash was a tiny plastic bubble. I leaned closer. It was a dollar store compass, like the one he had before, glued to the middle of the BullyBoy's dash.

"Head east," Chuck said.

"East?"

"Yeah."

"You sure? Isn't that toward Europe?"

"West, damn it. I mean west. Turn that wheel till we're heading due west."

I gritted my teeth and strained to push the accelerator as high as I could. I kept my eyes on the bobbling sphere in the middle of the compass and turned the wheel.

"Can I ask you something?" Chuck said. "Why did you kick Irena in the face?"

"Because she's with them."

"You're sure?"

My gut. My wife always said I trusted the wrong people, and I'd come to trust Irena and Terek completely. Feelings like that, I had to be wrong. Plus, those guys hadn't shot at them when they tried to get into the truck. I might be emotionally tone-deaf, but I did notice details.

I swallowed back a mouthful of bile and felt rage rising up over my fear. Where were my kids? That's what Billy had asked me, back at the house. That bastard better not be anywhere near them when I got out of this thing.

Chapter 45

D amon got up from the glass kitchen table to get his tenth cup of coffee. Maybe twelfth? He usually kept track with his health monitoring app, but today, all bets were off. Outside the kitchen window, the wind picked up again.

He could hear a news update from the TV in the living room. "The DC area will be experiencing hurricane-force winds by 3 p.m. this afternoon as the eye of Hurricane Dolly makes its way up the Chesapeake Bay toward Washington. The governor is alerting everyone to stay indoors and avoid—"

Damon checked his watch. 12:15 p.m.

It was time.

He refilled the coffee machine with grounds and water and set it on again. Might need another pot before this was over.

The leaves and branches of the oak beyond the patio door buffeted back and forth. A smattering of raindrops. Low clouds scudded by like mustangs charging away from capture.

He sat back down in front of his machine and tapped a key to open the network monitoring app. The attackers were still chasing his fish, but he had to set the bait. The way that wind was coming up, there was no telling how long he would maintain power out here. All it would take was one branch coming down.

With his index finger he pushed the button.

One keystroke.

He let the firewall open a crack. Seconds later they took the space surveillance file he had weaponized.

A minute later, a message pinged.

Damon got excited, thinking it was Chuck and Mike, but it was another update from the StarCorp satellites.

Exactly three hours again.

He suspected it was a real connection, but a stage-managed one. Real and fake at the same time. Like what he'd sent them. The only reliable information he could glean from it was that the satellite node still uplinking must have passed an active ground station.

He hoped his timing had been right.

The trap had been set. It didn't matter if he alerted the attackers anymore.

He needed to find a way to contact the outside world. Maybe get in one of the cars? Warn Mrs. Seymour not to come back to the house, but given the approaching storm, he assumed she had already found somewhere safe with the senator.

He needed to warn the senator as well, tell him to stop using the meshnet app. Damon needed to warn everyone.

He flexed his fingers and typed out the first message, checked the message twice, and pushed send.

An error message: *No network access.*

He tried his browser. No internet.

The lights went out. TV went silent.

That's what he thought would happen, right? The wind would bring down a tree branch? Take out the power? Or maybe this was one of the rolling blackouts.

He sat motionless for most of a minute and listened to the wind echo through the empty house. He stood, put his coffee down, reached over to the kitchen counter, and selected the biggest knife he could find.

Damon set the drone down in the grass by the edge of the garage. He could get into a car, but he wanted some intel first. What was around the house?

This drone was the heaviest of the four, and the weight should provide some stability in the gusting wind, but he still wasn't sure if it would fly.

It would *fly*, that was for sure, but would it be able to maintain position?

He laid the kitchen knife down in the grass next to it, then stood and used one hand to hold his phone, the other to control the drone. Its motors whirred to life and it sprang into the air. He set it to hover at two hundred feet and watched it ascend, the wind buffeting its control systems and pushing it back and forth.

Overwatch, that's what Damon needed.

He checked the camera on the drone, then brought it up on his screen. The drone went higher and higher. The house came into view, then the trees surrounding it, and then the other houses nearby.

Something wasn't right.

The other houses had their lights on. Only this house was totally dark.

Something else.

On the street in front of the senator's house, beyond the wrought iron gates and brick walls and hedges, were two parked cars. Someone got out of one of them, but it was hard to see in the dim light. Was it the senator? The Secret Service? But that wasn't a limo. That was a Jeep.

Terek had gone out in a Jeep.

Damon pocketed his phone and knelt to pick up the knife. His breath quickened; his heart thumped. Blade held high, he edged around the corner of the garage and into the circular driveway.

Fifty feet away, the iron gates swung open. Someone needed the code to do that.

That someone stood in the middle of the driveway. Terek. He held a gun to Luke's head and pincered his other arm around the kid's neck, choking him into submission.

Damon felt the blood in his face drain away. The knot twisting in his gut almost made him want to retch. He'd been trying to control the future, trying to bend a path through a needle's eye, but he had been fooling himself.

Behind Terek stood a man in camouflage with a shaved head and a beard. He held an assault rifle, pointed right at Damon.

A man laid face down on the road between them. A dark pool spread onto the rain-soaked pavement around Secret Service Agent George Dunbar.

Parked behind the Jeep was a Mercedes. Damon recognized it. That was Mrs. Seymour's. He edged forward. The kitchen knife held like an ice pick in his left hand. He put his right into the pocket of his jeans.

The trees swayed in the wind. Dark clouds sped by.

"Everything is going to be okay," Damon said to Luke.

The kid trembled and sniffled. One small white-knuckled hand gripped Terek's forearm.

Terek moved up the driveway, one deliberate step at a time, keeping Luke in front of him. "We go back in the house. Nobody gets hurt."

"What about your wife?"

"I have no choice. You don't understand."

"It's all a lie, isn't it?"

"You think I didn't check the hash on my memory key? I know you hacked me. They've been watching the whole time. It's too late. They know everything."

"Who are 'they'?" Damon sensed someone behind him, a presence that melted from the shadows behind the garage.

"We go inside," Terek repeated. "Get the power back, and we call in the senator again. Tell him you cracked the satellite uplink, but you need him—and only him—to come back here."

There was more than a little desperation in his voice. Whatever the plan had been, it had deviated.

Damon peered at the Mercedes.

Mrs. Seymour was in the back with Olivia on her knee. There didn't seem to be anyone else in the car. The bearded man in camouflage advanced, ten paces behind Terek.

From the corner of his eye, Damon noticed a distinctive flash of light. It went out a split second later, but more lights blinked in the distance between the trees. Blue lights. Red.

"Okay," Damon said.

He lifted the knife high and knelt, making a show of putting it on the ground. He lifted his left hand. The shadow moved behind him. Soft footsteps under the noise of the wind. Then louder, a thrumming sound through the trees.

"Both hands," Terek said. "Put them up."

Damon still had one hand in his right pocket. He closed his eyes and concentrated and slid his finger forward. He had to get this right.

The whining buzz grew louder behind him.

Someone cursed in a foreign language as the drone closed the last ten feet and slammed into them. Damon ducked, sprinted forward two steps, and then skidded to a stop.

The driveway flooded with light.

A four-ton metal tank exploded over the top of the brick walls.

Chapter 46

I wiped the stinging sweat from my eyes and tried to focus. Agent Coleman had regained consciousness when we'd made our way out of the water, but he was bleeding badly. The man struggled to stay awake and gave instructions as we wound our way off the highway.

I slowed as I approached Potomac Falls Road and the senator's house came into view. I clicked the headlamps off. One thing about electric cars—they were quiet as hell if you wanted to sneak up on someone.

Mrs. Seymour's Mercedes was parked out front. That was odd. Why wouldn't she park inside in this rain? I crept up the last two hundred feet of the road toward the gate and saw the Jeep.

My stomach fluttered.

They were already here. A man in camouflage cradled an assault rifle and walked through the open gates. And then I saw the unmistakable outline of Luke in someone else's arms in front of him.

Not just someone.

That was Terek.

He was in the middle of the parking circle holding my son. I gripped the steering wheel so tight I felt like I might snap it off.

"Motherf—"

Lauren was in the passenger seat next to me. She nodded. Chuck's head was between the two of us. He nodded as well.

You only get one chance at surprise.

I put my foot down on the accelerator. Angled the truck at the man walking through the gate. Only one guy with an assault rifle that I could see. I made my best guess. Made sure we would be well clear of Luke.

"Hang on," I said from between gritted teeth.

We barreled toward the brick enclosure. I braced myself against the steering wheel to keep from getting thrown back. Flipped our headlamps on at the last instant.

The truck plowed *through* the wall more than over it.

Terek was fifty feet to our left as we went airborne in the crunching impact with the four-foot-high brick wall. I caught a quick glimpse of the guy we came down straight on top of, his hands up in futile defense.

I hit the brakes.

Tapped the door switch at the same time.

Water sluiced out as the gull-wing opened and we skidded to a stop. The muzzle of Lauren's rifle came up beside me as I tumbled onto the pavement.

Damon was splayed out in front of the garage.

One of his drones in pieces behind him. He pointed to his left and said, "They went that way."

"How many?"

"Terek and some other guy."

"Mike," Chuck called from the back seat of the truck, "be careful. Don't do anything stupid. The cops are coming."

I heard Agent Coleman moan.

Lauren opened the passenger door and stepped out. Scanned back and forth with her rifle. Lights lit the trees red and blue in the street behind us. Sirens wailed over the wind swaying the trees.

"Oh, thank God," said Mrs. Seymour.

She stepped out of the Mercedes. Olivia cried in her arms. Mrs. Seymour was bawling her eyes out as she ran toward Lauren.

My wife said, "Mom, stay back, the police are coming." She kept the rifle's muzzle moving.

I was already on my feet, running in a crouch past Damon.

"Mike!" Lauren called out. "Goddamn it, Mike, get back here!"

"Luke!" I screamed as loud as I could. "Where are you?"

The wind intensified. A fat raindrop fell. Then another.

A sleeting downpour began. Thunderclaps rolled over the hills. I slicked the water away from my face. Ran around the back of the garage.

"Dad."

I stopped.

Was that left or right?

The ground ahead sloped down to the rushing white water of the Potomac. I turned right.

"Dad," called out Luke's voice again.

Behind me. *Other way.*

I spun on my heel. Turned and sprinted hard. The pain in my ankle disappeared in a blinding surge of adrenaline.

Might be running into a trap.

Didn't care. If they touched him, if they hurt him in any way…

"Stop."

I stumbled and skidded. Terek stood to the side of the path in the wet grass, next to a big old oak. He held Luke up off the ground in one arm, and pointed a sidearm at me. He set Luke down, his arm still around him, and held the gun to my son's head.

Terek said, "Walk away, Mike."

I held my hands up. "Whatever you think you're doing, it's over." I took a step toward them. Scanned the trees for dark shapes. Expected a muzzle flash at any instant.

The sirens louder.

Red-and-blue lights blinked through the trees, even back here.

"They left you." I took another step. "I know they took your wife."

"Stay back."

He swung his handgun at me. That was what I was waiting for. I wiped my hands as best I could on my wet shirt.

"Mike, put your hands up."

"Legook," I yelled. "Geget degown. *Geget degown.*"

Terek blinked, lowered his gun an inch as he tried to process what I was saying.

Luke dropped to his knees and then fell to the grass.

Terek raised his weapon. I reached into my belt and got out the gun as fast as I could, aimed square at his chest. His muzzle flashed as I pulled my trigger. The recoil flung the weapon from my hand.

It felt like someone punched my chest and knocked the breath right out of me.

I gasped. Kept my feet moving.

Luke curled into a fetal ball in the grass. Covered his head.

Momentum carried me forward. I let out a roar. Wrapped my arms around Terek as he fired again.

I collided into him.

We spun together. With one hand I caught his shirt, held on with every ounce of strength I could muster.

Pulled him toward me as I fell.

My knee glanced off Luke's head.

I tumbled into open space. My head flew back. Feet followed.

A second later, a crunching impact as the back of my head smashed the ground. I rolled wildly down the wet slope and tumbled to a stop in a wet heap, entangled with Terek.

We both slid into the water. The swollen Potomac swept us downstream.

Terek clutched at reeds and branches. He tried to get up. I grabbed a fistful of his pant leg and dragged him with me into the rushing water. I swallowed a mouthful and gagged. Held Terek's leg and twisted savagely.

My head submerged for a second, but then we both bobbed to the surface.

"Mike," someone screamed from a distance.

I spotted Lauren through the rain, up on the hill behind me. She pointed down. Luke was in the water as well, fifty feet upstream from me.

Terek pushed me away and slapped one arm and then another as he tried to swim away. I grabbed his shirt and pulled, and used my other hand to shove his head under the water. I kicked at him. Tried to scramble on top and launch off him toward my boy.

A deep thundering roar beyond the wind and rain.

The river opened up and slanted down. A churning mass of boiling white water. What had the senator said when we arrived? That aw-shucks story he must tell everyone who came into his house? *Keep your toes up.*

I swirled over the edge of the watery precipice and was pulled into the roiling maelstrom, turning and tumbling. No idea where my toes or feet or even head pointed. Flailed my arms and kicked in desperation.

Had I told my wife I loved her? My kids?

I swallowed a mouthful of water and screamed into the seething white. Please, God, I'm not ready. Turning and spinning, my last thoughts churned with me. *Would I even know if I was gone?*

Darkness closed in as I was dragged under. My body relaxed. My mind slid away. *I love you, Lauren.*

Luke, Olivia, I...I...

Chapter 47

Damon held Lauren's shoulders as she gently opened the door to the darkened room. Intensive care. Machines beeped in the silence. Voices murmured in the hallway. Mike was on a gurney in the middle of the room, a nest of tubes and wires coming out of him. Her husband's eyes were closed, a blue sheet drawn all the way to his neck. She brought one hand up to her mouth and held back tears.

After a few minutes, they closed the door behind them, leaving just the beeps of the machines.

Even through the thick glass of the hospital window, Damon heard the wind hiss and hum, trying to get in. Almost the middle of the night. The hurricane had passed. It had weakened as it had traveled inland but had flooded the entire Chesapeake area. Left shattered houses and ruined trees in its wake.

Damon hated hospitals.

The smell of antiseptic, the hushed voices. The quiet but polite way pretty women in scrubs told you things you never wanted to hear.

He retreated. To another hospital. He sat on his Grandma Babet's lap. A nice lady asked to speak to her. Alone. So, Damon stayed on the chair. Alone. The lights bright white. And far away,

way down the hall, Babet cried and cried and cried. And Damon knew. His mother was gone. He was six.

Years later, in the snowstorm. The train hammering off the tracks. Hands numb. Her face, her hair. A man in scrubs telling him to stay outside, just stay outside. What was the last thing he said to Cindy? He wanted a chocolate bar. I'll go get a Twix, she said. So we can share. He'd rolled his eyes and laughed. He was still holding her half when the doctor told him. She was gone.

Damon hated hospitals.

Please, don't let it happen again. He prayed, and he wasn't a praying type.

A Styrofoam cup of weak coffee in his trembling hand. Fifteenth? Twentieth? Might as well start injecting caffeine. A nurse offered him anti-anxiety meds. He didn't like taking pills, but maybe today would be the day.

The hallway of the intensive care unit was packed.

Men and women, all in dark suits. Secret Service. Local police. State. FBI. CIA. Every three-letter agency that saw fit to name itself, and probably some that didn't. Lauren sat across the hall from Damon with Olivia in her lap, her face streaked with mud and tears.

Everyone, uniform or not, gave her space to breathe.

Two seats down, Senator Seymour stood to one side of his sister.

Damon heard the senator's phone ping quietly. He held the device up and read something, glancing at Damon every few seconds. Then he pocketed the phone and walked over.

"Can I speak to you for a second?" the senator asked. "Somewhere more private?"

"With respect, sir, I'm not moving. Who are you going to keep a secret from? We've got half the country's intelligence services in here."

The senator admitted the point with a twitch of his shoulders. He leaned down, and said in a low voice, "It worked."

Damon had almost forgotten. "What are you seeing?"

In an even lower voice, the senator said, "Lockheed reports radar bounce backs from a whole lot of the SatCom fleet. Maybe twelve thousand satellites left up there, but they're all de-orbiting. This time tomorrow, most of the little bastards will be burning up in the atmosphere."

"All of them?"

"Every one that we can see."

Damon's ploy must have succeeded.

He'd inverted the security breach, the one that had compromised him. Terek becoming his "friend" must have been a long-planned social engineering attack. It was a two-pronged assault, first to get access to the Space Surveillance Network data Damon had privileged access to, and then to implant themselves within the meshnet they knew Damon would become a focal point of, once the mobile networks went down.

It was the only thing that made sense.

When he realized what Terek was up to, Damon had set up a Trojan attack.

He had casually mentioned to Terek that he had not only space surveillance data, but also location data on US military satellites. That information was two levels of secret above his meager rating, but the attackers didn't know that. It was a prize too valuable to resist, and Damon made it just difficult enough to get at.

He defended his system, watched them try to hack into it. Watched them steal his encryption keys on purpose. Once they'd taken the data, they must have unpacked it quickly in their system.

He faked as much data about military satellites as he could, and only in the second layer did he hide his exploit. A simple virus that replicated quickly and would be detected just as fast, but not before it spawned and executed a simple command protocol on every piece of equipment it could find.

End of life.

The "end of life" command sent to a satellite, and specifically the SatCom ones, was an irrevocable self-destruct signal. It triggered an automated feature that oriented the satellites relative to the Earth's horizon and fired all thrusters to de-orbit the birds. Slowed them down until they dropped and burned in the atmosphere.

No other instructions needed.

He had needed a little luck, but only required one or two satellites still communicating with the ground station to be in range when his virus spread through their network before they could stop it.

Any other time, he would be jumping up and down with excitement, but right now, he hardly cared.

What had the victory cost? Was it worth it? If he hadn't been so obsessed with the satellites, he might have been able to figure out some other way to help Mike and Chuck.

He had crashed that truck through the wall. Blunt force. Almost zero finesse. It wasn't his normal style, but he had been in a hurry.

He hadn't been able to control this future.

Did he hurry because he was obsessed with the thrill of defeating an adversary in cyberspace? He might have found a way to alert the authorities about the location of the terrorists sooner.

Not only that.

He was responsible.

He brought Terek and Irena into their lives. He'd been so stupid. He might be a genius behind the keyboard, but in real life? This was all his fault.

Damon said, "What about Irena? The terrorists? That house on Virginia Beach?"

It had only been about four hours since the events at the senator's house, but in that short time, the whole world had changed.

"We sent in another SEAL team," the senator said. "But that whole stretch was ground zero. The house is nothing but wooden posts and flotsam. The entire area still under six feet of water. The

Russians say they found the group's other bases in Chechnya and Ukraine. Wiped them out."

"Did you get my voice files? The images? Have they been analyzed?" Damon had sent the video and audio from inside the house.

"We have teams working on that. We did get some papers out of the truck. They must have gotten in there when you smashed it through the walls of that house. They were cleaning up."

"What's on them?"

"The names and addresses of US citizens, as if they were targeting them, but as far as we can see, those people are still around. It's strange. The FBI is starting to round up the ones we have names for, see if we can find a pattern."

"But you didn't get any of the terrorists?"

"Only the one Mike landed the truck on top of. And your friend, Terek."

"He's not my friend."

"They're not going to get far. Trust me."

It didn't give Damon much comfort. Those animals were still out there somewhere, unless they'd been killed in the hurricane. He doubted it would be that easy. But they were on the run, and their weapon had been dismantled.

Damon asked, "Was Terek his real name? Irena? Are they even related?"

"All this is coming in live, but now we have a face and DNA. We got a thick file from the Russians. His name is Pyotr Okuev, and the woman you called Irena, her name is Amina. She's an assassin. One of the top ten on Russia's most wanted. We think she was the leader."

"But Terek, I mean, Pyotr—is he really her brother?"

"Seems that way. She might have coerced him. Damn Russians are still barely speaking to us. Hard enough to get what we did. Their military still thinks there are bogeymen around every corner.

Ours too. In a few weeks, we should be able to stabilize the situation."

Stabilize. The word made Damon look at the ICU room's door.

"I was so stupid," Damon said.

"You identified them in the end. Slowed down enough that we can catch them."

The door to the ICU room opened.

A doctor appeared and pulled down his surgical mask. The men and women in the hallway turned to him.

"He's alive," he said. "But I'm not sure for how much longer. He's lost a huge amount of blood with that gunshot to the chest, so if you go in there, please, be mindful. I'm not even sure he's going to wake up."

Chapter 48

A bubbling cauldron hung over a fire, the heat searing into the bones of those trapped inside, the water churning and boiling and frothing.

I opened my eyes.

The mind-fog of the dream faded, replaced with a dim vision of squinting blue eyes, a mess of blond hair, and week-long stubble. I'd recognize that face anywhere.

"Am I in hell?" I croaked.

"What?"

"Because I figure this is what hell would look like."

Chuck stood over me with his face inches from mine. "Is that a joke?"

"Does the pope poop?"

His face disappeared from view and I heard him whisper, "Guys, he's awake."

I closed my eyes and winced. My head throbbed. My entire body ached.

I fought my way back to consciousness and won the struggle to open my eyes again. It was dark. Not quite dark. I was flat on my back in a bed, in what had to be a hospital from the beeping machines and antiseptic stink. I smiled, or tried to. I managed a grin.

"You guys can turn the lights on," I said in a thready voice.

Damon said in a hushed voice, "You sure?"

"Speak up. I think my ears are still full of water."

Chuck said, louder, "You should have seen how much they pumped out of you. I didn't think anyone could swallow that much."

"How long have I been out?"

"Maybe four hours. Got you on the good stuff now." Chuck pointed at an IV bag hanging next to a battery of beeping machines.

Someone flicked a switch. The fluorescent tubes in the ceiling blinked on. Chuck had a sling on his left arm, the prosthetic hand dangling in it.

My wife came rushing through the door. Lauren held her arms as wide as they could get and walked to me. "Oh, my baby."

She started crying, leaned over, and gently scooped me into her arms. She kissed my cheek, my forehead, my eyes. Under a patina of hand soap, she still smelled of blood and sweat and vomit and I'd never smelled anything so sweet in all my life.

She squeezed my ribs. I grunted in a flash of pain.

She let go, gently. "The doctors say you're going to be fine, honey. But we almost lost you."

"Terek's not going to be so lucky," Damon said. "Docs say he has multiple organ failures. Might not wake up."

"Good thing you brought most of Virginia's finest with us to the house." Chuck laughed encouragingly. "We had half a dozen EMTs on hand the second they fished you out."

The memory was hazy.

Once we got Chuck's amphibious monster truck back to land, we had raced back to the senator's house. That damned truck, shot through and banged up and waterlogged, still managed over a hundred miles per hour on the highway and shoulders. There was even self-healing glue in the wheels. The doors almost flew off, but the thing held together.

We blew through police barricades.

By the time we turned off the highway to Potomac Road, we must've had a trail of twenty cruisers and State Troopers following in our wake.

"No sucking chest wounds?" I asked. "No limbs missing?"

I still had no idea what shape I was in, beyond Lauren assuring me I was going to be okay.

"Agent Coleman's vest did its job," Chuck replied, "but you'll be sore for a while. Me too." He tapped his arm in the sling. "Took one in the shoulder. Mostly a flesh wound."

When I ran at Terek, I wasn't suicidal. Not entirely.

I had taken Agent Coleman's bulletproof vest, put it on in the mad drive back to the house. His idea. He wouldn't be able to get out of the car, he said, as he had handed me his sidearm. Point and shoot. Make sure the safety was off.

I said, "Speaking of?"

"Agent Coleman is going to be okay," Damon said. "He took three in the vest. One broke his clavicle, and another one in his arm caused all that bleeding. I mean, I'd be pretty much dead, but that guy will probably be doing laps at the Georgetown track next week."

"Where's Luke?" I asked.

"Over here, Pops."

Pops? When had he started calling me Pops?

I strained to look left over my bed's guard rail. I discovered a half-dozen wires and tubes coming out of me, like a science experiment gone wrong. Or maybe right. I was alive, whatever they'd done to me. Luke appeared from the dark corner of the room where the daybed was.

"He wouldn't leave your side," Lauren whispered and wiped away a tear.

"Dad, that was *awesome*." Luke beamed his gap-toothed grin at me and raised both arms in a victory salute. "You were like Superman or something. You *flew* at that guy."

"Your kid's quite the swimmer," Damon said.

Chuck said, "You got sucked down those rapids like a drunk possum, but Legook here swam his way out like a champ. He ran down through the woods and dove back in. He's the one that got to you first in the pool at the bottom of the rapids. You know that?"

I didn't know that.

My memory was blank after I went under.

My boy. The hero. I lifted my head and wanted to get up and hold him, but I was afraid I'd rip a tube out of me. I laid back down.

The door creaked open an inch. Senator Seymour came in, along with someone I didn't recognize in a dark suit.

"You owe me a new truck, by the way," Chuck said. "You definitely drove that one like a rental. Wheels shot through, windows wrecked, door falling off."

"Done." I laughed, then groaned in pain once more.

"Son," Senator Seymour said, "I know this is a bit soon, but we have some questions for you. National security kind of stuff. The country is still in a shambles."

I winced and tried to edge myself higher in my bed.

"You stay still. We have a few questions."

The clean-cut man in the dark suit asked, "This man you called 'Terek.' Your first meeting with him was through Mr. Damon Indigo?"

"That's what I already said," Damon protested.

"We need to verify, please."

"Yeah."

"He's in the next room over. You put a bullet next to his heart, and while they got you out of the water quick, he was submerged for longer. He's in and out of consciousness."

They asked me questions about things I'd seen at the house, which wasn't much, and whatever I could remember seemed more of a dream.

They explained how the Russians had stamped out what was left of the Islamic Brigade and that they had them on the run here. It had only been a few hours, so they hadn't caught anyone but the guy I'd run over. Of course, they hadn't really *caught* that guy as much as shoveled his remains off the cobblestone driveway.

And Terek. Or Pyotr, they explained, which was his real name.

I wondered why he would go to the trouble of changing his name, but then change it to a Chechen name, the name of the biggest river through that area, but everyone shrugged. People do stupid things, they said. I told them they insisted on speaking English. The clean-cut guy didn't have an answer of why they did that either.

Then they told me how Damon had hacked back their satellites.

We won, the senator said.

"Are we getting GPS back?" I asked.

"It's not that simple," the senator replied. "We still have a few GPS satellites left up there, but we need more to re-establish location fixing. In big cities they're starting to set up local GPS, and going forward, we're switching to wired timing signals. Don't need this mess again."

"How long?"

"Weeks. Maybe months. Longer in rural areas. Heard you boys ran into some Kentucky militia?"

"I think I'm going to go back," Damon said.

I was puzzled for a second, but then said, "Ah, that girl, Pauline."

"To add to everything else, this hurricane has caused one hell of a nasty mess," the senator said, "And like your friend Joe, it looks like we'll lose a whole season's crops. Whole country will be shut down for months. Again. People might go hungry for a bit, but we're going to get those stock markets back open in a few weeks."

I raised my eyebrows. "Stock markets?"

If they were talking about stock markets, then things had to be back on track, or at least on a road leading to it.

At least it hadn't come to nuclear war.

India was still protesting that it hadn't launched the anti-satellite weapons, but that was posturing, the intel guy said. He explained how the terrorists had used the initial confusion of the anti-satellite attacks between India and Pakistan to obfuscate what they were up to, at least at the start.

When GenCorp lost uplink with the first few dozen—and then few hundred—satellites, the fact of their losing comms was obscured in the discombobulation of the moment. Another strike team of terrorists attacked the GenCorp headquarters and killed everybody there. That's what the SEAL team that arrived in the morning found.

No trace of the second team of terrorists yet.

The senator and the clean-cut man explained how the terrorists hadn't only hit commercial satellites. The operators had started to move satellites around once the threat surfaced, when the Islamic Brigade announced what they were doing.

Problem was, the attackers also hit a lot of dead satellites that couldn't be moved. A massive debris field was still spreading in several orbital planes. It might take a decade or more to de-orbit by itself from the lower orbits, and maybe never for the stuff higher up.

Even medium Earth orbit was compromised, but they said they had ways to work around it. Get satellites up higher, punch missions through the debris. It might take years, but there were ways to fix it.

Not everything added up, but it had only been a few hours since it had all gone down.

The senator and the intelligence guy excused themselves, and Lauren brought Olivia and Susan in. We laughed and cried a bit more, then Damon offered to take everyone down to the cafeteria. Lauren said I must be tired.

Only Chuck remained.

The machines beeped in silence for a few minutes as he hovered by my bed.

"What?" I asked.

"Making sure you're okay. I called your brothers. Terry is coming down. He said he's going to tear Oscar a new one next time he sees him."

"My brother is coming?"

"It's a zoo out there, but he's going to try. You have a nice room, but the rest of the hospital is a mess. They're running out of supplies and the hallways are crammed with people."

"That bad?"

"Not as bad as last time."

I put my head back down. That sounded slightly reassuring.

"Makes sense now," Chuck said, "why my Jeep didn't work in New Orleans. Terek or Irena must have done something to it. Anyway, I'm enjoying no GPS. Makes me use my own head a bit more."

And here came that smile I'd seen too many times before.

I said, "I can see from that jasshonkey grin on your face that you've got something you want to say."

"Jasshonkey? Now I *know* you must be feeling better."

"Out with it. Come on."

He paused, just long enough to be theatrical. "I was right."

"About?"

"Conspiracies. Remember, at the start of all this, I said it wasn't an accident?"

So that's what he'd been waiting for. He was gloating. He had to be right. Even with me half-dead in a hospital bed, he needed to get his digs in.

Chuck added, "*And* I didn't like those two, Terek and Irena, or Pyotr and Amina, whatever they're really called. I pegged them right from the start."

That they were terrorists? He knew that? I shook my head in amazement. He was stretching the truth a little, or more than a little, but who was I to burst his bubble? And when was stretching the truth ever a crime between friends?

So I said, "Yeah, you were right, Chuck."

He beamed. "I told you. Sometimes conspiracies *are* real."

Epilogue

I waited till the tiny hours of the morning, until Lauren and the kids had gone back to the senator's house and even Chuck had left. I was fine, I said. The nurse made me a mobile station, an IV rack on wheels, so I could get up out of the bed and walk around a bit.

I was fine, I kept telling them, and the senator's house was only fifteen minutes away. There were nurses and doctors here. I told them to go shower, change into fresh clothes, and get some sleep.

They needed it.

We all needed it.

But I really needed to be alone for another reason.

Through the slatted blinds, the hallway outside my ICU room looked like it had emptied out. I listened past the beeping machines, strained to hear voices. Nothing. Five minutes past three. Outside my window, the night was pitch-black.

The wind had died down. The storm had passed.

Or had it?

Grunting with effort, I swung my legs off the side of the gurney bed and eased myself to the floor. Lauren had left slippers. Leaning against the bed, inched my toes into them. Unclipped the finger sensor monitoring my heartbeat and blood oxygenation. One of the machine's beeping noises slid into a single flat note. I gritted my teeth, took the pain, and forced myself to my feet.

And stood unsteadily.

Two seconds later, my door opened.

A nurse, the dark-skinned one who was a sweetheart, appeared. "You okay, honey?" she said. "You want me to put that back on?"

I held onto the metal upright of my mobile IV rack on wheels and shuffled across the linoleum floor toward her. I tried not to grimace at the lancing bolts of pain in my side. "I need to go to the bathroom."

"You got one in your room, sweetie."

"Can I stretch my legs?"

"You sure that's a good idea?"

I reached the door and opened it fully. "Please."

The hallway was mostly empty.

Three nurses on duty.

And of course, several men and two women in dark suits sitting across the hallway, half-asleep, and a half-dozen young men in khaki holding assault rifles, not asleep, but alert and upright and silent. There were two police officers in uniform at either side of the room next to me.

They weren't here for me, all these people.

They were here for *him*.

Them still being here meant he wasn't dead. Yet.

The nurse asked, "You want some help, darling?"

"I'm fine." I checked the tubes snaking out from under my hospital gown and made sure none of them were hanging so low they'd get stuck under my IV trolley's wheels.

I shuffled forward a few more steps and felt a cool breeze blowing up my backside. I realized the back of this gown wasn't tied up, that my naked ass was hanging out in the breeze.

I didn't care.

A few more steps and I was at Terek's ICU room door. Or Pyotr. Whatever his damn name was.

The two cops manning either side roused themselves. "Yes, sir?" the one on the right asked. "Can we do something for you?"

"I need to speak to him."

"You can't go in there."

"The hell I can't. I'm the one that got him here in the first place."

"He's not conscious."

"Then I'll wake him up."

"Sir, you can't—"

"It's okay, officer, I'll take it from here." The intelligence guy that had come in with the senator had magically appeared, as if from nowhere. "My name's Tim," he added and extended his hand.

I held onto the metal stand with both hands, as much for balance as anything else. "Nice to meet you. I need to talk to Terek."

I couldn't stop using that name. What was the point of switching?

"Sure, sure thing. Why don't we try?" Tim nodded at the two officers, who looked at each other and shrugged. This was above their rank.

We opened the door.

I shuffled my feet forward into the semidarkness to the side of the bed.

There he was. Terek. Pyotr?

The same boyish face that looked like he hadn't started shaving yet. The thick mass of brown hair. He had always been pale, but in the dim light he looked almost translucent. His lips a shade of purple-blue, dark rings under his eyes.

Was this the face of a mass murderer?

He had tried to kill my son.

Tried to kill me.

Then again, he might have saved my life when I'd gone headfirst into the Mississippi. Something about it didn't add up. Or maybe it did? *Was* that his wife back at the house? What would I do for Lauren, if pushed all the way to the edge? If she was in danger?

A stab of guilt.

Had I left his wife behind?

When we took off in the truck, I knew my gut instinct was finally right. I made sure Irena—Amina?—didn't get in with us, but Katerina I hadn't been sure about. Not at the time.

"Terek," I said. And then louder, "Terek!"

No response.

I let go of my IV pole with my right hand and slapped his face. "Terek, wake up. It's Mike. I need to talk to you."

Tim, the intelligence officer, hung back in the shadows.

"Terek, I need to—"

His eyelids fluttered, and then opened. His lips were cracked. "Mike, I'm so sorry."

"Was that really your wife? Katerina?"

He nodded and closed his eyes.

I closed mine as well. "What color is her hair?"

The beeping machine tracking his heartbeat quickened. "Her hair?"

"You heard me."

A pause for a second. Then two. Finally he answered, "Blond, of course."

"You're lying. That woman's hair was brown."

"Maybe she, I don't know—"

The machine's beeps faltered into an irregular staccato.

I said, "Lauren told me she saw Katerina working with them. She saw her on the plane from Hong Kong. How do you explain that? You're lying. Why did you do it?"

"I had no choice."

"You're lying. Stop lying."

An alarm went off. His face contorted and he gasped, "You wouldn't understand."

"Understand what?"

The door opened behind me. One of the nurses said, "Mr. Mitchell, you need to get out of the way."

Another alarm went off. His body arched. Hands tried to pull me away, but I held onto the edge of the bed. I leaned to Terek's ear and said, "What wouldn't I understand?"

"He's going into cardiac arrest!" someone shouted behind me.

"Why us?" I said.

His eyes opened, so wide I saw the whites glow in the light of the fluorescent tubes that blinked on. "You think you were the only ones?" He spat the words out. "You have no idea what is coming."

He started laughing and coughing at the same time. Blood spattered from his mouth. "This is only the beginning, you didn't stop us, you have no—"

"Out of the way!"

I was dragged backward and lost sight of Terek behind a mass of white coats.

"We're losing him," someone in the pile called.

Sneakers squeaked against linoleum floors as nurses and interns raced up the hallway and into Terek's room.

The kid was dying, I realized. I was the one that shot him.

Killed him.

Holding my IV pole and trolley, I backed out of the way, straight into the steady arms of the intelligence officer.

I looked him square in the eye and said, "This is only the *beginning?*"

Note From The Author
Matthew Mather

Dear Reader,

A sincere *thank you* for reading.

The adventure continues in *CyberWar*, the final book in this series (search for *CyberWar* on Amazon).

If you are looking for more right now, and haven't read the prequel *CyberStorm*, I highly recommend it. It's been translated and published in over thirty countries around the world and earned close 10,000 reviews on Amazon (search for *CyberStorm* on Amazon).

Another connected novel in this world is *Darknet*, which is set in the same universe, but spaced in time between the events in *CyberStorm* and *CyberSpace* (search for *Darknet* on Amazon). This novel is set in New York, and follows one man's journey deep into the tech underworld of Wall Street.

Mr. Damon Vincent Indigo from this series also appears in my *Atopia Chronicles* trilogy. These novels are set fifty years in the future after *CyberStorm*, when Mr. Indigo is an elderly gentleman presiding over a trillion-dollar empire on the island colony of Atopia off the coast of California. *Atopia* was my very first novel, and the style is different—more high-concept sci-fi.

If post-apocalyptic is more your style, then try out my "Science Fiction Book of the Year" award-winning four-book series *Nomad*, where a mysterious deep-space object threatens to destroy the solar system (search for *Nomad* on Amazon). These novels follow the adventures of Jessica Rollins as she protects her family and navigates and new Earth after a truly cataclysmic disaster.

My novel *Polar Vortex*, a new stand-alone title, is about a mysterious aircraft disappearance, and is now under development as a limited TV series (search for *Polar Vortex* on Amazon). This is by far one of my favorite books, and is a great sci-fi mystery from start to finish in an homage to Agatha Christie.

And finally, I have a new sci-fi detective series, the *Delta Devlin Novels*, which follow the career of a rookie New York detective as she faces some harrowing cases. The first "prequel" in this series is *The Dreaming Tree*, which is available right now, as is the second book *Meet Your Maker*.

Thank you again for supporting my writing and my family, and all my warmest wishes to you and yours,

Matthew Mather, March 2020

p.s. **If you enjoyed this novel, please don't forget to write a review on Amazon**, not matter how short, because these very much help sales for indie authors like myself. Thanks in advance!

About The Author

Amazon Charts Bestseller Matthew Mather's books have sold millions of copies, accumulated over 70,000 ratings on Goodreads, Audible and Amazon, been translated and published in over 24 countries across the globe, and optioned for multiple movie and television contracts.

He began his career as a researcher at the McGill Center for Intelligent Machines before starting and working in high-tech ventures ranging from nanotechnology to cyber security. He now works as a full-time author of speculative thrillers.

Website:
www.MatthewMather.com
Facebook
www.facebook.com/Author.Matthew.Mather
Email
author.matthew.mather@gmail.com